PRAISE FOR HEIDI MCLAUGHLIN

Cape Harbor

"I love a good second-chance romance, and Heidi McLaughlin did NOT disappoint."

—*New York Times* bestselling author L. P. Dover

"This is a story that will stay with me for a long, long time."

—Sara, Goodreads

"A beautifully written story that will pull you in and tug at your heartstrings."

—Nikki, *Crazy Cajun Book Addicts*

"The reader will instantly fall in love with Cape Harbor."

—Nicki, *The Overflowing Bookcase*

"McLaughlin knows how to put a person in touch with their emotions."

—Isha Coleman, Goodreads

The Beaumont Series

"If you want to read a book that is all heart—full of characters you will instantly connect with and love from the first page to the last—then *Forever My Girl* is the book for you."

—Jenny, *TotallyBookedBlog*

"*Forever My Girl* is a sweet, loving, all-around-adorable read. If you, like me, have a thing for musicians and reconnections, then this read is for you."

[illegible] *Reads*

"This is an utterly moving story of second chances in life, of redemption, remorse, forgiveness, of loves lost and found again, of trust regained. Through alternating points of view, we feel both Liam's and Josie's emotions, fears, and sorrow. These are well-developed characters whose love for each other survives time and distance."

—*Natasha Is a Book Junkie*, on *Forever My Girl*

"*My Unexpected Forever* completely outdid my expectations and blew *Forever My Girl* out of the water. *My Unexpected Forever* is without a doubt a book that I would recommend, and Harrison is officially my new book boyfriend!"

—*Holly's Hot Reads*

The Beaumont Series: Next Generation

"Heidi McLaughlin delivers a breathtaking addition to the Beaumont series. *Holding Onto Forever* is everything you want it to be and so much more. I fell in love all over again."

—*USA Today* bestselling author K. L. Grayson

"A roller coaster of emotions. McLaughlin takes you on a journey of two hearts that are destined to be together."

—*New York Times* bestselling author Kaylee Ryan

"Heidi McLaughlin delivers yet another heartfelt, emotional, engaging read! I loved every second of *Fighting for Our Forever*! You will too!"

—*USA Today* bestselling author M. Never

The Archer Brothers

"I *loved* everything about this book. It is an emotional story that will have you begging for more. Even after I finished reading, I can't stop thinking about it. A *must* read!"

—Jamie Rae, author of *Call Sign Karma*

"McLaughlin will have you frantically turning pages and make your heart beat faster because each page has something more surprising than the one before it. You'll be dying to see what happens next!"

—*New York Times* bestselling author Jay Crownover

"I needed this book. I didn't even realize how much until I read it!"

—*USA Today* bestselling author Adriana Locke

The Boys of Summer

"Heidi McLaughlin has done it again! Sexy, sweet, and full of heart, *Third Base* is a winner!"

—Melissa Brown, author of *Wife Number Seven*

"*Third Base* hits the reading sweet spot. A must read for any baseball and romance fans."

—Carey Heywood, author of *Him*

"*Third Base* is sexy and witty and pulls you in from the first page. You'll get lost in Ethan and Daisy and never want their story to end."

—S. Moose, author of *Offbeat*

"McLaughlin knocks it out of the park with her second sports contemporary . . . This novel goes above and beyond the typical sports romance with a hot, complex hero and a gutsy, multidimensional heroine. McLaughlin keeps the pace lively throughout, and just when readers think they have the finale figured out, she throws them a few curveballs. This novel will appeal to McLaughlin's fans and will win her many more."

—*Publishers Weekly* (starred review), on *Home Run*

"Heidi McLaughlin never fails to pull me in with her storytelling, and I assure you she'll do the same to you! *Home Run* is a home run, in my book."

—*New York Times* bestselling author Jen McLaughlin

"Top Pick! Four and a half stars! McLaughlin has hit the mark with her third Boys of Summer novel. There's more than one great story line to capture the imagination."

—RT Book Reviews

Before I'm Gone

Other Titles by Heidi McLaughlin

THE BEAUMONT SERIES

Forever My Girl

My Everything

My Unexpected Forever

Finding My Forever

Finding My Way

12 Days of Forever

My Kind of Forever

Forever Our Boys

Forever Mason

The Beaumont Boxed Set—#1

THE BEAUMONT SERIES: NEXT GENERATION

Holding Onto Forever

My Unexpected Love

Chasing My Forever

Peyton & Noah

Fighting For Our Forever

THE PORTLAND PIONEERS:

A BEAUMONT SERIES NEXT GENERATION SPIN-OFF

Before I'm Gone

HEIDI MCLAUGHLIN

Published by Montlake, Seattle

www.apub.com

ISBN-13: 9781662513510 (paperback)
ISBN-13: 9781662513527 (digital)

Cover design by Ploy Siripant
Cover image: © THAIS RAMOS VARELA / Stocksy United
Design elements used throughout: Bird © Piyanat nethaisong / Shutterstock; Bow © Gizele / Shutterstock

Printed in the United States of America

Lana Del Rey
And her music that inspired this book
You're a master storyteller

ONE

Palmer Sinclair sat at her small table and looked out the grand picture window at the San Bruno mountainside. She saw a black-tailed doe and her fawn grazing on what little shrubbery the mountainside had to offer, and watched as the doe nudged her baby, guiding it to a food source. The sight of a mother caring for her child brought Palmer back to the DNA instructions and test that sat in front of her.

Today was the day, her self-imposed deadline to finally spit in the tube and send it off. Deep in her heart, she knew she had family out there, and desperately wanted to connect with someone. She hoped she had a sibling but would welcome an aunt or uncle or even a cousin, distant or closely related. Someone who could teach her and help her learn about her family, her heritage, and where she came from. Mostly, she wanted to know how or why she'd ended up in the orphanage so many years ago.

Palmer read the instructions aloud, picked up the vial, and began to fill it. Once she'd gone over the designated line, she added the stabilization buffer and secured the cap. She pulled out the form and printed her name. Palmer Sinclair wasn't her birth name or the name she'd used at the orphanage. The second thing she'd done after turning eighteen was to change her name. The first was to ask for her records. She also didn't know her birth date. The date on her file was the date she arrived. Why the orphanage never asked for her birth certificate still confused Palmer to this day. It was as if no one wanted her to know she existed.

She'd made up everything herself, which made her feel like a fake. She didn't care what her driver's license and social security card said her name was—it wasn't her.

With the package sealed, Palmer set it by her front door and made her way into her kitchen to brew a much-needed pot of coffee. She ran on caffeine. It was her lifeline. While the aroma of coffee beans began to fill the air around her, Palmer thought about the box that sat by the door and how she had put the test off for what felt like eons, and how well her life had turned out despite the odds being stacked against her.

All her life, Palmer had been alone. She'd never had someone in the corner rooting her on, or a mother at home to make sure her homework was done, to kiss her scraped knee or braid her hair. She didn't have a father to teach her about cars or sports or hold her when she experienced her first heartbreak. Growing up, any friendships she'd had never lasted long. It was an inevitable end. Either her friends went back to their homes or they went to another house. School friends were impossible. Telling the other kids she lived in a group home was never fun.

According to what little paperwork she had about herself, she was about three years old when she arrived at the orphanage. She was sure of that, at least in her mind, because of a reoccurring dream she had of a woman in a brown dress, holding her hand. The issue with the dream was she didn't know if what she remembered happened before or after she arrived. Back then, record keeping wasn't the best, and if someone had information about her, it had never made it into her file.

Not until Palmer was older and in elementary school did she realize she was different from the other kids. Her classmates teased her, ridiculed her. The teachers tried to make it stop, but they weren't around during recess or on the bus after school. She dreamed of being adopted or at least finding a foster family, someone to love her, and each day, she'd wait for someone to tell her she was going to finally have a mom and dad. Days turned into weeks, which turned into years.

On her eighteenth birthday, the state moved her into transitional housing until she was twenty-one. Palmer made the most of her situation, and by the time her twenty-first birthday rolled around, she had earned her associate's degree in accounting and secured a job as a teller at Bay Bank. At first, the pay wasn't great, but she managed. She rented a room in a house and then found roommates to share an apartment with, until she had saved enough for a down payment on an apartment.

Her apartment was a nice size, with two bedrooms and an open-concept layout; the kitchen had brand-new appliances and led into her living room. Her favorite part of the apartment was the view she had from her living room—San Bruno Mountain.

Now, she was within walking distance to work, South San Francisco's historic downtown, and all the artisan-enriched cafés where she loved spending her weekend mornings, drinking coffee and eating a scone or cinnamon roll. She was often by herself, which was easier than forging friendships that might not last.

The coffeepot beeped, and Palmer contemplated her next step as she poured herself a cup. She could take her cup of coffee and go sit by the window and admire her view, or she could take the packaged test to the post office instead of waiting until she went to work. Thinking about the box sent her nerves into overdrive. Despite having nothing to lose, she had a long list of what-ifs that plagued her thoughts. She didn't have a family now, and if there wasn't one out there for her, things wouldn't change for her, but she had to know.

Palmer drank her coffee as she made her way into the bathroom. She showered, dried her hair, dressed in a pair of jeans and a long-sleeved shirt, and made her way to the front door. She picked up the box, tucked it under her arm, and walked toward the elevator.

Outside, the sun shone brightly and warmed her skin. Spring was in the air. Flowers bloomed, trees flowered, and the birds sang louder than the city noise. As she walked toward her destination, she missed the blue mailboxes that used to be on every other street corner. Those were gone, right along with pay phones and the corner bodegas. The only nostalgic things left these days were fire hydrants. Those would never go away. Neither would her memories of the time the boys at the home figured out how to unscrew the bolt on the hydrant during one of the hottest days of the year. They all played in the water until the fire department showed up, and then still, the firemen let them play a little longer. Those moments were worth remembering.

"Good morning, Palmer," the post office attendant said as Palmer approached the counter. "I didn't see a package in your box, but let me check."

"Oh, no worries. I'm just dropping off today." Slowly, Palmer extended her hand. She watched as the clerk took the box, scanned the prepaid barcode, and waited for the receipt to print.

"Anything else? Do you need stamps? We received some new ones in. Do you want me to show you?"

"Not today, but thank you." Palmer took her receipt and stuffed it into her pocket as if it was going to bite her or held bad news. She knew once she was home, she'd read the tracking number, memorize it, and check the website every day. Once the company had it, Palmer would start the countdown. The time between the six- and eight-week marks would be torture for her.

Palmer stopped and bought the newspaper, and then went into one of the cafés near her apartment. She picked up a bottle of water and waited until it was her turn in line. She ordered a cinnamon roll and told the barista she would be outside. She sat in one of the metal chairs, took a sip of her water, and opened the paper. At times, she felt like she'd grown up in a different era, one where reading the paper was the norm, and not the one where everyone read on their phones or tablets. If she stared at the small screen on her phone too long, she'd get a migraine, and never mind working for more than an hour at her desk. Once a migraine kicked in, she was down for the count. Her worst one yet, which happened a few weeks back, had kept her out of work for almost a week. Thankfully, her boss didn't have a problem filling in for her. She supposed that was because she'd been with the bank for fifteen years and until recently had never used a sick day. It seemed, as of late, she was using them more than anyone else.

Her cinnamon roll arrived, and her mouth watered. They were her favorite treat, and she only ate them on the weekends. The second bite was as delicious as the first, but by the last, she felt a headache coming and wanted to get home. She cleaned her space, tucked her newspaper under her arm, and headed back to her apartment. Her day was ruined, all because she couldn't stop the migraines from coming. She'd done everything she could. She'd changed her diet, increased her caffeine intake, started drinking tea, and bought the most expensive head-and-neck compress on the market. At first, the migraines were manageable. Lately, they were becoming increasingly unbearable.

Palmer made it into her apartment in time to pull her light-blocking curtains over her window and heat up her compress. By the time she crawled into bed, her stomach felt queasy, and she was on the verge of tears. As the pain throbbed, she told herself when it stopped, she would make an appointment with her doctor and ask if there was something more she could do to curb the pain. She didn't want to admit it might be time to seek treatment, and that home remedies and homeopathy weren't working.

Two

Six weeks later

Palmer walked into her office, kicked her door shut with her heel, and set the heap of files in her arms onto her desk. She sat in her brown leather chair, toed her shoes off, and set her stocking feet onto the pressure point massager she'd found on QVC—guaranteed to cure headaches. She rested her head on her fingertips and added pressure to her temples and forehead and waited.

Since she'd started seeing a neurological chiropractor at the urging of her primary care doctor, she'd not had a migraine at work for a couple of weeks. Her doctor understood Palmer's desire for homeopathic treatment, while also explaining how medicine could help her. His stance was no one needed to live in chronic, debilitating pain.

The chiropractor was a happy medium. After the initial consult, Palmer was scheduled for a spinal adjustment three times a week for the first couple of weeks, and then they'd drop down to twice a week. The appointments would gradually decrease over time. The approach to curb and eventually eliminate the headaches was to get Palmer's nervous system back on track, and if a migraine happened in between appointments, she had pills she could take.

Blindly, Palmer reached into the top drawer and felt around for the bottle. She found it after a few seconds, and finally opened her eyes. The pressure wasn't that bad, but she knew it would get worse if she didn't take something. She twisted off the lid, shook out a pill somewhat larger than a Tylenol capsule, and took a drink from the bottle of water she'd placed on her desk earlier in the morning.

She spun in her chair and looked out her office window at the San Francisco cityscape. Palmer had worked hard to get an office with a view. She had put her time in as a teller, and then a loan officer, and finally the branch manager. She loved her job and the people who worked for her. She knew that if she went to a bigger bank, she'd be able to climb the corporate ladder much faster. Her heart was here, though, and she couldn't see herself working for anyone else.

It was dreary out, having rained the night before and most of today. Until the headaches started, she'd never enjoyed the fall and winter months or the gray days that the spring rain brought. Now, she welcomed them just like she welcomed her oversize sweatshirts, a warm cup of soup, and her heated blanket. She also enjoyed the sun but was thankful she didn't have to keep her curtains closed or her lights off.

There was a knock on her door, and she told whoever was there to come in while she quickly slipped her shoes back on. Long ago, she'd grown accustomed to wearing heels and could do so for hours on end, but as with anything constricting, it was a relief when she could take them off. Shaunie Janes stood in the doorway. "Are you okay, Palmer?"

"Yes, of course," she replied, as she always did. It was her canned answer. She didn't want anyone to fret over her, especially for something trivial like a headache. "Is it lunchtime?" Palmer looked at the clock on her computer and confirmed her own question. "I'll be right out."

Ever since becoming branch manager, she'd made it her duty to cover the lunch shift. Prior managers wouldn't help out and often left the tellers with long lines and angry customers. Since Palmer took over, she had changed things. It was important to her that her employees and patrons have a stress-free lunch.

Palmer stood, brushed her hands down the front of her skirt, and tugged on her jacket. Appearance meant a lot to her. She wanted people to see her as put together and professional. When she came out of her office, she noticed the lobby was beginning to fill up with the lunchtime crowd.

She walked behind the long counter and greeted each of her tellers. When she came to Shaunie, she quietly told her to go to lunch once she finished with her customer and then made her way to the workstation Palmer kept available in case of emergencies. At her terminal, she logged in and called for the next customer to step forward without looking up. When she did, she saw a man who often made her heart skip a beat or two—Kent Wagner.

Kent was a client and off limits as far as Palmer was concerned, not that she'd ever shoot her shot or let anyone know she had a crush on him. He was a favorite at the bank. All the tellers liked him and thought he was too cute for words. Palmer thought he was handsome, with his deep-blue eyes and dirty-blond hair. Kent kept his hair short and often buzzed it during the summer months.

"Hey, Palmer," Kent said as he approached her station. Today, he wore normal clothes, or what he referred to as his "street clothes." Most of the time when he came in, he was in his EMS uniform. "How are you today?"

"I-I'm well," she stammered. "How are you?"

Kent smiled the most adorable, crooked smile Palmer had ever seen. "I'm well. How are you?" He ducked his head and his cheeks flushed with a pink hue, probably realizing he'd asked the same question twice. "I've missed you the last couple of times I was here."

Over the years, Palmer had gotten to know most of their long-term clients, whether it was from being their bank teller, opening new accounts, or helping them with loans, which was how she'd met Kent. She had a knack for memorizing the little things when it came to the clientele, although lately she'd felt her memory slipping more than usual. Palmer loved to listen to their stories, always fascinated by what they could tell her in their minutes-long transactions, but it was her interactions with Kent that had left a lasting impression. He was a kind man and always had a compliment for the staff.

"You have to come at lunchtime," she told him. "What can I help you with today?"

Kent slid a check toward her. "Just paying my car payment."

Palmer brought the thin paper toward her and typed his name into her computer. "You know, you can make this payment online."

"I know," he said. "But then I wouldn't get to come in here and say hi . . . to you." He muttered this last part, so Palmer barely heard him. She tried not to smile, but the giddy emotions she felt took over. It was her turn to duck her head and be coy.

Palmer typed the information into the computer and began processing Kent's payment. Her terminal was slow, and most days she hated it, except for now because it gave her a longer moment with Kent.

"Are you working today?" she asked, even though she already knew the answer.

He shook his head slowly and never took his eyes off her. "Tomorrow," Kent said. "Then I'll be off for two days, and then work for another twenty-four hours."

"I'm sorry this is taking so long. My terminal is slow." Palmer was embarrassed by how slow her machine moved. As much as she enjoyed having Kent at her window, she was sure he had other plans.

"It's lunchtime," he pointed out. "Everyone's at the bank right now." He looked around as if to prove his point. There was a line behind him, which increased Palmer's anxiety.

"Thank you for being patient."

"Of course. I don't mind." Kent leaned his elbows onto the counter and stared. Palmer looked everywhere she could except for at Kent. She didn't want to let on that she had a crush or anything.

Finally, her computer seemed to kick into high gear, and all the extra clicking and key pressing she'd done now needed to be undone. She exited out and started over by typing his name into the system and then choosing the account for his car loan.

"Have you ever thought of a home loan?" she asked while she waited for the computer to register her request.

"Nah," he said. "I sort of like living in an apartment."

Palmer did as well. The complex she lived in was equipped with everything she needed, and by moving there, she'd been able to cancel her gym membership. Not that she ever went, but it still felt good to finally stop the autopayment each month.

"You know you could buy an apartment, right?" She processed his payment and went to press the enter key to produce his receipt. She could hear Kent talking, but his words were muffled. Palmer's vision blurred, and black spots started to appear. She tried to move her hand, but it felt heavy and pinned to the keyboard. Somehow, she was able to close her eyes and brace herself against the counter, and then, everything was clear again. The hustle and bustle of the bank washed over her, and she looked around as confusion set in. What had happened? Had no one else seen whatever it was?

She slowly made eye contact with Kent, who bore a look of deep concern on his face. "Palmer, is everything okay?"

Palmer nodded and smiled. "Yes, I'm just a bit dizzy."

"Are you sure? Because it looked like you had a stroke."

Palmer waved the handsome EMT off. Of course he would think that. He was in the medical profession. Weren't doctors, nurses, and the like always looking for some ailment to treat?

She checked her facilities. Other than being tired and feeling a tad weak, she felt fine. She touched her face, wiggled her fingers, and shifted her weight from one foot to the other. Nothing seemed off.

"I'm okay," she said again, hoping to reassure her customer. Palmer handed the printed receipt to Kent, who took it reluctantly.

Kent hesitated and leaned closer to the counter. "I think you need to see a doctor if you have dizzy spells often. You shouldn't mess around with those. There could be a wide range of things wrong."

Palmer nodded. She appreciated his concern, but she was certain that whatever happened was a mere fluke in her system. For all she knew, it was the pill she'd taken minutes before she'd come out to help him. Kent reached across the imaginary plane and took her hand in his.

"I'm just worried," he told her. "I see a lot of stuff in the field, and it's those 'you never know' moments that can really throw someone off kilter. It's better to be safe than sorry."

"Thank you." She squeezed his hand and then slid hers out from under his. Kent didn't look convinced at all. He took his slip of paper, tucked it into his pocket, and kept his eyes on Palmer until he was forced to turn around and watch where he walked. He gave Palmer one last look before he exited the building.

Palmer felt relieved when Kent left. The last thing she wanted to do was discuss her medical issues in front of her coworkers and the bank's patrons. She continued to work through lunch, and when the final teller came back, she took a few minutes for herself. On her way to the break room, she ran into Frank Martinez, a third-generation owner of Bay Bank who tended to stay in his upstairs office unless he was needed, which if Palmer had her way would be never. They had a stellar working relationship, and he allowed her the freedom to do as she pleased. He liked to joke around with the staff and never took things seriously. Palmer and Frank were night and day when it came to work ethics. She'd had to work for everything she had, while Frank had inherited his job. Still, she respected that this was his bank, and they both expected their customers to be happy.

"Hi, Frank."

"Good afternoon, Palmer."

They went into the break room together, which Palmer found odd. He had a full kitchen upstairs and didn't need to use the one everyone else used, and she wondered why he was downstairs if they weren't meeting. He used the microwave to heat up his coffee and whistled while he waited for it to ding.

Palmer pulled her bag of lunch out of the refrigerator. She sat down, opened her yogurt, and started reading the newspaper. As soon as the microwave dinged, Frank came over and sat down.

"I've been thinking of hiring another teller, maybe someone part time to help with the lunch rush."

"That's not a bad idea," Palmer said. "Doing so would allow the team to take lunches two at a time instead of staggering them. I think they'd like to have lunch with someone. I know a few of the staff would like to walk at lunchtime together."

Frank nodded. "That's solved then. I'll have Celine put an ad online or whatever we do these days. I think we'll hire at least two. This way, we always have coverage."

Frank stood and Palmer thanked him. As far as bosses went, he was a stand-up guy, but he didn't like to work, unlike his father, who'd been very hands on until he retired and turned things over to his son.

Palmer was halfway through her yogurt when her stomach rolled. She placed her hand over it and willed the nausea to go away. She could now mark yogurt off the list of things to buy. Every week, it was something new. She was the type of person who stopped eating whatever didn't settle well in her stomach. Unfortunately for Palmer, she was running out of things she could eat.

She threw her yogurt away and took a bite of her sandwich, but again, her stomach twisted, and she knew lunch was going to consist of her green tea. She went to the water cooler, added water to her mug, and put it into the microwave. While she waited for the water to heat, Frank's assistant walked in and went right to the refrigerator. Celine enjoyed eating lunch downstairs, where she could talk to people, and not be at Frank's beck and call.

"I heard the good news," she said, no doubt referring to Frank's suggestion about hiring more staff.

"I didn't even have to ask." The staffing situation was something Celine and Palmer had discussed numerous times, but neither had ever had the guts to bring it up to Frank. He liked to pinch his pennies when it came to the bank. He was more the "in my pocket" type of owner.

"Sometimes he gets it." Celine took her lunch to the table and sat down. "Are you still reading this?" She pointed to the newspaper.

"Go ahead." Palmer neglected to mention her vision kept blurring and the print was too fine for her to make out. She'd stared at the newspaper for five minutes, squinting to see the muddled print before finally giving up. The optometrist was another doctor she needed to add to the lengthy list of physicians she needed to see. She turned and faced the counter and counted the seconds on her mug of water. When it was ready, she took it out, dunked her teabag in, and carried her cup over to the table. She sat down with a heavy sigh.

"Migraine?" Celine asked, and Palmer nodded.

"It's different," Palmer said. "It starts and then stops. As much as I hate to say it, I wish it would just knock me out so I can get it over with."

"The medicine isn't helping?"

"It was. It worked for a few weeks, but now they're back."

"You should probably see a neurologist."

"I have an appointment in six weeks. Until then, I have to manage the migraines on my own."

"Six weeks?" Celine looked shocked.

Palmer nodded and sipped her tea. "I'm on the cancelation list, but the receptionist told me not to hold my breath. The appointment times are coveted. I feel like I'd win the lottery before I actually get in to see one."

"I bet if you go to the emergency room, you'll see one faster."

Palmer gave Celine a sideways glance. "It's a migraine. The staff at the ER have more important things to worry about."

"Just saying. You look more tired than normal, and no one would fault you for going. Are you sleeping at night?"

"Surprisingly, I am. The blackout curtains help a lot."

"Well, you need a vacation then." Celine studied Palmer for a moment. "Come to think of it, I can't recall you ever taking a day off, let alone a week for vacation. You're burned out. Seriously, use the time you've accrued and get the hell out of town. I know a great spa up north. They'd treat you well."

"I'll think about it," Palmer stated, knowing full well she would never go. It wasn't in her nature to be adventurous. Something she wished she could change about herself.

Celine finished her lunch, and, on her way back to her office, Palmer detoured to check on the tellers, making sure they were all set until the end of the day. She had a pile of accounts to finalize and wanted to hammer them out before she went home. She rested against the counter and surveyed the lobby until her earlier stomach issues came roaring back.

Palmer rushed to the bathroom and splashed cold water on her face. She practiced some breathing techniques and worked to quell her uneasy stomach. It was then that she remembered she was supposed to take her pill when eating. She dabbed her skin with a paper towel and made her way back toward the front.

She stood there, watching people turn from humans to blurry blobs of nothing. She needed to get things under control, sooner rather than later. Palmer hated the way she felt, and didn't really understand why she couldn't kick this illness with everything she'd done.

THREE

Kent Wagner stretched and allowed the soft sounds of his alarm tone to settle over him. He spent enough time with the emergency bell waking him that he preferred something gentler for home. It took him a bit of time to find the right sound, but once he had, he basked in the calming chimes.

"Turn it off," the voice next to him grumbled.

He rolled to his side, did as requested, and then turned toward the form buried under a pile of blankets. Kent liked his apartment to be chilly. He slept better that way. His girlfriend, Maeve, favored warmth. To her, a room needed to be seventy or higher for a good night's sleep.

A year into their relationship, and this was one of the two things they hadn't seen eye to eye on. The other being if they should move in together. Early on, when they couldn't get enough of each other, Maeve had brought up cohabitation. Kent wasn't necessarily ready at the time. When he brought it up months later, Maeve brushed it under the rug, where the topic seemed to stay. It bothered him, her change of heart. He thought they had a great relationship . . . when they were together. Lately, Maeve seemed off. Kent couldn't pinpoint what "off" meant, though, and kept his thoughts to himself.

Kent lifted the blankets, brushed her tangled hair aside, and kissed her cheek. "Have a good day at work." He slipped out of bed and went into the bathroom to shower and get ready for work. Maeve would text him later after she left, and they'd text throughout the day, but they wouldn't see each other for a couple of days. Kent worked twenty-four on, forty-eight off, for the San Francisco Fire Department as a paramedic, while Maeve had what she called a boring nine-to-five office job.

On his way to the station, he stopped at his favorite coffee shop, RoccoBean. He stood in the doorway for a second longer than he needed and inhaled deeply. He loved the smell of freshly ground coffee beans, which was the main reason he stopped there every day. The shop was one of those blink-and-you'd-miss-it places, and the only reason he knew about it was because he once responded to a call there. Ever since, it had become part of his morning routine. Sure, they had coffee at the station, but nothing beat RoccoBean.

He placed his usual order, added a slice of recently baked banana bread, and waited off to the side. By the time his name was called, he had finished the pastry and desperately wished he had bought two pieces, but he needed to get to work before shift change and made a mental note to double up tomorrow morning.

Kent arrived at the station an hour before his shift started. He had a routine and rarely deviated from it. The ten years he'd spent in the army as a medic had trained him in ways only other soldiers could appreciate, and because of this, Kent liked things a certain way. He set his coffee, and the one he'd bought for his partner of three years, Damian Caruso, down on a bench and went to his rig. It was his and Damian's responsibility to restock the bus before their shift started, although most medics would do this after every call, unless they'd been out on calls all night. It was a rarity for Kent and Damian to have to fully restock before their shift.

Kent opened the back door and climbed inside. He checked the oxygen levels on the portable units and verified that they were securely in place. He ran his hand over the stretcher to confirm it was ready for use. Finally, he checked the first aid supplies and made a note on his phone of what they needed. In the event the alarm sounded now, they would have sufficient supplies in the field. Once Kent was satisfied with the inside, he went around to the driver's side door, hopped in, and started the rig. While he waited for the red dial to reach the *F* on the gas gauge, he flipped the lights and turned on the siren, although the currently sleeping crew probably wasn't thrilled. With the tank full, Kent turned off the truck and hopped out.

By the time he finished, the new shift crew had arrived. With both coffees in hand, Kent said good morning to the crew that was about to leave. Most were groggy, and he wondered if there had been a lot of calls the night before. Before he met Maeve, Kent would often volunteer to cover shifts or come in to help if needed. When they became serious, he scaled back and kept his days off for her. He even went as far as turning off his scanner when she was there. He had a fascination with needing to know where his coworkers were going when he wasn't there.

Kent climbed the stairs to the third floor, where the medics spent most of their time if they weren't out on calls. There was a fitness center on this floor, a kitchen and dining room, a lounge, and their dorm area for sleeping. He entered the locker room, went to his assigned space, and set the coffees down. He stored his keys and wallet and changed from his street clothes into his blue work pants and shirt and made sure his name tag and badge were straight.

The smell of bacon led Kent to the kitchen. His stomach growled despite the banana bread he'd eaten earlier. He found Damian at the stove, scrambling a large batch of eggs with some other crew members seated around the table drinking the unfavorable coffee brewed in the station's coffeepot.

Every shift the medics took turns with the chores. Paramedic Isha Cortez had graciously made a monthly calendar for everyone to follow. For the next twenty-four hours, Kent had sweeping duty, which was much better than cooking for everyone. Kent was an okay cook—when he cooked for himself or Maeve—but add in a dozen or more people, and he didn't know what he was doing. Doubling or tripling recipes never worked out well for him.

"Thanks for the coffee." Damian set the spatula down and took a sip of the large, undoubtedly lukewarm or cold black liquid. He closed his eyes and then quickly spat it out. "I will never complain about you stopping before every shift, but if you value our partnership, please bring it to me before you check the rig."

Kent laughed. "I wish they'd get delivery." If RoccoBean delivered, Kent could have his favorite coffee any time of the day, whenever he wanted.

"No, you don't," Reeva Kingsland, one of their other paramedics, said. "If they delivered, you'd have no reason to stop and enjoy their coffee."

"Is that some twisted version of 'If you build it, he will come'?" Damian asked Reeva, who shook her head.

"I have no idea what you're talking about," Reeva said to Damian.

"*Field of Dreams*?"

Reeva shook her head.

"Baseball?"

She shook her head again, and Kent laughed. "Sometimes, words are just words. Don't look too deeply into things," Kent said. "Reeva's right. I get it. When you have too much of a good thing, it becomes something you take for granted. Besides, I enjoy stopping in there before every shift. This morning, they had slices of banana bread, and it was delicious."

"Oh, so you're not hungry for what I'm cooking?" Damian set his hands on his hips and glared at Kent until he couldn't seem to hold his expression any longer and snorted with laughter. "I'm sorry. I can't even stay mad at you because you bring me liquid gold." He picked up his paper cup and took another drink. "The best, even if it's not as hot as I'd like it, and the lack of warmth caught me off guard."

This shift, Reeva was to set the table, or at least put enough plates and silverware out for people to use, and because Kent was already in the kitchen, he helped her. When Damian yelled that breakfast was ready, the cacophony of thundering footsteps came from all over the building. Mumbled thanks, scraping chairs, and chatter filled the kitchen space. Most of the crew ate at the table, while some took their plates to the lounge, where they watched the morning news.

After breakfast, Damian and Kent hopped into their rig and set off for the Financial District of San Francisco, their assigned coverage area. When they arrived at the station, they went in and shot the shit with firefighters until their first call of the day came in. It wasn't too long ago when paramedics and firefighters were in the same house. After the new construction of the Ambulance Deployment Facility, however, medics had their own house.

By the time they sat down to eat lunch, Kent and Damian's radio sounded. Everyone went silent so they could hear the call. As soon as the dispatcher called their rig number, Damian and Kent stood and left their lunch on the table. The others would wrap it up and put it in the refrigerator for them.

"Unit 81, possible stroke, female, thirty-seven, Bay Bank," the dispatcher said over the radio. "Patient is prone, and the guard has escorted everyone out of the building. Patient collapsed against the wall."

Kent and Damian rushed to their truck. Damian climbed behind the wheel and turned on the lights and sirens, while Kent went to the passenger side. Kent reached for the dashboard radio. "Unit 81 en route." Thankfully, they were already near the bank and would be there quickly.

"I was just there yesterday," Kent said as they turned the corner. He feared he already knew what they were going to walk in and find.

"They're small and personable," Damian added. "I've banked with them for years."

They pulled up to the front, and Kent radioed dispatch to let them know they'd arrived on the scene. He was thankful to the San Francisco PD parked along the curb. Damian grabbed his clipboard and started the necessary paperwork while Kent went to the back of the bus and pulled the stretcher and his medical bag out. They walked into the bank, and the manager led them to the patient.

"She's over here," the manager said.

"What's her name?" Damian asked.

"Palmer Sinclair. She's my branch manager."

Kent's heart sank, and his fast walk turned into a run as he headed toward Palmer. The surrounding crowd parted as he and Damian approached. Kent took his medical bag and squatted down next to her, while Damian started taking her vitals.

"Hey, Palmer. It's Kent," he said, his voice cracking as he conducted his visual assessment. He liked her and enjoyed coming in to see her. "Can you tell me what happened?"

She tried to raise her hand to touch her head, but Damian asked her to hold still. He placed a c-collar around her neck and then monitored her blood pressure and oxygen levels.

"N-no," she stammered.

Kent looked at Damian and watched him make a note of Palmer's motor skills.

"Palmer's battling some migraines," one woman near Kent said. "She's seen her doctor, but the medicine isn't working. I was behind her when she sort of leaned into the wall and fell."

"Did she hit her head?" Kent asked.

"I didn't see," the coworker said.

"Do you know what medicine she's taking?" She shook her head and said she'd be right back.

"Palmer, we're going to put you on the backboard."

Damian and Kent worked as a team to get the board under Palmer. Once they had her situated, Palmer put her hands over her stomach.

"Do you feel sick?" Kent asked.

Palmer tried to nod, but her head barely moved.

"I can take care of that for you," Kent told her.

"Here's what was in her drawer, and this is her purse," Palmer's coworker said when she returned, holding a pill bottle.

"Thank you." Damian took the bag and set it at the end of the stretcher.

"Okay, Palmer. Are you ready?" Kent asked, trying to lighten the mood. He'd known something was wrong yesterday when he saw her, but he wasn't a doctor, and there wasn't much he could have done unless she'd collapsed in front of him or asked for him. Kent was certain she'd had a stroke when she'd helped him, and she may have had another one.

Once they'd loaded her into the ambulance, Kent sat on the bench and started an IV. "I'm going to give you something for your nausea, which will definitely help on the ride over to the hospital. Is there anyone you need the nurses to call?"

He looked at her for an answer and received none.

"How about you blink once for no and twice for yes. Okay?"

She blinked twice.

"Okay, good. Is there someone you need us to call?"

She blinked once.

Kent didn't like that answer. No one should be at the hospital alone. Damian started driving, and Kent notified dispatch that they had cleared the scene. He then radioed the hospital to let them know about their transport and her symptoms. The entire time, Palmer never took her eyes off him.

He looked down at her and wished he had insisted on doing something yesterday for her. A tear slipped from her eye, and he wiped it away.

"Don't cry," he told her. "Everything will be okay. They'll run some tests, and then you'll be on your way with a three-page printout of doctor gibberish." He laughed and hoped she understood his joke.

Kent watched her vitals. Palmer's oxygen levels and blood pressure were good. Heart rate was faster than normal, but given the circumstances, he wasn't too worried. Damian radioed the hospital to inform them they had arrived. He reversed in and went around the back to open the doors for Kent. Together, they brought the stretcher out as smoothly as possible, trying not to jostle their patient. Once the stretcher was at full height, they wheeled Palmer into the emergency room and to the critical care room directed by the staff.

They waited until the attending nurse came in and gave her a full rundown of the situation. Before they left, Kent went to Palmer. "We're leaving you in expert hands," he said to her. "Whatever you need, the nurses will get it for you. Your purse is on the chair next to the bed. Are you sure there isn't someone we can call for you?"

"No," she said hoarsely as she blinked once.

"Okay, well, I hope you feel better. I'll stop in and see you when I make my next car payment."

Palmer smiled and blinked twice.

"All right. Feel better."

Kent left the room and found Damian finishing his paperwork at the nurses' station. Back in the rig, Kent said, "Yesterday, when I saw her, I swear she had a stroke. She told me she was fine and that nothing was wrong. I pressed her, but she was insistent. I should've called it in." He shook his head and looked out the window.

"She's really young to have a stroke."

"Yeah," Kent sighed. He didn't understand why she affected him so. Normally, he did his job and moved on. "She doesn't want anyone to know she's here."

"Maybe she doesn't have any family."

Kent looked at Damian. "Who doesn't have family?"

Damian shrugged and pulled out of the parking lot.

Four

Nurses bustled around Palmer. They talked to her, over her, and asked her questions that they didn't wait for her to answer. Their movements made her dizzy, and she was thankful for the antinausea meds Kent had given her. When he arrived at her side and started his assessment, she was embarrassed. The last thing she wanted was for him to see her like this—weak and unable to find her voice. It was there; she was just afraid to use it.

While Kent and his partner helped her, the memory of when he'd first come in for his loan flashed through her mind. He was charismatic and charming and had been very eager to buy his first new-off-the-lot car, but he wasn't looking forward to paying for parking. That was one expense she didn't have and something she didn't need. Besides, she rarely left the city, and could take the train if she needed to go somewhere. She loved the freedom walking gave her, and it allowed her to visit with the merchants near her home and office.

"Palmer, are you feeling any better?" The nurse picked up Palmer's wrist and then stared at her watch. Was she supposed to answer when it was clear the nurse was counting? After the nurse set her wrist free, Palmer nodded. "I am."

"Oh good, you're talking. The medics who brought you in noted you were having trouble speaking, but you sound clear. Can you tell me what happened?"

Palmer shook her head and then said, "I remember eating lunch, but it upset my stomach. I was walking back to my office, maybe? That's all I can recall."

"Your speech sounds great, which all but rules out a stroke. It's possible you have the flu, which could lead to fainting if you're dehydrated. The doctor will be in shortly," she said before she went behind the bed. "Can I get you something?"

"I'm a bit cold," Palmer said.

"I'll bring in a few more blankets. I put the call button on the side here in case you need anything. I'll be right back."

Everyone knew "be right back" in medical speak meant sometime in the next half hour. Hospitals were busy and their staff overworked. They all did their best to accommodate the emergencies as they came in.

Palmer lay on her side and watched the bag of saline drip into the tube. They were treating her for dehydration, but deep down, she knew something else was wrong. Ironic that Celine had suggested Palmer go to the emergency room to speed up her visit with the neurologist, and now she was there. When she saw the doctor, she was going to spill her guts and demand some sort of imagery testing. She could feel there was something wrong with her. By all accounts, the medicine her primary care physician had prescribed should've worked longer than the few weeks it had.

The nurse returned with two more blankets. She laid one on top of Palmer and then wrapped one around her shoulders. "Is there someone we should call?"

Palmer shook her head. "Thank you for the blankets."

"Of course. Do you want some water?"

"I'm fine, but thanks."

The nurse nodded, patted Palmer's leg, and then checked her vitals once again. Before she left the room, she reminded Palmer to press the button if she needed anything or felt worse than she already did. Palmer said nothing and continued to stare at the machine hooked to her arm. The IV hurt, but not as bad as her pride was hurting. She worked hard to keep up the facade that she was okay, and to collapse or faint at work in front of her employees and customers was embarrassing.

She shifted her focus to the concrete walls. They were a yellowish color, undoubtedly white at some point, and if she stared hard enough, she could find chipped paint in the creases of the walls. Not far from the ceiling, the metal rod holding the curtain started and formed what looked like a half circle. Palmer wondered why the rod hadn't been constructed to go straight across, instead of creating an odd-shaped space for privacy.

From what she could tell, there were four spaces or rooms. She wasn't sure what the hospital called them. But the rooms were in one large space, each with its own wall of medical gadgets and cloth partitions. The bed diagonal from hers had someone in it, but the other two spaces were empty. Palmer was closest to the door, and if she flipped to her other side, she'd be able to see people walking up and down the hall, which also meant they'd see her. She didn't want to see anyone.

Above, fluorescent lighting kept everything bright, which to her was a drawback, because she could see how dingy the wall color was. Plus, the lighting gave her a headache—well, made her existing one worse. She wanted her room to be dark and quiet, and the person sharing her room was now talking loudly on her phone. Palmer tried not to listen, but the boisterous and agitated voice echoed through the space, preventing her from hearing the one-sided conversation. Palmer deciphered that the other patient needed a prescription that no one wanted to refill or approve her for more.

Palmer finally turned toward the door when she heard a commotion. People in white coats ran down the hall, with one barking orders as they followed a stretcher and two paramedics. She wondered what had happened and guessed it was a car accident or a shooting. Both made her stomach turn. She hated hearing about all the trauma her beloved city experienced, and couldn't imagine what those families went through.

The intercom sounded overhead, and the automated voice repeated, "Code blue." More people ran past her room, and then she heard a scream. It was guttural and gut wrenching, and was followed by a string of "nos." Palmer turned over to face the wall and pulled the blanket from her shoulders over her ear. She appreciated the calm it gave her.

A woman appeared in front of her, dressed in a white coat, like the others she had seen running down the hall. "Hi, Palmer, I'm Dr. Molina. I was just going over your chart. It says you fell at work. Did you hit your head? Can you sit up for me?"

Palmer sat up and then shook her head. "I don't think I fell. It was more like a collapse."

Dr. Molina felt Palmer's skull, likely looking for any bumps or potential fractures. "Where does it hurt?"

"It doesn't hurt on the outside."

"What do you mean?" Dr. Molina asked without stopping the examination.

"The pain is on the inside. I think there's something wrong."

The doctor stepped back and sat on the stool with Palmer's chart in her lap. "There's a note here that says you suffer from migraines?"

"Yes, they're severe. Yesterday, I think I blacked out when I helped a customer, and then there was the incident at lunch today. I've had the migraines for a while now and finally went to the doctor for something to take, but it only worked for a couple of weeks."

"Can you tell me about the blackout? What were your symptoms?"

"My pinkie finger on my right hand froze over the keyboard. I could hear people talking, but it sounded like I was underwater. My vision blurred, and I had these black spots every time I blinked. And then it was like I woke up and everything was fine, except I felt dizzy. Kind of like . . . " Palmer paused. "Like how you feel when you get off a carnival ride."

"How were you treating your headaches before you sought medical treatment?"

"Anything holistic I could find. Changed my diet, increased my caffeine intake. I tried massage, herbs, anything marketed for migraine relief. I guess you could say I'm a walking, talking infomercial."

Dr. Molina chuckled and wrote in the chart. "I'm going to order a CT scan. I want to see what's going on. We're going to start at the top and eliminate the most obvious suspect. Sometimes migraines can be environmental. But there's a reason you blacked out and collapsed, and I want to determine what caused it." Dr. Molina gave Palmer a reassuring pat on her shoulder and stood. "An orderly will be in to take you to imaging. I need you to change and remove all your jewelry." She went to the portable cart next to Palmer's IV and rummaged through the compartments. "Here's a gown and a bathrobe. You can change in here, or I can get a nurse to escort you to the bathroom. I don't want you walking alone."

"I'll be fine in here," Palmer told her.

"Okay. I'm going to close the curtain to give you some privacy. When you've changed, just open it a bit, so the orderly knows you're ready. You can put your stuff in the bag on the counter there."

"Thank you."

"You're welcome. I'll be back as soon as your scan results are back."

Palmer pushed the blanket off and discovered she was barefoot. She couldn't remember if she'd taken her shoes off or where they would be and hoped someone had the keen sense of mind to put them in her purse.

She set her stocking feet onto the linoleum. It was cold and likely slippery if she were to walk anywhere without shoes on. She stood slowly and kept her legs pressed to the bed for some stability. She didn't trust herself right now. The first item of clothing she removed was her nylons. Once she had them off, she threw them into the trash. She didn't want them after her feet had touched the hospital floor. After removing her skirt and blouse, she slid one arm into the itchy gown. She had to undo the snaps on the shoulder area because of the IV. She wished she had a nurse or someone to help her but didn't want to bother anyone with what was likely a mundane task. After snapping the shoulder piece in place, she tied the strings on the side, and then folded her clothes. As much as she wanted, she wouldn't be able to wear the robe until someone had unhooked her from the machine.

Palmer took a very unassured step toward her purse, and then another, until she felt a small tug on her IV. The length of the IV tube confined her movements, but thankfully she could reach the tray where her purse was and pulled it closer. She put her folded clothes into the hospital-issued bag, removed all her jewelry, and then opened the partition for the orderly. She carefully climbed back into bed, mindful of her IV.

She paid attention this time when a paramedic brought another patient into the room. She tried not to be nosy, but the action across the way fascinated her. It was only when the medic turned enough for her to see him that she recognized him. He continued to help the nurses with their new patient, which gave her time to stare a bit longer. She felt sort of stalkerish, but she was fascinated by his job. Kent was caring and sweet with the elderly patient in the space across from her. He leaned toward the woman and must've said something because she giggled, which in turn made Kent smile. *He is handsome*, Palmer thought.

It was as if Kent sensed Palmer watched him. He glanced over toward her bed and smiled. She expected him to leave the room and return to work, but instead, he came over to her. "You look much better," he said when he stopped at the end of her bed. "Any prognosis?"

"They haven't said, but I don't believe they're treating me for a stroke or anything. They're definitely not rushing around like my life's in danger, for what it's worth."

"That's great," he said and then motioned toward her IV. "Anything good?"

She looked at the bag for a brief second and then said, "Saline for dehydration."

"That's good."

"Thank you, for earlier."

"I'm just doing my job, Palmer."

"It's more than that," she told him. "I should've listened to you yesterday. Maybe I'd have some answers already."

"Most people don't want to believe anything is wrong, until it's too late. You're in the best place now. The staff here is amazing."

"I'm sure you have to say that."

Kent laughed. "I don't, but I do like the people here."

"They seem very nice." Palmer trailed off and let her eyes wander a bit before looking back at Kent. "Thank you again, especially for the lift. I suppose if I had to take a ride in the back of an ambulance, I'm happy it was with you." Her cheeks flared instantly as Kent blushed. She had no idea why she said what she had and wished she could take it back.

He laughed at her humor, which she appreciated, and told her he'd see her at the bank the next time he went in.

Not long after he left, a nurse came in to shut off her IV and helped her into the wheelchair with the waiting orderly. His name was Victor, and he liked to sing, according to the nurse. He asked Palmer what her favorite song was.

"'Ride' is my favorite song."

"Lana Del Rey?" he asked, and she nodded.

Victor started humming her favorite song as he pushed her down the hall. She felt woozy and closed her eyes for the duration of the ride. She also wanted to be in the moment with the melody coming from Victor. Palmer took deep breaths to ward off the feeling in her stomach and was thankful when they arrived at the room for her CT scan. The orderly helped her onto the table, while the radiology tech prepared her for what was going to happen inside the tube. She had to lie still, and it was best if she kept her eyes closed. The technician showed her where the emergency stop button was, if Palmer felt claustrophobic.

The table moved into the tube before the machine turned on. It was loud, and it clicked every couple of seconds. The sound of Lana Del Rey's voice played from the speaker, and it took everything for Palmer not to smile or to sing along. Victor, a man she didn't know at all, had brought her comfort in such a brief span of time. Palmer concentrated on her breathing and listened to the music. She thought about the places she liked to spend her time: the coffee shop by her apartment, the park overlooking the bay, and somehow work popped into her mind. She enjoyed her job and the people she worked with, but she wouldn't call it her happy place. She hadn't forged any genuine connections.

Palmer tried not to let the lack of togetherness bother her. If she wanted to change the way they perceived her at work, she would.

The scan took thirty minutes, and by the time it was over, Palmer had fallen asleep. Victor was there when she came out of the tube, and she smiled at him. He helped her back into the wheelchair, and once again, she kept her eyes closed until they got back to her room. Victor helped Palmer into bed and made sure the call button was accessible.

"Normally they take about thirty minutes to read the scan, so the doc should be back in forty-five minutes to an hour."

"Thank you, Victor, and thank you for the music."

"My pleasure, Ms. Sinclair."

Palmer wrapped the blanket around her shoulders, lowered the top part of her bed a bit, and turned onto her side. Her head hurt, and she knew it was a matter of time before a full-on migraine would appear. She covered her face, brought her knees up to her chest, and prayed the scan would show them something . . . anything, because she desperately wanted to be free of the pain.

When she heard the metal clank from her partition, she didn't move. "Are you feeling okay, Palmer?" Dr. Molina asked.

"Not really."

"Okay, I'm going to get you hooked back up to your IV and give you fentanyl for the pain."

Palmer unearthed herself from the cocoon she had made and gave Dr. Molina her hand. She felt a slight tug on the IV, and then Dr. Molina pressed some buttons, and the saline drip began again.

Dr. Molina sat on the stool. "I'm also going to admit you."

"What? Why?"

"Because I don't like what I see on the scan," she said pointedly. "I've called a couple of colleagues in for a consult."

"Wh—" Palmer cleared her throat. "What did you see?"

"A large mass. I've ordered a biopsy to happen first thing in the morning."

FIVE

While Damian finished the paperwork from their last transport, Kent took a few minutes to check in with Maeve. They shared a few texts back and forth when they could. Maeve had a strict no-phone policy at work, and Kent only texted when he had some downtime. He preferred to be in the present when working with Damian and felt that if his face was stuck to a phone all day, they wouldn't be as close as they were. Kent considered Damian to be his best friend. After Damian completed the forms, he and Kent told the nurse at the desk they'd see her later. Their return was inevitable. It was an unfortunate fact, but they were paramedics in a city with over eight hundred thousand people, and that didn't include the daily tourists.

Back on the rig, Kent silenced his phone after climbing in. Damian let dispatch know they were back in service and heading toward the main facility, but available for Basic Life Support calls. They were low on supplies and needed to restock. Most BLS calls wouldn't require much more than a ride to the hospital. Despite Damian being on cooking duty, he knew he would ditch his responsibilities if someone needed help. He was, first and foremost, a paramedic. Everything else came second. Kent felt the same way, which was one of the reasons he enjoyed working with Damian.

They arrived back at their facility and gassed up their rig, and Kent began restocking while Damian headed to the kitchen once they'd pulled their rig into the bay. Someone yelled, "The cook is back!" and then others took turns on the intercom to complain about how hungry they were. They worked with a bunch of jokesters—a sense of humor was a definite plus with this job, and was needed due to everything they saw. Nick Martin and Isha Cortez were the biggest pranksters on their shift. If your birthday fell on a day you worked, it was inevitable they would fill your locker with balloons, shaving cream, or confetti.

After Kent finished the restock, he went upstairs to join his fellow paramedics. Most had gathered in the lounge. Their captain, Brenda Greig, sat in the recliner with her feet up, holding a can insulator that looked like a Bud Light can, although it was really a can of soda.

"Rough day?" Kent asked.

"Lost one," she said as she continued to stare at the television.

"I'm sorry." Kent sat down on the sofa next to his captain and put his feet up. Downtime was rare, but when they had some, they took full advantage. Kent pulled his cell phone out and checked his notifications. He texted Maeve to check in and then went to social media and scrolled. His favorite posts were those from other stations because someone always had a funny story to share from their shift. Of course, the stories were never funny as they happened, only afterward, when everyone could look back on the situation and laugh.

Kent's phone vibrated with a text from Maeve.

Having dinner with my mom tonight. Today is blah. Can't wait to be out of the office.

He frowned. He was certain Maeve's parents were out of town and not due to return for a few more weeks. Kent prided himself on listening when Maeve told him things, and he remembered how jealous she was of her parents touring Central America with a travel company.

Kent texted back: I thought your parents were out of town?

The chat bubble appeared, went away, and didn't come back by the time Kent pocketed his phone. He figured her boss was nearby. Maeve hated her job but wouldn't leave. She had great benefits, and she insisted on keeping them. He'd encouraged her to go back to school, even if she had to take night classes, and get a degree in something she wanted to do. No matter what Kent suggested, Maeve wasn't interested, which brought him back to her parents and their vacation. He was certain they were still out of town, so why would Maeve lie?

She wouldn't.

Would she?

Kent had a hard time shaking the feeling that something was amiss. Lately, Maeve had been noncommittal whenever he wanted to make plans. When they'd first started dating, they couldn't get enough of each other, and now . . . well, now everything felt like a chore. He wondered if they were still on the same page when it came to their relationship. Kent wanted to be with Maeve, but what had started out as a one-night stand before turning into something more had stalled along the way. They were in a scheduled rut, in part because of Kent's job; at least that was what he told himself.

Kent pulled his phone out of his pocket. He clicked on the phone icon, and his thumb hovered over Maeve's name. Texting wasn't his favorite form of communication, but Maeve insisted they chat throughout the day. He felt it was often informal, and the tone of the message on the other end depended on the receiver. Kent was someone who picked up the phone to call his parents and tell them something, regardless of how minute. He was also known to show up at their house just in time for dinner. He liked the face to face because he loved seeing people's reactions.

He wanted an answer to his earlier text because something wasn't sitting right with him. He went back and forth in his mind on what he should do. Nothing made sense. He *knew* her parents were out of town. So why was she lying?

On the other side of the lounge, some of the other medics played pool. Kent pocketed his phone and went to watch the game. Ruben Cross and Jenny Dillard were in a heated match, playing to see who would clean the toilets. It was Jenny's assigned duty, but she'd challenged Ruben and said she could beat him. He'd agreed, and they were currently tied at two games each. Kent sat on a stool and watched his friends go back and forth. The trash-talking was both out of hand and comical. Every time Jenny lined up for a shot, Ruben would start dancing or whispering in her ear. When it was Ruben's turn, Jenny pretended to undress. There was a long-standing rumor that they were a couple, but neither would admit to it. They rode together, and it was against policy to date your partner. Asking for a new partner would mean a different shift, and it would also mean disciplinary action for Ruben. He outranked Jenny.

When the eight ball sank, Jenny threw her arms up in celebration, and then started dancing. Ruben tossed his stick down and muttered something unintelligible about everyone's bathroom habits. No one enjoyed cleaning the bathrooms.

Kent followed Ruben out of the lounge, and headed to the first floor, where another rig pulled in. The back door opened, and Zach Lacey climbed out. He looked exhausted, and Kent could guess why. Not all calls were easy. Some were downright hard and unbearable. Their captain had lost someone today, which was never good, and by the looks of it, Zach had as well.

"Dinner's cooking," Kent said after Zach had hopped out of the rig. "Do you need help to restock?"

Zach shook his head. Most medics preferred to restock on their own. It was their rig for twenty-four hours, and they needed to know what supplies they had. Kent wouldn't take Zach's refusal of help personally.

Kent started sweeping. His method was to push the dirt toward one wall and scoop it up from there. Everyone had their own way of doing things, and their deputy chief didn't care as long as the facility looked clean all the time.

By the time he'd finished, it was time for dinner. They all sat down, thanked Damian for their food, and took their first bite. Some got three or four bites in before the alarm sounded.

Structure fire.

Kent listened clearly. He didn't want to miss any of the important details. It was unlikely he and Damian would go, but they'd be on standby. One by one, the others stood and raced downstairs. Within seconds, sirens blared through the building as buses left. Six of them remained. They would wait for their captain to tell them where to stage and be there to help if needed. Kent hated fires. Anytime he was on scene, he felt helpless. He needed to do something when he responded to a call, and waiting patiently wasn't a strong suit of his. He welcomed action and blamed his years of deployment with the army. This unit never had a dull moment.

The remaining medics finished dinner, stored and marked the leftovers, and cleaned. Kent cleaned the bathrooms to help Ruben out, while Damian tidied the lounge. The entire time, the radio told them what was happening at the scene, and when the second ambulance left, Damian and Kent made their way to their rig. They set off with only their lights on. There was no need for a siren until a call came in requiring their services.

They staged two blocks away and shook their heads as onlookers went to the scene. Neighbors and lookie-loos often clogged streets and access points for emergency personnel. They could be bothersome unless they had valuable information. The people walking by now were nosy. Nothing more to it.

"What satisfaction do they get?" Damian asked.

Kent shook his head. "I don't know. Social media fame? I know if that was my house, I wouldn't want this on the internet for everyone to see all the time."

"They're glory hounds," Damian said angrily. He wasn't wrong. Anyone taking video or pictures of the burning house and the unfolding scene out front wasn't doing it for anything but social media likes. They weren't part of the press, and Kent was certain the family hadn't asked their neighbors from blocks over to come record everything. It was rare that an onlooker's video actually captured anything important, but it had happened. The fire marshal had learned a long time ago to make public pleas for content whenever he had to look for arsonists. This could be why people did what they did—they wanted to help. Still, it bothered Kent.

Their radio crackled, and Damian flicked the lights and sirens on before Kent could tell dispatch their ETA. "Unit 81 responding, sixty seconds. Someone needs to clear the barricade."

"Roger, Unit 81."

Damian drove to the end of the street. Thankfully, people moved out of their way and also covered their ears with the piercing scream the sirens made. Kent was out of the truck before Damian came to a full stop, and he slipped his hands into his latex gloves. He came around the rig and saw a firefighter carrying a body out of the house. This spurred Kent into action. He opened the back of the truck and yanked the stretcher out with one powerful tug.

"What do you have?" Kent asked as the firefighter approached.

"Found him on the second floor, in the bathtub. Smoke inhalation. Other injuries are unknown. He's young." The firefighter laid the young boy on the gurney and walked off, but Kent stepped in front of his colleague.

"Are you okay?" Kent looked for any signs of injuries.

"I'm good," he said as he patted Kent on the shoulder. They both knew he wouldn't admit to having any issues, but Kent had to ask, regardless. Kent went to the stretcher. Damian had turned the boy onto his side and strapped him in for transport. He and Damian slid the stretcher back into the bus, and Kent climbed in.

"Hey there, I'm Kent," he said as the doors closed. "I'm going to put this around your nose and mouth. It's going to give you some oxygen to help you breathe. You can move it when you need to talk. I'm also starting an IV. You're going to feel a little poke, but it only hurts for a second. Can you tell if anything hurts?"

"My chest," the young voice croaked.

"Are you dizzy?"

"Tired," he said.

"We're almost there. What's your name?"

"Clark."

Kent laughed. "Clark! I'm Kent. That makes us Superman. Do you know what this means?"

The little boy shook his head.

"It means the two of us are stronger than one."

"Is my mom okay?" he asked.

Kent hadn't heard if the first victims had succumbed to their injuries or not. It wasn't his place to tell the boy, but he also didn't want him to worry. Too much stress could cause issues for the young man. He also didn't have an easy way to answer his question. Kent tried, though. "I only know she went to the hospital. They don't tell us anything after that."

"Oh," he said, and closed his eyes.

"Just hang tight, Clark. My buddy Damian is pulling into the parking lot now." Kent radioed the nurses' station and asked where they should take their patient. They rushed him into the ED triage unit and met with the head RN. It was a madhouse, which was normal when a massive incident had occurred.

Damian and Kent ran the stretcher down the hall, and Kent rattled off the information he had stored in his brain. Smoke inhalation, chest pains, and irregular breathing. As soon as they got into the room, the nursing staff and ER doctor took over. Every transport was different. Sometimes they would linger with the patient a bit longer if the staff was busy, or, like now, they rushed out of the room to give the staff the space they needed to work. Damian scribbled on the paperwork and handed their call sheet off to the desk nurse, and they made their way back to their rig.

"I hate fires," Kent said before he radioed to dispatch that they were back in service. They were told to stage at the hospital for transport to Saint Francis.

"Fuck," Kent muttered. He never asked questions but assumed one of the fire victims needed to go to the burn center.

Damian threw his clipboard on to the dashboard and sighed. Kent got out of the truck and went to the back. He pulled the stretcher out of the rig and moved it inside the private ambulance entrance. Whoever they were about to transport would come out on a stretcher. No one was dying on his watch. Not tonight. Not ever.

Six

It was after dinner when the hospital staff moved Palmer into a room. She hoped it would be Victor who moved her, but it was two nurses who chatted aimlessly about the weather, the food, and how they'd bring her a menu, and they asked her if she had called her family. Palmer told them they were aware of where she was, even though she hadn't. She hated the lie just as much as she hated the question. Not everyone had family or even close friends. It was a hard notion for some to believe, but those people usually had a support group, a network of friends and family who would do anything for them. Palmer suspected Frank was her network, or even Celine, but she refused to be a burden to anyone.

Luckily, Palmer's room had a view of the city and all its glory. She could stare out the window and watch the night sky turn into speckled dots from the lights. The downside was that she had to share the room with someone. Palmer had little experience in hospitals—none, in fact—but from what she'd seen on television, room sharing went one of three ways: they talked too much, had too many visitors, or were quiet. Palmer hoped for the third option.

When dinner came, the orderly gave her a tutorial on how to change the functions on her bed and how to use the TV. Palmer didn't have the heart to tell the young woman she had already mastered the bed part, but she appreciated the lesson on how to make the television function. She wanted mindless entertainment to take her mind off things. Ever since the ER doctor had told her about the mass they'd found during the CT scan, Palmer had imagined the worst-case scenario. She didn't even know what that could be. Nothing was ever simple in her mind.

The orderly removed the lid from her tray of food, and the aroma of chicken, vegetables, and potatoes filled the room. While the smell was pleasant, the presentation was lacking. Still, her stomach growled, which she took as a good sign. Palmer cut her chicken and took a small bite. She waited to see if her stomach would protest before continuing. She glanced at her hand and then followed the tube until her gaze reached the pole and finally the bags hanging from it. Earlier, Dr. Molina had given her fentanyl, and currently Palmer was pain-free, something she hadn't experienced in a long time. She knew it masked the real issue, but that was for another day. Right now, the drug kept her mind clear, and once it wore off, all she'd have to do was press a button for more.

Palmer listened as the orderly helped the person next to her. The partition curtain kept them closed off from seeing each other, but that was where the privacy stopped. She was curious why they were there and suspected they were wondering the same about her. They were already in the room when Palmer had arrived on a bed.

She turned on her television and pulled the handle until it was in front of her. She pushed the channel button until she found a rerun of *The Brady Bunch*. When Palmer was little, she used to fantasize about being a part of a family with so many siblings. That was until they started fighting, and then she wondered what it would be like to be an only child. She supposed the "only child" part wasn't much different from what she had, except that she would have her own room and not have to share with five other girls. The holidays were the hardest. The group home would put up a tree, and they'd each get a present, but nothing like what she'd ever seen on TV or heard about in school. She stopped believing in Santa when she was six or seven. No one with the magic he had, according to the books and her classmates, would allow children not to have a family.

Palmer lost her appetite when she thought about Christmas. She pushed the tray away, lowered the headrest, and turned onto her side. She left the television on to drown out the noise her neighbor was making and stared outside. Off in the distance, she saw what she thought were the red lights of an emergency vehicle. She watched until the vehicle turned a corner. She was humiliated about everything that had happened at work, from collapsing to the paramedics arriving. Since she'd left the foster system, she hadn't depended on anyone but herself. To be reliant on someone for help bothered her. Yet, here she was, in the hospital, waiting on people to help her.

She could tell when visiting hours had ended and when the nurses wanted everyone to go to sleep. The lights in the hall dimmed, and voices quieted. A nurse came in to check on Palmer, offered her a snack and something to drink, and turned the volume down at Palmer's request. She declined the offer of food and kept staring out the window, unwilling to accept where she was. Deep down, she knew the news was bad. Otherwise, why not just ask her to return in the morning?

In the middle of the night, Palmer got up to use the restroom. Afterward, she walked the halls. It wasn't against the rules or anything, and she wanted the exercise. She saw her shadow as she approached the end of the hall, where there was a window. She had blue slipper socks on, with a matching robe and a gown. Her right hand clenched the pole of her IV cart, and she tugged it alongside her. Aside from the mass in her head, she wasn't sure why they were keeping her hooked to the machine.

She found a window seat at the end of the hallway and sat down. The view differed from the one in her room. From here, she could see the entrance to the emergency room. There wasn't an empty spot in the parking lot, and she wondered what had brought so many people into the hospital that night. Whatever it was, she prayed everyone was okay.

◆ ◆ ◆

The next morning, a new nurse came in, checked her vitals, and asked how she was and if she needed anything, and then Palmer's stomach dropped as a doctor walked in.

"Good morning, Palmer. I'm Dr. Doty Hughes, the chief neurologist on staff here. Dr. Molina and I briefly spoke this morning about your CT scan. How are you feeling this morning?"

"I'm okay."

Dr. Hughes sat in the chair next to Palmer's bed. "According to the notes, you've experienced blurred vision, constant headaches, and dizzy spells? It says here that they brought you in for a possible stroke?"

Palmer nodded and tried to sit up straighter, but the IV in her hand prevented her from doing so.

"How long have you had these symptoms?"

"The migraines started first. They used to come and go once a month or so, but in the past few weeks, they've been almost every day. When they first started, I'd have one, but it wouldn't be bad enough that I had to stop working or anything. The blurred vision started about three months ago, and the dizzy spells every now and again, but nothing like yesterday or the day before. That was a first."

"It says here you've taken Imitrex and Nurtec?"

"Yes, those are recent prescriptions."

"What were you taking before?"

"Nothing," she said, and Dr. Hughes looked at her. "I changed my diet, increased my caffeine, sought homeopathic remedies. I'm not a big fan of medicine."

"I can understand." Dr. Hughes wrote in the file she had.

"Tell me about yesterday and the possible stroke."

Palmer cleared her throat. "Did I have one?" she asked. "No one confirmed with me or not, so I'm not sure it was a stroke, but while I was helping a customer, my pinkie seized, and my vision blurred. I could hear my customer talking to me, but his voice felt muffled. He's a medic and was concerned, but I told him I was fine. The next day, after lunch, I collapsed."

"What do you remember from that incident?"

"Not much. I remember putting my tea down and feeling nauseous."

"Are you nauseous a lot?"

Palmer nodded. "Last night's dinner is the first thing I've kept down all week, but then I didn't eat much of it."

Dr. Hughes frowned and flipped the previous page back. "They gave you fentanyl in the ER. Did that help with your pain?"

"Very much so. It's like there was a veil over my eyes, and nothing is muddled."

Dr. Hughes stood. "We're going to get you in for an MRI with contrast and move forward with a biopsy to see what we're dealing with."

"Okay, what does that mean, exactly?"

"Your CT shows a mass, but we don't know the extent of it, what it is, or how it relates to your symptoms. An MRI with contrast will essentially light you up so we can see better and give us a more concrete understanding of what's going on. For the biopsy, I'll make a small hole in your skull and guide a needle into the mass to take a sample. The procedure is called a stereotactic needle biopsy. This will help us confirm whether the mass is malignant or benign."

"Are you saying I have a tumor?"

"No, you have a mass, and that's what we're going to call it until we know more."

"And we'll know more today?"

Dr. Hughes nodded. "We'll know more by lunch. We're going to get you down to imaging, and from there they'll take you to the OR. When I see you next, I'll have a mask and cap on, but it'll be me."

"Thanks. I think."

"Regardless, we'll have a solution and know how to move forward. I know it's not a lot of information, but it's where we have to start. I'll see you soon." With those last words, Dr. Hughes walked out of the room, and an orderly and a nurse came in. The nurse unhooked Palmer's IV and attached the pole to her bed, while the orderly released the bed's brake pedals. Once given the all clear, the orderly, who didn't offer her a name, wheeled Palmer out and to the elevator.

Palmer thought about introducing herself, but the person pushing her bed didn't seem like the chatty type. Besides, Palmer did not know what she would even say if they asked her how she was. "I'm fine, but I have a thing growing in my head" didn't seem like the right answer. So, Palmer said nothing and kept her eyes closed for the duration of the trip.

In imaging, the radiologist added gadolinium to her IV and explained that this contrast metal was going to help them see her brain better. She climbed onto the table and lay down, with her arms prone at her sides. The process was the same as the day before, but this time, Victor wasn't there to make sure she had music playing. Instead, she heard the constant clicking of the machine, and wished for it to end quickly. They knew where the mass was; surely it shouldn't take them that long to get pictures of it.

When it was finally over, and she was back on her bed, her heart rate picked up. This biopsy would be a first for her. In fact, she had made it her entire life without having any sort of surgery. The incident yesterday, along with the IV, MRI, and hospital stay, were all firsts for her. She was ready to stop having firsts now.

Once they'd wheeled her into the operating room, the scene surrounding her grew hectic. Everyone moved rapidly and barked orders at each other. Her eyes darted every which way as she tried to watch people move. The headrest lowered, and Palmer came eye to eye, albeit upside down, with a masked stranger.

"Hi, Palmer. I'm Dr. Garrison. My friends call me Simeon. I'm going to administer your anesthesia this morning."

"Is this where I count backward from ten?"

Simeon laughed. "Or we could do something else. It's your choice."

"I don't think it matters."

"Everything matters, Palmer."

What mattered was what was about to happen. The doctor was going to put a needle into her brain and take a sample. What if she didn't wake up? What if she never got to go home? On her desk sat the envelope with the results of her DNA test. It had arrived weeks ago, yet she couldn't bring herself to open it. She wanted to know if she had family, but what if she didn't? All her life, she'd felt like someone out there missed her, but what if those feelings were self-induced and not from something greater? A tear leaked from her eye, and she reached up to wipe it away. She'd procrastinated, and now it was likely too late.

"Hi, Palmer," Dr. Hughes said as she stepped to her bedside. "This procedure should only take an hour or so."

"Are you going to shave my head?"

"Just a little spot. It won't be noticeable." Palmer wanted to balk, but said nothing. If everything mattered, everything was noticeable. Dr. Hughes nodded and Simeon started talking.

"Okay, Palmer, name all the US capitals for me."

Palmer started, "Sacramento, Salem, Olympia . . ."

When Palmer opened her eyes, she was in a new room with a machine beeping next to her. She was groggy, but her head didn't hurt like she'd expected. She raised her hand to feel around her skull but hesitated and dropped her arm back to her side. Palmer was easily grossed out by the littlest things, and this most certainly qualified as something that could gross her out.

There was a knock on the door, and then it opened. Dr. Hughes came in and stood near the end of Palmer's bed. "I'm happy to see you awake."

"Did I die or something?"

"A sense of humor. I like it. No, you didn't die. The procedure took under an hour. You have four small puncture wounds"—Dr. Hughes pointed to her forehead and the back of her head—"from the head ring, but those will heal nicely. You have sutures from where I conducted the biopsy, so no showering for a few days."

"What are the results?"

Dr. Hughes inhaled deeply and pulled a chair from the corner to sit next to Palmer. "Most of the time, the results take a week to get back, but I put a rush on them after seeing your MRI."

Palmer swallowed hard and nodded.

Dr. Hughes stood, pulled a film from her file, and placed it on the white box on the wall. She flicked a switch, and Palmer's head appeared. "Your MRI showed a clawlike tumor here." She pointed to the mass on the x-ray and then formed her hand into a claw to show Palmer what the tumor looked like. Dr. Hughes turned and faced Palmer. "After getting the preliminary results of the biopsy back and conferring with my colleagues, we're confident in the diagnosis of a grade-four glioblastoma."

Palmer heard the word, but was unable to fully process what Dr. Hughes said. "Gilo—"

"Glioblastoma, or GBM for short," Dr. Hughes corrected. "The causes of a GBM are unknown. The tumor and your symptoms support our findings. However, if you want a second opinion, I can give you the names of my colleagues."

"Would my diagnosis be different?"

Dr. Hughes shook her head. "No, it wouldn't."

"And the four means what?"

Dr. Hughes cleared her throat. "Grade one is nonmalignant, grade two is relatively nonmalignant, while grade three is low-grade malignancy."

"And I have the worst kind?"

Dr. Hughes nodded. "The next steps would be to perform a craniotomy and then start you on radiation or chemotherapy. The oncologist will talk to you more about that."

"Will a craniotomy fix this?" Palmer waved her hand in the air as her throat began to close and tears threatened to spill over. She had a headache—that was what had started all this, and when she went to the doctor, he'd prescribed pills. If he'd ordered further testing, maybe . . .

"It may help," Dr. Hughes said honestly. She sat down and cleared her throat. "I really wanted to give you better news, Palmer. Glioblastoma is terminal at any grade, but a grade four . . ." Dr. Hughes trailed off.

Palmer nodded and let her tears flow. "How long?" she croaked out.

"Six months, maybe a year, depending on surgery and chemotherapy."

"Are there risks with the surgery?"

"Yes, there are risks."

Palmer looked toward the window. "I'd like to be alone now."

Dr. Hughes stood. "Can I call someone for you?"

"There's no one."

"I understand needing time to process, but you shouldn't do it alone. Is there a friend or coworker we can call?" Dr. Hughes placed a soothing hand on Palmer's leg and gave her a sad smile.

Palmer shook her head and saw pity mixed with sympathy in Dr. Hughes's eyes. She rolled onto her side and whispered, "I have no one."

"I'm going to have the patient advocate come in and speak with you, Palmer. I'll be back later to discuss how we're going to move forward." Dr. Hughes touched Palmer's foot in what she probably considered a soothing gesture. Palmer wanted to pull her foot away. She wanted to kick and scream at Dr. Hughes, even though she was only the bearer of bad news. It wasn't her fault Palmer had a tumor growing—it was Palmer's own. She'd ignored the signs, and now she was faced with knowing she was going to die alone.

She heard the door close and let out a wail. How could the world be so cruel to not want her? First as a child, then a teen, and now an adult. What had she done to earn this sort of treatment?

Treatment. Something she wouldn't do. There was no way she could do this alone. She had no one to drive her to appointments, help her when she couldn't help herself. Palmer had to work. Her job was the only source of life she had. She couldn't count on her coworkers to be there for her because they had their own lives. What would she do, hire a live-in nurse? No, that wouldn't work.

Besides, what was the point? If she was going to die, why bother with any treatment at all? If she was going to be sick, vomiting, and losing her hair, why bother? If the surgeon was going to have to cut her head open, why should Palmer live with a scar, to maybe live six months?

No one had cared enough to find or adopt Palmer; she wasn't going to care now. She had nothing to prove to anyone. She wasn't strong or brave. She was alone and always had been. That was exactly how she wanted to die.

Seven

After two days off, Kent was happy to be back at work. He loved his job and the crew he worked with, and he genuinely loved helping people. It was the terrible accidents, the ones where he couldn't save someone, that tore him up. Thankfully, since leaving the army, those accidents were few and far between, but they happened, and each day Kent went into work, he prepared for the worst but expected the best.

Every call he went on had purpose. At least that was what he told himself. Case in point, he and Damian were currently at the mall, having responded to someone fainting. Only when they reached the sufferer did they discover she'd only fainted because her fiancé had proposed.

"This was a call for BLS," Damian said on their way back to their rig. "Now I have to file paperwork on someone who passed out because her boyfriend of ten years finally proposed."

"Don't sound so heartless." Kent laughed.

"When are you proposing to Maeve?"

Kent grew silent for a moment and then sighed heavily. Ever since he'd sent the text, asking about her parents, Maeve had been aloof and had every excuse under the sun she could come up with for not coming over. "Not even on my radar."

"Why not? You've been together for a year now, right? And doesn't she stay at your place all the time?"

Kent shrugged. "Something's up. I can't pinpoint what, but our relationship feels off. It doesn't help that she lied to me the other day and I called her out on it. Now, it seems like she's avoiding me." Lately, Maeve's behavior had seemed odd to him. When they'd first started dating, she was at his place all the time, mostly because she lived with her parents. But recently, she only came over the night before Kent had to go back to work. He'd go a full day off without seeing her, and it bothered him. He didn't want to think she had grown tired of him, but it was a possibility.

"Damn, I thought you guys were in it for the long haul. I remember when you introduced her, she was all over you."

Those days were long gone.

"She's stressed." It was easier for Kent to use her work life as an excuse than to think otherwise.

Kent and Damian made it back to their rig and loaded the truck. With Damian behind the wheel and Kent in the passenger seat, he radioed dispatch to let them know Unit 81 was back in service.

"You know what fixes stress, right?" Damian pulled out of the parking lot and turned onto the road.

"Don't say it." Kent rolled his eyes. The last thing he wanted to do was discuss his sex life with Damian. Although sex was a very common subject at the station, he avoided it. He never wanted to disrespect Maeve or anyone else he had ever been with.

They weren't back on the road for long when their next call came in. "Unit 81, please respond to Birchwood Park Health Center for an out-of-control patient."

Kent picked up the radio. "Unit 81 en route. Please send the police."

"Roger."

The lights and sirens blared, alerting traffic to clear a path for the ambulance. Kent held on to the stationary handle in the truck as Damian took a sharp corner. They were only a block away when the call came in, which made their response time immediate.

As soon as Kent and Damian exited the vehicle, a light rain started to fall. Kent looked to the sky, closed his eyes, and hoped drivers would take it slow. Standing out front was Paula, the director of the facility and the person they dealt with anytime they responded there.

Kent carried his medical bag in, opting to leave the stretcher in the truck for now. The center could administer aid, but there were times like this when they needed help. "What seems to be the problem?" he asked Paula while they walked in together.

"Bert's finger is stuck in the tub drain."

Damian cackled, and Paula glared at him. "Sorry, that caught me off guard. Dispatch told us you had an out-of-control patient."

"Oh, he is," she said as they rounded the hall. "I called for a plumber as well, but I'm concerned his antics in the bathtub are going to give him a heart attack." They rounded another corner and heard exactly why Paula worried about Bert.

"Who's dying in there?" Damian asked.

"Bert and his finger." Paula sighed at the dramatics coming from Bert's room. The loud screeching forced Kent to cover his ears.

Kent walked into Bert's room with his hands over his ears. He peered into the bathroom, and Bert stopped screaming.

"Why do you look like that?" he asked Kent.

"Because you're about to burst my eardrums."

"My finger is stuck and . . ." He looked past Kent. His eyes widened at the sight of Paula. "Get out of here! I'm naked, woman."

"I'm not looking at you, Bert," Paula said sarcastically as she waved him away.

Kent slipped a pair of gloves on and squatted to get a better look at Bert's predicament. Kent reached forward, and Bert screamed before Kent could touch his finger. He jumped and smacked his head on the porcelain toilet. "I'm going to need you to look away while I assess the situation," Kent said through gritted teeth.

"Fine," Bert huffed. "But hurry. I'm naked!"

Damian stepped forward and placed a towel over Bert to give the man some privacy. Something Bert could've done himself if he'd put a little effort in. Bert quietly thanked Damian.

Kent came as close as he could to the drain and shook his head. He grabbed Bert's hand and gave it a slight tug, and he was free.

"Are you kidding me, Bert? All this drama and for what?" Paula threw her hands up in the air and groaned.

"I don't know what you're talking about." Bert cradled his hand to his chest. "My finger was stuck."

Kent stood, pulled his gloves off, and made eye contact with Damian, who burst out laughing. "Sorry for the bill you're about to receive," Kent said as he passed Paula.

"Oh, Bert's paying for this one," she said. She looked into the bathroom and finally closed the door. "I am so sorry you came out for this. It's almost embarrassing."

"No worries. We're just doing our jobs," Damian said. Paula followed the men, apologizing again for wasting their time. By the time they stepped outside, the earlier drizzle had turned into a torrential downpour.

"We're going to be busy," Damian lamented.

Kent acknowledged neither the rain nor Damian's comment. Superstitions ran rampant among emergency personnel, and Kent believed it was best to say nothing about everything.

Back in the truck, they let dispatch know they were back in service. Their last two calls had required no supplies, and they didn't need to go back to the facility to restock. While Damian drove, Kent checked his phone. He sent a text to Maeve, asking how her day was going, and then deleted unnecessary emails. It didn't matter how many times he unsubscribed to newsletters; they kept cropping back up. He didn't mind his favorite retailers emailing him, but once a week was more than enough to keep him in the loop.

They reached their staging location and got out of the truck. Inside the fire station, the crew told him and Damian to grab lunch, which was chili and cornbread. One of the member's wives had made their lunch, which was perfect for the weather.

Kent ate greedily. It was by far the best bowl of chili he'd had in a long time. After he filled his bowl for a second time, he couldn't eat another bite, and thanked the crew member for sharing. The alarm bell didn't startle him or anyone at the table. The firefighters moved with rushed precision as they put their turnout gear on.

"Station 49 and all ALS units, please respond to a two-car MVA with injuries and entrapment."

"Shit," Damian muttered as he tossed his napkin onto the table. He and Kent stood and ran out to their rig in the pouring rain.

"We knew it was going to happen," Kent said after he'd alerted dispatch that they were headed to the scene.

"Never fails. It's like people forget how to drive in the rain, when it literally rains every spring." Damian sped toward the accident, which wasn't far from the waterfront. Traffic had already backed up, and Damian had to lay on the horn to get cars to move. He yelled "Move!" many times, but some people wouldn't budge. "We should be able to write tickets to these assholes."

Kent agreed. "Not a small fine either. Something substantial. A grand, at least."

"And more than three points on their license. They ignore us now. Need us later." Damian shook his head as he maneuvered the rig around a car. Kent glared at the driver as they passed by him, but it didn't matter. Some people flatly refused to move out of line.

Once they arrived on scene, Kent was out of the truck and at the rear in a rush to grab his things. He ran toward the first car, knowing Damian would take the second car until the other medics arrived. He crouched at the driver's side of the mangled sedan and immediately sought the pulse of the driver. "Hold on. We're going to get you out." In the distance, Kent heard the blaring horns of the firefighters. The trucks had the hydraulic rescue tools, which they would need to use to get the driver out of his car.

Kent viewed the passenger and froze. She had an eerie resemblance to Maeve, but that was impossible. She should be at work right now. Not in some stranger's car.

Maybe this is her boss?

No, that thought made little sense to Kent. Maeve hated her boss. She wouldn't get into a car with him. Yet, his mind screamed at the woman in the passenger seat, referring to her as his girlfriend. He left the driver and raced across to the other side. Kent yanked on the handle of the door, and it easily opened. He dropped to his knees and surveyed the woman.

Somewhere a bloodcurdling scream erupted.

Damian sprinted toward Kent and stopped next to him. "What is it? Are you hurt?"

"Maeve!" Kent screamed. "Oh, God, Maeve." Kent ignored Damian and reached for the c-collar. He fumbled with placing it around her neck, his fingers unwilling to work the way he needed them to. Damian pulled his hands away and took over, aggressively moving Kent out of the way. Kent fell onto his ass but scrambled to his knees and crawled toward Maeve.

"I need to help her." Kent tried to force Damian out of the way. He yanked on his partner's arm to clear the way. Damian's strength prevailed, and he shoved Kent back again.

"Stay there."

Kent sat on the sidewalk with his knees drawn to his chest. He watched the scene unfold around him, unable to do his job. Two of the firemen he had eaten lunch with were busy taking the car apart with the jaws, while his partner prepared Kent's girlfriend for transport. The loud crunch of metal and glass being torn away from the vehicle made Kent's stomach twist into knots. He had never been on this end of an accident before, and he wasn't sure how to cope.

"Where do you need us?" Reeva asked when she and Isha arrived at the car.

"I need one of you to help the driver and one of you to stay with Kent until Captain Greig gets here."

"I'll stay with Kent," Reeva said. She went over to him, squatted, and looked for any signs of injury. "Are you injured?"

"No."

"Why are you sidelined?"

"That's Maeve in there."

Reeva asked him to repeat himself.

"That's my girlfriend." Kent pointed to the car. Reeva turned and examined the wreckage. Her expression told Kent everything he needed to know. He started to get up, but Reeva placed her hands on his shoulders and pushed him back down.

"You need to sit here and let Isha and Damian do their jobs."

"*That's* my job," Kent wailed. "It's *my* job to protect her, and she's . . ." He couldn't finish his sentence. He was angry and confused, hurt and worried. With so many emotions coursing through him, he couldn't tell right from left. All he knew was his girlfriend had been injured when she was supposed to be at work. And who was the man? Her boss? Brother? Uncle? The list in Kent's mind went on for a mile, with no answer in sight.

In the time they'd been together, Maeve had never once mentioned a brother or a favorite uncle that she'd leave work to visit. She'd told him she was an only child who lived with her parents uptown. The site of the accident wasn't anywhere near her office either. The more Kent thought about the sight unfolding in front of him, the more questions he had.

Damian and Isha laid Maeve onto the backboard, strapped her in, and carried her to the stretcher. Kent followed, with Reeva hot on his tail. "I'm riding with her," Kent said as he climbed in behind Isha. Damian said nothing as he slammed the doors shut, and Reeva sped toward the hospital.

Eight

"You have to let me work," Isha told Kent. He gave her the space she needed to monitor Maeve. Kent held her hand and gave Isha pertinent information about her while he stroked her hair, careful not to put any pressure on her neck.

"Show me those beautiful blue eyes, Maeve." The desperation in Kent's voice filled the small box.

"She has good vitals," Isha told him. "She's in shock."

"I need to know she's okay." He gazed at Maeve and tried not to think about the man in the car. There was a plausible explanation, and she'd let him know what it was as soon as she woke up. They turned the corner, and Kent told Maeve they were almost at the hospital. Today was the first day in his career when he hated his job. He wasn't allowed to do what he had trained his entire adult life for, and he didn't know how to process the fact he felt like a failure. When someone he loved needed him the most, he couldn't function properly.

Maeve opened her eyes, much to the delight of Kent. He greeted her with unshed tears in his eyes and reassured her everything was going to be all right. She lifted her hand and cupped his cheek. She mouthed, "I'm sorry," and Kent shook his head. "Later," he told her as he kissed her hand.

Kent felt an overwhelming sense of relief at seeing Maeve's eyes, but that soon dissipated when she closed them again. He said her name, but she didn't wake. He shook her a little, but still nothing. Isha checked her vitals. Maeve's heartbeat was strong, and Isha assured Kent that she was probably in shock.

They arrived at the emergency room entrance. Kent exited first and allowed Isha and Reeva to do their jobs. He kept his hands in his pockets, afraid he might try to help his coworkers, until they were ready to take Maeve into the ED. Kent trailed behind them, but stayed close enough that he hoped Maeve knew he was there. Because of his uniform, he was able to follow them into the trauma room, where he stayed while Isha gave the RN the rundown. Kent never took his eyes off Maeve until Dr. Molina's voice rang out.

"What's going on here?"

"Kent was just leaving," Isha said as she pulled him away from Maeve.

Kent shifted his weight and refused to move. "This is my girlfriend, Maeve Hickman."

"I'll let you know when I'm done," Dr. Molina said. She didn't have to tell Kent to leave, but the pointed look she gave him and the door spoke volumes.

Seconds turned into anguished minutes. Kent drummed his fingers on the Formica countertop, and when that didn't curb his anxiety, he paced. The driver from the other car finally arrived. He was alert and talkative and had a bandage over his head. Kent could read the police report later to find out who was at fault. His gut said this guy was. As soon as that thought entered his mind, his blood boiled with rage. Why were people so careless?

Finally, Dr. Molina came out of the trauma room and headed toward Kent. "Maeve's unconscious. They're taking her for a CT scan right now. I'll let you know when you're able to go in and see her. Have you called her parents?"

"No, not yet. They're traveling, I think." Kent thought they were, but had no clue since Maeve said she'd had dinner with her mom the other night. "I'll call them."

Dr. Molina placed her hand on his bicep and gave a reassuring squeeze. "She'll be fine. This is her body's way of healing. Before they take her, I have to ask—is there a chance she might be pregnant?"

The question caught Kent off guard. He wanted to say no because they were careful, but "careful" was a relative term. "We're active" was all he could think to say.

Dr. Molina nodded and went toward Maeve's room. She met the nurse in the hallway, they spoke, and then she disappeared into another room.

Isha came down the hall toward Kent. She stopped at the nurses' station and gave him a once-over. "Need a ride back?"

"No, I'm going to stay and wait for Maeve to wake up. Someone should be here when she does, and I need to call her parents."

"You're right. I don't know why I asked if you wanted to leave. Sorry."

"It's fine. Thank you. I mean it, Cortez, thank you. You and Damian stepped up when I couldn't do my job."

"No one expects us to work on our family members. It's one thing if an accident happens at home, but when you roll up on one, it's a whole other ball game. This could happen to any of us. We're a team and we're family."

Kent choked up at her words. He nodded, unable to find his voice. Isha patted him on his shoulder and told him to call her or the house if he needed anything, and she'd make sure Damian showed up after his call. Once she was gone, Kent sat down in the waiting room and worked to keep his emotions at bay. He wasn't a crier, although he thought he'd start crying once he could relax. Yet, the tears didn't come.

Kent sat back and wondered. He felt worried and scared for Maeve—a normal reaction for someone he cared about . . . there it was. Kent *cared* about Maeve, but he wasn't in love with her. That's why he didn't push on the dinner issue with her mom. Deep down, he knew there was a reason neither of them had professed their love for each other—neither of them was there. They were very much "in like" with each other, but that seemed to be as far as their relationship had gone.

He expected his heart to hurt, more than it did, at the realization that the woman he'd spent almost a year with wasn't someone he was in love with. Kent was sad that Maeve was in that car, sadder even that he couldn't help her. Despite the standstill in his feelings, he still wanted things to work out for them because he still had feelings for her.

After they'd brought Maeve back from her scan and she still hadn't woken up, Kent made the trek downstairs to the cafeteria. He needed coffee and didn't want to drink the stuff in the staff lounge, mostly because he needed some space away from the noise.

Kent's stomach growled when he stepped off the elevator. The sweet smell of baked apples wafted in the air. He had no desire to eat, but the sudden onset of hunger pangs said otherwise. He got into line, picked the first available tray, and followed the person in front of him. Nothing looked appetizing, even when he came to the apple pie. Still, he placed one on his tray, paid for the slice and a large cup of coffee, and went to a table near the window.

He made eye contact with the woman one table away and grinned when he saw that it was Palmer. "Fancy meeting you here," he said and then shook his head. "Probably something I should say when I see you at the bank."

Palmer smiled, but it didn't reach her eyes. She looked lost in thought. "Thank you again for helping me the other day."

"Of course, I'd say it's my job, but it's more than that. I sincerely enjoy helping people."

"Well, you're very good at your job, Mr. Wagner."

"Kent," he said. "Call me Kent."

She gave Kent a shy nod, and he noticed that her smile never went away, but it had finally reached her eyes.

"You're not a patient still, are you?"

"Not really. I had to have some testing done," she said. "One more and then I'll go home. Why are you here? You don't really eat . . ." Palmer paused and glanced at his table. "Is the pie good?"

Kent laughed. "It looks like it, and yes, you're right. We don't normally eat here. My girlfriend is upstairs." He left it at that. He didn't want any sympathy and definitely didn't want to answer more questions about the car accident. "Do you mind if I ask what's wrong?"

"I don't mind."

Kent moved seats and sat across from her. Palmer straightened and faced him. She tugged the cardigan she wore closed and set her hands in her lap. She cleared her throat and focused on the table. "I have a tumor, frontal lobe."

Realization dawned on Kent. She'd definitely had a stroke when he was at her workstation the other day. A million things went through his mind as he second-guessed his actions. He should've taken her to the hospital when he saw the signs, but he'd chosen to believe her when she said she was okay.

"Operable?" he asked.

She nodded. "Dr. Hughes wants to operate."

"She's a stellar surgeon," Kent said. "One of the best in the state."

"I've read as much online."

"You're unsure?"

Kent's cell phone dinged with a message. He glanced at it briefly and saw it was from the nurses' station, letting him know Maeve was awake. As much as he wanted to stay and chat with Palmer, he needed to see his girlfriend.

Palmer shrugged. "The decision I make will change my life, no matter which path I choose."

"Brain surgery is no joke," Kent said. He pulled a pen from his pocket and wrote his name and number down on the napkin. "If you ever need anything, call me. Don't hesitate. And if you call 911, you can ask for me to respond. I can't guarantee it'll be me, but if I'm available, I'll be there." Kent slid the napkin toward her.

"They do that?"

"Sometimes. It depends on the dispatcher and how their shift is going. It doesn't hurt to ask, though."

"Thank you."

"I gotta run," he said and stood. He pushed his pie toward her. "I didn't take any bites, if you're interested. See ya around, Palmer." Kent winked and strode toward the exit. Maeve was on his mind, and he wanted to get back to her.

Back on the main floor, the hecticness of the emergency department had calmed down a bit in his absence. Kent went past the desk and ran right into Dr. Molina.

"You can go in and see her. She's in and out of consciousness. I expect her to wake fully in the next hour, maybe two. Her CT came back clear, no head trauma. Once she's awake, I'll be in." Dr. Molina gave him Maeve's room number and pointed in the direction he should go. It was funny to Kent that Dr. Molina seemed to have forgotten that he spent a lot of time in her ER and was aware of where the room was. They had moved her from a trauma room to a critical care room, still in the care of Dr. Molina, which meant they intended to keep her overnight for observation once she woke up.

He thanked Dr. Molina and went into Maeve's room. The door was open, and he went right in and stood at the end of her bed. Maeve had bandages on her right wrist, and her left arm had a splint. It was likely broken, and if that was the only thing wrong, then that was a win in his book. He was there. He saw the car. Maeve was very lucky.

Kent sat down in the chair next to her bed. He rested his head on the edge of the bed, careful not to touch her, and let his tears flow. The feeling was cathartic. It was freeing. He sat back in the chair and watched the rise and fall of Maeve's chest. Kent tried to compartmentalize being a medic, but he'd never be able to stop his training. When he wasn't focused on her breathing, he paid attention to the sphygmomanometer when it started up. Kent liked the number he saw, and deduced Maeve was going to be just fine once she fully woke up.

Maeve's hand twitched, and then her forehead creased. Kent's heart raced with anticipation. "Please open your eyes," he begged.

Her eyes fluttered, and hope sprang for Kent. He carefully touched her hand and said her name, coaxing her awake. Maeve blinked a couple of times before she opened her eyes fully. She looked at Kent and smiled, and then something shifted. Her eyes became frantic, and she cried.

"Hey, hey, hey, it's okay. Everything is okay." Kent gently wrapped his arm around her shoulders and consoled her.

"What happened?"

Kent gave her a muddled version of the accident. She didn't need to relive the memories playing in his head. He left out the man she was with, though, mostly because he didn't have any information on him.

"Am I interrupting?" Dr. Molina asked. Kent stood and helped Maeve wipe her tears.

"She just woke up." Kent beamed at Maeve, who stared at Dr. Molina.

"My timing's perfect, as always." Dr. Molina laughed at her joke. She held the chart open in front of her, closed it, and then looked at Maeve. "You have a broken arm, which we've set and will need to cast once the swelling goes down. You have a right wrist sprain, and you have ten stitches in your arm where we pulled out shards of glass. You also have a concussion, and some deep contusions on your thigh, which we need to watch for hematomas. That's all the bad news," she said with a wry smile.

"What's the good news?" Maeve spoke for the first time.

"The accident didn't cause any harm to the fetus. The ultrasound shows you're around ten weeks. An obstetrician will be in to speak to you later. We're going to keep you for two to three days for observation. Congratulations."

"A baby?" Kent whispered. A baby changed everything.

Maeve turned slightly and gazed into his eyes. Right then, everything he'd thought earlier about her aloofness went out the window. They could easily fall in love with each other, share a place together, and raise their family. Kent would make every declaration possible to show Maeve how much he wanted to be with her. He was confident everything would work out for the best.

"I'm so sorry, Kent."

"Shh, it's okay."

"No, it's not." Maeve shook her head.

"It is. Everything will be fine. We'll figure it out."

Maeve cried. "You don't understand. I've been having an affair."

It took a moment for the words to register, and when they did, Kent sat back in the chair. He opened his mouth to ask the mountain of questions forming, but the words wouldn't come out. An affair?

Why?

Was he not good enough for her? Had he not shown her how much he enjoyed having her around?

"Wh-what?" he finally croaked out. "What?"

Kent stood and took a step toward the door and then turned to look at Maeve. She was helpless in the hospital bed, bandaged and banged up due to an accident. "The guy in the car with you?"

Maeve nodded. "Let me explain."

Kent shook his head slowly. "There really isn't anything to explain, Maeve. I rolled up to an accident today and found my girlfriend with another man. I couldn't even do my job today because you were in the car, and I thought . . ."

"I'm married, Kent."

"What?"

"The man . . . oh, God. Where's Enzo?"

"Who?"

"Enzo. He's my husband. Where is he?"

Kent's vision blurred, and the room spun. He gripped the end of her bed and tried to process her words. Kent heard Maeve calling his name, but he couldn't bring himself to look at her.

"Please listen."

"I don't think I want to," he said. "I don't think I can even comprehend what you're saying right now."

"When I met you, Enzo and I had separated. We recently started talking, and he asked me to try counseling. I agreed."

"While sleeping with me? While being my girlfriend?" Kent walked toward the door.

"It wasn't like that."

"Then how was it, Maeve?" He kept his voice low and closed the door. "You had an affair with me without even asking me. You gave me no say in this matter. Is that what you're telling me?"

"I don't know, but it's not the way you're saying it is. I thought I was heading for a divorce, and I met you, and we had an amazing night together, and then it turned into something more—"

"You mean it turned into an affair. Congratulations. This explains why you wouldn't move in with me, and why you lied to me the other day about having dinner with your mom. I knew they were out of town, and when you didn't respond, I didn't want to believe something was amiss." Kent turned toward the door just as it opened. He shook his head when he saw one of the RNs he'd worked with before. She closed the door quietly. "You're pregnant."

"It's yours." Maeve's voice was quiet.

Kent scoffed and ran his hand through his hair. "I'm going to go out on a limb here and say I don't really believe you. I want a paternity test. Now. Not later. Not after the baby is born. I don't want to wait for the next eight months, wondering if I'm going to be a dad or not." Kent paced. "This is epically shitty, Maeve. All you had to do was be honest from the get-go. Instead, you used me and made me some innocent pawn in your twisted little game. If you want to know about your husband, ask the nurse to call the other hospitals. He's not here."

"Kent, wait."

He paused with his hand on the door. He stared at a pattern on the wood. "I wish you'd just been honest from the start, Maeve. When I started talking to you, all you had to say was that you were separated. There wasn't a need to lie and get feelings involved. I want a paternity test, Maeve. Don't make me go to court to get one." With those last words, he walked out of the room, out of the hospital, and into the pouring rain.

Nine

Kent stood in the parking lot of the hospital, with his face turned upward. He closed his eyes and welcomed the peppering of raindrops coating his skin. He basked in the cold, and only shivered when a gust of wind blew over him. People drove by with their windows down and asked if he was okay. He said nothing. He wasn't worried someone would go get a security guard because he was still in his uniform. To outsiders, he simply looked like an EMT who needed a moment.

And Kent definitely needed more than a moment.

He wanted, no, he needed, a reset button. He wanted to go back to the night he met Maeve and ask more questions. That night should've been a hookup, nothing more. And yet, it became something that would stick with him for the rest of his life. No matter how things turned out. He'd always have *this*, whatever the hell *this* was.

Kent sighed heavily and glanced around the parking lot. He hoped to find an ambulance to take him back to the station. Or he could call Damian and ask if he could pick him up. That would be the smart thing to do, but Kent didn't want to be smart. He wanted to walk down the street to the corner bar and drown his sorrows in pint after pint of his favorite IPA. Technically, he was still on shift, and hadn't reached out to his captain about any time off, and he never saw her at the accident scene to explain why he couldn't perform his duties. Drinking on the job would mean automatic removal from his duties, and there was nothing more important to him than his job.

Soaked, he finally sought shelter under an overhang and pulled his phone out. He'd call Damian because they were partners. Damian would come and take him back to the station. He'd stand by Kent and be his friend.

After he made the call, Kent stayed outside despite the urge to go back into the hospital. He wanted to see Maeve and ask her more questions. Mostly, why. Every question in his mind started with why, and to him, there wasn't a reasonable answer. She'd lied to him. She'd put him in a situation he did not want to be in, and now she was pregnant. Expecting a child that may or may not have been his. He was right to ask for a paternity test now, and not later. It wasn't fair to him to have to wait seven to eight months to find out if he was a father or not. He didn't ask for this. He didn't ask to be someone's affair.

Damian pulled into the parking lot not long after Kent called. He hopped into the truck, slammed the door, and thought about waiting for Damian to say something first. He told his friend the entire story on their way back to the station.

"Are you going to go home?"

"No, why would I?" Kent asked. "There isn't anything at home but wallowing and self-pity, neither of which I need right now. I need to work and be around friends."

Damian said nothing as he parked. "Captain Greig wants to see you."

Kent waited, and then finally opened the door. "I figured. I'm probably suspended. I failed to do my job out there and could've cost people their lives. Thanks for picking me up."

"Do you want to know about the driver?" Damian asked.

Kent paused for a moment and then shook his head. "No, I don't." He got out of the truck and made his way to the second floor, where the offices were. He hoped he wouldn't run into the deputy chief of EMS, Jacob Matthews, but it was likely. Kent enjoyed working for the deputy chief, and they got along well, but he wasn't naive enough to think a good working relationship outweighed his actions earlier.

He knocked on Greig's door and was told to come in. Deputy Chief Matthews sat in the chair across from Greig, as if he'd expected Kent to show up. They probably knew Damian had picked him up from the hospital. It wasn't like they could drive an ambulance around town without tracking their mileage.

"Have a seat," Greig said, her hand out over her desk, signaling where Kent should sit.

"I know why I'm here, and I want to apologize for my behavior. It was very unprofessional of me to not function at a call today."

Matthews turned slightly in his chair and let out a low, deep rumble as he cleared his throat. "We called you in here to see how you're doing and whether you need any time off. You're not in trouble for your reaction at seeing your girlfriend. You're human, and it's in our nature to react the way you did."

"I'm a medic," Kent said. "I was in the army. I knew better."

"Regardless, we don't hold it against you," Greig added. "Now, about time off—"

"None needed," Kent interrupted. "Everything is fine." There was no need for him to explain. He was a private person, and if the accident hadn't happened, neither of his bosses would know about his girlfriend. Now ex-girlfriend. "Am I cleared to return to duty?"

The deputy chief and captain excused Kent. He took the stairs to the third floor and found Damian sitting in the lounge. "Where is everyone?"

"Staging or on calls. Ready to roll?"

Kent needed a minute and went to the bathroom. He stood in front of the mirror and gripped the edge of the counter. What he saw before him was a man filled with rage and anger, and he wondered how he'd let himself get there. What signs had he missed? Where were the red flags?

What he'd thought was a relationship, Maeve had considered a fling. He was nothing more than a toy to her, something she could toss by the wayside when she was done. She didn't even have enough respect for him to be honest about her life. He understood shit was complicated, but honesty went a long way in his book.

Now, it all made sense on why she'd rebuffed him about getting more serious than they were. Maybe Kent ought to thank her for sparing him the awkward conversation on moving out of his place. He could easily put what she had in his apartment in a box and leave it for her. As he stood there, thinking about *his* apartment, it hit him that he had no idea where Maeve lived. Was it with her parents? Had she moved back in with her husband? Did her husband know about him?

None of it mattered from this point forward. Kent was done with her. Even if the baby Maeve was carrying was his, he could never trust her again. He would take care of his child, but that was as far as any relationship with Maeve would extend.

Kent splashed water on his face, dried his hands, and took a deep breath before heading back to find Damian. He found his partner where he'd left him, sitting in the lounge with his feet up. Kent sat down next to him with a heavy groan and relaxed into the sofa. He was tired and looked forward to hitting the sack later, even though the beds in the dorm weren't that comfortable.

Damian's radio crackled. "Unit 81, are you in service?"

Kent and Damian stared at each other to see who was going to answer. Kent raised his eyebrow at Damian and then smirked. Damian rolled his eyes and pulled the radio off his belt.

"Unit 81, staging."

"We have a caller on the line. She's asking for Wagner to respond."

Kent took Damian's radio and pressed the button to open the channel. "Who is it?"

"Palmer Sinclair. She called reporting complications and asked for you."

Kent stood and motioned for Damian to follow. "Unit 81 responding."

"Roger, Unit 81, Cypress Ave, apartment 400."

"Unit 81 en route."

They booked it to their truck and headed toward the address. Kent filled Damian in on his earlier conversation with Palmer and reminded him she was the woman they'd picked up at the bank a few days prior.

"She doesn't know if she wants surgery."

"Damn, it must be bad." Damian shook his head.

"I can't imagine."

The neighborhood Palmer lived in was part of a revitalization project that had done very well. People flocked to the area, mostly because of the view the area offered, and it was close to public transportation services. They pulled up to the apartment complex and took the stretcher out of the back. The lack of a doorman or security guard surprised Kent. He thought all the new apartments took extra precautions these days.

Kent knocked on Palmer's door and announced himself. When he didn't hear a response, he tried the doorknob, and was thankful it was unlocked. He didn't want to have to call the police for help. Damian entered first, followed by Kent, who called out for Palmer. They surveyed the apartment. It was impeccably clean and had a beautiful view of the mountains.

"Ms. Sinclair?" Damian said her name louder. "It's the paramedics."

They looked at each other, both worried. Kent headed down the hall, with Damian following behind. He was in the middle of radioing dispatch to confirm the address when Kent moved rapidly into the bathroom.

"Palmer? Can you hear me?"

She opened her eyes, barely a slit, and nodded slightly. "Yes, sorry I didn't answer."

"It's okay. Did you fall?" Kent asked.

"A little." She mumbled her words. "I was sick, and when I stood up, I got dizzy and hit my head on the tub when I sat down."

As Kent spoke with Palmer, Damian went back to the living room to retrieve the backboard and medical bag. He handed the bag to Kent, who went to work, making sure Palmer was okay. He explained everything he was doing when he saw her watching his every move. As soon as he had the c-collar secured about her neck, Damian maneuvered the backboard under Palmer. With limited space, they had to work effectively and make sure not to jostle her too much. After strapping her in, they carried her out to the living room and placed her on the stretcher.

"Purse," she said as she pointed to the desk. Kent went to her desk and picked up her purse and cell phone. The note next to her phone gave him pause. Written at the top of the paper were the words *Before I'm Gone*. Thinking it might be something she needed, Kent put it in his pocket.

On their way to the hospital, Kent made small talk and asked Palmer about the list he'd seen. "It's a list of things I've always wanted to do. I'm going to try and plan, if I can get the medications under control. It doesn't look like I'm off to a good start."

"Are you doing chemo or anything?"

"No, I decided not to."

"How come?" He knew chemo destroyed the body and sometimes the spirit.

"Because being sick and dying at the same time doesn't sound like the best way to go out."

Palmer left Kent speechless. He swallowed, trying to find something to reply with, but came up empty. Everything within him told him to play it off, to act like her words didn't affect him, but he wasn't sure he could. It wasn't like he'd never dealt with death before. He had. Too many times he cared to count. This time it was different, though, and he couldn't put his finger on why.

"How'd your family take the news?"

"I don't know my family," she said. "I was a ward of the state until I aged out at twenty-one."

He found himself speechless again. A rare occurrence for him. He focused on her vitals, checking them two and three times over because he didn't have the words to respond. He thought back to her list and remembered one place she wanted to visit, and then he remembered her words from moments before about dying, and he wanted to share his experience with her. He hoped that by telling her, maybe she could imagine herself there in case she never made it. "When I was stationed in Texas for training and went to the Alamo. I don't know . . ." He paused. "I thought it was going to be this immense place, kind of like how they make it look in the movies, and it wasn't."

"Are you happy you went?"

"I am. I think it's important that we visit our landmarks, but do you know what's better?"

"What?" she asked.

"That random hole-in-the-wall restaurant that only locals know about or driving all day to get to the best food truck on the West Coast. I enjoy obscure trips. The ones that don't make the tourist websites. Ya know?"

Palmer shook her head. "I've never left San Francisco."

"You should," he said.

She shrugged. "Dying seems to be getting in the way."

Her words left him speechless for a third time. He was about to ask her why she had never left the Bay Area until Damian pulled into the EMS spot and radioed their arrival. Kent had work to do, and he told himself he'd ask her if he saw her later.

They brought Palmer inside and put her in a critical care room per the triage nurse's instructions. She was close to where Maeve had been earlier.

"Hope you feel better, Palmer," he said as he left her room. Kent strode to the nurses' station and waited for Damian.

"She's in room 230," the nurse said.

"Who?"

"Your girlfriend."

"She's not my girlfriend, and that's a HIPAA violation. Why are you telling me this crap?"

"First off," the nurse fired back, "she wanted you to know if you came back. Second, she called you her boyfriend. Third, don't tell me what is or isn't a violation. I know how to do my job."

Kent was taken aback by her response and immediately recognized that he was at fault. "I'm sorry," he told her. "I was out of line. Thanks for the information." Kent told Damian he'd be right back and headed toward the stairs, taking them two at a time until he reached the second floor. He walked right to her room and paused. Kent was raising his fist to knock when a man approached him.

"She needs time and space," the man said.

"I'm sorry?" Kent asked.

A woman stepped beside the man, and Kent thought they could be Maeve's parents. "We know who you are, and about the situation," the woman said. "Maeve needs time to heal. When the paternity results come back, someone will call you. We ask that you give our daughter the space she needs to figure things out."

Kent studied Maeve's parents and finally nodded. They were right to ask him to leave. His intention had been to go in there and fight with her, and neither of them needed that right now. One thing was certain: he was happy she had decided to take the paternity test now, rather than later. They both needed to heal, and having something as important as a baby looming over them wouldn't do either of them any good.

TEN

Palmer spent the night in the hospital. The on-call doctor, who unfortunately wasn't Dr. Molina, who Palmer enjoyed speaking with, wanted Dr. Hughes to see Palmer in the morning. As Palmer lay on the uncomfortable bed, her thoughts went to the list she'd begun writing with all the things she thought she'd have a lifetime to accomplish.

Then she remembered the envelope that haunted her. It was still lying unopened on her desk. She'd picked it up countless times and tried to open it, but the letter opener never seemed to move from the edge. Palmer was afraid of what the contents would tell her. For her, there wasn't a suitable answer. If she had family, she'd never get to know them, and if she didn't, she'd die alone. She *was* going to die alone, no matter what. The test seemed pointless now.

When Palmer had told Dr. Molina and Dr. Debra Drue, the oncologist, about her life, Palmer could see the pity in their eyes. The vibe in the room changed. It went from mildly hopeful to sad. Palmer had an uphill battle, a steep climb, and she had to do it with no support and a dull pickaxe.

"I don't want to do it," she'd told them with her chin held high in the air.

"Not doing chemo or radiation will allow the tumor to grow," Dr. Drue stated. "This could give you a chance."

"*Could*," Palmer repeated. "*Could* isn't enough for me to spend my last days being sick or housebound. If I have months to live, I want to live them on my terms."

It was the doctors' jobs to argue, to push for treatment and a risky surgery. They were healers and believed in modern medicine, but they couldn't force Palmer to do what she didn't want to do. She wanted to live out her days, as best as possible, and they respected her for her decision.

Now, as she lay in bed with machines beeping around her, she wondered if she'd made the right decision. Palmer had read the reports, the blog posts, and the pamphlets the doctors had given her. She knew the side effects, both with the medicine and how the tumor was going to inhibit her mental abilities if they didn't operate. Seizures would start soon, even though Dr. Hughes believed they already had. The headaches would get worse. Vomiting would happen. She could lose her sight and her ability to speak. The tumor was going to attack her nervous system if Palmer didn't start radiation or chemotherapy. Regardless, she was going to die.

The surgery was extremely risky, and if she went through with it and survived, it would leave her with a half-shaved head and a gnarly scar from where they'd cut her open. If Palmer went ahead with chemo, she'd lose the rest of her hair. Maybe she was vain, but she loved her long hair. She loved curling it, wearing it in a ponytail, and braiding it. And while she loved the story of Frankenstein, she didn't want to look like his monster, at least not now, and not when her death loomed. Palmer wanted as much dignity as she could muster.

She slept off and on through the night. The hallway was busy, and despite her door being barely open, she could see people walking by in a rush. They never ran, she noticed, from her more-than-frequent trips over the last week. They walked fast. Palmer thought the staff here could compete in some speed-walking marathon, and they'd all be victorious. At one point during the night, she thought about getting up to open her door wider, but she didn't want to alarm the nurses or have one of them question her nosiness. She was curious, though, about what happened in the other rooms.

While growing up, Palmer had the same hopes and dreams most children did. Of course, at the top of her list was a family. She wanted to be loved and looked after. She had visions of coming down the stairs on the first day of school, with a mother waiting for her at the bottom, holding her lunch and backpack. As the years went on, that dream became nothing. Not even a wisp as she aged. Every day, she dressed in donated clothes and used a donated backpack. The only normal school thing for her was riding the school bus. But her classmates knew she didn't have a home. Her classmates mocked her for her clothing, saying, "I think my mom donated that to the homeless shelter."

By the time she reached high school, she had thick skin. She had stopped caring long before about what people thought of her unless it was the first Saturday of every other month, when the home would open its doors to prospective parents. It was then that she smiled, greeted everyone, and answered every question sent her way.

Most of the time, the questions centered around hopes and dreams. "What do you want to be when you grow up, Faith?" Faith was the name she'd received when she first arrived at the orphanage. It didn't fit who she was. She didn't trust anyone, and she lacked confidence in herself. When she was of age, she changed it to Palmer. It was a name she hadn't heard before, and she felt like it made her stand out. It was a name no one would forget.

She wavered from doctor to lawyer to princess (which, of course, she knew was impossible), to CPA. She wanted to be the CEO of a company and captain one of the cruise ships that came into port during the summer months. Palmer, or Faith back then, saw herself as one of the lead characters in her own rags-to-riches story, like Oprah Winfrey or Dolly Parton.

Palmer and the other kids would watch *Annie* on the home's VCR, thankful they weren't alive during the Great Depression and that their home wasn't like the Hudson Street orphanage. They were even more grateful they didn't have Miss Hannigan watching over them. But Palmer watched with rapt attention and saw how Annie got adopted.

Palmer told people about her goals and dreams, and she did it with flamboyancy. She practiced in the mirror the night before each open house. Her hands up in the air when she was excited, or on her hips when she was joking but trying to be serious.

Nothing worked.

Every dream she had about gaining parents, people who would love her and offer her a home, diminished after each open house. By the time she was seventeen, she didn't care anymore and rarely tried. If someone asked her a question, she gave one-word answers. She figured no one wanted to adopt a child who had big dreams and grand hopes. Children like that were expensive. No one, except for the kids in foster care and group homes, knew what it was like to dream of something as simple as a family. That's all she wanted. She would've given up every notion she ever had if it meant she had someone to tuck her in at night.

The hallway grew quiet, and she closed her eyes. Palmer counted sheep, took deep calming breaths, and tried to clear her mind. She was on the cusp of falling asleep, only to startle awake again because it felt like she was about to fall over the edge of a cliff—something she'd never stand on the edge of. She was afraid of heights. Even more scared of places with deep valleys, and she shuddered at the image of bungee jumping. Palmer had added the Grand Canyon to her list of places she'd like to see, because it felt like a bucket list item.

When Palmer started the list, she'd had good intentions of fulfilling as much as she could. The more she thought about it, the more she concluded she never would. She didn't drive, and even if she did, it would be unsafe to drive in her condition. She could have a seizure and kill someone. She could fly and hire a car service to take her places. That was much better than public transportation.

Palmer fooled herself with those thoughts. She would not be around long enough to accomplish any of them.

The following Monday, Palmer put her impending death aside, got dressed, and went to work. Hopefully, the meds she'd started over the weekend would allow her to function like her old self. So far, her pain was tolerable and nothing like the pain she felt when she had a migraine. She had missed a week of work since her ill-fated fainting spell and had told no one what was wrong with her. She wasn't going to either. Palmer had a plan. It wasn't a great one, but one that worked for her.

Palmer arrived at work, bright eyed and with a beaming smile on her face. She was in a fake-it-until-you-make-it mode and was determined to act like the week before had never happened. When she walked in, all eyes were on her. She waved, offered her normal smile, and went directly to her office. She was relieved that her desk looked the same as she remembered it. Palmer had spoken to Frank only twice during her absence, when he'd assured her that her health was important and to only return when she felt better.

She sat down at her desk, turned her computer on, and waited for the desktop to boot up. One by one, her coworkers came into her office. First Laura, who brought her a tray of cookies.

"Hey, Laura," Palmer called before she could leave. Laura turned and waited. "I never got the chance to thank you for inviting me out for your birthday. I had a really great time that night and wanted to let you know how much I appreciated it."

"Of course, Palmer. You're invited anytime. You don't need an invitation."

Palmer smiled softly and dipped her head in acknowledgment.

When Celine came in, she pulled Palmer from her chair and gave her a hug. At first, Palmer's arms stayed at her side, and then she relaxed and gently wrapped her arms around her. Palmer wasn't a hugger and rarely liked to be touched. Emotional contact of any kind made her feel uncomfortable, and it wasn't something she was used to.

Palmer stepped out of Celine's grasp within seconds, but she didn't get the hint and held on to Palmer's forearms. "I was so worried about you." She finally let go and sat in the chair across from Palmer's desk.

Palmer sat down and thanked Celine. "I'm good now." She had practiced the lie while in the hospital.

"Did the doctors tell you anything?"

I'm dying.

"No, unfortunately. They're stumped and say I'm prone to migraines. I'm on some new meds, so everything should be regulated now."

"What a relief. Well, Frank missed you."

"Did he?"

"Yes. He went on and on about how you made this place a well-oiled machine."

"Well, it's nice to be missed."

"Yes, it is," Celine agreed, and she stood. "I'll see you at lunch."

Palmer nodded and watched the doorway for a second and wondered who else would come in. People were funny. Most of the time, they didn't give you the time of day until something drastic happened, and then you were their best friend. Palmer was to blame as well. She could've forged relationships with people, but she wasn't good at it, and didn't enjoy telling people why.

She opened a document on her computer and started typing. Her words were to the point. She printed, signed, and carried the letter upstairs to Frank's office. His door was open. She went in and caught him watching videos on his phone.

"Hey, Palmer, I'm glad you're back."

"Thanks, Frank. I wanted to give you this." She slid the paper toward him and stepped back.

He picked it up, read it, looked at her, and then glanced at the sheet of paper again. "You're quitting?"

Palmer swallowed the lump in her throat. "Yes, a while ago I applied for a job overseas, and they offered me the position over the weekend. It's a dream, really." It wasn't, but the alternative was worse. She didn't want their sympathy. She didn't want to see the sorrow in their eyes if she told them she was dying.

What Palmer wanted was to say goodbye to her colleagues, pack her things, and sail off into the sunset. Maybe Celine would throw a nice office party, or they'd all go out to dinner and toast Palmer and her new adventure. She had peace in her heart, thinking her coworkers would believe she was moving on to a dream job versus succumbing to a brain tumor.

ELEVEN

The second day of Kent's scheduled days off meant laundry, groceries, and cleaning his apartment. Yesterday, he gave into the demons and drank himself into oblivion. When he had arrived home from his shift, all he could do was sense Maeve. She was everywhere. The book she was reading the other night sat on his coffee table. Her shampoo was still in the bathroom, and her pillow smelled like her perfume. That was when he let himself truly feel everything that had happened in the past twenty-four hours. In love or not, the woman he'd spent most of his nights with was gone, and there wasn't anything he could do about it. Kent needed to forget and opened a bottle of vodka for breakfast.

At some point, he called Damian, who came over and helped his friend through his heartache. Damian also took Kent's phone away. It was better to hide the device than for Kent to drunk text Maeve. His feelings fluctuated from anger to heartbreak. The brokenhearted version of Kent wanted Maeve back, even though she wasn't available. The smart part of Kent wanted to forget everything and move on. Damian said he hoped the smart part would win.

Today, he was determined to forget about everything. His eyes traveled over the empty bottles on his kitchen counter, and he groaned. Before he could clean the mess, he had to go to the store to get trash bags. He also needed to do his laundry before work tomorrow. The latter couldn't wait. He was out of clean uniforms and had to work in the morning.

"Laundry first," he said to his empty apartment. Kent loaded up his laundry into bags he'd found when one of the major box stores put everything out for back to school. They were perfect and lightweight, and they made carrying his laundry easy. Kent grabbed his wallet and made his way to the street. His apartment building didn't have a laundry facility, but there was one on the corner.

Only one other person was at the laundromat when he walked in. Kent breathed a sigh of relief. Sometimes, when he wasn't there first thing in the morning, laundry would end up taking him hours. He found two washers and loaded his clothes. The army had taught him about separating his darks from his whites, and even though it cost him more, he didn't care.

Before he tossed each pair of pants into the washer, he searched the pockets. He was checking his last pair when his fingertips met a folded piece of paper. He pulled it out of his pocket and held it for a moment before it hit him. It was Palmer's list of places she wanted to go to before she died. Kent slipped it into his pocket and finished sorting his clothes.

Once he finished, he went over to the soap dispenser, which looked like it was from the seventies, and bought his laundry soap. This was something he could buy at the store, but hated carrying it back and forth, and he wasn't a fan of those pods. They never broke open all the way, and often left stains on his clothes. Maeve never understood why Kent didn't buy his soap and fabric sheets at the store to save money. Kent got his soap and changed his dollars into quarters. He added the soap, closed the lid, and fed the machine.

The note weighed heavily on his thoughts. He took it from his pocket again, sat down, and opened it slowly. He hadn't read it fully the night he was at her house, but now that he had time, his eyes glossed over at her words. Palmer didn't just want to go to Disney World. She wanted to sit in the front of a roller coaster and feel the wind in her hair. She wanted to go to an animal sanctuary and touch the animals. Everything on her list had a reason. To Kent, this wasn't your normal bucket list. Palmer was trying to make her last days count.

Before I'm Gone

- ♥ Sit in the front seat of a roller coaster and feel the wind in my hair
- ♥ Eat tacos or tortillas from a roadside stand in New Mexico
- ♥ Shop at a large farmers market
- ♥ Meet Lana Del Rey and see her in concert
- ♥ Take a picture of the most-painted shed in the US
- ♥ Sit in the sand and watch the sunrise in Cape Cod
- ♥ Take the steps to the Lincoln Memorial
- ♥ Do yoga in Sedona
- ♥ Tour and feed animals in a wildlife sanctuary
- ♥ Stand under a waterfall
- ♥ See Elvis on the street corner in Las Vegas
- ♥ Hug an elephant
- ♥ Find my family
- ♥ Step on grapes and make wine
- ♥ Run through a wheat field
- ♥ Drive Route 66
- ♥ See the marquees on Broadway
- ♥ Ring the Liberty Bell
- ♥ Buy a quilt from an Amish stand

The line that struck him the most was "eat tacos or tortillas from a roadside stand in New Mexico." He had done that too many times to count. His friend Raúl was from El Salvador, and his family had settled in New Mexico. Throughout basic training, Raúl talked nonstop about his abuelita and how she was the best cook ever. After Kent left the army, he had to find out for himself and visited Raúl and his family. He wasn't lying. His family had the most popular roadside stand in the state. Kent ate there daily during his visit. The next time he visited, he and Raúl drove to Chicago to see a friend of theirs. They took historic

Route 66 because they weren't in a hurry. Those days were some of Kent's favorite memories.

Kent continued to read Palmer's list until he came up with an idea. It was far fetched, but it was something he wanted to do for her. He was going to help her cross off as many of these items as he could. He didn't know how, but he was going to do it. Kent had vacation time to use, and with everything happening with Maeve, he could use the distraction. He could take Palmer to meet Raúl and his family or take her to Santa Monica, where she could take a photo of the **End of the Trail** sign for Route 66.

The more he thought, the more his plan came together. He'd use his vacation time for places that required them to travel longer distances, and on his days off, they'd do what they could nearby. Santa Monica was an easy day trip. They'd go there, take a picture of the sign, and then head to Disney. Kent loved roller coasters and would take Palmer to Disney so she could feel the wind in her hair.

Kent impatiently finished his laundry. He wanted to tell Palmer his idea and start planning their trips, but his clothes wouldn't dry. It took two cycles for the waistband of his pants to not feel damp, and he was certain this was because he was now in a hurry. Kent rushed home, folded his clothes, and put them away, and then he saw the mess in his apartment. He had to go back to work tomorrow, and it would be another full day of looking like this.

Kent ran down to a nearby convenience store, paid for an overpriced ten-count box of trash bags, and ran back home. He separated the returnable cans and bottles from the trash. Kent would leave the bag of returnables downstairs for whoever needed them.

After cleaning, he showered. He couldn't get Palmer's list out of his mind and started adding other things to it. He'd always wanted to see the northern lights and wondered if they could fit a trip to Minnesota in. Kent also wanted to ride the Stratosphere in Las Vegas. They could knock a couple of things off this list . . . *their list* . . . if they went to

Vegas. Palmer could see Elvis and ride the roller coaster at the New York–New York Hotel.

Kent took a chance that Palmer was home and drove to her place. He found parking along the street, paid the meter, and noticed there was a thirty-minute limit on the parking spot. If it took longer than thirty minutes to convince Palmer of his idea, he'd happily take the parking ticket or feed the meter and hope there wasn't an attendant paying attention to his car.

Instead of waiting for the elevator, Kent took the stairs. Adrenaline coursed through his veins at the idea of helping Palmer. He couldn't quite pinpoint why she stood out more than any other patient. Maybe it was because she'd helped him at the bank or because she was determined to fight this battle alone. Either way, he wanted to be there for her.

Out of breath, he knocked on her door, and then rested his hands on his knees. He didn't realize he was out of shape until now. He should start using the workout equipment at the facility, especially the treadmill. Kent used to run five miles a day, and he bet he couldn't do that now.

Palmer answered her door, surprise in her eyes. "Mr. Wagner. I didn't call 911." He had it in his mind she would look frail and sickly. She didn't. Palmer looked exactly the way she did at the bank, and he had to remind himself that when he saw her last, she was sick and not the best version of herself.

"Kent," he wheezed and then shook his head. "Call me Kent. And I know you didn't." The air whooshed out of his lungs. He needed to get back into the gym. He was ridiculously and embarrassingly out of shape.

"Are you okay, Kent?"

He nodded and rested his hand on the doorjamb. "I just ran up four flights of stairs. I need a moment to catch my breath." He felt ridiculous.

Palmer leaned out the door and looked down the hall. "Is the elevator broken? I can call maintenance."

"No, nothing like that," he said with another deep inhale. His heart rate settled back into a normal rhythm. Kent cleared his throat and smiled. "I didn't want to wait to see you."

Palmer looked at Kent with inquisitive eyes. "Why?"

"May I come in?"

She stepped back and let him into her apartment. He looked around and noticed that a painting that had been over the sofa the other night was now gone. "Where'd your painting go?"

"I donated it."

"How come?" he asked. He wished he could take his question back. "Never mind."

"It's okay," she told him. "I've come to terms with my death."

"I can't imagine." He paused and shook his head. "Have you made any arrangements?"

"Not really." Palmer crossed her arms over her chest, pulling her sweater closed. "Why are you here?"

"Can we talk?" Kent motioned to the couch, and Palmer nodded.

"Would you like something to drink? I have water, soda, or juice."

"Water would be great."

Palmer went into the kitchen and returned with a glass filled with water and ice. Crushed ice. He loved crushed ice. "Thank you." He drank greedily and sighed.

"Kent, why are you here?" Palmer asked again.

"Right." Kent put his glass down on a coaster. He took a deep breath and leveled his gaze at her. He realized she was more than a patient to him; at some point in the last week or so, she had become important to him. She was someone he wanted to spend time with and help fulfill her journey. "I have a proposal for you. Today, while doing laundry, I came across the note I found on your table when Damian and I responded to your call. Technically, I should've given it back to you, but I forgot, or I wasn't meant to because there's something bigger at play here. While I read it today, I got this sense . . ." He paused and shook his head. "Do you remember when I told you I went to the Alamo, and it wasn't what I thought it would be?"

Palmer nodded.

"The way you wrote your list, the things you wanted to experience versus places to go. Like, you want to visit a large farmers market, but you didn't say where. I know there's a massive market on Saturdays in Portland, Oregon, and I want to take you."

"To a market in Portland?" she asked.

"Yes, and to the other places on your list. With my schedule, we can do something every other day. I work twenty-four hours and then I'm off for forty-eight. I also have a ton of vacation time. We can hit the places on the East Coast, and we can go to New Mexico. My friend lives there, and his family has a roadside food stand. Exactly what you're looking for."

Palmer stared at Kent for a long time, and Kent squirmed under the intensity. "Why?" she finally asked.

"Because I feel drawn to you, Palmer. Because I came across the list, and there's something about it that makes me want to make sure you accomplish everything on there, and then some."

"I'm dying, Kent. No one wants to spend their time with someone they don't know, let alone someone who's dying. The things my body will go through . . . no one wants to watch that. There are going to be days—" Palmer couldn't finish her sentence. She didn't need to. Kent already knew what she was going to go through. The more her tumor grew, the closer she'd come to death.

He shrugged. "I do," he said. "And who better than a paramedic? I can take care of you and make sure you're getting your meds." Kent rubbed his hands over his legs. "Besides." He looked at her and tried to smile. "You'd be helping me."

"How?"

"I'll be honest, Palmer. There's some stuff going on in my life that could mess with my head. Getting out of town would be a relief. And like I said, I'm drawn to you. I can't explain it, but there's something in here"—he pressed his hand to his heart—"that says this is something I need to do."

Kent cleared his throat. "I've seen death. I've held soldiers while they died. Most of them just looked at me, and when I saw your list, I wondered if they had one. I've lost people in the field or in the back of the rig. What would they have done if given one more day? Just thinking about traveling with you is exciting. I've already planned multiple trips based on your list. I know you're sick, and some days will not be good, but I want to give you as many tomorrows as possible."

Palmer stood and picked up Kent's water glass. She took it into the kitchen and refilled it. Kent waited. He felt as if he had made his case. He wanted her to say yes. Kent wanted to travel and give her the best last days possible while being out of town on his days off. Maeve knew his schedule, and if he didn't have to see her right now, it would be for the best.

"Thanks," Kent said when Palmer returned with a full glass of water. She went to the large window overlooking the road, with the view of the mountains, and stared. Kent joined her. He could see his car from the window but couldn't tell if he had a ticket or not. He was sure he'd been in Palmer's apartment for longer than thirty minutes.

"It's a lot to think about," he said. "You have a lot going on, but you have nothing to lose, right? And I'm guessing you have vacation time?"

"I quit my job."

"Really?"

Palmer nodded. "It's easier this way."

"How long did they give you?" Kent didn't need to expand on his question. Palmer's expression told him she knew what he meant.

"Six months."

He didn't have six months of time . . . unless. Kent needed to see his deputy chief. "What do you think?"

Palmer gazed at Kent and smiled softly. She was a beautiful woman with eyes that still had a sparkle in them. "I think it's a very generous offer, but I can't ask you to give up your life for me. You hardly know me, and the things you'd potentially see . . ." She sighed. "I know what's coming and am afraid of what they're going to do to me."

"Palmer, I want to do this. For you. For me. For us. For an adventure of a lifetime. Can you at least think about it for a couple of days? I'm working tomorrow, and then I'm off. Can I stop by?"

She nodded.

Kent did something so out of character he shocked himself. He pulled Palmer into a hug and held her. "Call me if you need me. If I'm working, call dispatch. I'll always respond." It was a promise he didn't know he could keep, but he'd try.

He made sure Palmer had everything she needed before he left. When he got down to his car, he looked toward her window and swore he saw her wave.

Twelve

She waved, but was it enough?

Even before Kent left her apartment, Palmer was second-guessing herself. He'd done something no one had ever done for her before—he'd offered to take her on a trip. Not just any trip, but one designed to fulfill the items on her list. She couldn't believe she'd shut him down without giving his proposal much thought. This was her automatic reaction to everything. She'd learned how to be independent, how to not rely on anyone but herself. Needless to say, Kent's kind gesture had shocked her.

As soon as he left her apartment, she realized her mistake. Even though he'd told her to call him if she changed her mind, she wasn't sure she would. She stood at her window and was certain it was Kent she waved to. He was motionless, at least to her. The person she watched opened their car door and then shut it without getting inside. They turned and waved.

It was Kent. She was certain.

She waved again, and instead of waiting for him to return to her apartment, she went to him. Thankfully, the elevator was already on her floor, and the ride down to the lobby was quick. When she stepped off, Kent was there. It was like he'd known she was coming to him.

"I'm sorry," she said as soon as she saw him. "I'm not used to people doing things for me, and your offer seemed so generous it didn't really make sense."

"You said you had no one, right?"

She nodded and looked around the lobby. "I grew up in the system." Palmer hated saying "the system" because everyone knew what it meant.

"Right, I remember from the other day." Kent stepped closer. "May I ask how you plan to . . ." He paused and shook his head. "I don't want to say—"

"It's okay." Palmer reached into her pocket and pulled out a small container. After her last visit to the hospital, she was determined to die on her own terms and had sought out the necessary pills. Walking down the back alley was the scariest thing she had ever done, at least until she'd started making her way home. She'd looked over her shoulder every ten seconds, expecting to find the police following her.

Palmer held it in her hand for a moment, knowing the pills inside were a means to an end. A quick, painless way to go out. She'd simply fall asleep. But then what? How long until someone found her body? She wouldn't want her neighbors to smell her rotting corpse. No, she'd take the pills and then call 911 and make sure they knew not to resuscitate. Of course, in order for that to happen, she needed to fill out her DNR paperwork, and she had yet to do that.

Kent's idea intrigued her. She liked the idea of taking mini vacations, if her health allowed, and seeing a couple of the things she had on her list. He was willing, so why was Palmer so hesitant?

Palmer held her hand out, with the tin box sitting there. She met Kent's gaze for a brief moment and then looked away in embarrassment. Kent's fingers grazed her palm ever so lightly, sending the tiniest of tickles through her hand when he took the box from her. Palmer winced when she heard the metal lid open.

Kent lifted Palmer's chin, so she'd look at him. For the first time, she noticed his blue eyes. They were sad, almost as if he hurt for the pain she was going to endure. "Where did you get these?" he asked quietly. He closed the lid and then slipped the container into his pocket. She wanted to protest, but held back. Those were her easy way out.

"I don't want to say."

"California allows death with dignity, Palmer. Your doctor can prescribe you the right drugs," he told her. "There are programs in place now to help people who have a terminal illness. I wish you hadn't shown these to me. I can't give them back to you."

"I know."

"Do you know what they are?" Kent asked. Palmer shook her head. "You don't want to do something like that alone. So many things could go wrong. This option isn't the only option, though. Have you considered . . ." Kent's brows furrowed in frustration.

Palmer took a resounding breath. "I've reached out to some hospice homes. I have a couple of meetings set up. They want to offer me a tour. I guess it matters where I spend my last days, and I figured dying with strangers around me is better than dying alone."

Kent closed the distance between them again. "I know this seems unconventional, but I want to be your someone. I want to help you live out your days the way you could've lived your life."

"And what do you get out of this?"

The lobby of Palmer's complex had a seating area, which the management company used mostly for prospective clients, and while she thought they should go back upstairs to her apartment, Kent motioned for her to sit down on the leather sofa. There was a light chill in the air, and Palmer shivered. Kent went over to the gas fireplace, which was directly across from them, and turned up the heat. He faced Palmer and pulled his leg underneath him.

"You asked what I get out of this. I get a chance to escape," he told her. "Do you remember when I saw you in the cafeteria and I told you my girlfriend was in the hospital?" Palmer nodded. "She'd been in an accident earlier that day. My partner and I were first on the scene. When I got to the car, I saw her in there, unconscious and with another man. Turns out, she was having an affair."

"Oh, Kent. I'm so sorry."

"Not on me, but with me."

"Oh!" Palmer said, shocked.

"It gets worse," Kent said.

"I can't imagine how," Palmer added. Kent chuckled, and she wondered what could make him laugh at a time like this.

"She's pregnant. She says the baby is mine, but she's also been seeing her husband, so I don't know what to believe."

"Oh . . . wow, that's a lot for someone to process in a day. I'm sorry for what you're going through."

"I just . . ." Kent pounded his fist into his thigh. "I really think that I hate her," he said as he looked away. "Like, all she had to say when we met was that she and her husband had separated, and we could've kept things casual, but to lie . . ." He trailed off.

"'Hate' is such a strong word, Kent." Palmer used to hate everything. The orphanage, the kids at school, her life. After three years of therapy, she'd learned there was a reason for everything. There was a reason her parents had put her up for adoption, and why kids were so mean to her in school. She couldn't care less about those kids. She never thought about them. But Palmer did think about her family, more so recently, because she was out of time. Kent could help her find her family, if there was one out there for her.

"If she turns out to be the mother of your child, you don't want to hate her for giving you the greatest gift of your life. You especially don't want your child to know that you hated his or her mother at one point. Your girlfriend made a mistake, and I'm sure she's distraught over it, and probably confused. Believe me when I say if I had the chance to be a parent, I'd be ecstatic."

He sighed. "It's what I feel. I thought we had a good thing going, and to find her like that, so helpless and with another man, I was beside myself. I couldn't do my job. Like, I'm there to save lives, and then I see her trapped in the car with him. And when she wakes up, I'm so happy, and then for her to tell me the rest? I think what broke me was how worried she was about her husband. I get it, but it was like she stabbed me in the heart and then twisted the blade until she could cut a piece of me out." He shook his head. "I don't want to see her or have anything to do with her."

Palmer mirrored the way he sat. "I think you'll change your mind once the hurt has worn off and you've had time to process everything. What if the baby is yours?"

He shrugged. "She's married, and, according to the internet, her husband will show as the father on the birth certificate, although I've asked for a paternity test, so not sure what happens then. It's a waiting game."

"You might have to hire a lawyer, or at least talk to someone about your rights."

"We have a program at work that can help me find someone. I've never had to use it before, but I guess there's a first time for everything."

Palmer cinched her sweater tighter around her. "Are you cold?" Kent asked, and she nodded. He got up and went to the fireplace and turned the dial even higher and then held his hands over the vent to make sure it blew hot air. He stood there and looked at the framed picture on the mantel. It was Alcatraz.

"Have you been there?" Palmer asked.

"No, never had an inkling to go. It's not on your list," he pointed out.

"I haven't finished my list. Honestly, it's depressing knowing I'll never go to half of those places, and yet I used to think I had all the time in the world."

Kent reached into his pocket and pulled out the piece of paper. He opened it and then handed it to her. "We'd be doing this for the both of us. I love to travel, and I've been to a lot of the states on your list. We'd see a lot of places together for the first time."

Palmer took the paper from him and studied her words. He questioned why she'd put finding her family so far down the list when it should be at the top. Suddenly, she knew why. She was dying. What was she going to do? Have a glorious reunion with her long-lost mother or father and then say, *Oh, by the way, I'm dying, but it was great to meet you?*

Prospective tenants came into the lobby with someone from the management company. Palmer stood and asked Kent to come back to her apartment. They rode in the elevator in silence, but she noticed he stood next to her. He could've stood against either wall, but he took the spot on her left. When they arrived on her floor, he put his arm out to make sure the door didn't suddenly close, and when they got to her door, and she opened it, he kept his palm flat on the door to keep it open.

Palmer once again offered Kent something to drink, but he had other plans. "What do you say we order in?"

His suggestion took her off guard, and she stammered over her words. Kent held his hand up, and his face beamed. "We're going to be spending a lot of time together. We should start with dinner."

Kent had a very valid point, and Palmer found it hard to argue with him, but she was still going to try. "I haven't agreed to be your bucket list buddy."

"It's your bucket list," he pointed out. "In fact, I think you titled it 'Before I'm Gone.'" He leaned forward to look at the paper in her hand, but she hid it behind her back. "Sort of morbid, don't you think?"

"I'm dying."

"So you've said. But right now, we're living. Let's live like we've never lived before for the next however many months we have."

"It's just me."

Kent shrugged. "Don't be so sure of yourself. What if—"

"Don't say it," Palmer said, pointedly. "You have a child on the way. You need to live."

"Might," Kent corrected. "And I have every intention of living a long, happy life. And those same intentions plan on giving you the happiest of days until you say stop."

Palmer needed a break from the back-and-forth. She went to the drawer in her kitchen and pulled out the stack of takeout menus. She turned and, much to her surprise, saw Kent standing on the other side of her kitchen island. Palmer set the menus down and gave him a pointed look.

"If we're going to do this, it's only fair that you add to the list as well. It can't be all about me."

"Deal," Kent said.

"And you let me pay for everything."

Kent's mouth dropped open, and he slowly shook his head. "Absolutely not."

"It's only fair."

"I don't see how."

Palmer crossed her arms over her chest. "You're going to see me at my worst, and I'm going to have to depend on you, and you're doing this out of the kindness of your heart. I already feel like a burden. You shouldn't have to bear any financial responsibility for these trips. Besides, I can't take the money with me, so I might as well spend it . . ." Her words trailed off.

"I'll tell you what." Kent picked up the stack of menus, waved them in the air, and fanned them out on the counter. "We eat first, and then we make a game plan. We'll budget everything, and we'll look at my work schedule. For the longer trips, I'll use my vacation time. When we go east, we can either make a couple of trips, or we can go for, like, two to three weeks."

"Are you sure about this?" she asked.

Kent held his hand out, and Palmer shook it. "Without a doubt. I'm ready to start our adventures."

Kent's additions to Palmer's list

- ★ *See the northern lights in Minnesota*
- ★ *Visit Plymouth Rock*
- ★ *Touch Babe Ruth's bat*
- ★ *Travel the Loneliest Road*
- ★ *Visit the Muhammad Ali Center*
- ★ *Dance in the rain with someone I love*
- ★ *Take the ferry to the Statue of Liberty*
- ★ *Check out the Grand Canyon*
- ★ *Take every picture I can of Palmer*
- ★ *Make Palmer smile*

THIRTEEN

The sun shone brightly and forced Kent to squint as he approached the door to RoccoBean. He smiled warmly at the people he passed as he made his way to the counter. Kent placed his normal order and then stood off to the side while he waited. He scrolled through the news apps he had on his phone and avoided social media like the plague. He and Maeve were friends on there, and the last thing he wanted right now was to see any updates from her. Kent was happy, and he wanted nothing to dampen his day.

Kent loved his new routine. He'd thought he would hate waking up alone on the days he had to go to work, but not this morning. He woke up rejuvenated and with a new purpose in life—to make Palmer's last days her most memorable.

With coffees in hand—one for him and one for Damian—he thanked the barista and made his way back to his car. He thought about Palmer and their dinner the night before. They bantered like siblings. They had decided on pizza for dinner, but they couldn't figure out toppings. She wanted veggies, and he wanted meat. Kent suggested half and half, but Palmer said there was no way she'd eat half a pizza, and it made sense for her to pick off whatever she didn't want. Kent refused. He wanted her to have whatever she wanted.

They instead went through the stack of takeout options and finally agreed they wanted Italian. Kent ordered pasta, salad, and breadsticks, and then Palmer called back and added to the order because she wanted

Kent to have leftovers for his lunch the next day. No one had ever done something like that for him, and he gave Palmer the biggest hug he could. He may have held on longer than was casually acceptable, but she didn't seem to mind. Kent liked being around her, more than he probably should.

Palmer offered Kent wine, but he never took a risk. He had to drive back to his place and was fine with water. After dinner, Palmer showed him her prescriptions. He made a note of them in his phone, and also added all her information, along with her physicians' number in his contacts. He suggested they meet with Dr. Hughes because he wanted to make sure he had firsthand knowledge about Palmer's condition. It was paramount that he'd be able to take care of her on the days she was with him.

At the station, he set Damian's coffee down and went to their rig. He went over his personalized checklist and made sure the rig was fully stocked and ready for the day. Afterward, he checked the calendar and saw that he and Damian didn't have any assigned duties for the day. This pleased him, even though they'd both help where needed. He grabbed Damian's coffee and climbed the stairs to the third floor. He found his partner in the gym, finishing a workout.

"Thanks." Damian took a quick drink. Kent eyed him oddly. He could never drink coffee after a workout. "You look happy."

"I am. I have some irons in the fire that I'll tell you about after I put in for some vacation time. See ya for breakfast."

Kent made his way back downstairs and over to the employee notice board. He scanned it and saw one of the new hires looking for an apartment, someone looking for a dog walker, and a flyer about free kittens needing a good home. Kent reached for the slip he'd need to fill out for time off and then read the instruction sheet pinned to the board. He scanned it mostly and then did a double take when he came across the word "sabbatical." Kent read and reread the rules for taking an extended period of time off and thought they could apply to him.

Instead of filling out the vacation slip, Kent went upstairs to the second floor, where his command was. He first knocked on Captain Greig's door, but there was no answer. He then went to the deputy chief's door.

"Come in," Jacob Matthews barked. Kent entered and suddenly lost his nerve. Matthews was a force of a man. He'd been with the department for over thirty-five years and was in the running to make chief of the department when the current one retired. Matthews was a favorite among most of the medics, as well as the firefighters. Everyone thought he was a fair man.

"What can I do for you, Wagner?"

Kent cleared his throat and then looked down at the sheet in his hand. Was he making the right decision? He thought about Palmer and how she only had six months to live her life. If he took a sabbatical, they could do everything on her list and then some. He had some savings and could cash out his vacation time and sublet his apartment.

"Sir." Kent stepped forward. "I'd like to request a sabbatical."

"Oh? What's the reason?"

"Well, after the other day, I realized I need to get away." Kent inhaled and cleared his throat. He would be honest with his command. "And also, I have a friend who's dying. She has a grade-four GBM, and I'd like to be there for her."

Matthews looked defeated, as if he'd been to battle. "That's unfortunate," he said as he glanced at his desk. His brow furrowed, and then he motioned for Kent to sit down. "Are you aware of what it means to take care of someone with a GBM?"

"I am, sir. I've done a lot of research, and I plan to meet with her neurosurgeon soon. The thing is, I came in this morning to put in for time off because I want to help her with her bucket list, and to get away from the situation I'm in. I saw the option of a sabbatical on the form and thought it would be easier. Palmer—my friend—she doesn't have anyone. I'm her person, and I'd really like to be there with her through all of this."

"You're one helluva guy, Wagner. I hope you know what you're doing."

"I do, but I don't. I just know I need to be there for her."

Matthews nodded. "Fill out the request, give it to Greig, and make sure I get a copy. The sooner the better. I'm in a good mood today, but I may not be tomorrow. I'll fast-track it through HR and give it my approval."

Kent stood. "Yes, sir. Thank you."

"Wagner?" Kent turned from the door. "Never hesitate to call me if you need something."

"Thank you, again, sir."

Kent went to one of the open conference rooms and filled out the form. He wrote as clearly as possible, read over his statement clause on why he needed the time off, and then made a copy for Matthews. He'd led Kent to believe they would approve his request, and now he had to plan. This wasn't something he had discussed with Palmer, but he needed to. There he went, thinking before he even consulted her. The worst she could do was say no; then he'd stick to his vacation time and deal with whatever came his way. Kent was truthful when he told Matthews he wanted to be there for Palmer, and he fully intended to be. Kent was going to hold her hand until the end. He would be her someone from this point forward.

Back upstairs, Kent found Damian at the table. Kent thanked medics Nick Martin and Zach Lacey for breakfast and made himself a plate. He joined the chatter around the table as they talked about the Golden State Warriors and how they used to get tickets for thirty dollars, and how the best way to watch them these days was from the privacy of your own home. Kent preferred college basketball over the NBA, but he kept his thoughts to himself.

When they finished, Damian and Kent went downstairs and got into their rig. They would stage at Station 49 until they got a call. On the drive there, Kent told his partner about his plan and waited for him to respond.

"Why are you doing this?"

Kent rolled his eyes. He was growing tired of answering the same question. "Too many reasons to list," he said.

"Do you like her or something?" Damian asked.

Kent thought about the question and smiled when the answer presented itself with an image of Palmer in his mind. "Actually, I do. She's definitely someone I would've asked out."

Kent's phone vibrated in his pocket, and an uncomfortable feeling rose. He kept it off during his work shift, but he had promised Palmer he'd leave it on, just in case. He took it from his pocket and saw Maeve's name on the screen. Kent sent the call to voice mail. He had nothing to say. If it was important, Maeve could leave a message.

"You're going to have to talk to her sooner or later."

"Preferably, later," Kent said. "How'd you know it was Maeve?"

Damian pulled their rig up to the curb and put it in park. "Because if it was anyone else, you would've answered it."

"I have nothing to say to her, and I don't want to hear her excuses. After the first night together, she should've said something. Hell, she could've said, 'I'm separated and looking to be wild.' I would've been okay with that. But she led me on."

"Yeah, that's messy."

"See why I want to leave?"

Damian shrugged. "I do, but I don't. It's your life, though, and you seem to have a connection with the banker."

"Palmer—that's her name," Kent said. "You'll like her."

Damian laughed. "I don't envy you."

Kent didn't need Damian to expand on his comment. He had spent last night scouring the internet for everything he could find on glioblastomas, and what he couldn't find on the web, he searched for through his textbooks. Kent wanted to be prepared for everything and anything that might come his way. He also wanted to make sure they equipped his car with what they might need. He started for a list of what they'd need for their road trips. Extra clothes and water were at the top.

"Where are you taking her?" Damian asked, interrupting Kent's thoughts.

"I don't know. I'm going over tomorrow with an atlas. We'll plan it all together."

"Does she know you're taking a sabbatical?"

"No, I haven't told her yet. I decided this morning to ask for that instead of time off when I saw the option."

"What am I supposed to do while you're gone?" Damian asked.

Kent hadn't thought about Damian. Instantly, he felt like shit. Like he had quit on his partner. "I'm sorry," Kent said. "I know this sucks, but I have to do it. I want to do it for her. For me."

"I get it." Damian opened the door and got out of the truck. Kent gave him a head start and then followed. When he walked into the station, Damian wasn't in their normal spot. Kent had upset his partner, and there wasn't much he could do about it. He would not take his offer off the table where Palmer was concerned.

His phone rang again, and this time it was Palmer's name on his screen. "Hello, Palmer? Is everything okay?"

"Yes, Kent, it is. I'm calling because my office is throwing a goodbye party."

"I'm sorry, they're what? Giving you a party because you're . . ." He still couldn't bring himself to say "dying" to her.

"Oh, God, no," she whispered. "I told you the other day that I quit my job."

"Oh, right. I'm sorry. I forgot. But why not just tell them the truth?"

"Because I didn't want their pity or to hear how sorry they were."

"Makes sense. So, why the call?"

"My boss told me to invite my friends, and well, you're my only genuine friend." Her words broke him. She added, "Do you want to come to the bank for cake? There's other food as well."

"I'm working, remember?" He was afraid her memory had already slipped.

"I remember, but you're in the Financial District, right?"

"We are. Tell you what, I have to find my partner—he's around here someplace—and then we'll be over unless we get a call."

"That will be great," she said. They hung up. Kent went to look for Damian and found him coming out of the bathroom.

"There's food and cake down at Bay Bank. They're throwing Palmer a going-away party."

"Uh . . . that's extremely disturbing."

Kent realized his mistake and shook his head. "She told them she's moving. It's a long story, but Palmer's alone in more ways than you think. I'm pretty much the only person in her life who knows what's going on."

"Well, I've never been a man who says no to cake."

The men made their way over to the bank. Their entrance seemed to scare everyone. The tellers and customers frantically tried to figure out who'd called 911. Palmer came forward and greeted them. Kent couldn't take his eyes off her. He smiled as she approached.

"The food is in the back. Follow me."

Damian fell in step behind Kent, and he could hear his partner saying hi to everyone. They both knew how women felt about seeing a man in uniform, even though they wore pants and a short-sleeved button-down.

Kent caught his breath when he stepped into the back room. What would normally be a generic break room had become a room with streamers, balloons, presents, and a sign wishing Palmer good luck. Kent's heart broke at the scene in front of him. He went to Palmer's side and whispered in her ear: "Are you okay?"

She nodded, but the movement was ever so slight. He hardly knew her yet could read the emotions on her face clearly. Palmer strained to keep her emotions in check. That was why she'd called him—to give her coworkers something else to look at and talk about. Kent was going to make sure her coworkers never forgot about him after this.

Fourteen

Kent wanted to be Palmer's person. Deep down, she knew he wouldn't leave when the going got tough—and it was going to be tough—but she expected he wouldn't want to deal with the mundane tasks of what would happen after she was gone. She wouldn't ask him to either. Her life was hers to clean up, and as odd as it was, she had time to get her affairs in order. Few had an opportunity such as this.

Palmer went around her apartment and pulled the curtains back to let the natural light in. The gray sky and slight drizzle of rain matched Palmer's mood perfectly. "Somber" was the word she used to describe herself. She couldn't quite grasp the magnitude of what lay ahead of her. She was dying. There would not be some breakthrough medicine or some state-of-the-art technology that would miraculously save her. Palmer had an end date. If she went past the six-month mark, she'd be lucky, especially since she was refusing treatment. The pills she would do, and if they gave her four or five months, then she'd take it. The chemicals, the radiation, and losing her hair, only to die anyway, didn't appeal to her. Palmer wanted to go out with some grace and dignity because she was going to die in the company of strangers. There was still a chance she'd end up in hospice.

Palmer pulled a garbage bag from the box she'd bought at the store and shook it open. She started in her closet, pulling each suit out and laying them on her bed. She carefully folded the skirts and trousers, then the blazers, and bundled them with a rubber band. Palmer wanted the pieces to stay together and felt like if she'd haphazardly tossed them into the bag, no one would take the time to match the pieces together. Her plan was to donate her work clothes to the women's shelter. She wanted them to be free. She wanted someone to benefit from her clothing without it costing her anything.

Suit after suit, she folded, bundled, and set the items in the bag. When the bag was half-full, she'd open and fill another one. By the time she got to her dresser, she had half a dozen bags near her front door. She'd ask Kent to take her or ask him to drop them off for her.

Her casual clothing she would hold on to until the end and leave a note for the hospice. Or maybe even Kent, if he wanted the responsibility. She wasn't sure about their budding relationship, even though she'd called him to come to her going-away party a day after she'd agreed to travel with him. Palmer considered him a friend, and that day, she needed someone. With him and his partner in the room, everyone focused on them and not her. Palmer's coworkers gushed over the medics, often causing them to blush. She appreciated Kent coming to her rescue. Later, after she'd gone home for the night, Kent called to check up on her. He thanked her for inviting them to the party and thought that Damian might have a crush on Laura. Kent and Palmer laughed about it for a bit. She offered to give Damian's number to Laura if he wanted. Kent asked the standard questions and reminded her to call if she needed anything.

What she needed, no one could offer her. She *needed* to go back in time to her first migraine, to the time when she could've gone to the doctor for help. Palmer couldn't dwell on what she couldn't change, though, and pushed herself forward. For the rest of her days, she'd live life to the fullest and be the most positive person she could. She at least owed it to herself to go out with a smile.

The knock on her door brought a smile to her face. In the very short amount of time she'd known Kent, he'd given her some hope. He couldn't cure her, but he was determined to give her a lifetime of memories in the time she had left. He was, by far, the most selfless person she had ever met. As she unlocked the door, she thought he should have a key to her apartment.

Kent greeted Palmer with a smile that made her knees shake. He was dashing, with an air of confidence that Palmer wished she had. He carried himself in a way that made him look fearless, yet he had a softer side to him. She sensed he cared deeply about her and would do anything to make her last days worth living.

His arms were full of books, as were his hands. She took the two coffee cups from him and set them on the island in her kitchen. He dumped the pile he carried onto her small dining room table and sighed.

"Good morning." Kent pulled Palmer into a hug. Startled, it took her a second to wrap her arms around him, but once she had, she sank into his embrace. This was new to her, a physical connection to someone she barely knew. Palmer wasn't a toucher. She didn't randomly touch people to get their attention. Call it an adverse effect of growing up in the system. The director of her group home didn't go around offering affection, and the only people Palmer would've ever considered asking for a hug from would've been a teacher. Yet, she never had the courage to speak those words.

Kent let her go, and the grin he had when he walked in was still there. Palmer didn't know who to thank for his presence, but she was grateful. She still wasn't sure about his offer and felt like he was giving up his life for a complete stranger, even if it was a few days a week and for a limited time.

"Thank you for the coffee." Palmer took a sip and closed her eyes as the rich flavor met her taste buds. "This is good." She held the cup out to look at the logo.

"I'm surprised you don't go there. It's not far from the bank."

"Don't be surprised," she said. "I don't do a lot of the things a typical person would do. I've learned this recently. I'm boring and live by a routine because I thought that was how adults did things. On Saturdays, I go to the café down the street and order a cinnamon roll with a cup of coffee or tea. The same brands I have in my cupboard."

Palmer glanced at the cup she held and then took another drink. "The other night, I sat on the couch and tried to look at my life from an outsider's point of view. Do you want to know what I saw?"

"What's that?" Kent asked.

"I saw someone who waited until she had an end date to start living, and then it hit me that's not the case at all. I'm only living because of you. If you hadn't offered to travel with me, I'd still be sitting on the couch, making plans for what hospice center I'm moving to. You're the knight in shining armor I didn't know I needed."

Kent went to Palmer and set his hands on her upper arms. "Just call me Super Kent."

Palmer repeated his new moniker over in her mind, and that's when it hit her. "Kent," she said softly. "You're my Superman."

He was, and he knew it. "The next time I talk to my mom, I'll thank her for naming me Kent. It seems she knew what she was doing."

"Will you tell me about your parents?" Palmer asked with genuine interest.

"I will, but let's save it for one of our drives," he said. "Speaking of which, I have some news. Let's sit down."

They sat around the table. Kent moved his books to the side and relaxed against the chair. "Before, I suggested we go somewhere every couple of days, and plan a couple of weeks on the East Coast. Do you remember?"

Did he ask if I remembered because memory loss is part of my symptoms?

"I remember," Palmer said. "My memory is still intact."

"Okay, I just wanted to make sure. Anyway, that plan is off the table."

"Oh?" Palmer's voice cracked, despite her attempt to remain calm. She knew the trips were too good to be true. Tears pricked her eyes, and she had no choice but to look away.

"Hey, no." Kent reached for her hands. "I'm sorry, but what I have to say is good. I promise. We're going on this trip. We're just doing it differently."

"We are?" She tried to keep her voice level.

"Of course. Yesterday, instead of asking for the time off, I asked for a sabbatical instead. My deputy chief told me he'll approve it as soon as my captain signs off. So, it looks like I'm going to be off and we're going to travel, with no time constraints."

The words soaked in as Palmer sat there, stunned. "Uh . . . what about my doctor's appointments?"

"Yeah . . . that's the only thing I haven't worked out. I can administer your meds, track your symptoms, and we can do telehealth with Dr. Hughes. If things get bad, we can stop at the hospital. Of course, if Dr. Hughes approves."

"She won't," Palmer said. "She wants me to have chemo or radiation, and she's vehemently against forgoing any treatment."

"Well . . ." Kent paused and looked at Palmer. "We could go and not tell her."

"Okay." Palmer shocked herself by her quick answer.

"Can I ask? Since you quit your job, what are you doing for health insurance?"

Palmer stood and went into her bedroom. When she came back, she placed a pile of papers in front of Kent and sat down. "I bought a six-month plan. I suppose if I make it past the six months, I'll wing it." She shrugged. "I also added you as the person who can make decisions for me if I'm incapacitated."

"And what is the decision?"

"DNR. I'm terminal. If it's my time, I want to go."

Kent swallowed hard. "This brings me to my next question. On the list you wrote, it says, 'Find my family.' Now, I know you grew up in the system, so what does this mean exactly?"

Palmer stood and walked over to her desk and brought the envelope back to where they were sitting. "I've taken a DNA test, and these are the results." The paper-thin shell felt as though it weighed a hundred pounds, sitting there on her lap.

"And you haven't opened them?"

She shook her head and looked at him. "Months ago, I was eager to know the results, and now . . . well, now, what's the point? Either I go on living the rest of my days the way I have, or I open it to find that I have a slew of family out there that I'll never know because it took me far too long to take this test."

Kent rested his hand on Palmer's knee. "I'm sorry," he said.

"Because I'm dying?"

"Not only that, but because of the way you grew up. It doesn't seem fair, not to you. Not to anyone. There's someone out there who belongs to you, and I'm sure they're missing you just as much as you miss them."

"I doubt it." She set the envelope onto the table. If they missed her, they would've looked for her or not left her at the orphanage to begin with.

Kent nodded and cleared his throat. "All right, let's shift to something happy." He pulled the stack of books in front of him. "We need to figure out our plan. Do we start here? Do we fly east and start there? We have options. What's your flavor?" He spread the books across the table, opened the atlas, and took out the highlighters he'd bought.

"Everything I marked with a red dot are the things on our list."

"Our list?"

"Yes." His eyes met hers. "You told me to add to the list, so I did."

Palmer smiled. "Okay." She leaned forward and studied the map of the United States.

"Flying east means we have to rent a car."

"Money isn't an issue," she told Kent. "I told you I'd pay for everything."

"And I told you no. We'll split or figure something out. This is our trip. We make all the decisions together."

Palmer nodded and ducked her head. She tried to hide her smile, but Kent saw it. "So, Ms. Sinclair, are we flying east?"

She nodded. "I think we should rent a convertible. I've never been in one, and I've always wanted to feel the wind in my hair."

"Yes." Kent fist pumped. "I've always wanted to drive one. Look at us, working together." Kent wrote on his notepad. "On your list, you said you want to watch the sunrise in Cape Cod, and it just so happens that I want to see Plymouth Rock, and they're close to each other." He flipped to Massachusetts, which shared pages with Connecticut and Rhode Island in the atlas. He showed Palmer where Plymouth and Chatham were and estimated the travel time to be a little over an hour without traffic.

"We'd fly into Logan Airport in Boston. Now we can either stay in Boston or Cape Cod. Your choice."

"I want to see as much as possible. So, maybe Boston?"

"Boston it is." Kent wrote another note. "We definitely have to eat New England clam chowder while we're there."

"Chowdah," Palmer corrected.

"Excuse me?" Kent laughed.

She shrugged. "People in Boston drop their *r*'s. I thought I'd try it out."

"I like it. What's next?"

Palmer picked up one book and began flipping through. Kent did the same thing. They spent the rest of the morning making notes about places they wanted to see and places they wanted to eat.

Palmer and Kent's List

- *Eat chowdah in Boston, per Palmer*
- *Eat pizza in Chicago*
- *Try frozen custard in New York City*
- *Get coffee in each city*

FIFTEEN

Word spread quickly between the department, the fire stations, and the hospital. People called Kent a hero. They patted him on his back, told their own stories of places they had visited, and offered to help fund the trip he was about to take with Palmer. This last point caught him off guard, as he hadn't expected that sort of kindness.

He declined, of course, and thanked them for their generosity. He didn't see himself as a hero, but a friend to Palmer. It wasn't like she had a dying wish and he was her savior. She had six months or less to live, and he was going to make sure she lived her last days to the fullest. If she had family, they would've done the same thing. At least, that's what he told himself. For him, this wasn't out of the ordinary. It was in his nature to be giving.

Their shift had ended, and everyone had said goodbye to Kent. They wished him well and asked for postcards, and Reeva asked for souvenirs. She said she didn't care what he brought back, as long as it was something cool, unique, and special to the place they visited. Palmer and Kent talked about keepsakes, the pros and cons of them.

"They'll be good for you, Kent." That was all Palmer said on the matter.

Kent went into the locker room to finish packing his things. He found Damian in there. He sat on the bench and stared at the ground. In the past couple of weeks, since Kent had asked for the sabbatical, the tension had been thick between them. Damian was upset, and rightly so.

Damian was a drawback of leaving. When Kent returned, it was unlikely he and Damian, still fully employed, would be partners. That hurt Kent, and Damian as well. They'd been partners since they'd started, and they had a great relationship. They worked well together and could sense what the other was about to do beforehand. Kent definitely didn't want his partner to be stuck with someone who was uptight or unfriendly, and he didn't want that when he came back to work.

It was unlike Damian to linger after his shift ended. He usually wanted to get home and start his two days off. Kent went to his locker and pulled out the extra set of clothes he kept there and the many bags of snacks Kent liked to munch. He set those on the table in the locker room for anyone who wanted them. It made sense for Kent to take them home, but over the past week, he had cleaned out as much of his cupboards and refrigerator as he could to prepare so the subletter could move in.

The tension between Kent and Damian was palpable. They had lost their rhythm. Their cohesiveness. Kent chalked it up to him being distracted. He couldn't blame Damian for anything. He was the perfect partner, and whoever ended up with him would be damn lucky.

Damian sighed, and Kent looked at his back. "When are you leaving?" Damian asked.

"We fly out tonight," Kent said.

Damian turned. "What are you going to do if she gets sick? Has a seizure or a stroke? Then what?"

Kent held his breath for a moment and then relaxed. He'd been through these questions and more with Dr. Hughes. They'd agreed on weekly telehealth check-ins, and in the event Palmer needed medical care, Kent was to call Dr. Hughes at once so she could consult with whoever saw Palmer.

"I'm not doing this by the seat of my pants, Damian. Palmer and I have spoken with her neuro."

"Still doesn't answer my question."

Kent slammed his locker door, and then immediately regretted it. He shouldn't be angry at Damian, not over something like this. He was asking valid questions, but he also made Kent feel like he hadn't done his due diligence. Was there a risk? Yes, and it was mountainous.

"I'm prepared to take care of her, Damian."

"Should she even fly?"

Another question Kent and Palmer had posed to Dr. Hughes. "Yes, she can fly. Dr. Hughes prescribed anticonvulsants and corticosteroids for her. Many people in her condition fly to see specialists all the time. We're prepared."

Damian shook his head. "Listen, I'm not trying to be a jerk here. I'm just really worried that you'll be in over your head."

"I was a combat medic, Damian. I can handle giving Palmer a shot in her hip." Kent put the rest of his clothes in his bag. "I'm sorry this sucks for you and I get that you don't agree, but it's something I have to do both for her, and for me. If you were doing something like this, I'd support you."

Damian sighed. "You're right. I'm sorry. Getting a new partner is a big change for me."

"I get it." Kent went to Damian, and they hugged. Kent would miss his friend. "I may call you from time to time, so have your phone handy."

"You better bring me a present or something."

"Yeah, like what?"

Damian laughed. "When you see it, you'll know it's for me."

Kent rolled his eyes. "No pressure."

"Nope, none. Come on, I'll walk you out."

After Kent had stopped at his apartment to pick up his things, he stopped at RoccoBean for his and Palmer's caffeine fix. He told the barista he wouldn't see them for a while since he was taking the most epic road trip ever.

"That's so cool," the barista said. "What's your Instagram? I want to see your photos."

"I don't have one."

"You should totally create one and post your photos!"

"Thanks, I'll think about it." He would bring the subject up to Palmer, who had no social media presence at all. The more he thought about it, the more it made sense for Palmer to create some sort of profile if she planned to look for her family.

Kent drove to Palmer's and pulled into the parking lot across from her complex. The plan was for him to leave his car there for the duration of their trip. It was the cheaper option, and he had told his subletter he could have his parking spot while he was gone. Before he could get into the elevator, his phone rang. He glanced at the screen and froze.

Maeve.

He hadn't spoken to her since the day in the hospital when everything went south with them. He didn't know how she was or what was going on in her life. Her parents said she needed time and space, and that's what Kent was giving her. Seeing her name made his heart race. Kent had cared for her, but those feelings went out the window when she told him about her husband. He hesitated before answering.

"Hello?" He intended to answer with a firm, nonchalant tone, but his voice cracked, much to his dismay. Kent didn't want to show Maeve any emotion. He didn't want her to know how she had hurt him.

"Hi, Kent," Maeve said and then sighed. "Um, how are you?"

"I'm fine."

"Good, good. I was wondering if we could get together and talk?"

They could. He had time before he and Palmer needed to be at the airport, but he couldn't bring himself to say yes. Did he owe it to Maeve to hear her out? Possibly, and only because she could be carrying his child. If she wasn't pregnant, he would've deleted her number by now and forgotten all about her.

Before he could tell her off, he remembered what Palmer had said. Maeve could be the mother of his child, and while he was hurt by what she had done, she was hurting just the same. Somehow, in the short amount of time he had spent with Palmer, she'd changed his view on how he should interact with Maeve. "I can't right now, Maeve," he said. "I'm about to leave town for a while."

"Oh, where are you going?"

"On a road trip to everywhere. My friend is dying, so we're doing the ultimate bucket list tour of the US."

"I'm so sorry, Kent." Was she sorry for the situation she'd put him in or that his friend was dying? He said nothing. He didn't want to tell her things were okay because they weren't. What did she expect him to say?

"Anyway, I wanted to let you know I did the paternity test, like you'd asked. Enzo isn't happy—"

Hearing that her husband wasn't happy with something Kent had the right to didn't sit well with him. "Look, I don't mean to be mean or anything, but I don't really care about Enzo and his feelings. I will not be a third wheel in your marriage problems. If the baby is mine, I'll be there. I'll be a hands-on dad and do my part. I'll take care of what's mine. But I won't be this extra person in your life, Maeve."

"No, I know, and I told him as much. If the baby is yours, Kent, we'll work something out. I won't be *that* person—the one who keeps the father away from his child. I know I messed up, but I hope that someday, you can forgive me," she said quietly. "I'll call you when the results come in."

"Thanks. I'd appreciate knowing, either way."

"Well . . ." Maeve sighed. "I guess I'll call ya," she said quietly.

"Maeve," he said before she could hang up. "Listen, if you need anything, call me. I can't promise to always answer, but I'll call back when I can. I care about you and know you're going through a tough time right now, and with everything . . ." Kent paused. He pinched the bridge of his nose. "Just know that I'm here if you need anything."

"Thank you. Again, I'm sorry. Have a safe trip, Kent."

"Thanks." He hung up before she could prolong the conversation. He closed his eyes and took a deep breath to calm his nerves before getting into the elevator.

When Kent reached Palmer's door, he paused and listened to the music coming from the other side. Palmer had eclectic taste when it came to the music she listened to. Every time he'd come over, she had something different playing. He mostly caught her listening to songs that seemed like a tragic romance, but they made Palmer smile, and that was what mattered these days.

He rested one cup on top of the other and used the key Palmer had made for him. She'd given it to him the other night and was nervous about it. They'd taken a step in their friendship that most wait years to take in their relationships.

"Good morning," he called out as he entered. "I brought the goods." Palmer came out of her bedroom, looking worse for the wear. "What's wrong?" Kent asked instantly.

"Nothing," she said.

"You mean 'something.' You've been crying, and before you can argue with me, I can tell by how bloodshot your eyes are. Spill. What happened?"

Palmer shook her head. "I just realized some things today, and they sort of hurt, ya know?"

Kent nodded and set the stack of cups onto the counter before handing her one. "Are they things we can add to the list?"

"Maybe, but one is unlikely."

"What is it?"

Palmer took a drink of her coffee, closed her eyes, and sighed. Kent smiled at the vision. They would have to seek a new coffee place in each town they visited because seeing Palmer enjoy a simple thing like that would be worth it.

"I'll never see Lana Del Rey perform in concert."

"Would you have gone if she had come here?" Kent asked.

Palmer shook her head. "Unlikely, but I would've liked to have had the option."

Kent took Palmer's coffee from her and set it down, along with his. He then took her hands in his. "We can make list after list of things we're going to miss," he told her. "From rainbows to new movies, from thunderstorms to our stupid rolling blackouts. All we can do is live in the moment. Moving forward, we live for now. We can sign up for alerts or something, and if Lana goes on tour, we're there—front row—I promise you."

"Do you think I'm being silly?"

"Not in the slightest." He squeezed her hands. "Palmer, I can't imagine what you're going through. This must be the scariest thing ever, and I'm watching from the outside. I want to treat you like a fragile flower or a delicate egg, but I also want to bungee jump off bridges with you and scream from mountaintops. I also wouldn't mind sitting on the couch and watching your favorite movies while sharing a bucket of popcorn." Kent paused, shook his head, and then looked into her eyes. "What I'm trying to say is we can only live for the moment, but I promise you I'm going to give you as many tomorrows as I can. That's my goal. I know it won't be easy, but each day is a new day, a new adventure, and we're going to make the most of it."

Palmer grinned. "You're rambling."

"I am because my mind swirls with everything I want to say but sometimes have trouble with. All I know is I want you to live. Live for tomorrow."

"I'm trying."

Kent nodded. "That's all I can ask. Now come on. We have coffee to drink. We need to finish packing and who knows what else, but we're about to embark on a cross-country trip, and I feel wholly unprepared."

Palmer reached for the coffees and handed Kent his. "My meds are packed."

"Well, that's the important part. Those are the things we can't buy at the store. We can forget everything else, I suppose."

"I'm going to miss this coffee." Palmer held the cup close to her nose, inhaled, and then shook her head. "I wish I'd found it sooner."

"That's the beautiful thing about coffee, Palmer. It's everywhere we go. We'll find our favorites in each state."

She held out her cup and said, "To the memories we're about to make."

Kent tapped his cup to hers and said nothing. He would be the one with the memories. Soon, her meds would stop working and her mind would shut down. Kent was nervous about the tomorrows he'd promised Palmer. They were going to be hard, a challenge, but he was going to do everything he could to make each day the brightest for her. He had to.

Before I'm Gone

♥ Sit in the front seat of a roller coaster and feel the wind in my hair

♥ Eat tacos or tortillas from a roadside stand in New Mexico

♥ Shop at a large farmers market

♥ Meet Lana Del Rey and see her in concert

♥ Take a picture of the most-painted shed in the US

♥ Sit in the sand and watch the sunrise in Cape Cod

♥ Take the steps to the Lincoln Memorial

♥ Do yoga in Sedona

♥ Tour and feed animals in a wildlife sanctuary

♥ Stand under a waterfall

♥ See Elvis on the street corner in Las Vegas

♥ Hug an elephant

♥ Find my family

♥ Step on grapes and make wine

♥ Run through a wheat field

♥ Drive Route 66

♥ See the marquees on Broadway

♥ Ring the Liberty Bell

♥ Buy a quilt from an Amish stand

★ *See the northern lights in Minnesota*

★ *Visit Plymouth Rock*

★ *Touch Babe Ruth's bat*

★ *Travel the Loneliest Road*

★ *Visit the Muhammad Ali Center*

★ *Dance in the rain with someone I love*

★ *Take the ferry to the Statue of Liberty*

★ *Check out the Grand Canyon*

★ *Take every picture I can of Palmer*

★ *Make Palmer smile*

- *Eat chowdah in Boston, per Palmer*
- *Eat pizza in Chicago*
- *Try frozen custard in New York City*
- *Get coffee in each city*

SIXTEEN

San Francisco's airport was busy at night. The cab driver double-parked and helped Kent with their luggage, while Palmer stood on the curb and waited. For some reason, she expected there to be fewer people than during the day, but something told her she was wrong. The terminal was packed with people. They stood shoulder to shoulder in line or rushed by one another to get to wherever they needed to go.

Kent used the kiosk to check them in for their flight while Palmer looked around. The bright lights, the loud sounds, and the intercom voice that seemingly talked over itself made Palmer wish she'd worn headphones and a blindfold. There was too much going on, and she feared the worst.

They waited in line to drop their bags off for what felt like an hour, when it was probably twenty minutes. After she and Kent had made it through security, they found their terminal, and then went to the nearest restaurant to waste some time. Prior to leaving, Kent had given Palmer a corticosteroid shot in her hip to help combat a seizure and would give her the anticonvulsant before they boarded their flight. He wanted her to walk around to keep her hip from tightening up, but she wanted to eat. Kent wouldn't fight her on anything she wanted. She knew this.

They sat down at a chain restaurant, and Kent suggested she order a glass of wine. She looked up when he said this and swore she saw a glint in his eyes. He smirked, and she wondered what he had up his sleeve. When the server took their order, they both ended up with soda. Palmer wanted the caffeine and planned to get more before they finally got on their plane.

"How about an espresso martini?" he proposed without looking up from the menu.

"If I didn't know better, I'd think you're trying to get me drunk before our flight."

Kent closed the menu and set it down. "You fidgeted the entire drive here and seem on edge. I can assume why, but I want to make sure you're comfortable. Are you having second thoughts?"

"No," she said. "I want to do this. I just can't help but think about . . ."

Kent reached across the table and took her hand in his. "I get it. Anytime you want to come back, you just say the word, and we come home."

She nodded and mouthed "Thank you" to him. She confided in Kent that she feared she wouldn't return to her apartment or the city she loved so much. Kent hadn't wanted her to think like that and tried to assuage her thoughts by telling her how amazing their trip was going to be. Anything could happen to either of them at any given time. Their future was a bunch of unknowns, but he promised to make sure she made it back to say goodbye.

While they waited for their food, they looked at the travel books Kent had purchased and discussed whether they should take the ferry to Nantucket or Martha's Vineyard when they were in Massachusetts, or keep moving south to New York City and save the ferry ride for when they visited the Statue of Liberty.

"I say we wait until New York," Palmer said. "The trip to Nantucket is long, and I'm not sure there's anything I want to see there."

"And you can get clam chowder in Boston," Kent pointed out.

"New York it is." They had started a journal of sorts, writing what each other wanted to see in each state. Realistically, they knew they wouldn't get to all the states, but their goal was to knock off as many things on Palmer's list as possible.

"When are you going to open that?" Kent motioned to the envelope protruding from the journal.

Palmer sighed. "I don't know. I'm torn. What if it says I have a family and I meet them, only to die months later? Or what if it says I don't have a family, and then I die knowing I'm alone?"

Kent reached for her hand. This had become common for them, him holding her hand. In the short time they'd known each other, he'd quickly become someone she could count on. He'd shown her what it meant to have someone who cared about her for no other reason than for who she was. She never thought she'd be excited to see someone every day, but Kent had changed that for her.

"You're not alone," he reminded her. "I'm here, and I'm going to be here whether you have a family waiting for you or not."

Palmer glanced at the envelope, closed the journal, and slipped it into her bag. "Later," she said. "I'll open it later."

After dinner, Kent insisted Palmer walk. He was afraid her hip would tighten up during their long flight and didn't want her to be in pain.

"Do you think people know?"

"Know what?" he asked as he walked alongside her.

"That I'm dying?"

Kent shook his head. "How could they? It's not like you're wearing a shirt that says as much or have a beacon shining on you."

"I don't know. Sometimes I feel like people are staring."

"Maybe they're looking at me and thinking, 'Wow, look at the beautiful woman by his side. He's one lucky dude.'"

Palmer blushed. Kent was quick with compliments for her. It was something she secretly appreciated about him. If she felt down, she knew he'd pick her up with either a comment or a lingering look. At night, after he'd gone home, she'd lie in bed wondering what life would've been like if they'd dated. She was angry at his ex and everything she was putting Kent through. He had said very little about the situation, but Palmer suspected Kent held a lot of animosity toward her.

They finally sat down at their gate near the window, where Palmer could see the other planes taxiing and taking off. Kent took his phone out of his pocket. Curiosity got the best of Palmer, and she leaned in to see what he was doing.

"We need a name."

"For what?" she asked.

"For our Instagram." Kent looked at her and could see her confusion. "The barista at RoccoBean suggested we create an Instagram of our trip. She said to post pictures of the places we visit."

"Who's going to want to see photos?"

Kent shrugged. "Maybe us, in two months, when we're eating tacos on the side of the road."

"Yeah, maybe." Palmer wasn't convinced. She couldn't imagine anyone caring about their photos.

Kent stood and matched his shoes up toe to toe with hers. He moved his phone up and down until he got the right angle and then took the photo. He sat back down and hid his phone from Palmer so she couldn't see what he was typing out until he was ready, and then he showed her. It was a picture of their feet, with the caption "Our journey starts tonight."

"Cute," she said.

"You don't like it?"

"No, I do. I just don't understand it."

Kent spent the next however many minutes explaining Instagram, hashtags, followers, and what the heart meant. He told her how they could tag places they'd been, and sometimes people would reshare their images. Social media was lost on Palmer. She'd never jumped on the trend of having multiple accounts for her to post what she had for breakfast each day or how someone had upset her. She wasn't one to air her dirty laundry. But if Kent wanted to chronicle their trip, she wouldn't stop him. In the end, he would be the one with the memories. Maybe something like this would be therapeutic to him later on.

They stood, and Kent gathered their things when it was time to board. He handed Palmer his phone for her to scan their tickets when they got to the front of the line. "I can't believe we're in first class," she said to him as they moved forward.

"If all goes as planned, this is our first and only flight. I wanted to make it count."

Palmer placed Kent's phone down on the scanner, waited for the beep, and then did it again. They walked down the jet bridge and onto the plane and turned to the left. "This plane is huge," she said over the roar of the engine.

"Yeah, one of those jumbo jets."

They found their seats. Palmer sat next to the window and took her bag from Kent. He stowed their luggage in the overhead bin and then sat down with a contented sigh. "Do you want to take your pill?" he asked her.

She nodded. Palmer had yet to have a seizure, but Dr. Hughes said they were imminent. It would be extremely rare for someone with Palmer's diagnosis to go through her remaining days without having one. At some point, they were going to be unpreventable. Kent and Palmer knew that day would be soon. In their meeting with Dr. Hughes, she had shown Kent the tumor and said it would grow until it took over Palmer's brain and work into her nervous system. He needed to be prepared for everything coming Palmer's way.

Kent opened the small med kit he'd put in his backpack and took out the anticonvulsant. The rest of his equipment—the syringes, additional medications, and other essentials—he'd checked for the flight. He handed Palmer the pill and then opened the complimentary water bottle for her. She took the water and sipped until she could no longer feel the capsule in her throat.

"Good evening," the flight attendant said when she stopped at their seats. "What can I get you to drink?"

Kent took the liberty of ordering hot water for Palmer's green tea and asked for a soda for himself. Palmer rested her head against the back of the seat and looked at Kent. "I don't remember if I thanked you or not."

"For what?" he asked.

"For all of this," she said. "For taking care of me. If it weren't for you . . ." Her words trailed off. If he hadn't come to her apartment that day and proposed this trip, she wouldn't be on the plane right now. She'd be in the morgue, waiting for the year to expire so the city could cremate her. Palmer had had every intention of ending her life. When she thought back to those days, not too long ago, and how she could've gone to a hospice or just ended things on her own terms; tears fell from her eyes.

Kent brushed her tears away softly and spoke quietly to her. "Something bigger than us brought us together, Palmer. I'm right where I want to be." He kissed her forehead and then wrapped his arm around her shoulders. She hid her face in his chest and cried. It wasn't the first time she had shed tears about her impending death, and it wouldn't be the last.

The flight attendant returned with their drinks. Kent took them and waited for Palmer to situate her tray. He set them down and then took two of each snack offered, even though they had just eaten.

"Once we take off, we'll dim the lights. We have dinner service available as well, if you're interested." Before she left, she handed them a package that held an eye mask, wired earbuds, and slipper socks.

Palmer made her tea while Kent fiddled with his screen. He found something to watch, plugged in the headphones, and let them dangle.

"Should I get mine out?" she asked Kent.

"I thought we could share," he told her. "I'll use one, and you can use the other. This way we can watch something together."

"I like that."

"As soon as we're airborne," he told her. "The screen is going to show preflight announcements, so we might as well wait."

She sipped her tea and watched out the window while they taxied. Kent leaned over the armrest and pointed to the other planes in line to take off.

"Such a well-oiled process," she said as they inched forward.

Palmer reached for Kent's hand when the plane began gathering speed. He held her tightly and spoke calmly in her ear as the plane took off. The initial bounce the plane made once it was off the ground jostled her, but Kent was there describing everything to her.

"Look out the window," he said in her ear. She leaned forward and let out a small gasp. "The city at night, from this elevation, is beautiful."

"It really is."

By the time they reached elevation, she had her arm wrapped around his, and she rested her head on his shoulder. At some point, they fell asleep like that.

It was the sun that woke Palmer first. It beat through the tiny window and caused her to squint. She moved to close the shade and then screamed out in pain. Her hands went to her head instantly as a sharp stabbing sensation coursed through her.

"Breathe," Kent said. He reached for her seat belt, released it, and gently guided her until her head was between her legs. Kent knelt there, between the seats, and rubbed her back. "It's the air pressure," he told her. "We're going to be on the ground soon."

"Open," he instructed when his fingers touched her lips. She did so without reservation. "Give it a minute to work." Whatever Kent had given her dissolved on her tongue. She was grateful she didn't have to move because she wasn't sure she could sit up right now. Kent kept his hand on her back, moving it up and down. The motion soothed her.

Palmer turned her head slightly and saw that Kent had blocked her from view. He had the keen sense to shield her from the people across from them. She wanted to cry and crawl into his arms. She stayed where she was and met his gaze.

"Sir, I'm going to need you to take your seat," the flight attendant said as she came by. Kent scowled but did as she asked. He still angled his body to keep prying eyes away as best he could.

"Better?" he asked.

Palmer nodded. "I'm queasy."

Kent took the emergency bag from the pocket in front of him and handed it to her. "Just in case."

"I'm so embarrassed."

"Don't be. Everyone has issues with the air pressure. You're just more susceptible because of your situation. We knew this could happen."

"Everything had been going so well."

"It still is, Palmer. This isn't a setback. Hell, it's not even a hiccup. I probably could've prevented it, but we were both asleep."

"The sun woke me, and as soon as I moved . . ." She sat back and buckled her seat belt. Palmer reached for Kent's hand, clasped it, and then rested her head on his shoulder. She stayed like that until after they'd landed. He was a comfort to her that she didn't realize she'd needed until this flight. Now more than ever, she wished they weren't friends and taking this trip because she didn't want to say goodbye to him.

SEVENTEEN

They arrived at Logan International Airport, collected their luggage, and then took a shuttle to car rentals. Kent kept the style of car he'd rented for their trip a secret. Palmer had one request—a convertible. He'd searched every rental agency until he'd found the one he wanted. The car had to have unlimited miles and no end date on returning. The latter was difficult, but he'd worked out the details with an agent. Kent didn't want to put an end date on their trip, and he wanted to return it at any location.

After he filled out the paperwork and took the keys, he and Palmer walked through the garage until they stopped in front of a Jeep Wrangler. It was brand new, according to the clerk, and the top went back easily with the push of a button. Kent had done his research and knew the top had a panoramic roof, and if they wanted, they could recline their seats and look at the stars during the night.

"Is this what we're driving?" Palmer asked as Kent went to the rear and opened the tailgate. He peeked around the side and smiled.

"It is. I found a beach we could drive on in Plymouth," he told her as he loaded their luggage. "We need a permit, but I already took care of that." Kent came around to the side and opened the passenger door for her.

"It's so purple."

"Also, in my research, I found out that Jeep comes out with some cool color every year. This is it." He also found out that renting an exclusive color was near impossible unless the company ordered a handful for their fleet.

Kent ran around to the other side and climbed in. He pushed the button to start the engine and then spent some time hooking his phone up to the navigation system. Once it was set up, he got out and took a picture of their car and uploaded it to their Instagram account.

"Do you think people will care?" she asked him.

"I think so. Besides, it's a cool-looking ride. Don't you think?" Kent pushed the open button on the panel near the roof and watched as the roof retracted. Palmer suggested she get a sweater for the ride in case she got cold, and Kent agreed. He reached into the back and grabbed the sweater Palmer had packed for the plane and handed it to her. "If it gets too cold, we'll close the top."

"I feel silly because I asked for a convertible."

"By the time we get south, we'll want the top closed because it's too hot," he joked.

He drove out of the parking garage, showed the proper information for the rental, and followed the GPS guidance. Their first stop, after coffee and donuts from the nearest Dunkin', would be to a medical supply store. Kent hadn't brought this up with Palmer, but he'd bought a wheelchair for her. He wanted it on hand for when they'd need it, which could be anytime. He didn't want anything to damper her trip, even though he knew seeing the chair would probably do so.

When they were a block away, Kent told her what he had done. "Please don't be mad."

"I'm not mad," she said, but her voice didn't match her expression.

Kent pulled into the parking lot and shut the car off. He turned in his seat to face her, but she kept her gaze forward. "Hey," he said as he took her hand in his. Palmer didn't fight him, but she also didn't turn to look at him. "I'm not saying we have to use it at all, but we'll have it in case of emergencies. We're going to do a lot of walking, and I don't want you to miss out on anything."

"It's just—" Palmer didn't finish her sentence because Kent pulled her into his arms.

"I'm sorry." He soothed her. "I should've talked to you about it. I knew it would be a hard choice for you to make, and I'm trying to make things easier on you. It's going to stay in the back until we need it." He hoped that day wouldn't be anytime soon. She nodded against his chest and pulled away.

"It's like the next nail in the coffin," she mumbled. "Right now, I look like I'm a healthy thirty-seven-year-old, but once I'm in that chair and you're pushing me around, everyone is going to know I'm sick."

Kent was at a loss for words. They sat there in the parking lot and watched people go in and out of the building. On one end, there was the medical supply store, and on the other, a pizza parlor.

"Do you want me to cancel the order?" he asked, breaking the silence between them.

Palmer thought for a long moment and then finally shook her head. "No, you're right. I'm going to need it. I just wasn't prepared."

He said nothing as he hopped out of the Jeep and hurried into the store. He hoped the transaction wouldn't take too long because he didn't want to leave Palmer alone for long. Kent had upset her, and he had to make it up to her.

While the clerk processed his paperwork, he meandered around the store and tried to spy on Palmer through the window. He didn't have a clear line of sight, but he could see her sitting in the passenger seat. He went to the counter and read the advertisement for a medical identification service. It wouldn't be a bad idea to get something for Palmer, but the likelihood he would be away from her when she needed medical attention was slim. Kent had already upset her with the wheelchair; he didn't want to add insult to injury. Still, he pocketed the flyer and decided he'd research it later, after she'd gone to sleep.

The salesclerk brought the wheelchair around and gave Kent his receipt. He was now the proud owner of a lightweight folding chair with hand brakes. He wasn't sure which part was light. It was anything but. Kent half carried, half wheeled the chair out to the car and placed it in the back. He then climbed in and hoped everything would be okay.

Palmer greeted him with a smile, which made him happy. "It's only if we need it," he reminded her, and she nodded.

"I think I'll have you push me in it while we're on the beach. I don't want to get sand in my shoes."

Kent studied her for a long moment with a blank expression. He waited for her to crack under pressure, and when she finally did, her laughter filled the car. "I'm on to you, Sinclair."

"Me too, Wagner."

Kent redirected the GPS, and they started their trip toward Plymouth. This was a stop he'd added, since they were going to see the sunrise in Chatham the next morning. He wanted to see the famous rock, walk the waterfront town, tour the replica of the *Mayflower*, and drive what many called "the old road to the Cape" highway.

"This traffic looks like San Fran," Palmer said when they hit the first of many backups.

Kent laughed. "Unfortunately, I think we might hit a lot of traffic on this side of the country. The infrastructure is much older than on the West Coast."

"And they're not always rebuilding after earthquakes," Palmer stated matter-of-factly.

What should've taken them fifty minutes, not counting their stop for breakfast and the medical store, took them about an hour and a half. Once they came closer to town, the traffic eased up considerably. As they drove, Palmer read from one of their travel books, listing off historical information. They parked, closed the top, and set out on foot.

Kent held her hand as they walked along the seaport of Plymouth. They leaned over the seawall, pointed at the sailboats that drifted by, and walked through the park. When they came to the *Mayflower*, Kent had Palmer stand in front while he took a picture of her.

"Is this going on your Instagram?" she asked.

"Do you want me to post it?"

Palmer thought for a moment and then shook her head. "Maybe later, but not yet. Here, let me take yours." Kent handed his phone to her. He posed and then beckoned her over. Kent took his phone, held his arm out, and brought Palmer closer.

"Smile," he said to her. Instead of looking at the camera, she looked at him. He snapped the photo. It was a memory he wanted to keep for a lifetime. In her features, he could see the sheer amount of gratitude she had for him. His heart, when he looked at the picture of her looking at him, sprang to life. The sensation was different from what he'd felt for anyone else. He thought it odd, but Palmer brought him a comfort and ease, a longing, he hadn't noticed before.

Kent reached for her hand. He wanted to be close to her, touch her, without her thinking he was being too forward. He hoped she wouldn't pull away. If she did, he would have to find some other subtle way of expressing his desire to be near her. He kept his pace slow as they walked toward the rock, and checked on Palmer often for any sign of distress. The seizures would come whenever they felt like it, with or without the medication. Her headaches would return as well as the dizziness. The medicine Dr. Hughes prescribed was a stopgap and could cease working at anytime.

There was a small gathering at the portico where people stood behind the wrought iron railing and looked down at the rock. Kent and Palmer waited their turn, and when they finally had a clear shot, they both said "Huh" at the same time. Kent took a couple of pictures, and then they walked across the street to Pilgrim Hall Museum, which sat atop a hill, with a steep incline of stairs. He stopped them there and looked at Palmer.

"Okay, so it wasn't some magnificent . . . heck, I don't even know. I thought the rock was going to be this giant formation."

"And not a pebble?"

Kent laughed, and Palmer followed suit. "We can't talk about history that way," he said, even though he didn't believe a word coming out of his mouth. "What about this?" he asked as he nodded toward the museum.

"Sure."

Kent matched Palmer's pace. She moved slowly, each step taking more and more of her breath away. They weren't halfway up the flight of stairs when she needed to stop. He stood behind her and placed his hands on her hips, fearful she might fall if she were to lose her balance. She leaned into him and sobbed quietly. "I can't do it."

"Okay. There wasn't anything in there I wanted to see anyway. Can you walk, or do you want me to go get the car?" He didn't want to leave her, but he couldn't make her walk if she wasn't able. This was why he'd bought the wheelchair: for moments like this when her body refused to cooperate and she needed a little help.

Kent sat them down on a step. It was awkward, but it gave Palmer a reprieve. He held her with his arm around her shoulder and waited for guidance from her. They were in no rush and could sit there as long as they needed.

People walked by and asked if they required help. Each time, Kent thanked them and said they were fine. They would be once he got her back to the car. He couldn't begin to understand what her body was doing to her, and why it picked the moments it did to be a nuisance. This was just the beginning, though. They had a long road ahead of them, and he was still determined to give her everything she wanted.

"I think I can walk now."

"Okay," Kent said, but before standing, he gave her a once-over. "Everything working?" he asked as he picked up her hands and wiggled her fingers. She had minimal mobility in her right pinkie, but it still functioned. "What about your vision? Are we clear or blurry?"

"A little blurry on the edges, but that's going away."

"Do you think you had a seizure?"

She didn't answer him, and that was enough for him. When they got to their hotel later, he would document everything and email Dr. Hughes. Kent all but picked Palmer up from the ground. He didn't let go of her until they were back in the car. He gave her another dose of the anticonvulsant and waited while she washed the pills down with water.

Kent waited for traffic to pass by before he went around to the driver's side. He climbed in, reached for her hand, and kissed the back of it. "We're good," he told her. "There's a beach calling our name." He put the car into drive and headed out of town. This time, he didn't set the GPS and followed the signs. They drove through Plymouth and its outskirts until they had to get on the interstate to cross into Cape Cod.

"It's like a mini Golden Gate," Kent said.

"More like micro," Palmer added. "The Sagamore Bridge is one of two bridges accessing Cape Cod. The only other way onto the island is by plane or boat."

"Is that so?"

"Yep. We're about to drive through some very old towns and a lot of history," Palmer told Kent.

"I'll be sure to drive slow," he replied as he winked at her.

EIGHTEEN

The soothing sounds of Kent's alarm clock started at 4:00 a.m. He grumbled, rolled over, and shut it off. He lay there in the darkness and cursed his poor planning. Kent had forgotten about jetlag and how the three-hour time difference between the West and East Coasts would affect him. He sat up and groaned. His body was sore from traveling, and it had been a while since he'd worked out last. Come to think of it, the last time he'd worked out was prior to him responding to the call from Palmer's work. After that, life went to hell in a handbasket when he responded to the accident involving Maeve. He would have to make it a point to work out while he and Palmer were on their vacation, but that would mean leaving Palmer for long periods of time, and Kent wasn't sure about that.

The soft snores of Palmer reminded Kent they were getting up this early for a reason. He hated to wake her, but they had something to cross off their list today. He stretched, threw the covers back, and placed his bare feet on the threadbare carpet. Kent and Palmer were at an inn near the Chatham Lighthouse, where they planned to watch the sunrise. Palmer called the inn "quintessential New England" and had fallen in love with the photos online. They'd booked one room with two beds. It wasn't because they were trying to save money but because Kent didn't want Palmer out of his sight. If she seized in the middle of the night, he wanted to be there to help her. At first, she'd balked. They barely knew each other, but she came around after Kent showed her how many hours they would spend together in the week's course, not to mention the duration of their trip.

They had left the bathroom light on, in case Palmer needed to get up in the middle of the night, and the glow that peeked out from the barely open door gave Kent the opportunity to stare at Palmer without her sticking her tongue out or asking him what he was doing. He wanted a moment to take her all in.

When they'd checked into the inn and opened the door to their room, Kent was a bit sad that there were two beds. He wanted an easy excuse to sleep next to her, to be close to her, even though his thoughts were on a ridiculous level. They were friends. He was there to support her in her time of need, not explore these new feelings he had.

Except, he couldn't stop his thoughts. She was naturally beautiful. Kent noticed that the first time he'd met her at the bank. Whereas most of the women he knew wore makeup, Palmer didn't. Her cheeks had the perfect pinkish hue, turning red when she was embarrassed, and embarrassing her was quickly becoming a favorite trick of Kent's. He loved it when Palmer ducked her head shyly or turned away because she didn't want him to see her smile.

She wasn't very good about hiding things from him either. Her brown eyes were expressive and full of life despite her battles. Kent could look into them for hours, and he swore he'd be able to see her soul if she gave him the chance.

Kent stood and tiptoed to Palmer's bed. He touched her shoulder and whispered her name. "It's time to get up," he said. He then went to the bathroom they shared with the room next door. He didn't like the sharing part and was thankful that they'd be in a hotel when they got to Boston. This was only one night, and soon they'd be on the road heading back to the city.

He turned on the light and waited for his eyes to adjust. He used the facilities, washed his hands, splashed some water onto his face, and then brushed his teeth. When he came out of the bathroom, Palmer had turned on the bedside lamp and was moving about the room.

"It's so early," she said quietly, as if to not wake the neighbors. "I never got up this early when I had to go to work."

"The only reason I'd be awake at this hour is if I had a call." He went to his suitcase and pulled out a pair of sweats and a sweatshirt. "I'm sorry. I forgot about the time change. I should've planned this for tomorrow so we could adjust."

"Nothing a nap won't cure," she said as she passed by him. Palmer went into the bathroom, and Kent finished dressing for the beach. The weather app on his phone told him it was chilly out, and he was concerned for Palmer. She was cold all the time. It didn't matter what the temperature was outside. She always wore a sweater. Kent grabbed another sweatshirt from his suitcase and found an extra blanket in the closet.

"I need coffee," Palmer said when she came out of the bathroom. "I think the owner said they have some downstairs."

"We can check," Kent said, needing a cup as well. There wasn't a coffee maker in the room, which didn't surprise him. What caught him off guard was that there wasn't a Dunkin' on every street corner. The nearest was a three-mile drive away from where they wanted to be.

Kent prepared Palmer's meds and gave them to her with a bottle of water. While she took them, he checked her pulse. Satisfied with the results, he asked if she was ready to go.

They walked quietly down the hall and cringed when they hit a creaky step or two on the staircase. Halfway down, Kent could smell coffee, bacon, and something fruity. Palmer's stomach growled, and she placed her hand over it to dampen the loud rumble.

The innkeeper startled Palmer and Kent when she came around the corner. The two women screamed, while Kent gripped the railing for support.

"Oh goodness, you about gave me a heart attack," the owner stammered.

"Same," Kent said.

"He's a medic." Palmer pointed to Kent. "He would've saved you."

"A knight in shining armor. Be careful, dearie, I might keep him." She winked at Palmer, who blushed. "Come along, I have coffee, and then you can head out for the sunrise."

They loaded up with two large metal cups of coffee and headed outside. It was a short walk to the beach, but risky with the dark sky. Kent used the flashlight on his phone to alert any oncoming motorists, and then again when he read the sign about sharks being in the area.

"It's a good thing we aren't going swimming."

"Do you think they come close to the shore?" Palmer asked.

"Not this early in the morning. Even Jaws needs his sleep." They descended the wooden staircase and had no choice but to slip their shoes off.

"I didn't realize the sand would be so deep," Palmer said. Kent set their shoes off to the side. He wasn't worried about anyone stealing them at this hour. They trudged through the sand until they came to the edge of the dividing line where sand met surf. The tide wouldn't shift their way until long after sunrise, negating any chance of them getting wet.

Palmer sat first and brought her legs to her chest. Kent watched her as the disappearing moon glowed on her. Each day he grew fonder of her. He sought reasons to hold her hand, to be close to her, and was secretly thankful she didn't push too hard on wanting her own room. Kent didn't want to be far from her. Not because of fear, but because he felt alone when she wasn't by him.

"Do you want to wear this?" He offered her his extra sweatshirt. She smiled and reached for it. The idea of her wearing his clothes made him giddy, and he welcomed the feeling. After she slipped it on, he covered her with the blanket.

"You're going to be cold," she said as he wrapped her up in the blanket.

"Nah." In what would be considered a smooth move, Kent moved in behind Palmer and pulled her to his chest. She now had his body warmth to keep her comfortable, and he had . . . *her*. Deep down, he knew these budding feelings were wrong, but he wasn't sure if he'd be able to stop them. Palmer was everything he looked for in a relationship. She was smart, determined, and caring, and the fact that she was beautiful hadn't gone unnoticed by him at all. He couldn't deny he was attracted to her, even if the timing was all off. The last thing his body and mind should feel right now was a longing for Palmer. Neither of them was in the right headspace, and time was their enemy.

Palmer rested her head against Kent's chest and sighed. "The sun isn't even up yet, and this is already the most beautiful thing I have ever witnessed."

Kent felt the same way. He wrapped his arms around her and rested his chin on top of her head. He was gentle, wary of causing her any undue pain. "I can't remember the last time I watched the sunrise," he said. "It had to be when I was deployed."

"Do you miss it?" Palmer asked.

"Deployment? Hell no. The army, sometimes. I don't know, it's hard to quantify. At times, I miss the structure the army provides, but I love the freedom I have now. I can do whatever I want whenever I want, like now. But I miss my friends."

"I had nothing like what you experienced, even as an adult."

"Who's your best friend?" Kent asked her.

After a long moment, where the only sounds around them were nature and the waves crashing into the shore, Palmer said, "You." Kent turned slightly to look at her, but she avoided eye contact. "Growing up, I didn't trust anyone and kept to myself. The relentless teasing and bullying kept me guarded. By the time I aged out of the system, I'd learned to depend on myself. I didn't need anyone to go to the library with me or out for coffee."

"What about the ladies at the bank?"

Palmer shrugged. "They're friendly. Before my diagnosis, I went out for Laura's birthday. I had a good time, but I was their boss, and it felt strange. Celine was probably the closest to a friend, but we rarely met outside of the bank."

Listening to Palmer talk about her life broke Kent's heart. He wanted to give her a lifetime of memories, but there was no way he could. He should've thought ahead and bought a sand pail and asked her to build a sandcastle with him. That was something he had done as a kid with his parents.

"Well, I'm glad I'm your friend."

Palmer pressed into Kent. "You're more than that. It's hard to explain."

You're telling me.

Somewhere in the distance, a horn sounded. Kent thought it was a foghorn or the kind you'd find at a mill, signaling everyone back to work. He imagined the horn would be for fishermen to get up and get out on the water. Kent knew absolutely nothing about deep-sea fishing or what it was like to be out on a boat all day long.

Palmer pointed. Along the horizon, the once-dark sky began turning a vibrant orange, pink, and yellow. Kent likened the color to sherbet. He tightened his arms around Palmer and held her. Her hands gripped his forearms, and she sniffled. This was the first thing on her bucket list, and he'd made it happen for her. He'd never forget this moment—the two of them sitting like this—watching a new day unfold.

They stayed there, on the sandy beach in Chatham, for an hour until the sun was high in the sky and everything around them came to life. It was still early, but they could hear traffic on the road behind them, and they could see boats heading out to sea to work for their daily catch. After a bit, Kent suggested they walk on the beach. They left their blanket there and held hands. They walked toward the surf and took in the beauty around them. Birds squawked at other birds, while some scoured the sand for morsels of food.

Palmer looked over her shoulder and laughed at their footprints in the sand, and the whole time Kent never stopped looking at her. His determination to make this trip happen was worth everything he saw in this moment. He stepped away from her, took his phone out of his pocket, and started snapping photos. It was as if Palmer sensed that

Kent would need these photos later and posed. She turned, tilted her head toward the sun, and gave him the time to capture her. He stepped to her and put his arm around her waist. Kent wanted these memories for the rest of his life.

"We need a selfie."

"But I look—"

"Perfect," he said as he interrupted her. "You're stunning, Palmer."

She looked at the camera and rested her head on his shoulder. Kent snapped the photo. The way Palmer looked in the photo spoke volumes to him. He saw how shy she was, and how thankful she was for him. When she turned to look at him, he snapped another photo, and then he looked at her. If there ever was a perfect moment to kiss Palmer, it was now. He cupped her cheek and then hesitated. The way she made him feel came rushing forward. He had no problems looking past her illness. He would be with her through it all. He wondered what would happen if he inched closer to her. If he licked his lips and turned his head slightly, would she do the same? Would she close the gap and press herself to him?

Palmer looked away, the connection between them broken, at least for the time being. Kent pocketed his phone and took her hand in his as they started walking again. They moved closer to the water, where the cold sand formed around their feet.

"I dare you to go in," Palmer said to him.

"Easy." Kent pulled his sweatpants up to his knees and walked into the water. It was freezing, and he wanted to run back out, but he stayed.

"Is it cold?"

"It is," he told her. "But you might like it." He turned and looked out over the water as waves washed over him. "It's not on your list, but something you can definitely add."

"What's that?" she asked from shore. "Getting eaten by Jaws?"

"Yes, of course." Kent laughed. "Being eaten by a fictional mechanical shark should be on everyone's list."

Palmer snorted. Kent walked toward her. His feet were numb, but he didn't care anymore. He only cared about making Palmer laugh and smile. Seeing her happy was all he needed right now. He crouched down and pulled her yoga pants up to her knees to keep them from getting wet. Kent righted himself and reached for Palmer's hand, and as soon as their fingers touched, he brought her into the water. She gasped on contact but didn't let go of Kent's hand.

"It's cold."

"It is, but now you can say you've been in the Atlantic Ocean. Few can ever say that."

"Just one more thing on my list, right?"

Kent nodded. "For every one we tick off, we'll find something to add." He pulled her into his arms and hugged her while the ocean lapped at their feet.

He never wanted to let her go.

NINETEEN

After breakfast and showers, Palmer and Kent packed up, loaded their things into the Jeep, and set off to walk the streets of Chatham. The quaint village was a tourist destination with its one-of-a-kind shops, classic New England ambiance, and old-town feel. They window-shopped, went into a few of the stores, admired the wares of the locals, and listened to a tour guide tell a group of visitors about the local church.

They made it back to their car with only one purchase—a magnet for Kent's refrigerator. It was a gift from Palmer. She'd picked it out for him and suggested they get one at every stop because they were easier than coffee mugs or other items, which would take up space in their luggage.

"Can we put the top back?" Palmer asked. It was chilly outside, but she wanted to feel the sun on her while Kent drove.

"Of course."

Kent pushed the button to open the top while Palmer reclined her seat a smidge, enough to relax and yet still see out the window.

"We're going to take Route 6A," he told her. "It's historic and will take us through most of the towns. If you see someplace you want to stop, let me know."

"And we'll stop if you see someplace you want to visit?" She wanted this trip to be about him as much as it was about her. Granted, the day before, they'd visited Plymouth, which was on his list, but she wasn't sure if he'd added it because they would be in the area or not. So far, anything Kent had jotted down seemed close to the places she had.

"I'm driving, so I'm going to depend on you to tell us where we have to stop." He winked and pulled out onto the road. He was clever in how he turned things around, but Palmer was onto him and his sly antics.

When she shivered, he turned up the heat, pressed the button for her heated seat, and told her they were going to buy some throw blankets to keep in the car. Palmer agreed. She wanted the best of everything right now. She loved having the roof open so she could smell the salt air and feel the warmth of the sun, but she was cold. Sometimes, teeth-chatteringly cold. Palmer still wore the sweatshirt Kent had lent her. It was hers now, and except for the times she'd need it to smell like him again, she had no intentions of giving it back to him.

Palmer watched out the window, taking in the sights. She did what she could to avoid looking at Kent because he gave her butterflies. She'd had them one time before, back in high school, when she had a crush on a boy. He was nice to her, and they studied together, but their relationship went no further. Palmer dated a classmate from one of her accounting classes for a year after they graduated, but the feelings she had then were not the same as those she felt around Kent. There was something about him that exuded self-confidence and kindheartedness, and it didn't hurt that he was sexy. Being near him gave Palmer hope everything would be okay.

When she saw the sign for Hyannis, she told Kent a story. "When I was little, we'd get asked these questions about what we wanted for our futures, and I remember I'd seen a documentary about the Kennedys and how they were this perfect family marred by tragic events, and their escape was Hyannis. I thought this was a magical place," she said as she looked around the busy town. "But the traffic is so heavy, unlike Chatham or the towns we drove through yesterday. Do you think people flock here because of the Kennedys?"

"Could be," he said. "I suppose if people as influential as the Kennedys paint something as idyllic, others will flock to it."

"The power of a name," she mumbled. "Do you want to stop here?"

"I don't have a reason to," he told her.

"All right, let's keep driving."

They made it through the hectic roundabout in Hyannis and continued toward the bridge. Palmer took Kent's phone and snapped a few pictures. "Have you loaded any more photos to that site?" she asked him.

"One from Plymouth," he said. "And I'll load one or two from Chatham. If you look through the photo album, you'll see one I took of the town. It's pretty neat."

"I don't want to go through your phone."

"I have nothing to hide from you, Palmer."

How could those words send a zing through her body? They shouldn't, and she needed to shut her feelings off. Palmer was afraid she was going to blurt out how Kent made her feel, and that wouldn't be fair to him. She had an expiration date. Palmer set the phone down and glanced out the window to hide the tears in her eyes. She wanted to forget she was dying, but the tumor wouldn't let her. She could see it in her mind, gnarly, mean, and with tentacles pushing deeper into her brain. It was going to cut her off from life as she knew it, strip her of her memories, decimate her motor functions, and destroy her humanity. Palmer was going to change from someone who could do things for herself to someone who would have to depend on a man she barely knew yet was certain she was falling in love with.

Kent's hand found hers, and he squeezed it. "Hey, are you okay over there?"

How had he known she was upset?

"I'm fine," she told him despite the pain clear in her voice.

Kent pulled over into the nearest parking lot and put the Jeep into park. He unbuckled her seat belt and pulled her to him as much as he could with the console in the way. Kent didn't ask her what had made her cry or why she felt down. He held her because he knew. Palmer sobbed into his chest over the sudden onslaught of emotions brought on by the trip, her budding feelings for Kent, and the realization that her time on earth was almost over. With the tears came the anger. The hurt and frustration. And the questions. Why her? Hadn't she sacrificed enough already?

Not once did Kent tell her everything would be okay. He faced the same battle of watching her die in front of him. He would be the one to take her to the hospital when the time came. Death with dignity no longer applied to her, unless they returned to California. Kent would shoulder the brunt of her death and had never wavered in his decision to take her on this trip. For what was left of her life, she couldn't fathom why someone would be so kind.

Kent continued to hold her, soothing her with soft strokes up and down her back. He only asked her once if she was in pain, but she told him she wasn't, even though she was. The pain was different. It was gut-wrenching, rip-your-heart-out, pointed pain. It was her reality, and nothing could take it away from her. Not a pill, not a shot in the hip, not even her personal medic.

When Palmer pulled away from Kent, he wiped her tears and kissed her forehead. She wanted more and hated that she couldn't have it. She wouldn't put him through any more heartbreak than he'd already experienced.

"What can I do?" he asked.

Palmer cleared her throat. "They're my demons. I'm the only one who can combat them," she said.

He understood. "If they were physical, I'd beat the shit out of them for you."

"And I'd let you." The tumor was physical, but it had a grip on her, and it wasn't letting go until it won.

Kent waited until he was sure Palmer was okay before he started driving again. He turned the GPS on and set their destination for Boston. When they were back on the road, Kent reached for Palmer's hand and held it. She appreciated the gesture and clung tightly to him.

It was early afternoon when they checked into their hotel downtown. They'd specifically chosen one within walking distance of the historic features they wanted to visit. The valet helped them with their luggage and then took the keys to the Jeep. Inside, Palmer checked them in while Kent played with a dog belonging to one of the guests. When they got to their room, Palmer cackled when she read the pillow on the bed: "Wicked Smaht."

"What's so . . ." Kent didn't need to finish his question because he saw it too. "I think this might be our most interesting stop on our vacation."

"I agree."

They freshened up and then set out to explore. Their first stop was Quincy Market for lunch. Palmer had read about it and Faneuil Hall in a brochure back at the inn in Chatham and thought it would be a great place for them to eat. As soon as they stepped inside, Palmer felt overwhelmed. People were shoulder to shoulder, and the food selection was far more expansive than she had anticipated.

"I don't think I read the pamphlet clearly."

Kent laughed. "How about we get something from the vendor outside? I saw a food truck near the entrance of the marketplace."

"Sounds like a better option."

They stopped and watched a drumming street performer who used buckets and stainless steel bowls as his equipment. Palmer couldn't make sense of what song he was playing, but she enjoyed the rhythm. Before they left, Kent dropped a five-dollar bill into the man's tip jar. They found their food truck, ordered, and sat down at a picnic table, near dancers who tried to entice onlookers to join them.

"People who can dance like that have so much talent. I'm envious."

"You can't dance?" Palmer asked.

Kent huffed. "Nope. Can you?"

"Absolutely not," she chuckled. "I have two left feet, zero coordination, and have never been to a nightclub."

"I'd say we could add that to your list, but veto." Her eyes widened at him. "The noise would be too much," he said, and then took a bit of his clam chowder, or, as the sign said, **Clam Chowdah**.

Once they finished, they found the Freedom Trail and took it to the site of the Boston Massacre. Palmer marveled at how the city had memorialized the location right in the middle of traffic. The history of the United States of America fascinated Kent. He peppered the colonial soldier with questions and nodded along with everything the young man said. There was a tour of the Old State House, but they decided against taking it.

Kent bought two tickets for a hop-on hop-off trolley at a kiosk. This was the best, easiest, and fastest way to see the city. They could stay on for all the stops or get off, and tonight, if Palmer felt up to it, they'd take the ghost tour.

They walked three blocks to the waterfront and boarded the trolley. Palmer suggested Kent be near the window so he could take photos, but he refused. He wanted her to see everything. During their guided tour, they learned about the Great Molasses Flood of 1919 in the North End of Boston. At first, Palmer thought the tour guide was joking until the trolley paused in front of the small historic sign.

They swung by the USS *Constitution*, and then, after passing the TD Garden, home of the Boston Bruins and Celtics professional sports teams, the driver took them by the garage a now-famous mobster used to work out of while he infiltrated the FBI, which was right across the street. Palmer's eyes widened and her mouth dropped open, and Kent told her it was in a movie that they could watch some night.

When they arrived at the Harvard stop, Kent and Palmer got off the trolley. They both wanted to see the famous campus. Palmer walked under the wrought iron archway and took in the beautiful space around her. She had dreamed of schools like Harvard, Yale, and Brown. The guidance counselors always spoke of how important a high school education was and gushed about the Ivy League. People who wanted to be in politics, especially those who wanted to run for president, went to esteemed schools on the East Coast. This translated to Palmer as meaning those people who were rich attended schools with deep traditions and power—something she'd never have.

Kent stepped beside her and sighed. "This place is impressive."

"Did you know the campus used to be a cow pasture?"

"I did not," he said, laughing.

"I remember during high school when we'd have college fairs. I'd talk to every school away from California because I hated it so much there. I wanted to move and start over. My guidance counselor saw me once and suggested community college, which is where I ended up, because she said a prestigious school is not the place for someone like me." Palmer scoffed. "I wish I hadn't believed her."

Kent moved closer to Palmer, their shoulders touching. "My parents wanted me to go to college, but I chose the army. I always wanted to be a medic or a firefighter because I wanted to help people, and the army was the best way to do both. I proudly served my country and saved lives." He sighed. "I lost lives, too, and those are the ones I'll never forget." Kent held Palmer's hand. "We can't dwell on the past. We have to look to the future and be the people we want to be."

Palmer looked at Kent, with tears in her eyes. "I don't have a future."

He squeezed her hand and nodded. "You have tomorrow. I promise you that."

Twenty

At the first sign of exhaustion, Kent hailed an Uber and took them back to the hotel. Palmer protested until she got into the back of the car and fell asleep. They had toured the city of Boston via the trolley, taken a boat cruise on the harbor, and eaten more clam chowder, which Palmer proclaimed was the best she'd ever had. It was when Kent saw her hand trembling that he knew it was time to call it quits on the day.

Palmer was asleep on the bed farthest from the wall, bundled in his sweatshirt and the comforter he'd given her from his bed. When he'd given Palmer her meds earlier, he'd checked her vitals. With her being cold all the time, he worried her blood pressure was too low.

Kent sat on the window ledge and watched the taillights of the passing cars. The building across the street and all its businesses were dark, except for the restaurant and bars that occupied the bottom floor. The rain began, which added to Kent's melancholy. He couldn't pinpoint what was wrong besides the obvious—he was falling in love with someone who couldn't love him back, and for the first time in his life, he understood what heartache was.

When he found out about Maeve, he was mad. Pissed off, even. Sure, he felt a pang of hurt in his heart, but nothing like he felt when he looked at Palmer. He saw Palmer as someone he could love for the rest of her life. Someone who never got a chance to live, and now that she had the opportunity, it was being taken away from her viciously. He looked at her and saw someone who wanted to be loved and love back.

He saw someone who was dying.

For the first time since he'd approached Palmer with his idea, he regretted it. He could've taken his sabbatical and stayed with her in San Francisco, close to where they'd have all the medical care she'd need. Instead, he came up with this crazy plan to fulfill her bucket list, which was probably costing time and comfort.

Palmer moaned. Kent moved lightning fast to be by her side. He looked her over for any signs of distress and saw none.

"Kent," she mumbled.

"I'm here."

"Hurts."

"What hurts?" he asked before moving from the bed to his medical bag. "Is it your head?"

"Feet." Kent paused. Her answer caught him off guard. He looked at her and asked again. "Feet?"

Kent went to the bathroom, turned the faucet on, and started filling the tub with hot water. He then brought the desk chair into the bathroom and positioned it near the tub. He shut the water off and went back to Palmer.

"Are you awake?"

She moaned her answer.

"I'm going to pick you up. Okay?"

"'Kay," she mumbled.

After moving the covers, Kent scooped Palmer into his arms and carried her to the bathroom while mentally running through his research on GBM. He couldn't recall anything about lower extremities except paralysis, and he prayed it wasn't that.

He sat down with Palmer in his arms and set her feet into the water. She hissed when the hot water touched her feet, and he felt horrible for not checking the temperature. "I'm sorry," he said. "Let me add some cold water."

Palmer shook her head.

He held her, with her back to his chest and his arms around her. Kent rested his head on her shoulder and tried not to cry. This was going to be the hardest thing he'd ever done. He was a trained medic, but he patched people up enough to get them to the professionals. Kent was the professional now. They could quit and go back home, but that thought tore at him. He'd promised her this trip. He'd promised he'd take care of her.

"Does anything else hurt?"

"No," she said as she woke up.

Kent felt her shiver in his arms, and he tightened his hold. "Want me to get you a blanket?"

"Don't move," she pleaded. "This is perfect."

"But you're cold."

"I'm not."

They stayed like that until the water chilled. Palmer lifted her feet and rested them on the opposite side of the tub. "I don't know what that was," she told him. "It was like they were on fire or something."

"We did a lot of walking today. Maybe we should use the chair?" He hated suggesting the wheelchair because he knew how much the thought of it made Palmer feel degraded.

"Not yet," she said. "I think, maybe, I need some new shoes."

Kent hadn't thought of that. When she'd said she was in pain, he'd automatically thought about the tumor and what it was doing to her. "Are you being dramatic?" he asked with a hint of laughter.

Palmer cackled and shook her head. "I think I am." She turned and looked at him. "I blame my brain. It said 'pain' and went into extreme overdrive, and I thought nothing of it."

Kent shook his head and dropped it to her shoulders. "You scared me."

"I'm sorry. I didn't mean to."

"I know you didn't. Come on, let's go to bed," he said. "There's a place I want to take you before we head to New York tomorrow."

"What is it?"

"It's something you mentioned in passing, but I want to keep it a surprise."

Palmer walked out of the bathroom on her own and crawled back into bed. She pulled the covers to her chin and rolled onto her side and looked at Kent. "If I haven't said it before, I'm grateful for you. You didn't have to do this for me."

Kent sat on the edge of his bed and faced her. "Palmer, you have no idea how much you've helped me heal. I needed this trip and the time away as much as you did. Asking you to do this was the best decision of my life."

"You didn't really ask," she pointed out.

He shrugged. "Semantics. You could've said no."

"I tried, but you won me over," she said in a hushed tone. "Best decision of my life." She rolled over before Kent could react. The temptation to drop to his knees beside her bed and kiss her was great. He yearned for her, and he didn't know how to stop his feelings. He was in way over his head and was certain there wasn't anything he could do about it.

Kent woke and moved about the room before waking Palmer. He wanted her to get as much sleep as possible. He called the valet for their car and packed his things. He shook Palmer's leg and called out her name.

"Sleep," she grumbled.

"In the car. It'll be nice and warm when we get downstairs."

She groaned and sat up. "It's dark out, Kent."

"Yes, Captain Obvious. I want to detour, remember?"

Palmer got out of bed, grabbed her outfit for the day, and went into the bathroom. While she showered, Kent went to the Instagram account he'd created for the trip and was surprised to see they had a hundred people following them. He liked and replied to the comments, thanking each of them for their love, support, and recommendations on places to visit.

When Palmer came out of the bathroom, she smiled. "I need coffee."

"I've already ordered it. The delivery driver is one minute away. By the time we get downstairs, it'll be waiting."

"God, I could kiss you right now," she said. They made eye contact and paused. Kent swallowed hard. Was this an invitation? He stood, ready for her to make her move, and then Palmer asked, "What are you looking at on your phone?"

Kent felt foolish. For a second, he thought she was serious when she said she was grateful for the coffee. He cleared his thoughts and showed her the phone. "We have followers now, and they're leaving comments. The power of hashtags."

"Let me see."

He gave her the phone so she could look at the comments. Kent loaded his arms with their luggage, and Palmer held the door, even though she never looked up from the phone.

"How come there are more likes than followers?" she asked as she absentmindedly pressed the button for the elevator.

"Our profile is public, so anyone can see it, especially if one of their friends liked our photo or started following us or if they're searching under one of the hashtags we've used." They stepped into the elevator, and Palmer pressed the button for the lobby.

"Social media is so weird."

Kent laughed. The doors opened, and they stepped into the quiet lobby. It was still dark out, and aside from the people who worked in the hotel, no one was around. "It is. How come you don't use it to look for your family?"

"What would I even do?" she asked him. "Make a post about how a woman who I think is my mother, but I can't be positive, dropped me off at an orphanage?"

"While I see your point, I think the power of social is a resource that could benefit you. We're gaining a following. Someone's going to share and reshare our posts. If you make a heartfelt one about looking for your family, they may see it. You don't know that they're not looking for you. I think it's worth a shot, if you want to try." They walked toward the exit and then jumped when they heard Kent's name.

"Mr. Wagner, these are for you," the clerk said as he motioned at the two coffees.

Before Kent could move, Palmer stepped forward, thanked the clerk, and picked up the paper tray. Kent played it off and headed outside to the Jeep, where the valet held the door open for Palmer. When he got behind the wheel, she handed him his coffee, and then turned her seat warmer on and moved the heat dial to high.

"Take a drink before you drive. It'll help."

"Help what?" he asked her.

Palmer laughed and shrugged. "I have no idea, but I thought it sounded good in my head."

Kent did as she suggested and then set the cup into the holder. "Thank you, Dr. Sinclair."

While he navigated to the freeway, Palmer turned on the overhead light and wrote in the journal. "Are you going to tell me where we're going?" She finished writing, closed the book, and shut the light off.

"Nope," he said when they took the on-ramp for the interstate. "It'll be a quick stop," he said. "And we have to do some walking, but we're bringing the chair."

"That's embarrassing," she muttered.

He grabbed her hand and squeezed. "I'll push the damn thing while you walk next to me, but what I want to show you is a bit of a walk, and I don't want you to overdo it."

"Fine," she sighed.

Kent decided he would not tell her he planned to take the chair to Times Square later because he didn't want to ruin her day, but there was no way Palmer could navigate the crowds. She barely ate and had lost weight, almost to the point where he was going to have to give her nutritional shakes. Something she would for sure frown at, but would be a necessity.

"Are you going to post a photo from yesterday?" Palmer asked.

"*We* are. It's our account. Which photo should I post?"

Palmer went through their images and showed Kent which ones she liked, and then she took some pictures of Kent while he drove.

The **Welcome to Rhode Island** sign came into view, and Palmer looked at Kent. "What are we doing here?"

He chuckled. "I'm not telling you. Just believe me when I tell you you're going to love it, and you'll thank me later."

They drove over a bridge lit up in white, the lights dancing off the water. Palmer told Kent she could make out the shapes of boats in the water, and could tell they were in a residential area. She kept looking out the windows and would sigh in aggravation, which made Kent laugh. After a series of turns, the skyline opened up, and she gasped.

"We've already seen a sunrise," she told him.

"First of all, you can never see too many, and second, the sunrise is a bonus. There's something else I want to see and do."

Palmer put her window down as they drove along the shoreline. "I love the sound the water makes when it hits the rocks. It sounds like the ocean is angry, but yet it can be so calming. What a mix of emotions it can bring."

Kent agreed.

He parked, took the wheelchair out of the back, and set it up, complete with a blanket, and they started off on the natural trail. They walked until the path turned toward the east, and then they stopped and watched the sunrise. It was as beautiful as their morning on the beach in Chatham.

"The sun seems so close."

"I know, like we could walk to it from here," Kent said.

Palmer slowed down, and Kent suggested she sit in the chair. When he saw tears in her eyes, he pulled her to his chest. "It's okay to use it," he told her. "It doesn't make you weak or incapable. It's here to help you."

She hesitated and then finally gave in. She sat down and covered her legs with the blanket. "I feel like this is a sign, and I don't want to accept it."

"It's a sign that you just walked a mile and you're tired. If it makes you feel any better, you can push me later."

Palmer scoffed and rested her elbow on the armrest and her head in her hand. Kent pushed her into one of the benched areas meant for resting, and she perked up. "What's this?"

"Painters gather here every day and paint the skyline."

They sat there for a moment and watched a group of people with their paints and easels, painting the shoreline. "This is something you only see in galleries."

"Do you like it?"

"I love it. Thank you." She looked at him and smiled.

He reached into his back pocket and pulled out the envelope that held her DNA results. Last night's hiccup made opening this even more important. "I think this is the perfect spot to find out if you have family out there or not. I don't want you to open it in a hotel or while we're driving down the road. I want you to open it in a place you can remember, whether the contents are good or bad. If you have someone out there sharing your DNA, you'll think back to the moment when you saw something you've only seen in galleries. And if you don't, you'll remember the beauty of what we saw this morning."

Kent handed her the envelope. "Before you open it, I want to remind you, if it says there isn't a match, it's because they haven't taken a test yet. You have family out there, Palmer. Let's find them."

Before I'm Gone

- ♥ Sit in the front seat of a roller coaster and feel the wind in my hair
- ♥ Eat tacos or tortillas from a roadside stand in New Mexico
- ♥ Shop at a large farmers market
- ♥ Meet Lana Del Rey and see her in concert
- ♥ Take a picture of the most-painted shed in the US
- ♥ ~~Sit in the sand and watch the sunrise in Cape Cod~~
- ♥ Take the steps to the Lincoln Memorial
- ♥ Do yoga in Sedona
- ♥ Tour and feed animals in a wildlife sanctuary
- ♥ Stand under a waterfall
- ♥ See Elvis on the street corner in Las Vegas
- ♥ Hug an elephant
- ♥ Find my family
- ♥ Step on grapes and make wine
- ♥ Run through a wheat field
- ♥ Drive Route 66
- ♥ See the marquees on Broadway
- ♥ Ring the Liberty Bell
- ♥ Buy a quilt from an Amish stand
- ★ See the northern lights in Minnesota
- ★ ~~Visit Plymouth Rock~~
- ★ Touch Babe Ruth's bat
- ★ Travel the Loneliest Road
- ★ Visit the Muhammad Ali Center
- ★ Dance in the rain with someone I love
- ★ Take the ferry to the Statue of Liberty
- ★ Check out the Grand Canyon
- ★ Take every picture I can of Palmer ✓
- ★ Make Palmer smile ✓

- ~~*Eat chowdah in Boston, per Palmer*~~
- *Eat pizza in Chicago*
- *Try frozen custard in New York City*
- *Get coffee in each city* ✓

Twenty-One

Once again, the envelope that weighed a hundred pounds pressed heavily onto Palmer's lap. Kent was right: it needed to be opened, but there wasn't a perfect time or place to do it. Regardless of the results, they would taint her trip. She either had a family or she didn't, and if she did, they'd never know each other.

Palmer sighed heavily and lifted the corner flap until the paper tore away from the glue, but then she chickened out when it came time to pull the sheet of paper out. She stared at the open envelope. Flipping it back and forth in her hand. The printing on the outside had become faded, likely from being touched so many times.

Kent reached for her hand and gave it a squeeze. "I'm right here," he told her. "You can do this."

Palmer sighed again and nodded, as if she had given herself a mental pep talk. She tugged the trifolded sheet of paper out of the envelope and held it in her hand, trying to use the x-ray vision she didn't have to see through the linen.

"You have to unfold it," Kent said with a hint of laughter. She knew he meant well and was only teasing her about how painstakingly slow she moved. Palmer thought about asking him to unfold it, but knew she was looking for an excuse to ignore her fate.

"Here goes nothing," she said.

Before she could take the plunge, Kent put his arm around her and kissed the side of her head. She leaned into his embrace, wishing it was more, and not so friendly. If she wasn't sick, she could see herself with a man like Kent. Although, if she wasn't sick, they wouldn't be together right now.

"You can do it," he said, speaking words of encouragement. He leaned forward slightly to look at her. His eyes were expectant, eager. He wanted to know just as much as she did. She likened him to what she would look like on Christmas morning—if she were to have one.

Slowly, she unfolded the flaps and tried to process the words. Her vision blurred and then clouded instantly with unshed tears. She dropped her hand to her lap and shook her head.

"May I?" Kent asked. She handed him the paper and stared out into the ocean. She saw what the painters saw, and it was beautiful.

Kent read the letter to himself and then said, "It says here that you have a familial match and that it could be an aunt or sister."

Palmer turned quickly. Her mouth opened and then closed before she shook her head. "No match, right?" she asked, her voice quivering.

"A match, Palmer." Kent lowered the paper. "You have a family."

When the tears prickled in the corner of her eyes, she let them fall. She covered her mouth when a strangled cry released and was in Kent's arms instantly. "You have a family," he repeated in her ear. "There's a part of you out there, waiting to meet you."

"I don't have the time," she whispered back.

"We'll make the time," he told her.

They stayed in each other's arms until her tears dried. She tried to read the letter, but her focus was off. Kent was excited and pumped up, to the point that he almost tipped her over when they hit a rock on the way back to the car.

As soon as they were situated, he turned the music up, and he sang loudly to whatever song played and sang to Palmer. He got her to smile and feel a bit of happiness, which was easy to do because he was her savior. Her guiding light through the worst of everything.

It was because of Kent she'd know her sister or aunt—whoever it was who had submitted their DNA—all Palmer had to do was send an email and introduce herself. She relaxed in her seat and held the paper to her chest while she stared at him, until she eventually fell asleep.

"How long was I asleep for?" she asked when she came to.

Kent looked at the clock on the dashboard. "About an hour."

Palmer looked out the window and saw the sign to New York City, their next destination. The Statue of Liberty was on their list of places to visit, but the more Palmer thought about it, the more she wondered if it was a place she absolutely needed to see. She pressed the button to open the top and then reclined her seat. Palmer gazed out of the open roof and watched as the clouds moved at a fascinating speed. She likened their movement to how fast her health had declined. She could feel herself dying and see the physical evidence on her face. Her once-visible cheekbones were now thicker and made her look puffy. Palmer could hardly stand to look at herself in the mirror anymore.

She reached toward Kent and touched a small curl at the nape of his neck. Kent didn't look at her but leaned into her touch. Something had shifted between them. Palmer wasn't sure when, but she was certain they both had the same feelings for each other. Although hers were stronger by far. It made sense they would be. He'd come to her in her time of need. He'd stopped her from taking what many considered the easy way out.

Nothing was easy when it came to what her body would go through—what had already started. Palmer had yet to tell Kent, but her already-blurry vision had gotten worse. She used to have perfect vision. She couldn't pinpoint exactly when it had started changing. Sometimes when she woke up, her eyes would be blurry, and she'd rubbed the sleep away. When the muddied edges started, she asked the eye doctor—normal age progression or common with people who stare at computers all day, he'd said. Except, she wasn't old, and while she did work on a computer, it wasn't for a straight eight hours. She took breaks and made sure she sat the correct distance away. Palmer went as far as buying reading glasses, even though she didn't need them, to help with the blue light from her screen and take the pressure off her eyes.

Now, when she looked at Kent or stared through the open roof, she knew her vision was worsening. The tumor was growing and progressing faster than she thought it would. She'd hoped she'd have more time to explore and see the country she lived in. Palmer had already wasted years and years of her life working and saving, and for what—to take a trip before she died? If everything she researched was true, she wouldn't remember most of it by the time they got to the end. Her memory was going to fail. It was going to slip, and she'd be left fumbling through a thick haze of nothingness.

Palmer dropped her hand. Not because she'd tired of touching Kent's neck, but because the strenuous activity hurt her. To think that touching someone would physically hurt her brought tears to her eyes. Her body was failing her with every breath she took. She could no longer walk long distances, sleep through the night, see well, or even sit for any amount of time. Yet, if she moved, she would be in pain. Palmer's life was the definition of a no-win situation.

She shivered, and the motion caught Kent's attention. "Are you cold?" he asked. He reached for the dial to turn on the heat.

"I didn't think I was."

Kent frowned and signaled to change lanes. He worked hard to mask his emotions when something happened, and Palmer appreciated him for being a stoic medic and a friend. She never saw pity in his eyes, only concern. He cared for her like he'd care for anyone else. Her heart longed for him in ways she had never experienced, and each day they were together only deepened her feelings for him. Kent had gotten Palmer to do what no one else had been able to—fall in love.

The Jeep slowed, and Kent pulled off the road. Palmer sat up and saw they had turned into a rest area. Kent found a spot nearest the building, which would shorten the walk for her. He closed the top and turned off the car. "We can get something to eat here."

"I'm not hungry," she said, and he frowned.

"I know, but you need to eat something." He got out and went to her side, opened the door, and held his hand out for her. Her body hurt. The other night, it was her feet. Today, it was her torso. She felt like she had run a marathon or ten and hadn't rested for weeks.

Kent kept his arm around her and tucked her into his side, instead of letting her hang on his arm for support. They looked like a couple, and not travel companions or a medic taking care of his patient.

Inside, they parted ways when they got to the bathroom. Thankfully, she wasn't at the stage in her life when she needed him to help her. Those days were approaching fast, and there wasn't anything Palmer could do to slow them down. It seemed that once she'd accepted her fate, her body had stopped fighting.

Palmer used the facilities and then went to wash her hands. Next to her, a little girl stared. Palmer tried to smile, but her thick cheeks prevented her mouth from lifting. When the little girl looked at Palmer, she wondered what she saw. She looked at herself in the mirror and wondered how she'd gotten where she was now. She'd listened to her body and taken care of herself. Palmer had been to the doctor, but he'd only prescribed pill after pill. He'd never suggested she go for testing. "Take this," he'd said to her. "Drink more caffeine," he'd told her. "It's only a migraine."

Only it wasn't a migraine. It was a tumor. The neurologist had called it a claw. Palmer called it an octopus whose tentacles continued to grow, sucking the life right out of her and taking up every free space she had left, until one day her head would explode.

Back in the food court, Palmer found Kent sitting at a table with a tray of food. Her stomach rolled, and she felt queasy. She sat down across from him and looked at the pile of junk he'd accumulated while she was in the bathroom.

"I'm not eating any of this," she told him. The food was deep-fried or fake meat from the fast-food places. He handed her a cup of yogurt and a bowl of fruit.

"No, you'll eat this."

"You're awfully bossy," she snapped.

Their gazes met, and Kent's eyebrow raised. "Nice attitude."

She glared and ripped the lid off her yogurt. She was mad at him for making her eat. Deep down, she knew she had to, but for some reason, Palmer wanted to fight about it. Mood swings were a part of her diagnosis. Kent knew this as well.

Palmer added the fruit to her yogurt and then threw the empty cup onto the table. Kent watched as it slid across until it fell off. He looked at her again and shook his head.

"What's your problem?" she asked.

"I'm not the one with the problem."

"I'm allowed to be angry," she told him. "I have an octopus growing in my head."

Kent scoffed. "Is that what we're calling it now?"

"Yes. It's ugly and large, and it's eating my brain."

Kent nodded. "You can be angry, Palmer. But you don't have to be disrespectful," he told her. He bent down and picked the cup up off the floor and set it in a pile of garbage. "I'm not the octopus."

"I never said you were."

Kent said nothing as he ate his lunch. Palmer studied him. She waited for him to look at her, but he wouldn't. She picked at her yogurt, taking only a couple of bites until her stomach protested. Palmer pushed it away and sighed.

Kent ignored her.

"I'm sorry," she said as she leaned forward to rest her head on her hands. "This thing . . . one minute I'm fine, and the next it's like a demon who's trying to get out."

Kent rubbed his hand up and down her arm. "I know, and I'm sorry. I didn't mean to goad you earlier."

"What else are you supposed to do?" she asked. "Placate me? Ignore me? Either way, I'm sure the ugliness will come out in full force." Palmer covered her face for a moment and then looked at Kent. "I'm not that type of person. I don't smart off or say mean things, and I hate that this thing makes me act like an a-hole."

Kent laughed. "I think you've earned the right to cuss, if you wanted."

Palmer shrugged. "It's not who I am."

"It doesn't make any difference if you need to express yourself. Maybe we should find a place where you can stand and scream. Say everything you want to say, without anyone hearing you."

"You'd hear me," she said.

"I'll cover my ears."

Palmer smiled softly and reached for Kent's hand. "You're too good to me."

Kent raised their hands and pressed a kiss to the back of Palmer's. He released her hand, gathered their garbage, and took the tray to the trash. Palmer followed behind him.

They made their way to the Jeep. Kent helped her in and then got into the driver's seat. He drove over to the gas pumps, filled up, and then checked the navigation. "We're almost there, but we're going to hit a lot of traffic."

"Can we skip New York?" she asked him.

He glanced at her and waited.

"I'd rather head to Washington, DC." In her mind, some sights were far more important than others, and this was one of them.

"We can do whatever you want, Palmer."

"Will you be mad?"

He shook his head. "Absolutely not. Besides, I love DC, and I can't wait to show it to you. Going now will give us more time."

"Thank you."

Kent smiled at her and reached for her hand. "You don't have to thank me. I'm right where I want to be."

"Me too." Only she wanted to be alive and with him.

Twenty-Two

They arrived in Washington, DC, in the late hours of the night, or was it the early hours of the morning? Kent's job often required him to stay awake for hours on end, and he'd mastered the art of the quick twenty-minute catnap, but the endless driving wore him out. When Palmer was awake, she kept him company, and when she slept, he let his thoughts wander.

He worried about her and, not for the first time, questioned whether this trip across the country was a good idea. Each day, Kent saw something new in Palmer that showed her health was failing her. The outburst at lunch caught him off guard. He'd expected the behavioral changes but had prayed they wouldn't show up for another week or two. His sweet, shy, and reserved Palmer had disappeared before his eyes in a matter of minutes, and he hated it.

And he hated knowing and visualizing the tumor taking over her brain. Maybe Palmer was right in calling the tumor an "octopus"—they were always growing and could mimic their environment. The clawlike mass in Palmer's brain presented like a migraine, but now that its presence was out in the open, the headaches weren't as bad because everywhere else hurt.

Kent pulled into the check-in-only space in front of their hotel. They didn't have a reservation there for two more days. Palmer's request to skip New York City had thrown his planning off course. Palmer was sound asleep, and Kent didn't want to wake her. He leaned forward and confirmed she was breathing, though, for his own peace of mind. Kent kept the car running, made sure the fob was in his pocket, and exited the vehicle as quietly as possible. He locked the door before closing it and made his way into the hotel, ready to plead with the night manager.

The lobby was quiet and absent of any life. The decor reminded Kent of the lobby at Palmer's apartment complex, complete with a fireplace. Kent felt the warmth radiating and somehow found the entire setup inviting. The pictures on the internet did not do this place justice.

He stood at the counter and fiddled with the jar of pens that sat there, hoping the noise would encourage the night clerk to come out from the back office. When that didn't work, he tapped his fingers and coughed, and even hummed loudly. The clerk finally emerged, wiping his face as he came out of the office. Kent mentally kicked himself for being obnoxious and interrupting the man's dinner.

"How can I help you?" the clerk asked when he stepped up to the terminal.

"Sorry for coming in so late or early. I have a reservation, but it doesn't start for a couple of more days. Our plans changed, and we arrived early. I'm hoping you have a room available?"

"Let me see," he said as he began typing. There was a lot of mouse clicking, typing, and some sass as the computer froze. All of which gave Kent zero hope that the hotel had a free room. "I have a room now, but it's booked tomorrow."

Kent groaned.

"What I can do is put you in the room now and move you to the suite, if you don't mind paying, and then put you in the standard room for your existing reservation. I know it's a lot of moving, but that's the best I can do."

"That's fine, we'll take it."

"Very well, I'll just need to see your driver's license and a credit card." Kent fished his wallet out of his back pocket and handed over his credentials. "What brings you to town early?"

"My . . ." Kent paused and thought about how he should title Palmer. "Travel companion" seemed wrong, as did "friend."

"My partner and I are doing a bucket list tour sort of thing, and she wanted to skip NYC and come to the nation's capital early."

"Oh, that sounds fun. I've always wanted to write a bucket list."

"Do it now, before it's too late." The clerk's eyes shot up to meet Kent's. He shrugged and said, "She's dying. Nonoperable brain tumor."

The clerk shuddered. "I'm so sorry."

Kent nodded. He was sorry too. He didn't want to lose her now that he knew her.

"I put you in the suite," the clerk said. "You won't have to move or pay the additional fees. I've comped tonight and tomorrow and will have my manager adjust your other two nights. If there's anything you need, press the front desk button on the phone, and we'll get it. Room service is twenty-four hours. There's a pool, hot tub, and gym available, and the breakfast buffet starts at six." The clerk handed Kent his key cards. "Please let me know if you need anything."

"Thank you for your generosity." Kent pocketed his ID and credit card and slipped the room keys into his front pocket. He got back to the Jeep and found Palmer still asleep, which surprised him. He found a parking spot, got out, and went to the back to get her wheelchair. She would need a good half hour of alertness before she'd be able to walk, and he didn't want her sleeping in the car anymore.

Kent opened her door and gently woke her, and a very groggy Palmer put her arm around Kent's shoulder when he scooped her into his arms. "Are we here?" she asked.

"Yep, at the hotel now."

"I'm starving."

Kent's steps faltered slightly. He had never heard her say those words before, but they elated him. Since he'd struggled to get her to eat, he was prepared to get her some protein shakes or other supplements to help give her some strength.

"What would you like?" he asked her. Kent set Palmer down in her wheelchair and covered her lap with a blanket. The chill in the air made him shiver, and he couldn't imagine how it made her feel. She'd lost a lot of weight since he'd first met her. He pushed her toward the lobby and hunched over her to encourage an answer. "I'm waiting."

Palmer tilted her body so she could see Kent and rolled her eyes. "You must be so happy."

"I am. Now tell me what you want to eat so I can order it."

"You'll laugh."

"Highly unlikely. I'm elated," he told her. "Overjoyed."

"I want chicken nuggets from Mickey D's. Honestly, I want a Happy Meal."

She was right; he did want to laugh, and now that she'd said it, he sort of wanted one as well. He couldn't remember the last time he'd gotten a toy with a meal. No one remembered when they went from the kids' menu to the adult menu at their favorite fast-food place. Sure, the sign said they were for children aged twelve and under, but who followed that rule? And how come there wasn't a ceremony or some recognition when you graduated from the small section on the right side of the menu to the large one on the left? Palmer was spot on for suggesting a Happy Meal.

When they entered the lobby, the clerk stood at the counter. He offered a genuine smile and asked if they needed any help. "Actually." Kent stopped in the lobby. "We'd like to order from McDonald's. Is there one near us that's still open?"

The clerk nodded and wrote down the address. "All the food apps will deliver, and if not, let me know and I'll arrange with the concierge to get it."

Kent assured him that wasn't necessary but thanked him for his generosity. They continued on to the elevator, and Palmer pressed the button for their floor. "He seems nice."

"He's outstanding," Kent said. "We're going to leave him a very nice review. He went above and beyond."

"How so?"

"You'll see." Kent hit the button for the top floor and waited next to the chair. "So, nuggets? Anything else?"

"Maybe a cheeseburger."

Kent fist pumped and shouted "Yes!" with so much enthusiasm that he startled Palmer. "Sorry," he muttered. "I'm excited."

Palmer gave him a dirty look. "I think you're tired."

She had no idea. "Nothing a nap won't cure." He needed about ten hours, but he'd hold off as long as possible if it meant spending time with her.

The elevator doors opened, and he pushed her toward their room. After swiping the key card, Palmer opened the door. Kent secretly loved how she tried to keep as much independence as possible. She might have been slowly dying, but her spirit wasn't. It was going to take death to dim her shining light.

"What in the banana sundae is going on here?"

Kent stood behind her, speechless. They had a view of the Mall and could see the Capitol. "Wow."

"How much did this cost us?"

"It's free," he muttered.

Palmer stood, turned, and placed her hands on her hips. "Say what?"

Kent nodded and moved the wheelchair off to the side. He took her hand and led her over to the window. The lights from the Mall and the monuments cast the perfect glow into the night sky. "The clerk and I had a conversation about bucket lists, and I told him not to wait to do his. I also told him what we're doing and why. He comped this room for us."

"I don't want to use this"—she pointed to her head—"to get free stuff."

Kent looked at her. "I know you don't. It wasn't my intention. It would've been rude to tell him no."

Palmer sighed and nodded. "I know. Remind me to thank him."

"I will."

Kent left her at the window to go back downstairs and retrieve their luggage. He placed an order for their food, grabbed their bags, and headed back to the room. He fully expected to find her in the same spot, but she wasn't there.

"Palmer?"

"In here," she called out. He searched for her, with his arms still full, and found her sitting on the edge of the tub with water coming out of the faucet. "I've never been in a jetted tub before."

"And you thought now was the time to take a bath?"

Palmer beamed. "I'm awake."

"Are you still hungry?"

"I am."

He wouldn't argue. "There's only one bed," he said. "At least it's a king." Kent went into the bedroom and set their stuff down. He unpacked his clothes and put them in one half of the dresser, and made a dirty pile. They would do their washing tomorrow and forgo some sightseeing. Palmer came into the room and sat on the edge of the bed.

"Your tub will overflow if you don't watch it."

"I'll be quick," she said. "Can I use your phone?"

He checked the delivery time on their food order and handed his phone to her without question.

"I want to email my aunt or sister—whoever she might be."

"I think that's a great idea." He went into the bathroom and shut off the water. It was fuller than it needed to be, and he was thankful she hadn't seen the bubble bath, or they'd have issues on their hands.

"Our food should be here soon."

Palmer gave Kent his phone. "I hope I get a fun toy."

He laughed and wondered if she'd ever had a Happy Meal before. "You should go get into the bath before the water cools."

She looked surprised, and he suspected she'd forgotten about filling the tub. Forgetfulness was another side effect they'd have to deal with as the tumor progressed. Kent pulled up a music app on his phone and handed it to her.

"Play some music while you're in there."

"Okay," she said, taking his phone again. "Aren't you going to ask about my email?"

He sat down next to her and rubbed his hands down his legs. "If you want to tell me, then yes, but I don't want to pry."

Palmer bumped her shoulder into his arm. "You're not prying. I feel like this is as much your journey as mine, and besides, you'll end up meeting whoever it is." Kent nodded, and she continued. "I introduced myself and told them I'd recently done a test, although that was a lie, and said I'm interested in meeting members of my family." She paused. "I thought about going into the whole foster care thing, but it's hard to write about sometimes."

"Makes sense. I'm sure whoever gets that email will be happy to hear from you."

She leaned into him, and Kent put his arm around her. He kissed the top of her head and sighed. "Thank you," she said to him.

"For what?"

"For all of this. For being my friend." He loved being her friend and possibly a bit more if he could muster up the courage to tell her.

"You don't need to thank me, Palmer. You're doing the same for me."

"Have you heard whether the baby is yours?"

Kent shook his head. "You'll be the first to know when I do."

His phone vibrated in her hand, and she looked at it and then showed it to Kent. Not only was their food at the hotel, but they had a new comment on one of their posts. Kent clicked it and told her to read all the comments. In the short time they'd been on their trip, they'd amassed a following. Strangers from every corner of the world were interested in their journey, and some had even asked to see their faces.

"You have fans," Kent told her. "They want to meet you."

"Absolutely not," she told him.

Kent chuckled. "Not physically. Social media makes things so easy these days. Let me go get our food, you hop into the bath, and then we'll discuss it while we eat." He kissed her forehead and lingered there longer than a friend would. How she had turned his bitter heart around in such a short time amazed him, but it also devastated him. He was going to lose her before they even had a chance to be more for each other.

Twenty-Three

There was a park near the hotel. Palmer had spotted it from their room after the sun rose and asked Kent if they could go. He agreed, even though he was tired. Kent would do anything she asked and could figure out his sleep schedule later.

They held hands as they walked through the park. They smelled the flowers, pointed at birds and wondered what kind they were, and sat on the bench to people watch. At a food cart, Kent bought them freshly squeezed lemonade and cookies to enjoy while they basked in the sun. It was a beautiful day with warmth and nature surrounding them.

Kent pulled out his phone and scrolled through their messages on Instagram. It seemed like overnight they had become some sort of sensation. They'd gone from a couple hundred followers to close to ten thousand. Their comments had tripled, and they had many messages waiting for them. Kent went through the notifications and clicked on one that mentioned their page name. A video played, and he recognized the clerk from the hotel.

"Y'all, I gotta tell you about this couple that came in while I ate dinner. I didn't get a whole lot of details at first, but now I know more. Anyway, the guy checking in tells me they're early for their reservation and that they're in town because he and his partner are doing this bucket list thing. And I tell him I want to create a list. He tells me not to wait and then says his partner is dying because she has a tumor. After I got them their room, I started thinking about how short life can be, and here's this couple trying to live their best life and make all these memories. And I just know this man is doing it so he can see his lady smile every day. If that's not love, I don't know what is. Anyway, they have an account and I'm going to tag it below. I want you all to follow them on this journey. I know they're not posting a lot, but each recap of the stops they've made is worth the read. If my man sees this, I got you for dinner tonight. Come see me in the lobby."

The video ended and then restarted. "What was that?" Palmer asked.

"The clerk from last night," Kent said. "Did you listen to what he said?"

Palmer nodded.

"I don't think he meant any harm by telling people," Kent said when he saw the look on her face. It was a cross between confusion and hurt, both of which she had the right to feel. It wasn't lost on Kent that she'd told her former coworkers she'd taken another job because she didn't want them to worry about her, and something like this could reach them. Not only that, but she was a private person—even before her diagnosis—and now her business was all over social media, and people were clamoring for information.

"I'm confused," she said. Again, he understood.

"We can ignore it, or we can embrace it."

"Embrace it how?"

Kent turned slightly to face her. "We can tell your story, Palmer. Despite the outcome, you've persevered and done something with your life. Others in foster care might not see the positives in front of them. You could give them hope."

"How would I do that?"

"We can go live. All I have to do is press this button, and all those people who are following us will get a notification on their phone telling them we're live, and they'll tune in or watch later. They can ask us questions by typing them out for us to read. Maybe they'll even suggest a couple of places not on our list. We can try it and see how it goes, and if you don't like it, we won't do it again."

Kent went back to his phone, found the video again, and followed the clerk. He then commented on the video, thanked him for all his help, and said they'd see him for dinner later, but only if they could have Happy Meals. He closed the app and set his phone down. Palmer was deep in thought and biting her lower lip. Kent pulled lip balm from his pocket and handed it to her. Dry lips—another side effect—mostly caused by dehydration. He wasn't doing a good enough job of taking care of her. Kent headed to the food cart, bought a bottle of water, and brought it back to her.

"You need to drink more."

"You're so bossy," she said, but this time she followed it up with a smile instead of the poor attitude she'd had at the rest stop.

"Do you think people care? About me?" she asked after taking a drink.

What a loaded question. How could he answer that when she'd lived her life in a place where people didn't care? Kent leaned forward and rested his elbows on his knees. The question hurt his gut. It made his insides twist and turn. He took a deep breath and then glanced at her. She smiled at him, and he melted. It wasn't the first time she'd evoked this type of reaction from him, but this moment stood out. The sun shone behind her, and birds chirped close to them. Palmer had called Kent her knight in shining armor, and right now, she was his princess. The only thing missing was her big fancy dress.

"I think everyone is going to care. People are going to see you as a fighter, someone who's facing adversity head on. I also think you don't give yourself enough credit. You're the strongest person I know, and you're letting a tumor take you down without a fight."

"Octopus."

Kent chuckled. "Should we name the octopus?"

Palmer scoffed. "As if it deserves a name."

"You're the boss." Kent rested against the bench and watched a couple walk by with a stroller. That could be him in a few months, or he could still be the guy on the bench. He couldn't really picture himself as a dad, but he was eager to find out if the baby Maeve carried was his. Kent picked up his phone and sent her a text asking if she'd received the results yet. Before he sent it, he showed it to Palmer.

"You don't think she'd tell you?"

"No." He shook his head. "I don't know. Maeve is in a tough spot with her husband. When I spoke to her last, I tried not to ask any questions because I don't want to know about their marriage, but I told her if she needed anything to call me. I know this isn't easy for her." Kent was still upset at Maeve for what she'd done, but he'd had time to think, and he worried about how her husband might react if the baby wasn't his.

"I'm glad you spoke to her and told her to call you."

Kent bumped shoulders with Palmer. "I have you to thank for helping me see the error of my ways."

"Life's too short to be mad at a mistake," she said. "Are you going to send the text?" Palmer eyed his phone and then him.

"Do you think I should ask her how she's doing?"

Palmer appraised Kent for a moment and then shook her head. "I've never been in a relationship to answer that type of question, but yes, I think you should."

We could be in one.

"This is hard because as upset as I am, if the baby is mine, I want to know whether Maeve is okay. Does that make sense?"

"It does." Palmer paused for a moment. "Do you miss her?"

Kent shook his head instantly. "Not at all. Not even a little. I think about what she did to me and how she put me in this situation." He stared at his phone and frowned. "I'm just going to check in."

"That's a good idea." Palmer rested her hand on his leg and smiled. Kent matched her expression, typed out his text, and then set his phone down.

"What else do you want to do today?"

"We could do that live thing, if you want."

He met her gaze. "It's not about me, Palmer."

"What do you mean?"

Kent turned, brought his leg up to rest on the bench, and placed his ankle on his knee. Palmer did the same, matching his pose. "I'm not trying to hide this part of my life. You told your coworkers you moved, and they may or may not see this. I see the comments and how people are behind us, encouraging us, and it makes me happy. We're doing something good, something others can get behind. But we're doing it for a reason. If you hadn't been diagnosed with a tumor, we'd be at work right now. You'd be processing loans, and I'd be sitting next to Damian in the rig, waiting for a call." Kent sighed. "I don't know. I think if you're willing to share, people will listen, but you have to accept that your coworkers back home might see this, and they might be hurt."

"I'm not sure anything you just said makes sense," she said sarcastically.

Kent laughed loudly. "You're right. Bottom line, if you want to go live or start posting your face on the app, we can. If not, no biggie."

"My story could help, though, right? Like, if I tell people I've had these migraines and encourage them to seek image testing, I could save a life."

"You absolutely could. You could also show people that life is short, and if there's something you want to do, you get out there and do it."

"Manifest your happiness."

"Exactly," Kent said. He smiled and loved how amazing Palmer was.

"Let's do it."

"Okay, when?"

"Right now," she said enthusiastically.

Kent picked his phone up off the bench and moved closer to Palmer. He took the steps to go live and waited. After a few seconds, people started watching. At first, there were ten viewers, then twenty, and then over a hundred.

"Hey, everyone," he started, and then positioned the camera to include Palmer in the frame. "I'm Kent, and this is Palmer." She waved and then giggled. "We want to start off by saying thank you for all the love and support you've given us. We are in awe, and you've made us feel very special." Kent paused for a minute and showed Palmer the comments that flowed in. "We're going to answer a couple of these questions for you." He elbowed Palmer and asked, "Do you want to read their name and their question?"

"Sure." She leaned forward and squinted. Kent knew instantly she'd have trouble seeing the scrolling, faint script and regretted asking her if she wanted to read the comments.

"Someone wants to know who your favorite musician is," Kent said to Palmer.

"Oh, that's easy—Lana Del Rey." Palmer squeezed Kent's hand to thank him.

"Excellent choice. We're going to have to listen to her when we head to our next location." He beamed at Palmer. "Okay, they want to know why we're taking this trip." He glanced at Palmer and cocked his eyebrow.

She inhaled and stared at her reflection on Kent's phone. "I have . . ." She paused and shook her head. "I guess if you're following us, you already know. I'm not well . . ." She trailed off. Her eyes found Kent, and he took over, answering a handful of questions while she sat next to him. He read each one to Palmer, who added commentary every now and again. They finished and promised to go live again in a few days.

"What happened?" Kent asked her after he closed the app.

Palmer shrugged. "I just . . ." She shook her head. "I guess I never really said it out loud, except to you, and I don't even remember if I said it to you." She wiped at her tears. "The thought of saying it made my heart hurt." Palmer sobbed and covered her face.

Kent brought her into his arms and held her. The magnitude of the moment washed over him, and he cried with her. Admitting that you were dying was a hard thing to do, but to tell strangers—that was overwhelming.

People walked by and stared. Some stopped and asked if they were okay. Kent nodded and thanked them. He kept Palmer's face buried, to protect her dignity from onlookers. He held her to his chest and let her cry until her tears ran dry. They had nowhere to go and nowhere to be unless they wanted. That was the beauty of their situation. No one depended on them for anything. They only needed each other.

A dark cloud covered the bright sun, and rain fell. Kent tapped Palmer's shoulder and told her they needed to head back to the hotel. She sat up and tilted her head back. Kent sat there, watching as raindrops dotted her face. An idea struck.

Kent turned on his music app and looked at his recently played songs. Palmer was the last one to listen to music, while she bathed in the tub. He pressed the first song and then reached for her hand.

"What are you doing?" she asked.

"Dance with me," he said as he stood and pulled her up with him.

He stepped them away from the bench and spun Palmer around, surprising her. Their hands connected, and they swayed to the melodic sounds of Lana Del Rey's "Young and Beautiful." Kent held Palmer tightly, with his arm pressed to her back and his hand clutched in hers. Palmer pressed her face into the crook of his neck and hummed along.

"I've never danced in the rain," she said when the song ended and the next one began.

"Me neither. I love that we're doing something together for the first time."

"Me too," she whispered against his neck. Kent desperately wanted to kiss her, but he was afraid she would rebuff him. She had every reason in the world to stop his advances. She didn't need a lover, she needed a friend, and he had vowed to be that for her.

Twenty-Four

"Put that aside," Palmer told Kent after she stood and faced the massive granite steps of the Lincoln Memorial. All morning, Kent had pushed Palmer and her chair down the sidewalks of the National Mall, acting as if he were some race car driver. He even added sounds, which were meant for her entertainment. At one point, he wove in and out of foot traffic while making honking noises with his mouth. When they halted at the crosswalk, Palmer asked for a seat belt because she was afraid he was going to inadvertently dump her onto the ground. She was being facetious, of course. Kent would do nothing to hurt her.

"Are you sure?" he asked. "They have a ramp and elevator."

"I'm not disabled," she said as she stared straight ahead. The steps loomed in front of her, inviting yet challenging. She could walk, but she tired easily. And sure, at the end of the day, she'd soak in a tub of epsom salts. Palmer didn't want pity or help, not right now.

"I never said you were," Kent said. "I'm sorry if you think I'm treating you like you are."

They exchanged glances, and she smiled at him, aware that she may have accused him of doing something he hadn't. "I'm sorry," she said. "I'd like to try the steps."

"All right. Let's do it then."

The smaller steps were no problem for Palmer, and walking the space between each set of three stairs was a piece of cake. She turned and looked at the Reflecting Pool and then the Washington Monument, and felt small. The memorials were impressive, and she wondered what it had been like when people flocked there to protest the Vietnam War. The movies she'd seen likely didn't do that moment in history any justice.

They'd visited the Vietnam Memorial earlier in the day. Palmer had trailed her fingers over the names and wondered if anyone of them had been in her family. She had yet to hear from her aunt or sister and thought they'd given up their search. She had no idea when they'd taken their DNA test, and for all she knew, the service might not have an updated email for them. Kent reminded her often that not everyone checks their email daily and to give them time.

With a big intake of air, she faced her self-created task. Kent was next to her, poised to catch her if she faltered and ready to celebrate after she succeeded. The chair, however, was next to him. It was probably for the best. Someone could easily walk away with it, or she could need it when she finally made it to the statue of Lincoln.

"How many steps?" she asked Kent.

"Eighty-seven from where we started." He had the number memorized. In fact, he had every aspect of DC memorized, which astounded Palmer. Any question she threw at him, he had an answer, and if he didn't, they looked it up together.

"I can do this."

"Of course you can." Kent stretched. He brought his ankles up to his butt and brought his arms over his chest. He bent at the waist and did some side-to-side exercises while Palmer stared at him.

"What are you doing?"

"I'm going to race you," he joked.

Palmer scoffed. "Okay, but you start over at the Washington Memorial."

He turned and laughed. "Come on, we don't have all day."

"Wow, you're a laugh a minute."

"I know." He picked the chair up and took the first step, and then the second. He wouldn't go too far away from her, but enough to get her moving.

"Look at you," he said when she stepped onto their shared step. "Only like a million more to go."

Palmer nodded and moved closer to the wall. There wasn't a rail, but the wall would give her some stability if she needed it. She stepped again and again until they reached the next platform. Kent set the chair down, opened it, and asked if she wanted to rest.

"I do." She turned and sat on the steps, mimicking what others had done. Kent did the same and slipped his backpack off and opened it. He handed her a bottle of water and a protein bar. She wanted neither yet took both.

"Do you ever wonder why we memorialize some, but not all?" she asked as she took a bite. "So many people have shaped American history."

"I think DC does an okay job of making sure they're honoring all."

"There's room for improvement."

"In everything we do," Kent said. They finished their snack and walked what many would consider a short distance to the next set of steps. "You know, when we go to Arlington National Cemetery, I'm going to insist on the chair until we get to the Tomb of the Unknown Soldier. The walk is daunting."

Palmer grabbed the railing and took the first step. "Do you have friends buried there?" she asked.

"I do."

"Are we going to see them?"

"We are," he told her. It was important to Palmer that Kent pay his respects to the friends he'd lost. She insisted a trip to the cemetery be an item he could add to their list.

About halfway up, Palmer reached for Kent's arm. "Do you want to stop?" She shook her head and wheezed.

When they reached the top, Palmer sucked in a big gulp of air. Kent was next to her and spoke calmly in her ear: "I need you to bend over." She did, and he began rubbing her back and speaking in his soothing tone. "Short inhale, long exhale." Palmer nodded and practiced the breathing technique.

She stood and said, "I'm good. Let's do this."

Kent laughed at her spunky attitude. She rolled her eyes at him but couldn't hide her smile. Her mood changes often left a sour note in both their mouths. Step after step, she prevailed. When Palmer made it to the front of Lincoln, she marveled at the grand statue. She read the words behind his statue.

"Turn around and pose."

She did as Kent asked and put her arms diagonally in the air. Ever since they'd gone live on Instagram the day before, she'd been a bit more willing to have her photo taken and posted. She'd even insisted on taking some of Kent, taking selfies, and videotaping them on the train. Palmer even told Kent that when they went live again, she would tell the world what was wrong.

They swapped spots, and Palmer took photos of Kent, and some of the Reflecting Pool, and some of the Washington Monument. After another quick break, they made their way down the stairs, which was much easier than going up, and headed to their next destination.

As far as train stations went, Palmer thought the Metro was fairly clean. She wasn't a connoisseur of subway systems, unless she counted Boston's, but had heard horror stories about other cities and how filthy they were. They hopped on the Blue Line and rode the rails for just over thirty minutes. The escalator ride to get outside seemed to take forever, but once they reached the top, the sun shone brightly on them. Kent motioned for Palmer to get into her chair, and she did so begrudgingly.

"Maybe I should push you," she said as they crossed the street. He laughed.

"I'd like to see you try."

"Don't dare me," she told him. "I'm in rare form today and can do anything I set my mind to." Truthfully, she scared herself. She was having a great day, a perfect one, in fact. Her pain was minimal, she didn't have a headache, her stomach didn't hurt, and the blurriness in her vision wasn't affecting her much. Tomorrow, she expected, she'd go downhill. There was no way she'd have back-to-back great days without paying the price somehow.

Palmer gasped when they entered the cemetery and saw rows upon perfectly lined rows of headstones. The precision with which they lined up astounded her. No matter which way she looked, they all lined up.

"They're all the same," Kent told her. "Same height and weight."

"That's some amazing craftsmanship."

As Kent pushed her through the cemetery, she understood why he'd insisted she be in her chair. The ground was uneven in places and hilly. They came to their first stop. Kent helped Palmer out of her chair and held on to her while they walked toward the headstone of a man Kent had served with.

"Chuck was in my barracks during my first tour," he told her as he put a dime on top of his headstone.

"What's the dime for?" she asked.

"It tells his family that someone he served with came to see him. A penny means someone visited, a nickel means you trained in boot camp with them, and a quarter means you were there when they died."

"That's very . . ." She paused. "I guess I don't know. I think if he were my son, I'd be moved knowing his friends came to see him."

Kent nodded. They walked a couple of graves over, and he placed a quarter on the one they stopped in front of. "Brian is one I couldn't save," he said quietly. From that moment, Kent placed nickels, dimes, and quarters, along with some pennies, on the tombstones.

"So much death." Palmer placed her hand over Kent's as he pushed her up a hill. They came to the eternal flame of John F. Kennedy and Jacqueline Kennedy Onassis, and just beyond there, General Lee's home.

"Do you think she wanted to be buried next to her husband?" Kent asked.

"I don't know," she said honestly. "I think it's more for her daughter than anything." Palmer thought about her burial, or lack thereof. Prior to coming on this trip with Kent, she'd expected the city to cremate her, but now maybe she could ask Kent to do it and spread her ashes somewhere. Although she didn't want to burden him. Taking her on a trip was one thing; to dispose of her remains was something wholly different.

Kent and Palmer made their way to the Tomb of the Unknown Soldier. They sat in front and watched the sentinel march his twenty-one steps down the black mat before turning, and then another twenty-one steps to the other end of the mat. Everyone around there was quiet or used a very hushed tone to speak to the person next to them. Palmer couldn't take her eyes off the man marching in front of her. His precise movements mesmerized her, and she counted each step and jumped when he reached the end of the mat and tapped his shoes together.

The relief commander appeared and asked everyone to stand and remain silent. Palmer held on to Kent and watched with rapt attention at the changing of the guard. In the background, taps played, and the sound of the bugle brought tears to her eyes.

When the ceremony was over, she hugged Kent. "Thank you for bringing me here."

"Thank you for coming with me."

They stayed for a few more minutes and then made their way out of the cemetery. Off in the distance, they saw a horse-drawn carriage and people gathered. "Another soldier," Palmer said.

"Upward to thirty a day are buried here."

She shook her head and placed her hand on top of Kent's, thankful to know him and be there with him as he honored his friends.

Palmer wasn't ready to call it a day, so they headed to another museum. She needed something to cleanse her emotional palate. Kent gave her two options: the Air and Space Museum or the National Archives. She chose the latter.

When they finally made it inside to see the US Constitution, Palmer was less than impressed, mostly because the dim lighting and the yellowish faded documents were unreadable to her. Still, she walked around and pretended to enjoy the moment. In the gift shop, she insisted Kent buy a magnet—his collection was growing tenfold—and suggested they watch *National Treasure* in bed later in the evening.

As dusk settled over DC, they sat on the steps of the Capitol, drinking soda and eating food truck hot dogs and fries shaped like the Washington Monument.

"Today was a good day," she said to Kent, meaning every word of it. No pain. She'd laughed and cried, and she'd enjoyed every moment, even the ones inside the stuffy archives, where you had to be quiet.

"We have another day tomorrow," he told her. "The National Museum of Natural History and the National Museum of American History, for sure."

"I really like it here."

"We can stay another day, if you'd like," he said. "Maybe go to the zoo. They have pandas there, or we could try the other museums. We have the National Museum of African American History and Culture, the US Holocaust Memorial, and the Smithsonian American Art Museum," Kent said as he read from the pamphlet he'd picked up when they'd first arrived at the Mall.

"That seems like a lot to tackle in a day."

"We can just stay another day."

"Well, before we decide, we should probably talk to the hotel."

Kent smiled and pulled his phone out. "Let me just text our friend Greg."

"He's a gem," Palmer said. While Kent texted Greg, she thought back to the night prior. When they returned from their jaunt in the park, he was waiting for them in the lobby, hours before his shift started. He'd decorated one of the square tables with a party tablecloth, added some plastic toys, and had three Happy Meals on the table. Kent and Palmer learned that McDonald's had indeed come out with adult-size Happy Meals, with toys, and Kent was over the moon.

"Ask Greg if he can join us tomorrow." Palmer nudged Kent's leg with hers.

"You want him to come with us?"

She nodded. "Why not?"

"You're the boss." Kent typed and then grinned when the response came in. "Greg says he called his manager. There's a room, and it's ours, and he's in for tomorrow. He says, and I quote, 'Tell Palmer she better be ready for IG because it's going to be lit.'"

"Greg is too hip for me with his lingo."

"Don't I know it. I'm thankful all the new recruits are in the know—otherwise I'd feel like an old man when someone says something. I swear, every day, there's a new word we have to learn."

"My favorite is when the meaning of a random word becomes sarcastic."

"Like, whatever," he said as he rolled his eyes.

"Exactly."

"Or when '-est' is added to everything."

Palmer cackled and bumped her shoulder with his. "You're the hippest, coolest, and most awesomest guy I know."

Kent blushed. "I like you too, Palmer."

TWENTY-FIVE

Kent sat in the chair beside the bed and watched Palmer struggle through a restless sleep. In the middle of the night, she'd had a seizure, one she wasn't even aware of, but he was. As soon as he saw her eye twitch, he fully expected the outcome.

They'd been sitting around the fireplace with Greg, who had taken a break from his night clerk duties to talk to them. It was late, and Palmer should've been in bed, but she'd had such an amazing day, and Kent didn't want it to end. When he saw the first twitch, he waited for her to say something, but she rubbed her eye and continued talking to Greg. After the second twitch, Kent asked her if she had any pain anywhere, and while she said no, her eyelid convulsed multiple times. He rushed to her side, checked her pulse as an automatic response, and told Greg he didn't need to call for an ambulance, even though he wanted to.

Kent carried Palmer to their room, much to her protest. He didn't want her falling down and hitting her head if this twitch turned into a grand mal seizure. When they got back to their room, he administered her meds and told her to get into bed. He hadn't meant to be snippy, but that was how he sounded.

All night, he watched her for any signs the anticonvulsant he gave her wasn't working. The convulsing in Palmer's eye had stopped, but he could tell she was in pain. Mentally, Kent was beating himself up. He knew better than to agree to more activities earlier, and they should've returned to the hotel after the cemetery. That trip was emotional, and while he appreciated Palmer's efforts, he needed to be the adult and say no.

Kent got up and paced the room. Palmer had insisted on keeping the curtains open so she could see the skyline at night. He stared out the window and prayed they'd have a few more days before they'd need to head back to San Francisco. Kent pulled up his calendar and looked at the date. If he were home, he'd be working, and he decided to text Damian to check in.

Damian: Where are you? How's it going?

Kent: We're in DC. Things were good up until tonight. She had a seizure.

Damian: Do you think it's time to come back?

Kent shrugged as he looked at the message. This wasn't a decision he could make on his own. Sure, her health was declining every day, but Palmer was a fighter. She worked through the daily pain, made things humorous, and tried hard to have a good time. She had a list of things to do, and he'd told her he'd help her get them done . . . until he couldn't.

Kent: I don't know. This is the first episode. I know there's more to come but to end her trip abruptly . . .

Damian: Well, you're missed around here. My new partner isn't as much fun and never stocks the rig.

Kent: LOL. I see that you only miss me for my stellar stocking skills. Chat more later it's late here.

Kent pocketed his phone and rested against the window. Palmer was sound asleep, for the most part. Along with the anticonvulsant he'd given her earlier, he also gave her some heavy-duty pain meds to help her sleep through the night. And in the morning, they'd leave. He wanted to get as much done as possible before they were forced to head home. He'd promised her as much.

In the morning they were going to leave and drive over five hundred miles to Louisville, Kentucky, on what most travel guides called the Loneliest Road. He hoped that whoever it was that Palmer had emailed about being related would email her back along the drive. If anything, Kent wanted her to meet at least one family member before it was too late.

While Palmer slept, Kent packed. He wanted to load the Jeep before she woke, mostly because she would fight him on leaving early. He had already canceled their added day when Greg called to check on Palmer. Kent felt the small seizure was a sign—they needed to get on the road and get their stuff done before it was too late.

With everything packed and their luggage by the door, he crawled into bed to catch an hour or two of sleep before the sun rose. He lay on his side and watched her sleep. Her body had finally calmed down, and she slept peacefully.

Kent slept maybe two hours, and when he woke—thanks to the sun rising through the curtainless window—he found Palmer staring at him. She had unshed tears in her eyes. He took her hand in his and placed them in the middle.

"I'm sorry," he whispered.

She nodded and the tears fell. He had no idea what was going through her mind, but he had a good idea. Palmer was dying, and the realization weighed heavily on her.

"I wish I could take it all away."

"I know," she said, matching the quietness of his voice. "I failed."

"At what?"

"Being a person," she said. "I waited to live until I couldn't live anymore, and I'd be dead now if it wasn't for you."

"Why do you say that?"

"Because had you not knocked on my door, I was going to take those pills and end things."

"When did you decide to kill yourself?" he asked and then wished he hadn't.

"After Dr. Hughes gave me the diagnosis," she said. "I have nothing. I have no one. There isn't anyone waiting for me at home, or anywhere else. Sure, I had my coworkers, but they all have lives. I went to church for the first time. I don't know how long I sat there, looking at the man on the cross and asking him why. What did I do to deserve this? Haven't I already suffered enough?" She started sobbing.

"I was raised in an orphanage. I've never had a Christmas morning where Santa left presents under a tree or had a mom to wake me up on my birthday with a cupcake and candle. I didn't have anyone in the crowd when I graduated high school. I never went to homecoming or prom, and never bothered to learn how to drive. I'm not a bad person, yet I have the shittiest hand dealt. I want to live but can't because I have this thing growing in my head that wants to control every part of my body, and I want to know why.

"After my second trip to the hospital, I sought out the drugs. I couldn't believe how easy they were to find. I told the guy I wanted to die. He disappeared behind a door and came back with that tin. I didn't even ask what they were, just handed over the money and left."

Kent let Palmer say what she needed to say. He wished he could give her the answers she desired. To say life was unfair would be an understatement. There wasn't a doubt in his mind this tumor could've been caught earlier. Even with her homeopathic take on medicine, someone could've recommended a brain scan to determine the cause of her headaches.

He moved closer and pulled her into his arms. He kissed the top of her head and held his lips there. "I'm so sorry, Palmer. I'm also so damn thankful I knocked on your door that day and took those pills from you. I believe we're meant to be on this journey together and you're definitely meant to be in my life."

"I'm thankful for you," she said into his shirt. "I've never been thankful for much, but for you, I am."

Kent leaned back so he could look into her eyes. He was on the verge of telling her that he was falling in love with her but thought twice. If he said those words, they could damage what they had between them, or they could hurt her in ways the tumor wasn't. More to the point, he could break her heart, and that wasn't his intention.

He returned to hugging her. It was his best defense against the sadness in her eyes. In another time, another place, they could've been something to each other, other than friends. When she sighed and disentangled herself from his hold, she sat up. Kent followed and broke the news that they were leaving. He expected her to put up a fight, but she nodded and slipped out of bed.

She closed the bathroom door, and within seconds Kent heard her crying. He wanted to go to her, but she needed her privacy. Palmer had demons to work through, and if she expunged them through tears, who was he to fault her.

When she emerged, she had blotches on her face, and her lower eyelids were red. Still, Kent said nothing.

Kent changed and finished packing what was left and walked around their suite one last time. Palmer would miss the garden tub, and he hoped he'd be able to find another hotel with one in the room for her, or at least a place with a hot tub.

Palmer suggested they put their luggage into the wheelchair to avoid making two trips. Kent agreed and even let her push it for a bit, knowing it would give her some stability. They walked through the lobby and out to the parking lot. While Kent loaded the back, Palmer climbed into the Jeep and wept. The seizure was a turning point for her. She had peaked and was now on a downward spiral.

After they stopped for breakfast, it took her a good two hours before she said anything to Kent, and it was only after she heard his phone beep with an incoming message. "May I check your email?"

"Of course you can. I told you, you don't have to ask." She looked at him oddly, and he wondered if her memory was starting to slip. She checked and saw that someone had responded to her email.

"Someone wrote me back."

"That's great," Kent said. "Do you want me to pull over?"

Palmer shook her head and enlarged the font like Kent had shown her. She read it once, and then again, before crying out. She cried and asked him to pull over so he could read it. He signaled and found a safe place.

"Read it to me," he said. Hearing this from her own voice was going to make a world of difference.

She cleared her throat. "Hello, Palmer. My name's Courtney Marsh, and I'm your half sister. I don't know about you, but I've been looking for you for some time now. When I saw your email, I thought for sure it was some kind of joke, so I'm hoping this is real, that *you're* real, because I'd really love to talk to you. No, strike that. I want to meet you. I'm not sure where you live, but I'm in Missouri and willing to travel to wherever you tell me. I can't thank you enough for your email, and for taking the test. I've waited for you for a long time. Your sister, Courtney."

Palmer wiped at her tears. "I have a sister."

"Yeah, you do." Kent threw his hands in the air and cheered, and then honked the horn a half dozen times in excitement. "Let's go meet her."

"What?"

"Let's do it, Palmer. Missouri is on the way to New Mexico. It's an easy stop for us. Unless you don't want to."

"I do. I think."

"What's holding you back?" He turned in his seat to face her. She started to speak and then stopped to look at the email again.

"I'm dying," she said so quietly he could barely hear her. This was something she rarely said, if at all, and he didn't know how to respond. Palmer was going to die; there wasn't a cure waiting for her when she returned home, and there wasn't going to be some miraculous breakthrough in the next day or two that would save her. She would succumb to the tumor, sooner or later.

But not today, if Kent had anything to say about it, or tomorrow or however many days it took them to get to Missouri. He'd driven through the night to get them to DC, and he'd do the same damn thing again if it meant meeting her sister.

"Here's what I propose. Tell her you want to meet, but you need three days. Ask her to find a restaurant where we can sit down and have a nice conversation."

"I want you there with me," she told Kent. "You know what to look for, in case . . ." She looked to Kent for help.

"You don't want her to know?"

Palmer shook her head. "I don't think so, at least not right yet."

"Whatever you want, Palmer. You're the boss."

Kent adjusted their GPS for Missouri and signaled to get back on the road. Palmer typed out a response and read it back to Kent.

"Dear Courtney, You have no idea how much your email has meant to me. I have waited a lifetime to find out I have a sister. This is such amazing news. I would love to meet you and can do so in three days if this works for you. My boyfriend and I are traveling and are on our way to Missouri right now. Would you be so kind as to find us a place where we could have a nice meal together and enjoy a conversation? I look forward to hearing from you. Palmer."

"Boyfriend, huh?" Kent waggled his eyebrows at her, and she giggled.

"Do you want me to change it?" she asked.

Kent waved her question away. "Absolutely not. Besides, we're always holding hands, or I have my arm around you. No one needs to know we're not. In fact, I sort of like the sound of it." He absolutely loved the sound of her calling him her boyfriend and needed to find a way to make it permanent. Kent was certain Palmer had similar feelings toward him as he did her, but he was afraid his declaration would scare her and ruin their trip. Their trip was far more important than a title.

"Okay, I'm sending it." The faint whoosh brought a smile to Palmer's face.

"How do you feel?" Kent asked her.

"I don't know," she said. "I'm excited, but nervous. I have so many questions that I want answers to, mostly about who my parents are, and who the woman in the brown dress was."

"What woman?" Kent asked.

Palmer leaned forward and pulled a photo out of her bag. She held it up for Kent to glance at when he had a quick second. "This is all I have from my childhood, and I think that's me. I don't know if the memory I have of this woman in the brown dress is mine or if it's something I generated from looking at the picture so much."

"Where did you get that?"

She shrugged. "It's always been with my stuff, so I assumed it was mine."

"Anything written on the back?"

"Just a year, and if it's accurate, I'm about three in the photo."

Kent told her to pick up his phone and to open his notes app. "Start typing your questions or using the microphone to speak into the phone. It'll transcribe. You should note them down while they're fresh in your mind."

"In case my memory fails, right?"

"So you don't forget," he countered. He would never tell her that he feared another seizure could wipe out her short-term memory. From this point forward, he would have her document everything they could.

Before I'm Gone

- ♥ Sit in the front seat of a roller coaster and feel the wind in my hair
- ♥ Eat tacos or tortillas from a roadside stand in New Mexico
- ♥ Shop at a large farmers market
- ♥ Meet Lana Del Rey and see her in concert
- ♥ Take a picture of the most-painted shed in the US
- ♥ ~~Sit in the sand and watch the sunrise in Cape Cod~~
- ♥ ~~Take the steps to the Lincoln Memorial~~
- ♥ Do yoga in Sedona
- ♥ Tour and feed animals in a wildlife sanctuary
- ♥ Stand under a waterfall
- ♥ See Elvis on the street corner in Las Vegas
- ♥ Hug an elephant
- ♥ Find my family
- ♥ Step on grapes and make wine
- ♥ Run through a wheat field
- ♥ Drive Route 66
- ♥ See the marquees on Broadway
- ♥ Ring the Liberty Bell
- ♥ Buy a quilt from an Amish stand
- ★ See the northern lights in Minnesota
- ★ ~~Visit Plymouth Rock~~
- ★ Touch Babe Ruth's bat
- ★ Travel the Loneliest Road
- ★ Visit the Muhammad Ali Center
- ★ ~~Dance in the rain with someone I love~~
- ★ Take the ferry to the Statue of Liberty
- ★ Check out the Grand Canyon
- ★ Take every picture I can of Palmer ✓✓✓✓✓
- ★ Make Palmer smile ✓✓✓✓✓

- ~~*Eat chowdah in Boston, per Palmer*~~
- *Eat pizza in Chicago*
- *Try frozen custard in New York City*
- *Get coffee in each city* ✓✓

Twenty-Six

"Welcome to the land that's round on the outside and high in the middle." Kent laughed at his joke as he pointed to the sign welcoming travelers to Ohio. Palmer scratched her head and gave Kent an odd look. "Do you get it?"

"Clearly not, and don't try to blame the octopus," she told him. Ever since she'd received the email from Courtney, Palmer had been on cloud nine—smiling her way through West Virginia. Kent had asked her if she wanted to stop at any of the attractions, but she said no. She was eager to get to Missouri, not that Kent could blame her. He was also on the edge of his seat. Not only with nerves, but trepidation. The last thing he wanted was for this meeting to not go as Palmer had planned in her head.

Kent feigned being hurt by her accusation that he'd blamed her tumor for her not getting his joke. Against his better judgment, he held his hands up and made an *o*, and said, "O-HI-O. Do you get it now?"

Palmer rolled her eyes and pointed at the road. "Eyes on the road, mister."

"Aye, aye, Captain."

"And yes, I get it now. That's sort of a dumb joke."

"What are you talking about? It's the classic dad joke." Again, he pretended her words hurt him. "Man, you're a tough nut to crack sometimes."

Palmer opened their travel book and used Kent's phone to magnify the pages. He tried not to frown, but knowing her eyes were deteriorating quickly bothered him. He needed to email her neurologist with an update and ask if there was something they should or could do to help her. Kent hated the idea of Palmer going blind before their trip concluded.

"It says here that for the next fifty miles we'll be able to see the remains of coal mines and overgrown rail-fenced cornfields, and apparently if we come across a gift shop, we can buy moonshine."

"Are you looking to get drunk?" Kent asked her. "Because that stuff will knock you on your tail, and you won't move for days."

"Hard pass for me," she said without taking her eyes off the book. "But if you want some, I'll drive." Palmer chuckled as Kent scoffed.

"Do you want to learn how to drive?" he asked her.

She studied him for a long minute and then shook her head. "I don't think so. I don't know that I'm missing anything from not driving. Honestly, it looks sort of boring."

"It is, unless you have the most amazing travel companion ever." Kent winked. She blushed and held his gaze before turning away.

He drove along US 50 and listened to Palmer read about Ohio. When they'd come across something she mentioned, he'd slow down and point to it along the side of the road. He told her about Ohio State University's long-standing rivalry with Michigan, among other schools, in college football, and how Ohio was known for the Rock & Roll Hall of Fame.

Kent signaled to exit and asked his GPS to send them to Court Street in Athens. From his research, they'd be able to get out, stretch their legs, explore, and have a sit-down meal. Palmer objected. "We'll be in Missouri to meet your sister, I promise you," he told her as he parallel parked. He shut off the car, got out, and went to her side. Kent would not give her an opportunity to tell him no or miss a stop because of something happening days from now.

Palmer accepted Kent's hand and stood on the sidewalk while he retrieved their jackets from the back. The chill in the air caused Palmer to tremble, and she thanked Kent for her coat when he slipped it over her shoulders. He held her hand because he wanted to. It felt natural—the way her hand fit into his.

They stopped for coffee and went into every store they came across. Palmer picked out another magnet for Kent while he bought her a sweatshirt. The purchase may not have made sense to Palmer, but it did to Kent. This was something she could sleep in, and it would keep her warm. As of late, she woke up shivering, and he wanted to help combat her chills.

Kent and Palmer somehow ended up at the college bookstore for Ohio University. Palmer shook her head when Kent held the door open for her. He shrugged. There was no way he could come all the way to Athens and not visit a bookstore. The fact that it was on the campus was a bonus.

Palmer left Kent to look at all the gear. He contemplated buying something but wasn't sure. He wasn't a fan, per se, but when he wasn't working he liked to wear paraphernalia from different schools. When Palmer found him, he was deep into the T-shirt section. She held a bag in her hand. Kent knew that whatever she had in there was for him, since she refused to buy herself anything.

"What did you buy?"

"I'm not telling you until later."

"Okay," he said with a chuckle. "Do you like this?" He held out a green shirt with Rufus the Bobcat on it. Palmer laughed and shook her head.

"I found one I like for you." This time, she took his hand and led him through the store. Kent appreciated the gesture and the moment. Palmer was having another great day. He didn't want to look a gift horse in the mouth, but a bad day or night loomed.

Palmer took him to another rack of shirts and pulled out the one she liked best. The gray shirt had a green Superman shield with Ohio over the top of it. Nothing about this shirt screamed sports, fan, or even college, but Palmer had chosen it for Kent, and he wanted it.

He carried his shirt to the checkout. Before he could place his card into the machine, Palmer sneaked hers in. "Hey," he said to her.

She shrugged. "I can't take it with me," she said pointedly. "Might as well spend it on the person I love." She walked away without meeting his gaze. There wasn't a doubt in his mind that he'd heard her correctly.

Once the clerk finished the transaction, Kent rushed to find Palmer. She sat outside at a bistro table. Kent sat across from her. She refused to look at him, even after he said her name.

Kent reached across the table and lifted her chin with his thumb and index finger until their eyes met. "Do you love me?" he asked, and then he wished he could ask again with more tact.

Palmer shrugged and tried to look away, but Kent held her gaze. "I've never loved anyone before," she told him. "I think what I feel is love, of some kind."

Kent's heartbeat soared. "Everyone feels love differently. For me, it's like if I don't see or talk to the person I love, I don't feel complete."

"Is that how you felt about Maeve?"

He shook his head slowly, hoping she'd understand that whatever he and Maeve had wasn't love. "It's how I feel about you, though. You've stolen a piece of my heart, Palmer. I don't even know how, but you have."

"I'll be sure to give it back."

"Don't. Don't give it back, and don't talk like that," he said. "I want you to keep it. I wish it were something tangible for me to give you besides words, though." He reached for her hand and held it. "Know this, I have never felt this way about another person."

"Me neither. Every time I think about the end . . ." She choked on a sob and covered her face. Kent tried to move his seat next to hers, but they were cemented to the ground. He went to her instead and crouched down.

"Hey, I'm here. I'm not going anywhere."

"But I am."

He said nothing. There was no point in arguing with reality. They both knew how their trip would end. Still, Kent wanted Palmer to enjoy herself to the fullest.

"Thank you for my shirt," he said to her. "I'm going to wear it with pride."

"And you'll think of me?"

Kent scoffed. "Palmer, there isn't going to be a day in my life when I don't think about you." He took her hand and placed it over his heart. "Like I said, you have a piece of me, and I don't want it back."

He finally convinced her that they should get a bite to eat and then hit the road. There was one more stop he wanted to make before they headed for Missouri. They still hadn't heard back from Courtney. Kent wasn't bothered. If it came down to postponing the rest of their trip, he would. Nothing was more important than Palmer finally meeting her sister. She had a list of questions and deserved every answer possible. They had her name, and while Missouri might be a big state, he wasn't opposed to searching every nook and cranny for Courtney. He refused to let Palmer down.

Palmer suggested they walk around campus. As they did, she used Kent's phone to take photos, and then posted them onto their Instagram story. She had yet to tell the world why they were on this trip. Kent wouldn't pressure her, even though Greg had pretty much told everyone. Palmer would say it when she felt the time was right.

The campus of Ohio University was quaint, with old brick buildings and a homely feel. Kent felt comfortable, even when they happened upon an old asylum. Palmer gawked at the four-story redbrick structure that looked like it belonged down south, with its fountain out front and the white wrought iron railings to keep people from falling in.

"Wow, I've never seen something so beautiful and scary at the same time," she said as they stood side by side.

"They say it's haunted."

"Of course it is. We don't even want to imagine what went on in those rooms. It was built in the late eighteen hundreds."

"How do you know?" Kent asked.

She held up a pamphlet. "I found this by the door at the bookstore. I wanted to see it."

"Clever."

Palmer turned around and walked away from the structure, and then abruptly stopped. "Come here," she said to Kent, who went to her right away. "Look." She pointed to the hospital, which was now part of the school.

"This place is enormous."

"I can't imagine living in a place like this," she said. "To think I almost went into hospice care to be another number." She looked at Kent. "Thank you for saving me."

He pulled her into his arms and kissed the top of her head. "You're saving me too. Don't forget." Palmer nodded against him. He turned her away from the building and guided her back toward where they had parked on Court Street. If they weren't going to go meet her sister, he'd suggest they stay a day or so, and really take advantage of everything Athens had to offer. He'd love to go sit by the lake and roast marshmallows or rent a canoe for the day.

They found a diner that was an old-school landmark near the college. Most of the patrons seemed on the younger side, which Kent hadn't expected despite the proximity to campus. It wasn't until after he'd opened the menu that it dawned on him: this place was affordable to college students, and it all made sense.

"Do you want to go someplace else?" he asked Palmer, who had her face in the menu. He slid his phone across to her, but she ignored it.

"Not at all. I already found something I want."

"You did?"

"Yes, don't be so surprised," she said. "The letters are really big." Palmer laughed, and Kent marveled at her ability to turn her situation into a joke.

"All right," he said as he continued to look over the menu. When the server stopped at their table, he ordered the firecracker burger, while Palmer ordered the open-face roast beef.

"I wanted the mashed potatoes," she told Kent when he eyed her suspiciously. "You can eat the rest of my food."

"Why didn't you just order a side then?"

She shrugged. "I like roast beef, and the Texas toast sounds good."

"You know we can go to Texas, if you want."

"Is that really where the toast comes from?"

Kent shrugged. He had no idea and watched Palmer reach for his phone. Instead of typing her question into the search bar, she voiced it. Over the course of their trip, she had become quite the cell phone user.

"The owner of the Pig Stand in Beaumont invented Texas toast," she told him, and then proceeded to read everything this restaurant had. His stomach growled at the mention of chicken-fried steak and pork sandwiches.

"Look on the map. Can we go to Beaumont?" he asked.

Palmer handed the phone back to Kent and let him do the honors. He pulled Beaumont up on the map and saw it was near the Louisiana border and out of their way. It was his stomach talking, and the idea of diverting to southern Texas flew out the window when the server set his burger down in front of him.

By the time he'd added the condiments, Palmer had already dug into her mashed potatoes. She closed her eyes when those Yukon Golds touched her palate. Seeing her this way made him happy. Food was a struggle. The stuff she loved often made her sick, and if she ate anything, there was always a risk she'd throw it up. Hopefully, that wouldn't be the case today.

"Do you want a bite?" She nodded toward her plate.

Kent was never one to pass up food and stabbed the roast beef and toast together and made sure the gravy coated his bite. As soon as the combo hit his tongue, he moaned. "Holy crap, that's delicious."

"I'm glad you like it because there's no way I'm eating all of this."

If she ate a fourth of her food, he'd be happy.

"I'll gladly finish what you don't. Do you want a bite of my burger?" He held it out for her and waited. She studied his burger for a second and then shook her head. It was probably for the best. The firecracker burger had jalapeños, and he'd pay the price for it later.

Palmer ate slowly, savoring each bite with a satisfying hum. By the time she pushed her plate toward Kent, she'd finished about half her meal. Kent dug in and devoured the rest, and then sat back in the booth and groaned.

"Now I wish you knew how to drive," he said, feeling very uncomfortable. "I ate way too much."

"Are you in a food coma?" she asked. She reached across the table and poked at his belly. "I think you have a food baby in there."

"I do and I'm naming it Palmer."

"Hey, that's not nice."

"What, why not?"

She shrugged. "Do you want to be the father of Maeve's baby?"

It was Kent's turn to shrug. "I don't know. I hadn't really thought of it. I guess I'm waiting for her to tell me whether I am. What about you—did you ever think about having kids?"

"Once," she said. "I dated this guy in college—he was my first and only boyfriend—but it never went any further than whatever we were. I used to dream about coming home to him and our children, but after about nine months, we went our separate ways."

"If things were different and you could have a child, what would you name them?" Kent asked.

"I'd want a girl, and I'd name her Juniper."

"Why Juniper?"

Palmer shrugged. "It's unique. Like Palmer."

"I wonder how your parents came up with your name?"

"They didn't." Her cheerful tone changed to sadness. "The orphanage named me Faith. I changed my name when I aged out of the system. I wanted a fresh start."

Kent masked his emotions. Her words gutted him, tore his heart into pieces.

"When's your birthday?"

"I don't know. Any paperwork on who I am or who my family is, the orphanage lost a long time ago. I was just a number in the system. That's one of the reasons I took the DNA test, to find out who I truly am."

"Well, let's hope Courtney has the answers."

When the server returned, Kent and Palmer passed on dessert, paid their bill, and headed toward the Jeep. Kent wasn't ready to leave Athens quite yet and decided to drive around.

Twenty-Seven

Palmer found herself checking Kent's phone more often than paying attention to the sights. Kent caught her a couple of times and chastised her, saying he was going to take it away if she didn't point things out to him. She was supposed to be sightseeing, not checking emails every ten seconds.

He didn't understand her, at least this part of her. At lunch, they'd talked about his potential child, and while she'd brought it up, she hadn't expected him to ask her if she wanted children. She had, when she was sixteen and yet another family had passed her up. She vowed she'd be a mother who loved her child, no matter what. Palmer would never abandon her child like her mother had done to her.

When she was a senior in high school, she'd hoped a boyfriend would materialize. She was friendly with a couple of the boys in her class, but that was as far as it went. When she got to the community college and met Rick, her classmate, she thought her life was going to change. For nine months, she was happy. The happiest she'd ever been. He didn't care that she lived in a halfway house because once she was done, they'd move in together. Rick allowed Palmer to hope and dream, until he wasn't in school one day. She took the bus to his apartment and learned from his roommate that he had moved back in with his parents—in Oregon.

That was that. The moment Palmer shut everyone out of her life. She'd live her life on her own terms and depend on no one. She didn't need a family, a boyfriend, or any friends. After graduation, she started her life, away from the orphanage, and not once had she gone back to visit.

Palmer pulled the screen down on Kent's phone to refresh his email and waited for the circle to disappear. A new message appeared, and Palmer's heart rate jumped. "She wrote back," she told Kent.

"Read it."

"Can she see that I've read it right away?"

Kent laughed. "No. At least I don't think so?"

"Maybe I should wait?"

"Why? Who cares if you read it right away. I think you've earned the right to be eager."

Kent was right. She tapped the screen, turned the phone, and read the large print. "She says she can't wait to meet me and gave us an address to meet her at."

"Does she say what time?"

"Yes, three in the afternoon. What do I say?"

"Tell her you'll be there."

Palmer voice texted her response and sent the email. She then sat back and smiled. Everything was right in her world—at least for now. Palmer wasn't going to think for even a single second her world couldn't shift on a dime. For now, she wanted to believe where she headed was the right path for her. She'd leave this realm knowing she had a sister.

With those thoughts, she also berated herself. Had she opened that damned letter months ago, she might have been able to have a real relationship with her family. She trusted no one, except for Kent, not even the company that had performed the DNA test or herself to do the test correctly. Palmer convinced herself she hadn't added enough saliva or enough time hadn't passed between drinking and taking the test. Moreover, she'd told herself no one in her family even cared about her because no one ever came looking.

"I wonder how Courtney ended up in Missouri?"

Kent gave her question some thought before answering. "Maybe her husband is from there or that's where she went to school."

"I should've asked her age. Wouldn't it be weird if we went to the same school together?"

"Yeah." Kent frowned. "I would hope your mother would've recognized you."

Palmer shrugged. "One thing I want to ask Courtney is where our mom is and how old she is. Maybe we can go see her?"

"Absolutely, if that's what you want," he told her. "We'll spend the rest of our time in Missouri, if that's what you decide. You're the boss here. You call all the shots, Palmer."

She nodded and rested her head against the window. "I definitely want to meet my mom, and maybe my dad if she knows where he is. I wonder if I have more siblings, or any aunts and uncles."

Kent allowed her to talk without interrupting. Palmer went on about nieces and nephews, cousins, and any other family members she could think of. They both laughed when she mentioned grandparents and figured if they were alive, they'd be in their eighties or nineties.

"My parents want to FaceTime later and meet you," he told her, catching her off guard. "I know I haven't talked about them while we've been on this trip, but they know about you. They know everything, really. My parents are super supportive of what we're doing, and my dad is jealous. He's always wanted to tour the US."

Palmer sat up and turned to face him. She moved her seat belt strap under her arm for more comfort. "I'm sorry, I never thought to ask about your family. I guess I assumed you were like me, in a way. Do you have any siblings?"

"Only child. My parents met in college and married right after graduation. My dad is an engineer, and my mom's a high school principal. They live north of the city."

"Do they know about Maeve?" Palmer asked, and Kent nodded.

"I tell them everything. My dad is my best friend. He also served in the army, as did my grandfather and uncles."

"How come you haven't talked about them?"

Kent pondered her question. "Our lives growing up were so opposite. I didn't want to sound like I was bragging or trying to rub it in your face. I grew up with a great family who supports me in everything I do, and it breaks my heart that you didn't."

"You shouldn't have to hide your family because I didn't have one," she told him. "That seems wholly unfair, and you're not being true to yourself or to me."

Kent glanced at her quickly and tried to smile. "I'm sorry. That wasn't my intent at all."

"I know," she said quietly. "Can I ask you a question? It's not something I've ever asked anyone before."

"Palmer, you can ask me anything you want."

"What are the holidays like?"

"Any one in particular?"

Palmer shrugged. "I know people go all out for Thanksgiving and Christmas, but I've never experienced any of the so-called magic that comes during the holidays."

Kent frowned. He'd been vocal about how he hated that she'd grown up this way. "Well, for the Wagners, we go see my aunt and uncles for Thanksgiving. They have a huge house that overlooks the bay. My uncle does all the cooking, and every other year we swap duties. Like last year, all the women set up and cleaned. This year, it'll be all the men. On Christmas Eve, we go to church with my dad's family and then celebrate at another aunt's house. There are so many aunts, uncles, and cousins, we do a gift swap instead of buying something for everyone. And then, for Christmas, we start off at home. My mom makes breakfast, and we open our stockings and then presents before heading to see my other grandparents. My mom and her sisters do all the cooking there, and when it's time to open presents, we cram into the living room, and my grandfather puts on a Santa hat and hands them all out."

Kent cleared his throat. "What was it like for you?" he asked nervously.

"For Thanksgiving, we'd have turkey for dinner and have to tell everyone what we were thankful for. I always said my good grades, because I honestly wasn't thankful for anything. We'd have a Christmas tree, and all the decorations were made by the kids who lived in the home, which was neat. The staff would draw names of who they'd buy a gift for. I'd get things like a new notebook and pen or some socks. Sometimes, Santa would come and ask us what we wanted for Christmas and tell us if we were good little kids, we'd get it. By the time I was eight, I realized he was fake and nothing but a liar. I could be the best kid in the house, and I never got what I asked for."

"All you wanted was a family?"

Palmer nodded.

"Jesus." Kent wiped at his face, but the tears kept coming. "I don't even know what to say." Kent slowed down when he saw brake lights ahead. He glanced at the map system on the dashboard and sighed. "Traffic jam." Kent pointed to all the red and moved the screen down to see how far the traffic was backed up.

"There's nothing really to say. My life is what it is, or was, and there isn't anything that can change things for me."

"Don't say that."

"It's true. My time's up," she said. "I definitely didn't live life to the fullest, and now it's over. I feel like I've wasted an opportunity." Palmer sat forward and looked out her side window.

They sat in silence for about a mile. Kent fiddled with the radio. He scanned stations to find something to listen to, adjusted the volume, and then finally turned it off. He groaned to get her attention, mentioned he was hungry (which Palmer didn't believe for a second because of the lunch he'd eaten), and played the drums on the steering wheel.

Palmer pressed the button to open the top and, for reasons unknown to her, she unbuckled and stood up.

"What in the hell are you doing?" Kent screamed.

"Living my life."

"You're going to get impaled by a pebble." Despite the traffic, the Jeep crawled along at a snail's pace.

"I see lights," she yelled.

"Don't go toward it." It was a dumb joke, but Palmer laughed at Kent.

"That's incredibly rude," she said as she ducked her head into the cab. "But funny. I think there's an accident up there."

"Lovely."

She stood back up and waved at people nearby. Whatever this was, it was fun. They weren't going fast enough that she'd get hurt, and honestly, she didn't care. She'd never done anything stupid or reckless in her life, and it was about time she started to live.

Palmer ducked her head in again and asked, "I'm supposed to live like I'm dying, right?"

Kent said nothing.

"I mean, I am dying, so why not start living."

He shook his head. Her comment agitated him. She could see it clearly on his face and, for right now, didn't care. Palmer stood up again and pretended she was Kate Winslet in *Titanic*, only at a standstill. She took in the noise from the oncoming traffic and welcomed the people who cheered her on. It was funny to her that something like standing up through the open roof of a car would get people to cheer.

When Kent picked up a bit of speed, she held on to the top as best she could, closed her eyes, and leaned her head back. She opened her mouth to shout but emitted a strangled scream instead. Palmer did it again, and again, until tears streamed down her face.

"I'm dying," she screamed into the universe. The pain and anguish in her voice caused her bones to ache. "I'm dying!" she said again as loudly as she could.

Kent pulled over and brought her back into the car. She fought him, punching his chest with her closed fist, repeating her words over and over through gut-wrenching sobs. Kent cried as he held her.

"Let it all out," he encouraged her. "You can hit, kick, and scream at me. I can take it. Use me as your punching bag, Palmer."

Palmer cried until she was hoarse, and hiccuping. She stayed in Kent's arms, with the traffic now buzzing by them and her fist clenching his shirt. She had accepted her fate back in the hospital, when she was told she had six months to live. Deep down, she knew she wouldn't make it six months. Palmer felt herself slipping away, losing a piece of her essence every single day. She was afraid of what lay ahead—the inability to do anything for herself, the seizures that would surely knock her unconscious, and finally, death. The grim reaper stood outside her door, waiting for her to open it and welcome him with open arms. She wanted to. She wanted to leave before the suffering began.

Palmer wanted to stay as well. Kent had given her the gift of life and had done so knowing the outcome. He'd dedicated his time, energy, and, most importantly, his heart to her. As much as she wanted to leave, she couldn't leave *him*.

Kent held her. He absorbed whatever she dished out and never wavered in his support. He cried with her. He cried for everything she'd been through, what she was going through, and what waited for her at the end of the road.

Palmer finally relaxed in his arms. Her grip on his shirt loosened, but his hold on her didn't. She opened her eyes and wondered how long her meltdown had lasted. She extracted herself from his arms and slid into her seat. Palmer was embarrassed to look at Kent, fearful she might see anger or hurt in his eyes.

"Hey," he said as he caressed her cheek in an attempt to look at him. "This is over when you say it's over."

His words were loaded with promise. Without her having to tell him what went through her mind, he knew. Kent would be there in the end, no matter what and no matter when.

Palmer nodded. "I'm okay now."

Kent waited a minute before signaling to pull back onto the highway. He pressed a button on the dashboard unit and asked his phone to play Lana Del Rey. As soon as her voice came over the speaker, Palmer sank into her seat, and let the music wash over her.

TWENTY-EIGHT

Kent debated whether to find a motel or drive through the night until they reached Missouri. Louisville, Kentucky, was on their list of places to stop—well, his list. He loved baseball and thought visiting the Louisville Slugger Museum would be a fun place to visit, as well as the Muhammad Ali Center. But Palmer's reaction in the car—he didn't want to call it a "meltdown" because that would lessen what she'd gone through—gave him pause and had him reconsidering his plans. She was slowly coming to terms with dying, and things weren't pretty. The more they talked about life, and the more they explored, the more he could see the realization settle over her—she'd missed a lot. It wasn't even the holidays. It was life itself. When she'd had the opportunity to live, she'd done so in a way that kept her sheltered. She might have been free from the system and the halfway home she lived in, but she wasn't free to live. Palmer hadn't allowed herself to come out from under the rock she'd placed herself under when she aged out. The life she had lived at the orphanage was the life she currently lived. Until Kent came along and showed her what living truly meant.

Palmer slept next to him. Kent had convinced her to recline her seat and try to get comfortable. He kept the music low and tuned in to her favorite artist to keep her calm. He'd never really listened to Lana Del Rey, unless it was her mainstream hits playing on the radio, and he found that he really enjoyed her music. She had an old-school vibe about her, and she sang whatever the hell she felt like. He liked the grittiness in her voice and her soulful lyrics. Kent could see why Palmer liked her so much.

A sign for hotels appeared, letting motorists know they'd find them at the next exit. He had a mile to contemplate what to do. If he got off the highway, he'd wake Palmer, and she desperately needed her sleep, although sleeping in a bucket seat wasn't exactly comfortable. If he didn't exit and she woke up, he'd have to explain why he'd given up something he wanted to do, which was a conversation he didn't want to have. The exit neared, and he signaled to leave the highway. At the light, he followed the directions and turned down the road. Kent drove slowly, looking at the names of the hotels. He wanted a Holiday Inn or something similar. They didn't need many amenities, just a bed and bathroom. From their stays, he'd concluded that he preferred rooms on the first floor, near the lobby or an exit. Those made it easier for Palmer to get in and out without having to use her chair. She loathed that thing and would rather suffer than sit in it.

When he saw a Comfort Inn, he turned in to the parking lot. He pulled up to the front and woke Palmer. "Hey," he said softly. "I'm going to check us in."

She was groggy, but she nodded and lifted her seat to the upright position. "Where are we?"

"Just outside of Louisville."

Palmer acknowledged him and started gathering her stuff. She surprised him when she followed him into the lobby. "What are you doing?" he asked her.

"I don't know. I thought I should come."

He chuckled. "Are you trying to get free stuff? You want another suite, don't you?"

She looked mortified and covered her mouth. "Oh my, is that what it looks like?" she asked as her eyes widened. "Holy crap, I'm one of those people."

Kent couldn't help but laugh. "Come on," he said and pulled her behind him.

"I'm embarrassed," she muttered.

He said nothing as they approached the counter. "Hi, do you have a room available?"

"We do." The clerk smiled and asked for his credentials. The transaction took about five minutes, and then they were back in the car, parking and unloading their stuff.

"What's on tap for tomorrow?" Palmer asked as they walked down the hall. "Oh, this is where the Baseball Hall of Fame is, right?"

"No, that's in New York. This is where they make the bats, and it's the home of Muhammad Ali, among many other things, but those are the two on my list."

Palmer stopped in the middle of the hallway and huffed.

"What's wrong?" Kent asked her.

"Why did we skip New York if there was something you wanted to see there?"

He motioned for her to follow him. "We didn't. Cooperstown isn't on my list of places to see. Besides, it was way out of the way, and I wanted to go to DC." Kent wasn't exactly being honest, except for the part about DC. He'd love to visit Cooperstown, especially during Hall of Fame weekend, but mostly if one of his favorite players was being inducted. He couldn't even begin to imagine the atmosphere in that place.

Kent opened the door to their room and held it so Palmer could walk through. As soon as he stepped in and the door shut, Palmer crumbled to the floor, smashing her head against the mirror on her way down. Kent screamed out her name and reached out to catch her, but he stumbled into the doorway of the bathroom with the bags he had in his hand. Finally free, he dropped to the floor and rolled her onto her side while she shook. Kent reached for a pillow and slipped it under her head to keep it from banging on the floor, and he started the timer on his watch.

"Fuck, fuck, fuck," he muttered as her body convulsed. He couldn't hold back his tears and let them flow down his cheeks. As much as he didn't want to admit it, they didn't have five months left. At some point, he was going to have to cut their trip short. The medic in him wanted to do it now, to say "Fuck it" and catch a flight back to San Francisco tomorrow. The friend and the man falling in love with Palmer fought him.

She needs this trip.

I promised.

The seizure stopped in under a minute. Even for Kent, that was too long. If it had gotten to the five-minute mark, he'd have had no choice but to call for an ambulance. There were some things even he couldn't do for her. Kent waited a long beat before helping Palmer into a sitting position. He kept the pillow behind her back for comfort and sat across from her. He needed his medical bag, but he wasn't thinking and had left it in the car. There was no way he would leave her now to go get it. Kent checked her pulse and listened for any signs of distress in her breathing. He kept quiet, afraid of what might come out of his mouth. The words were there, on the tip of his tongue, that he was taking her home.

Palmer's eyes met Kent's, and he saw nothing but confusion in them. While she was somewhat alert, he suspected she had no recollection of what had just happened. She looked at his hand on her wrist and pulled it free from his grasp.

"Sit still a little longer, please," he asked her quietly.

She ignored him and raised her hand to the side of her head and winced. Palmer pulled her hand away and looked at it. She saw blood on her fingertips and let out a high-pitched screech.

"Stop," Kent demanded of her as she moved her hand away from her line of sight. "I'll take care of that in a minute."

"Wh-what happened?"

"You had a seizure, and you hit your head on the mirror in the entryway."

"Oh."

"Yeah, oh." Kent was torn about what to do. He needed help or someone to watch Palmer, but he was it. He was the one-man show right now. Kent moved to her other side and assessed the cut on her scalp. He could see glass shards in her hair and deduced she wouldn't need any stitches. She also wouldn't be able to wash her hair for a few days either.

"I'll clean your scalp in a minute," he told her.

"Are you hurt?"

"No." He shook his head and followed her gaze. He had blood on his shirt and a cut on his arm. He didn't remember bumping into the mirror, but it could've easily happened when he struggled to drop their bags.

"I'll get you a tissue," she said. Palmer started to move until Kent told her to stay put.

"You need to rest."

He got up and went to the bathroom. He turned the water on and stared at his reflection. "What in the hell are you doing, Wagner?" Kent kept his voice low to prevent Palmer from hearing him. He shook his head and glared into the mirror. His hands gripped the counter, and he squeezed until his fingers throbbed. He told himself he could do this, he could be the man he'd promised to be, but even he was questioning himself.

Kent soaked a washcloth and used another one to clean the blood and cut on his arm. He needed a Band-Aid, which he had in the car. He took the washcloth to Palmer and wiped the sweat from her forehead, and cleaned the droplets of blood on her arm and her hand.

"I'll be right back," he told her. "Don't move and don't touch your head."

She nodded.

"Palmer, look at me."

She did as he asked.

"It is imperative that you stay where you are. There's glass in your hair that I need to get out."

"Do I need to go to the hospital?"

"No, I don't think you need stitches, but I won't know until I can clean your injury. Stay put." He placed a kiss on her forehead and left the room.

Kent ran.

He ran down the hallway as if her life depended on it. To him, it did. He was responsible for Palmer, and while seizures were part of the growing tumor, it was his job to make sure she was okay. Hitting her head against the mirror was far from okay. He knew better than to overload his arms with their luggage, and to let her walk more than a couple of feet after waking up.

Kent got to the Jeep, grabbed his medical bag, and ran back into the hotel. He was sure the clerk stared, but he didn't bother to slow down and look. When he arrived at their door, he paused before slipping the key card into the slot. *If Palmer's moved . . .* He refused to finish his thought.

Palmer sat in the same spot she was in when he'd left her. Kent helped her up and all but carried her into the bathroom, where he'd left his bag.

"Okay, sit on the toilet."

The lighting wasn't the best, and he finally understood what women meant when they posted about hotels and their lack of usable lighting in the bathroom. "I'm going to have you sit on the counter, so I can use that makeup light."

Kent helped Palmer get up onto the counter. He appreciated the longer counter space, and after getting her a pillow, he asked her to lie down. She did and faced the mirror. Their eyes met in the mirror, and Kent smiled.

"I'm sorry."

"For what?" he asked as he put gloves on.

"For this."

Kent couldn't look at her, out of fear he'd start crying. He didn't want her to apologize for being sick. This was out of her control. If anything, *he* should be the one apologizing to *her*. He should've caught her and saved her head from hitting the mirror.

"You have nothing to be sorry over, Palmer. We know what to expect." It was the best he could say. "This is going to sting."

Kent cleaned her wound with antiseptic. Palmer hissed when the liquid seeped into her open cuts and flinched when Kent removed the glass from her scalp.

"No stitches," he said in relief. "Also, no shampoo for a few days. The cuts need time to heal." He helped her sit up and get off the counter. "Are you hungry?"

"No, just tired."

"Okay. I'm going to clean up, and then I'll be in."

Palmer left Kent in the bathroom. He moved slowly, still working through his demons. Every logical part of him wanted to take her home, but then what—would he leave her in the hands of a hospice? No, he couldn't. It would break his heart not to be with her every day and be there for her. They could go home and do the day trips he'd initially considered before taking a sabbatical. Then they'd at least be home or nearby. He hated that option too.

Kent washed his hands, dried them, and turned off the light. Palmer lay in bed, facing the other bed. He turned off the light, changed, and crawled into the empty bed.

"Kent?" she whispered.

"Yeah?"

"Are you mad at me?"

"Why would you think that?"

"Because you're over there."

He got out of bed and crawled into the bed with her. He held his arm out, and she nestled into the space he created. "Is this better?"

She nodded. "Yes, now I can sleep."

Kent kissed the top of her head and sighed. "Me too," he told her. "Me too."

Twenty-Nine

Palmer rose early and made her way to the restaurant to order them breakfast. She wanted to do something nice for Kent. She knew the risks and what could happen to her by leaving the room alone or being out of reach from Kent. Palmer considered what the outcome would be if she were to have a seizure in the hall or someplace else. Surely, she'd end up at the hospital, and she could hurt herself. Still, she went. She would deal with the consequences later.

Kent was still asleep when Palmer returned. She sighed in relief when she entered the dimly lit room. She moved quietly and set the table as best she could in the dark. She opened the lid and waved it over the plate, hoping the aroma would entice Kent to wake up.

He shifted in bed and then asked groggily, "What do I smell?"

"Pancakes, bacon, french toast, eggs, home fries, and sausage. As well as orange juice and coffee."

Kent sat up and got out of bed. Palmer opened the blackout curtains to let some light in. She swallowed hard at the sight of his bare chest. This wasn't the first time she'd seen him without a T-shirt. Each time before had caused the same reaction from her. Palmer thought Kent was sexy. He was ruggedly handsome and had strong hands that always held hers. She felt safe in his arms and wanted to be there always.

Palmer sat down across from him and poured two cups of coffee. She handed one to Kent, took a sip of hers, and then cut into her french toast. She was midbite when he glanced at her.

"I didn't hear you call room service."

She could lie or be honest. All she ever wanted from people was honesty and suspected Kent would appreciate the truth. He'd be mad, but she was prepared.

"I went down to the restaurant to order our breakfast. They don't serve breakfast off the menu, only dinner, so I loaded up from their buffet."

Kent was silent as he set his fork down. Palmer saw the proverbial wheels turning in his head and imagined steam coming out of his ears. She remained poised.

"I know what you're going to say," she told him before he could muster a statement.

"And what's that?"

"That I shouldn't have gone down there by myself."

"Yep," he said. She expected him to pop the *p* at the end, but he held back. Palmer respected him more for not being obnoxious.

"And while you may be right, you also have to remember I am an adult, and I can make decisions for myself."

"And the decision you came up with was to walk down to the restaurant to get food after you had a seizure?"

"Technically, it's not after," she said. "But yes, I wanted to do something nice for you."

Kent was stoic at first. He blinked once and then looked at her. Within seconds, a smile broke out. He inhaled and cleared his throat. "While I don't agree with you going down there by yourself, I appreciate breakfast. It's very nice to wake up to. Thank you."

"You're welcome," she said with a smile.

"Did you use a cart to get all of this back here?"

"Yes," she said with a laugh. "Even without the tumor, there would be no way I could've carried all of this without some sort of help. Wonder Woman, I am not."

"True, but I find you to be pretty incredible."

No one had ever said that to her before. "You do?"

Kent nodded. "You have this inner strength that you don't see in many people. You could've given up, ten times over, but you keep trudging forward. You're by far the strongest and most resilient person I know. Last night, I was ready to give up and take us back home. That seizure scared the shit out of me because there's nothing I can do. The octopus grows daily, and we can't stop it. All I can do is make you comfortable. I can increase the dosage on your meds and be more aware, but that's it."

"I really don't want to go home," she told him. "There's nothing there for me."

"I'd be there, regardless. However, we're not going home. I promised you the trip of a lifetime, and I plan to deliver until you tell me it's time. There'll be times when I'm worried and angry at myself because I can only do so much, but I'm going to be here, right by your side, until we're done." Kent reached for her hand and pulled it to his lips. He kissed her knuckles and winked at her.

"We're meeting my sister tomorrow."

"I know. Are you excited?"

She shook her head. "I'm nervous."

"That's expected. It's like a blind date, except she's your secret keeper."

"I just want to know what happened."

Kent put his fork down and clasped his hands together. "She may not know, so keep that in the back of your mind. Although she knew you existed, so I think on some level she'll have the answers you're looking for."

"I hope so." Palmer turned and looked outside. The sun shone, and everything looked like it had a golden hue to it. "I think it's going to be a beautiful day."

"We'll be in museums today."

"As long as we're together, I don't care what we do. I do have one request."

"What's that?"

"Can you help me wash my hair? I know you said no shampoo, but the thought of touching my scalp is weirding me out." Palmer shuddered at the thought.

Kent laughed. "I didn't take you as a squeamish person."

"I hate needles too."

His eyes widened. "Now you tell me!" He threw his hands up. "I probably could've been a little nicer when I jabbed that sucker into your hip."

"That would've been nice," she fired back. "I was wondering about your bedside manner."

Her quip caught Kent off guard. He tossed his napkin at her and told her to wash her own hair. He got up and went to the bathroom, and she followed.

"I'm sorry," she said as he started filling the tub.

"Palmer, stop apologizing. You're not hurting my feelings. Please, continue to joke."

She leaned forward and inhaled. "You might want to shower."

"Okay, that was too far." He cupped a handful of water and threw it at her. She screamed and ran back into the other room. Palmer waited a few seconds before approaching the bathroom. Kent sat on the edge of the tub and had the stack of towels ready.

"I'm not going to wait here all day, especially when I stink," he told her, even though she wasn't in the room. She stepped into the bathroom and had forgotten he hadn't put his shirt on. Palmer had slept on that chest last night. Seeing it in the light was far different from feeling it in the dark.

"Bend over," he instructed her.

"Excuse me?"

"The tub, Palmer. Geez."

"Oh, right. Sorry." Palmer squatted until she could put her knees onto the towels Kent had placed near the tub. She bent over the edge, while he slid in next to her. The positioning was awkward, but Kent never complained.

He poured water over her hair until it was saturated, and then conditioned the ends. As long as he steered clear of her scalp, she would be okay. After rinsing her hair, Kent squeezed as much of the water out of her strands as he could and wrapped them into a towel. He helped her sit up and then stand.

"Thank you."

"You're welcome. Now, I'm going to take a quick shower."

"Okay, then I'll take one after you."

Palmer closed the door behind her and stood there for a moment. Until Kent, she'd never grasped the depth of physical attraction. He was her idea of the perfect man. He was beautiful, with the kindest eyes she had ever encountered, and when he looked at her, he saw her. Never mind what happened when he winked at her. That simple gesture turned her insides to goo and made her knees wobble.

Palmer pushed away from the door and went to her suitcase. She pulled out the clothes she wanted to wear today and set them in a pile on the bed. She didn't have to wait long for Kent to come out of the bathroom, and when he did, he did so with only a towel around his waist, with pebbles of water dotting his chest. Palmer stood and licked her lips, an automatic reaction to the sight before her.

"I should . . . uh . . ." Palmer grabbed her clothes and brushed passed him, and he chuckled. She closed the door behind her and leaned against it. Was Kent doing this on purpose? Did he know how she felt about him? Sure, he'd asked her if she loved him, and she did, but she'd assumed he meant as family.

Palmer cleared her thoughts. A man like Kent wouldn't date a woman like her. He likely saw her as the sister he never had, and that was how she needed to treat the situation. She showered, dressed, and pulled her hair into a messy bun. She wasn't about to run a brush through her hair and forget about her scalp.

She opened the bathroom door and studied the mirror in the hall. Kent watched her from across the room. "Crap," she muttered. "How much do you think they'll charge me?"

"The mirror is like fifteen dollars at the store, so it shouldn't be that much."

"Maybe I should just tell them."

"What are you going to say?"

She shrugged. "I don't know. I mean, I don't want to tell them I had an incident."

"Is that what we're calling it now?"

She nodded. "Yes, it sounds better."

"Got it."

"But I don't want them to think we go around damaging property either. I'll think of something by the time I get down there."

"Sounds good."

They packed their things, and Palmer insisted on cleaning their table so the housekeeper wouldn't have to worry about the garbage. Kent stacked their dishes and set everything outside their door. He cleaned the bathroom and inspected the sheets and pillowcases for blood. When he found none, he said the room was ready and left to get a luggage cart.

Palmer set their luggage near the door and held it open for Kent when he returned. They stopped at the front desk to turn in their keys, and Palmer told them about the broken mirror. "I'm sorry, but I've broken the mirror in the entryway, and I'd like to pay for it."

The clerk looked wide eyed at Palmer and said she would get the manager. Kent stood next to her. He leaned in and said, "They're probably shocked someone is admitting to the damage."

"It's only right."

"I know," he said.

The manager came to the counter and took Palmer's statement. Her version of events wasn't that far off from the truth. She made it sound as simple as possible. "We struggled with the door, and when I tossed my bag in, my aim was off. I'd like to pay for the damages."

"Uh, we're okay," the manager told Palmer. "Accidents happen. We're not going to charge you."

"You're sure?"

Kent bumped her hip, and she ignored him.

"Yes, of course. Thank you for letting me know."

As they made their way to the parking lot, Kent asked, "Why would you encourage him to charge you?"

"I don't want anything looming over me after I die," she said. "Whoever moves into my apartment is going to end up getting my mail someday, and I'd hate for them to get notice after notice that I committed some crime."

"Falling into a mirror is hardly a crime. You're being a tad overdramatic."

Palmer sighed. "You're probably right."

After Kent loaded their luggage, he returned the cart to the lobby and jogged back to the Jeep. Palmer already had the top pulled back and had her face turned toward the sun. "This feels good," she said.

"It does. What do you say we hit a couple of museums today? I know they're not really your thing, given they're about a boxer and baseball."

"If they're your thing, they're mine," she told him.

He stopped to fill up with gas, and then they got on the road. He drove the scenic route, and Palmer pointed out the historic features of Louisville. When they pulled into the parking lot at the Louisville Slugger Museum, she insisted Kent stand in front of the giant baseball bat so she could take a picture.

When he reached for her hand, she stopped him. "I want to thank you."

"For what?"

"For being you and keeping your promise."

Kent stepped toward her and caressed her cheek. She leaned into him and prayed he would kiss her, and she wished she was brave enough to kiss him.

Before I'm Gone

♥ Sit in the front seat of a roller coaster and feel the wind in my hair

♥ Eat tacos or tortillas from a roadside stand in New Mexico

♥ Shop at a large farmers market

♥ Meet Lana Del Rey and see her in concert

♥ Take a picture of the most-painted shed in the US

♥ ~~Sit in the sand and watch the sunrise in Cape Cod~~

♥ ~~Take the steps to the Lincoln Memorial~~

♥ Do yoga in Sedona

♥ Tour and feed animals in a wildlife sanctuary

♥ Stand under a waterfall

♥ See Elvis on the street corner in Las Vegas

♥ Hug an elephant

♥ Find my family

♥ Step on grapes and make wine

♥ Run through a wheat field

♥ Drive Route 66

♥ See the marquees on Broadway

♥ Ring the Liberty Bell

♥ Buy a quilt from an Amish stand

★ See the northern lights in Minnesota

★ ~~Visit Plymouth Rock~~

★ ~~Touch Babe Ruth's bat~~

★ ~~Travel the Loneliest Road~~

★ ~~Visit the Muhammad Ali Center~~

★ ~~Dance in the rain with someone I love~~

★ Take the ferry to the Statue of Liberty

★ Check out the Grand Canyon

★ Take every picture I can of Palmer ✓✓✓✓✓✓✓

★ Make Palmer smile ✓✓✓✓✓✓✓

★ *~~Eat chowdah in Boston, per Palmer~~*

- *Eat pizza in Chicago*
- *Try frozen custard in New York City*
- *Get coffee in each city* ✓✓✓✓

THIRTY

While Kent drove, Palmer scrolled through his phone. Ever since they'd gone live that one time in DC, she'd become slightly obsessed with social media. She loved to take pictures of Kent, especially while he drove, and post them onto their "travel story," as she called it. If Kent cared, he never said anything, and he never balked at having his photo taken. Palmer had, though, at first, and now she wanted him to have all the memories of their time together. She locked the phone and took out the journal she'd picked up a couple of stops back.

She propped her feet onto the dash and began writing, despite her fingers feeling useless. They seemed swollen, even though they looked normal. She flexed her fingers and shook her hand to regain some feeling. They were on the interstate, and there wasn't anything to look at or for her to point to until the next big city came along. Palmer wrote about their trip to the baseball museum, where they learned how they made the wooden baseball bats.

When you stood there and ran your fingers over the signatures on the name wall, I imagined you as one of the boys who used to play baseball at the park, across from where I lived. I never understood how poignant the crack of the bat was until you showed me.

Of course, Palmer insisted Kent get a personalized bat. What surprised her the most was the inscription he added: *Kent & Palmer*, along with their social media handle and the year. He'd memorialized their trip with one of his stops. She tried to hide her smile but failed. Palmer grinned, even though her heart broke. She didn't want their trip to ever end, or her life for that matter.

"What are you doing over there?" Kent asked. "You're awfully quiet."

"Nothing," she said as she closed her journal. When she'd bought it, Kent asked her what she was going to write about. She told him it was to track her health so she could see how her tumor progressed. Lying to him wasn't what she'd planned, but she had her reasons. She was thankful Kent never asked her what she wrote down because she wasn't sure she could make anything up on the fly. Somehow saying "The octopus hates me today" was not going to work for Kent.

Palmer picked up Kent's phone again and opened the Instagram app. She clicked "Live" and waited for a few people to start watching before she said anything.

"Hello," she said to the viewers. "Kent and I are driving again, but I wanted to come on and tell you what we did today." Palmer kept the phone on Kent, who laughed as he drove. "We went to the Louisville Slugger Museum and Factory, as well as the Muhammad Ali Center. So, Kent, what was your favorite part of the bat museum?"

"I think holding one of the bats used in a game and seeing the speed of my fastball."

"Which was?"

"Not very fast," he said, laughing.

"Our fans want to know whose bat you held."

"That would be Big Papi," Kent said with a smile.

Palmer added, "You know I have no idea who that is, right?"

They both laughed, and he reminded her that he played for the Boston Red Sox and was instrumental in helping them break the "Curse of the Bambino."

Kent showed Palmer a side of baseball that people didn't talk about—the fan side—such as Marilyn Monroe's stocking from the night she married Joe DiMaggio, which she left behind at the motel they stayed at. It was now on display. Or a vest made from potato chip bags and a dress made of Sprite cans. While these things fascinated Palmer, the sight of Kent admiring history mesmerized her. It was like he was a little kid again. He told her story after story of players like Babe Ruth and Pete Rose, and how he went to as many games as possible when he was younger. He'd go now, but the prices were a bit steep for him, and he was lucky to make it to one, maybe two games a season.

"What was your favorite part?" Kent asked her.

"Watching you—it was like meeting the kid version of Kent," she said. Palmer hid behind the phone, thankful Kent couldn't see her face. She could feel her cheeks flush with embarrassment. Speaking this way was odd for her, but the more time she spent with Kent, the more comfortable she felt around him.

Palmer wanted this live session to be about Kent. So many of their postings had been about her, and she wanted him to share in the limelight. No one had the full story yet on how these two strangers had ended up on the road together. She wasn't sure if they should tell everyone that if she hadn't passed out at work, it was unlikely they'd be together now. Was it fate that had brought them together? Palmer thought so.

"What was your favorite part about visiting the Muhammad Ali Center?" she asked him.

"Easy," he said. "Seeing his inspirational quotes in writing, front and center. Hearing his voice gave me chills. He was an icon, without trying to be one."

"He was more than a boxer," Palmer added.

"He was," Kent agreed. "He transcended expectations. He said he was the greatest, and he proved he was, whether in the ring or with the civil rights movement. He never cared what anyone thought. That takes a lot of courage, and he had it tenfold."

"Well, I thank you for taking me to those places today," Palmer said into the phone but at Kent. He smiled and said nothing. Palmer ended the live video and waited for the video to save, and then she posted it. When she set his phone down, he glanced at her.

"You only read one question."

"It wasn't even a question," she told him. "I can't see what they're saying because of the print, and everything moves so fast."

Kent sighed. "I mentioned the vision thing to Dr. Hughes the other day when we emailed back and forth about your seizure. She suggested you try some of those reading glasses that the drugstores sell. She said they might help. Do you want me to stop?"

Palmer thought about it for a second and then nodded. "I'd like to see better, even if things are still fuzzy around the edges." Ever since she'd had another meltdown about dying, she'd vowed to try and be positive. She realized the negativity she surrounded herself with made her angry and caused her pain. She didn't want to be remembered like that.

Kent redirected the navigation to the nearest store. While he followed the directions, Palmer slipped her shoes on and tied the laces, which took her longer than normal with her stiff and numb fingers. She hadn't told Kent yet and knew it was a matter of time before he figured it out. Palmer glanced at the clock and timed herself. As the minutes ticked by, she gave up and sighed heavily as tears fell down her cheeks.

"What's wrong?" Kent asked as he turned into the parking lot of a superstore. He put the Jeep into park and pressed the ignition button to turn off the engine.

"I think . . . maybe I had a stroke?"

His eyes widen. "What? When?"

Palmer shrugged. "I don't know. I may be wrong, but it's my hands." She held them up. "My fingers feel tight and thick, and they're hard to use."

Kent frowned. "Both hands?"

"Yeah."

"Okay, so I'm going to say it's not a stroke, which is good. Do your hands hurt?"

She shook her head. None of this was a good thing, but she understood what he meant. If she'd had a stroke, she would need medical attention, and their trip—mostly meeting her sister—would derail. "They feel funny. I don't know how to explain it."

Kent took her left hand and examined it, and then looked at her right. Since their trip had started, Palmer had learned how to read Kent's expressions, and she could tell he wasn't overly concerned but curious. "I'll email Dr. Hughes, but I suspect it's the tumor."

"Octopus," she reminded him. Not that either of them needed a reminder. She hated both words, but "tumor" was entirely too clinical for her, and calling the mass an "octopus" gave it a face she could pretend to punch.

They went into the store, and instead of bringing her chair or using one of the motorized ones the store offered, Kent insisted that Palmer push the cart. He walked next to her but focused on his phone. He told her he was searching her symptoms in hopes that someone else with a GBM had a blog post or something they could read. So far, the results came back with nothing of any importance to their current situation.

In the pharmacy section, they found the display with the reading glasses. She tested each pair she tried on by reading something on Kent's phone. He'd enlarged the font for her, but many of the apps didn't have a feature to make an adjustment. The strongest pair the store sold ended up helping Palmer see a little better. They had some time to waste and chose to walk around the store to help Palmer adjust to seeing through them.

"I think maybe I'll use them for reading," she told Kent. "I don't really like how they're making me feel."

"Nothing says you have to wear them all the time. Although you do look pretty adorable in them." He tapped the tip of her nose and smiled.

She turned away from him to prevent him from seeing her flushed cheeks. Every day they spent together, her attraction to him grew exponentially. She wondered what the opposite of the Florence Nightingale effect was because she was surely experiencing it.

Kent loaded up on what he referred to as "road snacks": candy, cheesy crackers, soda, and his favorite red licorice. He'd only eat one kind, and stores rarely carried it. As soon as he saw the pack, he raced toward it and loudly proclaimed that today was the best day of his life.

After they got back on the road, Palmer opened the licorice and gave Kent a piece. He asked for another and put it into his soda to use as a straw, which made Palmer's stomach turn. "That's so gross."

"Don't knock it until you try it, babe," he said, laughing. She scrunched her face at him in disgust.

"No way," she said. "I'm even on my deathbed, and that's not something I want to try." Silence filled the space between them. Kent's expression went blank, and Palmer regretted her words. She was dying and had made a joke about it. Sometimes she needed to say it aloud to remind herself that she was on borrowed time.

An hour later, they pulled into the restaurant to meet Palmer's half sister. Kent turned the Jeep off and waited for Palmer to make a move. She stared at the front door, watching people go in, and she wondered if those people were related to her. Would Courtney bring other people with her?

"Remember our deal," she said to Kent.

"Yes, we don't tell her you're dying."

Palmer nodded. "I'm just not ready."

"Your secret is safe with me."

"Do I look sick?" She looked at Kent. He studied her for a moment and shook his head.

"No, you do look tired, but we've been traveling, so I think that's to be expected. Honestly, I think she's going to be so excited to meet you, she's not going to notice if anything is amiss about your appearance. Besides, you're beautiful."

"You're just saying that because you're my pretend boyfriend."

Kent frowned, and then his expression went blank.

"Where are we again?"

"Columbia, Missouri. Halfway between Kansas City and Saint Louis."

"Right. Do you think this is where I was born?"

"There's only one way to find out," he told her.

Palmer picked her purse up off the floorboard and pulled out the picture of the little girl she thought was her and the woman in the brown dress. She tried to focus but couldn't. She put the glasses on, and while the image was better, it was an old photo and the subjects had blurred over the years.

"I'm going to come around and help you out. Remember, we're in love and you can't keep your hands off of me." He winked. It wouldn't be hard for her to pretend. When Kent opened the door, she greeted him with a smile and held her hand out. If it weren't for him, she wouldn't be there, meeting her sister. Kent had made all this possible and wanted nothing in return, except to stop at a few places, and to see his friend in New Mexico.

Kent held the door for Palmer to walk into the restaurant. She waited for him and took his arm, and they stepped up to the host stand. Kent leaned down and whispered, "I see your sister."

"You do?" She scanned the room, but everyone was fuzzy. "How do you know what she looks like?"

"She looks just like you," he told her. Kent guided Palmer to the table, and Courtney stood on shaky legs. She covered her mouth and held back a sob when Palmer smiled. The two women stood there, in the middle of the aisle, and studied each other. It was like looking in the mirror, with the exception that Courtney was taller by an inch or two. Their hair, eyes, and complexion matched.

"Wow, you ladies could be twins," Kent said.

The sisters looked at him, and Palmer mouthed, "Thank you."

"Hi, I'm Courtney," she said as she held her hand out.

Palmer stared at it for a moment and contemplated whether she wanted to hug the woman or not. Her resolved teetered between shaking her hand, pulling her into an embrace, or running for the door.

Kent tapped her lightly on the back, and Palmer reacted. She shook her sister's hand and said, "I'm Palmer Sinclair."

"Such a beautiful name. Shall we sit?"

Palmer slid into the booth, and Kent followed. He kept his hand on her leg, to keep the jitters away. She appreciated the comforting touch because she was about to jump out of her skin. The sisters stared at each other, neither of them saying anything, until the waiter came by and took their orders.

Kent ordered every appetizer on the menu because neither woman had bothered to even look at what was in front of them. They were both lost in each other's eyes.

"I'm Kent," he said.

"Oh, gosh. I'm so sorry." Palmer covered her face in embarrassment.

"Don't be, babe. This is a big moment for you."

"It's nice to meet you," Courtney said. "This is awkward, isn't it?"

Palmer nodded. "I'm sorry, but I don't . . . didn't know about you, but I get the impression you knew about me?"

Courtney nodded and leaned forward. "I've known about you my entire life."

Kent squeezed Palmer's leg. "Palmer has a lot of questions. We're hoping you can answer them for her?"

"I'll try my hardest."

Palmer looked at Kent, and he motioned for her to ask. This was the moment she had waited for. Now was the time to let everything out.

"What's my name?"

THIRTY-ONE

Courtney reached into her bag and pulled out a folder and a small wooden box. She set both on the table and nudged the box toward Palmer, who opened it. Inside were a dozen or more photos. Kent handed Palmer her glasses, and she slipped them on. The photos were of a little girl and an older woman.

"That's our mother," Courtney said, a confused expression crossing her face.

"Where is she?" Palmer asked.

"She passed away about ten years ago."

Years before DNA testing became popular.

"Our dad?"

Courtney shook her head. "We have different dads, and unfortunately, Mom never told me anything about yours. I'm sorry."

Palmer studied each picture and tried to find a memory, something she had hidden away, but came up blank. "I don't remember any of this," she said quietly. "Except this one?" She held up a duplicate of the photo she carried with her. "I have a copy of this photo. For the longest time I've wondered if that was me and my mom, or if this was something someone just gave me to keep."

"That's Mama," Courtney said. "And one of the last pictures of the two of you together."

"Where were we?"

"A train station, I believe." Courtney gave Palmer a moment before she asked, "I don't remember if Mom told me where you were going or not. Sometimes she'd tell stories, but she wasn't well, most of the time, and she'd mix the two of us up."

Palmer nodded and continued sifting through the photos.

"Did your family treat you well?"

Kent squeezed Palmer's leg as she stiffened. She looked up from the box and met her sister's gaze. "I was never adopted."

"What?" Courtney's voice broke.

"I lived in an orphanage—well, they call them 'halfway houses' now—until I was twenty-one."

Courtney looked stunned, angry, and confused. "I don't understand."

"It's a long, complicated, and emotional story for another day," Kent said, saving Palmer from having to tell her story when she was there to learn about where she came from.

"No, wait. I get that it's probably hard to talk about, but why change your name to Palmer? And why ask me what your name was? If you hadn't, Mom may have been able to find you."

Palmer met her gaze. "The orphanage called me Faith Smith. All children who came in or were dropped off with no paperwork were named Faith, Hope, John, or Luke—names with biblical ties."

Courtney shook her head as she processed everything. "Oh, God. I think I'm starting to figure things out," she said. She opened the folder and handed Palmer her birth certificate. "Your name is, or was, Abigail Weaver. Our mother's name is Donna Weaver. You were born in Dodge City, Kansas, but lived in a town called Hanston until you were two, and then Mama moved you back to Dodge City because she had to work."

"Until she gave me up for adoption," Palmer said as she looked at her sister. "Do you know why?"

"She didn't, Palmer. Mom had me when you were about five, and my entire life, she looked for you, but she was looking for an Abigail.

We'd move all the time, between Kansas, Missouri, Oklahoma, and Iowa, looking for you. Mom would sit at elementary schools and wait for recess to see if she could find you. She would volunteer at all my schools as the lunchroom lady, just so she could see all the kids around your age."

"I don't understand," Palmer said.

"Neither do I, but for different reasons," Courtney said. "When you were almost three, the babysitter kidnapped you. Mom hired her to watch you while she worked nights as a waitress. The sitter was a young girl, in high school. One night, Mama came home from work, and you were gone. She went to the girl's house, at least the address she had given Mama, and it was a vacant lot. Mama went to the police, but they thought she'd done something to you, and they didn't start looking for you until weeks later. Even then they only looked around the neighborhood where you lived at the time."

The waitress came to their table with their food and drinks. "We condensed and added things to save plates for you," she said. "And I'm going to leave this tray here for extra space."

"Thanks," Kent said as he helped arrange things. Palmer sat, stunned. Tears dripped down her cheeks. She did nothing to stop them. Someone had kidnapped her and left her at an orphanage, instead of keeping her as their own. They took her from her mom, from her home. Her mom had looked for her.

"Where do you live?" Courtney asked.

"We live in San Francisco," Kent told her. He glanced at Palmer, who met his gaze briefly. Courtney's revelations shocked her and left her speechless.

"Palmer's lived there her entire life," he said, speaking for Palmer.

Courtney's mouth dropped open, and she shook her head. "No wonder she couldn't find you. You were across the country with a different name."

"What about the FBI?" Kent asked.

"When I was about ten, I remember a man coming to the door. He was dressed in a dark suit, and he made Mom very nervous. She invited him in and told me I had to go to my room, but I hid in the hallway to listen. It was after he started talking about you that I realized he was some sort of agent or police officer. He told her they didn't have any updates, but they were still looking. He asked her if she'd remembered anything else from the day you were kidnapped, and she hadn't."

"What about age progression?" Kent asked, interrupting.

Courtney handed him a sheet of paper. It was a grainy image of a child. "That's what they gave Mom. Each time an agent would show up, there would be a new image, but the clarity was always horrible."

"Why didn't they use your likeness?" Kent asked.

"Honestly, I don't know," Courtney said as she glanced at Palmer. "Even I see how much we look alike. Maybe if they had, we wouldn't be sitting here right now."

"What about the milk carton campaign? Did anyone ever put Palmer's picture on there?"

Courtney shook her head. "Not that I know of. Every year, Mom would take an ad out in the paper detailing what she knew and whether anyone had seen you. She never gave up looking. When the DNA testing took off, I submitted to every database I could in hopes of finding you, and now I have."

Palmer covered her face with her hands and sobbed as Kent put his arm around her. He whispered for her to let it all out, and she did. If someone with some authority had gone above and beyond, she could've been reunited with her family. If someone had listened instead of blaming her mother, they might have been able to stop the person who'd taken her. Instead, whoever kidnapped her had left her at an orphanage with nothing but a photo of her and her mother.

"Do you know the name of the woman who took Palmer?" he asked while he continued to hold her.

Courtney sifted through the file folder and nodded. She handed him a sketch drawing and said, "Her name was Sarah Cousins. She'd answered an ad that Mom put up at the grocery store. She told Mom she was sixteen, new to the area, and had years of experience. Her parents didn't mind if she was out late, as long as she had time to do her homework. The police couldn't find her, and the FBI has interviewed other women by that name, but none of them were ever viable leads. The agent who was in charge of your case said it was likely she used an alias."

Every time Kent asked a question, the answer from Courtney made things worse for Palmer. She still didn't know how she'd ended up at the orphanage or why, and she didn't remember this Sarah person.

"I don't remember any of it," Palmer said in a hushed tone.

Kent pushed a plate of food toward Palmer, but she shook her head. He leaned into her and whispered, "You need to eat something. Even if it's a little bit."

She nodded and took one of the pretzel bites off her plate. She dipped it in the warm cheese and nibbled on it, only for her stomach to heave.

"How did our mom die?" she asked.

Although Palmer knew tumors weren't hereditary, she still wondered if her mom had died from the same thing Palmer battled.

"The medical examiner said natural causes, but I believe it was because of a broken heart," Courtney said as she took a deep breath. "I came home one day, and she was asleep on the couch. I didn't think anything at first. I knew it was a difficult day for her because it was the anniversary of the day you disappeared. That day, your birthday, and the holidays were always so rough on her. I tried my best to console her and help get her through them, but it was hard. Mom was depressed, and her life was hard after you left. I think her heart just gave up. When I went to wake her, she was cold."

"I'm so sorry," Palmer said.

"It was hard. All she ever wanted was to find you. She wrote to news shows like *20/20*, *America's Most Wanted*, and whatever else aired. No one ever responded. Your kidnapping didn't get the national attention like some had, no matter what she tried. A lot of people around town thought she had something to do with your disappearance, which was another reason we moved so much. Mom struggled. Emotionally, physically, and financially. She'd hold down a job or two, until the anniversary crept up, and then she'd hit a downward spiral."

"We're sorry you had to deal with that," Kent said.

"I had my dad for a bit, but even he got tired of it all and left her when I was thirteen. I chose to stay with her because she needed me." Courtney leaned toward Palmer. "She never gave up. I want you to know this. She loved you with everything she had."

Palmer nodded. The words were nice to hear, but that was all they were. She didn't have her mother, and she still had so many questions, especially for this Sarah person. Who takes a child and then dumps them off?

"What about you?" Kent asked. "What do you do for work? Married? Kids? Does Palmer have any other family?" Palmer was incredibly grateful to Kent for asking the questions she couldn't.

"Mom has one sister, Doris. She lives in Florida. We have five cousins, and they have their own kids. I'm not married and don't have any children. What about you guys?"

Kent cleared his throat. "We've been together for a while, but no kids yet." The lie sounded perfect. "I'm a paramedic, and she manages a bank. That's where we met." He nudged Palmer with his elbow and smiled at her. She appreciated him so much.

While Kent and Courtney munched on the appetizers and made small talk, Palmer looked through the box her sister had given her. Aside from the photos, she now had the pink newborn bracelet hospitals gave babies. The writing had faded, and she assumed it read "Baby Girl Weaver," like the others she'd seen. Her mother had saved a tuft of her hair, a pair of booties, and a certificate with Palmer's footprints. She picked her birth certificate up and elbowed Kent to get his attention.

"Can you read this for me?" she asked him quietly.

"What part?" he asked in an equally hushed tone.

"Birthday."

Kent stiffened next to her for a second and then read the document aloud. "It says April 24, 1986. When do you celebrate?"

"February second."

Palmer worked to process the dates in her head, but her ability to think straight had long gone out the window when she met Courtney. She asked her sister, "Do you know when I was taken?"

"It was January of '89." She went through the papers again. "Mom filed the missing persons report on the tenth of January. Do you know when you went to the orphanage?"

Palmer shook her head. "Sometime in '89. They don't have any paperwork on me anymore."

"They didn't keep records?"

Palmer shrugged. "I think maybe they did, but their record keeping was shoddy at best. They didn't even know my name."

"Can you tell me how it happened? Like, did Sarah just drop you off?"

Palmer took a deep breath and closed her eyes. "I don't remember much. It was like I woke up at the playground where the orphanage is. No one knew who I was, and that was that."

Courtney's mouth dropped open. "I don't understand why she would take you and then give you away like that. Why not just bring you back?"

Palmer wanted to know the same thing. She slumped against Kent out of pure mental exhaustion.

"I think that's probably enough for today," he said to the sisters. "What do you say we meet tomorrow?"

"I'd like that," Courtney said. "I'd love to show you where I live. Would you like to come over for lunch?"

Palmer nodded, and Courtney gave Kent her address. Kent paid the tab and then helped Palmer gather her things. The three of them walked to the parking lot together, and Kent insisted on taking a picture of the sisters.

"Text that to me," Courtney asked Kent.

The women hugged and went to their separate cars. As soon as Kent got behind the wheel, he pulled Palmer into his arms. He told her how sorry he was and wished he could do something to make things better for her.

"I want to leave," she told him.

"Yep, I'll find us a hotel, and we'll go chill for the rest of the night. Maybe we'll get lucky, and we'll find a room with one of those tubs you like."

Palmer sat up. "No, I want to leave here. I don't want to see her tomorrow. I just want to go and forget today."

Kent nodded and said nothing. He started the car, put in the address to his friend Raúl's in New Mexico, and pulled out of the parking lot.

Before I'm Gone

♥ Sit in the front seat of a roller coaster and feel the wind in my hair

♥ Eat tacos or tortillas from a roadside stand in New Mexico

♥ Shop at a large farmers market

♥ Meet Lana Del Rey and see her in concert

♥ Take a picture of the most-painted shed in the US

♥ ~~Sit in the sand and watch the sunrise in Cape Cod~~

♥ ~~Take the steps to the Lincoln Memorial~~

♥ Do yoga in Sedona

♥ Tour and feed animals in a wildlife sanctuary

♥ Stand under a waterfall

♥ See Elvis on the street corner in Las Vegas

♥ Hug an elephant

♥ ~~Find my family~~

♥ Step on grapes and make wine

♥ Run through a wheat field

♥ Drive Route 66

♥ See the marquees on Broadway

♥ Ring the Liberty Bell

♥ Buy a quilt from an Amish stand

★ See the northern lights in Minnesota

★ ~~Visit Plymouth Rock~~

★ ~~Touch Babe Ruth's bat~~

★ ~~Travel the Loneliest Road~~

★ ~~Visit the Muhammad Ali Center~~

★ ~~Dance in the rain with someone I love~~

★ Take the ferry to the Statue of Liberty

★ Check out the Grand Canyon

★ Take every picture I can of Palmer ✓✓✓✓✓✓✓

★ Make Palmer smile ✓✓✓✓✓✓✓

- ~~*Eat chowdah in Boston, per Palmer*~~
- *Eat pizza in Chicago*
- *Try frozen custard in New York City*
- *Get coffee in each city* ✓✓✓✓

Thirty-Two

Kent exited the interstate after what felt like a half hour of driving. Palmer glanced at him, the GPS, and then out the window. She may have drifted into her thoughts, but she wasn't that out of it. "Where are we going?" she asked.

"We're getting a hotel."

"Where are we?"

"About an hour from Kansas City," he told her. Much like their other stops, Kent pulled into the first hotel he saw and asked for a room. Unfortunately, they didn't have anything available, and neither did the next three they found. On his fourth try, he secured a room.

"I thought we were driving to New Mexico," she said when they got to their room. It was a standard room with a stand-up shower and no fancy bathtub.

"That was my intent," he told her. "But the more I thought about it, the more I questioned whether you would regret your decision. So, here we are. If in the morning, you still want to leave, we will."

Palmer wanted to leave, but what Kent said made sense. If they drove too far and she wanted to go back, she knew he would, but that would be unfair to him. But she was confident in her decision to leave.

Kent changed into a pair of shorts and a T-shirt and opened his laptop for the first time since they'd started their trip. Palmer sat next to him while he read and returned an email from Dr. Hughes, detailing

Palmer's issues, and asked what to do about her hands. He asked her if she wanted to add anything else, and she said she didn't.

Next, he typed "Abigail Weaver" into the search bar and waited for the page to load. Palmer expected there to be multiple pages about her, but there was only one, and it had three links. The first was a link to a missing children's database. It had all her basic information. Her height, weight, and age at the time of disappearance, where her abduction took place, and a horrible age-progression photo.

"I don't think they cared," she said.

"I agree. There's something odd about the whole thing. It's like they didn't do a nationwide search, which sort of makes sense, but it doesn't. I don't know. I can't put my finger on it."

Neither could she, nor would she be able to. Again, she wished she could turn back the clock and give herself more time.

The next link was a website that listed the same information the FBI had posted. It looked like one of those true crime sites, with an amateur sleuth. "Make sure you write to them after I'm gone and let them know my story so they can close their case."

"Do you really want me to do that?" Kent asked, and Palmer nodded. "Okay, I will."

The last link was to a profile page on a social media site. Abigail Weaver's age was listed as thirty-seven, and it didn't take much for Kent to speculate. "I wonder if this is the daughter of your kidnapper?"

"What on earth makes you say that?"

"She's the same age as you. What if Sarah kidnapped you to protect her daughter? You could've been a means to an end for someone who needed to escape. Maybe she stole your identity."

Palmer scoffed. "If that's the case, I hope she's lived a miserable life because she ruined mine. Besides, wouldn't the feds look into something like that?"

Kent couldn't disagree. "I'm just throwing stuff out there. I watch too much TV."

Palmer rearranged the pillows and lay down. Kent kept the font on the computer large enough for her to see. He scrolled for a bit, switched to a new site, and then checked on her, only to find Palmer with her eyes closed. He couldn't begin to imagine what went through her mind or how she felt. He felt sick to his stomach at how cruel people could be to one another.

Kent wrapped his arms around her. "I'm so sorry," he told her. "This is so unfair for you." Life had not treated her fairly, and he vowed to help her forget.

Palmer pulled away and angrily wiped at her tears. Kent wanted to find this Sarah Cousins and ask her why she did what she did. But doing so would have to wait. It would likely take years to even find a clue, unless the person he had found online was actually her.

"I don't want to know," she said out of the blue.

"Know what?"

"If that Abigail person is me or whatever. I don't want to go to my grave knowing someone has been pretending to be me, while I grew up with no one by my side."

"Okay." Kent closed his laptop and then lay down beside her. He rolled onto his side and rested his hand on her hip. "Do you feel better knowing your mother loved you?"

She shrugged. "Yes and no. It's so hard to wrap my head around it. I want to know why no one believed that I was missing and why she didn't check any references for the babysitter."

"It sounds like she was a single mom trying to keep food on the table."

Palmer closed her eyes and cried some more. Kent held her and told her everything would be okay.

"Do you think she's waiting for me?"

Kent stilled. Her question took him off guard. He pushed her hair behind her ear and let his hand linger there. "I do," he told her. "When you cross over, she's going to be waiting with open arms."

"Will I know it's her?"

This time, Kent couldn't hold back his emotions and began to cry. He swallowed the lump in his throat and nodded. "You'll know. Your heart will lead you right to her. Your mom passed away without any closure—you'll both be free once you get to her."

"That's all I want."

Palmer closed her eyes again. Kent kissed her forehead and held his lips there longer than what anyone would consider friendly. She cried, and he wiped her tears while telling her everything would be okay. His words felt empty because in the end, nothing would be okay. They had found her family, but at what cost?

Shortly after the sun came up, Kent slipped out of bed and went to the lobby to retrieve coffee. He thought about waking Palmer, but she needed as much sleep as possible, especially after the night she'd had. Between the octopus and learning about her mother, Palmer had been restless most of the night, which concerned Kent.

He opened the door to their room as quietly as possible, only to startle when Palmer came out of the bathroom.

She gasped and placed her hand over her heart. "Crap, you scared me." He held two large cups up and smiled. She closed her eyes and inhaled the aroma of coffee. Kent had never met someone who loved coffee more than her.

"I'm sorry. Peace offering." Kent handed her one of the cups and waited for her to step in front of him.

"What's wrong?"

"Uh . . ." He ran his free hand through his hair and sighed. "Maeve called."

"Oh?"

"Yeah, it looks like I'm going to be a dad." His face strained as he said the words. This wasn't what he wanted, but he'd accept the responsibility. "She's having a girl."

"Congratulations." Palmer seemed genuinely happy for him.

He set his coffee down and leaned against the dresser. "Maeve wants to meet and go over some paperwork or something."

Palmer's breath caught. She nodded and sat down. "Okay. Are we going to drive or fly back?"

Kent blanched. "What? Oh, God. No. We're not cutting our trip short."

"Oh, that's good."

He dropped to his knees and ducked his head until Palmer looked at him. "You're my priority. We're on this journey until you say stop, remember? Maeve . . ." He paused and shook his head. "I told her what we're doing, and she thinks it's great—not that I care what she thinks, but she knows, and she also knows I'm not on my way back just because the baby's mine. When the baby's born, I'll be there, but Maeve and I are over, aside from coparenting. I'm not leaving you to go back to her."

"Do you know what this means?"

"That I have to learn how to change diapers?"

Palmer laughed. "No, it means we're going to buy all the girly things every time we stop."

Kent dropped his head into her lap and groaned. Palmer brushed her fingers through his hair. He moaned in approval. "That feels good."

"I'm glad you like it." Palmer didn't let up and added some pressure, massaging his scalp. He could stay like this for hours and even fall asleep, but they were on a mission, and time was not their friend.

He lifted his head. "What's our plan?"

"I still want to leave," she said. "After yesterday and knowing my future. I don't want to develop something with Courtney that's going to hurt her later. She'll have known me for one day, that's it. She has the picture of us, and can say she found me, and can live her life knowing how things turned out for me, but I don't want to go back. Yesterday was a lot, and I don't want to do it again."

"Okay. Are you going to call her?"

Palmer eyed Kent, and he took that as a no.

"Then you need to email her. It's the right thing to do. Honestly, I'd tell her what you're going through. She may or may not deserve to know, but I think you'll feel better if you come clean."

Kent waited for her to say something, to either agree or disagree with him. When she finally nodded, he stood and retrieved his laptop. He offered to type for her as long as she told him what to write.

Hello, Courtney,

I want to thank you for taking the time out to visit with Kent and I yesterday. It was a very emotional day for me, to say the least. The information you provided about who I am was earth-shattering and a lot to process. I will never be able to thank you enough.

The reason for my email is to let you know Kent and I are leaving Missouri. I know we agreed to meet today, but I don't know what else there is to say or what else you could tell me.

If you have questions about me or my life, please feel free to reach out or call Kent, he can fill you in. I say this, because what I'm about to tell you is going to be hard to process. You see, the reason Kent and I are on this trip is because we're fulfilling a bucket list—a list I didn't start to make until I was diagnosed with a grade IV glioblastoma. Almost two months ago, I was given six months to live. Finding my family was on my list and you've helped me check it off. I'm grateful to have met you, and I thank you for the box you gave me. I hope you have closure on what happened to me and can live the rest of your life knowing I'm okay.

Your sister,
Palmer

When Kent finished typing, he had tears in his eyes. "That was beautiful, yet hard to type."

"She'll probably be hurt."

"Maybe, but you have to do things your way, not hers."

Kent sent the email and then closed his laptop. They packed their things and left the room. Kent was halfway down the hallway when he noticed that Palmer wasn't behind him. He turned and ran back to her. "What's wrong?"

"I don't know. I can hardly move, and everything hurts."

He looked up and down the hall, and then finally went to their room and opened their door. He pulled the security lock forward to keep the door ajar and went back to Palmer and their things. "I'm going to put our stuff back in the room and then carry you to the car." Palmer didn't object.

Kent scooped her into his arms and carried her out through the lobby and into the parking lot. When they got to the car, he set her down. "Wheelchair from here on out," he said as he unlocked the door.

"You've said that before."

"I mean it this time."

Kent held her hand while she climbed into the car. He was at the ready in case she staggered. He'd catch her. Palmer brought the visor down before he could shut the door. He watched her turn her face from side to side and poke at her cheeks. Her face was swollen as a result of the fluids building up. She turned slightly and pulled on her ear.

"You can't see it," he said.

"See what?"

"I'm assuming you're looking for the octopus's tentacle."

"Don't be silly," she told him. Her smile spoke volumes. She was trying to make light of the situation.

He shut her door and went back to grab their stuff. Palmer let out a squeak when Kent opened the back of the car. "Are you lost in your head this morning?" he asked from the rear of the vehicle.

"Just looking for those tentacles."

Kent chuckled. “If I see one, I’ll let you know.”

Once they were on the road, Kent pulled into a fast-food place and ordered their breakfast. He ate while he drove, and it didn’t go unnoticed that Palmer never touched her food. If he asked, she would say she wasn’t hungry, and the thought of eating made her stomach queasy. He’d let it slide for now, but later, he’d make sure she ate something; otherwise, she’d have no strength to do anything.

Kent turned on the playlist he’d created for her. She rested her head against the window and sang along. He would be forever grateful for Lana Del Rey and her music because it brought Palmer peace and soothed her.

Palmer cried while he drove, and he held her hand, hoping she understood that he was there for her, that he would do anything for her. As much as he wanted to know what her thoughts were, he couldn’t bear to ask. Her story broke his heart. She didn’t have anyone until he came along, and even then, he’d had to fight to be let into her life.

Hearing her sniffles broke him and reminded him of deployment and being in the field. His job then was to save his friends, his team. Palmer was a part of him now, and the one thing he couldn’t do was save her. But he’d do his damnedest to make her final days enjoyable.

Palmer screamed and held her head. Kent pulled over and gave her a couple of pills to take. He massaged her shoulders while she sobbed. It’d been days since she’d complained or shown any signs of how much pain she was in.

“I’m dying.”

Thirty-Three

Kent worried they were missing too much with Palmer's insistence that they get to New Mexico. He was also troubled by Palmer's mindset. It wasn't healthy for her to accept that the end was near. Kent firmly believed people who wanted to fight the inevitable could, and it seemed like Palmer had given up.

Each time they drove through a new city or saw a sign that Kent knew something about, he asked if she wanted to stop. The answer was no, even when it came to food. He felt like he was on this trip alone at times, and he wanted to shake her out of her funk. The thing was, he didn't fully understand her mindset or how she felt. Palmer knew her body better than anyone, and if she felt herself slipping away, piece by piece, then he had to respect her decisions. Even when it broke him. He wasn't ready to let her go.

Kent drove for eight hours and then stopped for the night. Palmer didn't fight him when he got the wheelchair out and pushed her through the lobby. She had lost a lot of spunk since her body had started deteriorating at their last stop. He wanted to help her, revive her somehow, but he wasn't sure how.

He also wasn't sure if some of this new, despondent Palmer was a result of meeting her sister, or if her spirit was ready to give up now that she'd fulfilled her biggest quest. Palmer knew where she was from and what had happened to her, and the person she longed for the most had already passed away. Palmer could be ready to meet her mom in the next realm, and there wasn't anything Kent could do about it.

After they settled in their room, Kent took a long hot shower. His bones ached and his back was stiff from driving. Jeeps weren't known for their comfort, and driving across the country was taking its toll on his body. Of course, sleeping in a different bed every night wasn't helping either. Never mind the added stress of Palmer. He wanted what was best for her but was at a loss about what that was.

"I think I'm going to book us a flight home," he said after he got out of the shower. Palmer perked up and glanced at him. Again, he'd come out of the bathroom with nothing more than a towel on because he knew this would get her attention.

She put her journal aside. "Why?"

He shrugged. He wasn't sure why he'd said that. "You're not having a good time." Kent looked through his suitcase and found shorts, boxers, and a T-shirt. They would have a chance to do laundry again when they made it to Raúl's tomorrow. He turned and went back to the bathroom. When he came out again, Palmer was waiting for him.

"I know I've been moody."

Kent nodded.

"I feel weak. Both physically and mentally. It's like a darkness took over after we met Courtney. I know I've talked to you about dying and having this tumor, but to say it to someone else . . ." Palmer paused and shook her head. "It feels final," she said quietly. "It feels like I have nothing left."

Kent sat on the edge of the bed next to her and brushed her hair behind her ear. "You have me. I'm not going anywhere until you tell me you don't want me around anymore."

"That's not going to happen."

Kent nodded. "I hear there's this great place called Saltgrass Steak House. What do you say we go there for dinner?"

"I'm not really hungry," she told him.

"I get that, but you can't take your meds on an empty stomach, and if you don't start eating, we'll have to go back to San Francisco because you'll need a feeding tube." The last part was a scare tactic, although he suspected that once Dr. Hughes took one look at how much weight Palmer had lost, she'd recommend hospice care until the end. Kent couldn't do that to Palmer. He knew, without her having to say the words, she didn't want to die in the hospital. Where she wanted to die or what she wanted to do with her body remained a mystery to him. As much as he needed to broach the subject with her, he couldn't bring himself to have that talk. To him, it would make things more final than they already felt.

Palmer went to shower, and for the first time since the mirror incident, Kent wouldn't need to wash her hair, which made him a bit sad. He enjoyed taking care of her. He sat in the hallway and waited for her, listening to her blow-dry her hair. When she opened the door and asked him to help her with her curling iron, he jumped at the opportunity. Once he finished, he excused himself and sat on the bed while she dressed.

"You're so beautiful." The words were out of Kent's mouth before he could change them to something like "You look pretty" or "You look nice." He meant what he said. She was beautiful, and she made his heart do things he hadn't felt in a long time—if ever. Somewhere along the Loneliest Highway, he had fallen in love with her. Kent should tell her. He owed it to her to let her know she'd done that to him. For him.

"Thank you." Palmer blushed and ran her hands down the front of her dress. She grabbed a sweater, and Kent helped her put it on. "Shall we go to dinner?"

Kent held her chair in place, and she looked from it to Kent. He motioned for her to sit, but she hesitated. Palmer frowned. "Just until we get to the car," he said. "You can hold my arm into the restaurant."

Palmer sat down and tucked her dress under her legs, away from the wheels. Kent pushed her down the hall. He made car noises and tipped the chair back so it popped a wheelie. He laughed while Palmer squealed and told him to knock it off. Kent only stopped when they entered the lobby. He didn't want people staring at her because of his actions, but because of how pretty she was.

Luckily the restaurant wasn't busy, and they were able to get a table rather quickly. Palmer shocked Kent when she ordered a cocktail. He couldn't believe his ears. Palmer had led a very straitlaced type of life, even when facing death's door. He liked the idea of her letting loose.

"Are you going to order something to drink?" she asked after the waiter had left with their order.

"I did."

"No, I mean a beer or a cocktail." Palmer leaned forward. Her eyes beamed with happiness. "You should get something."

"I'm good," he told her. He wouldn't indulge in an alcoholic beverage while her care depended on him. That would be reckless, and he'd never forgive himself if something were to happen and he couldn't take care of her. "Besides, I'm high on life." He tapped her knee under the table and grinned.

"High on life because you're having a little girl?"

Kent's face fell. He wasn't excited about becoming a father, especially a single dad.

"What's wrong?" Palmer asked.

Kent tried to shake off his disappointment, but to no avail. "Whenever I imagined being a parent, it wasn't like this. I feel duped and trapped," he said. "I was put into a situation without my knowledge, and now an innocent baby will end up paying the price. Can you imagine how confusing this is going to be for her when she's older?"

"I imagine it will be the same as if you and Maeve had been together and split when Baby Girl Wagner was two or three. Honestly, this isn't much different from parents divorcing when they have really young children and one of them is moving on. You gotta look at it differently."

"How?" he asked.

"As a blessing. You created a life, and that little girl is going to grow up with the best daddy out there. If you're half the man with her that you are with me, she's going to know you're always in her corner being her champion. That's something I wish I had—someone there at the end of the day to just ask me how my day was and mean it, to sincerely want to know. The people at the group home, they'd ask, but it was their job. They didn't care about the bullying or anything else that went on. They never checked homework or reprimanded the children because of a bad grade. You're going to do all of that and more for your daughter, and over time, you'll forget about the situation that brought her into your life and remember the first time you held her in your arms. I hear that's when people experience true love for the first time."

"I hadn't looked at things that way."

"No, you probably saw the burden, both financially and physically. Right?"

Kent nodded and felt horrible for doing so. The child shouldn't be looked at as a burden; she didn't ask for this. "I know I can support her. That isn't the issue. I just don't know what kind of dad I want to be, or if they'll allow me to be a dad at all. Her husband may not be on board with me being in the baby's life."

"He doesn't have a choice," Palmer said. "The DNA test will always prove she's yours. He has no say if you get to be in her life or not. If he thinks he does, you take him to court, and you fight for her."

Easier said than done. "Yeah." Kent sighed and wished he had a beer or five to numb the voices in his head. It wasn't that he didn't want to talk about this with Palmer; it was that he wanted Palmer with him when the baby was born. He wanted her by his side moving forward. Kent's needs were irrational, and he knew it. He'd just have to bring himself to think otherwise.

Their drinks came, soda for him and a tequila sunrise for her. She offered him a sip, and he took it. The quick taste wouldn't impair him. "Oh, wow, that's tasty," he said. Palmer sipped. She pulled the straw away, and her face contorted as the liquor hit her taste buds.

Palmer opened her mouth and let out an exaggerated breath. "Holy crap that's strong."

"Have you ever had liquor before?" Kent asked her.

She looked mortified at his question. "I'm not a prude."

"Didn't say you were."

"Of course I have. It's just not something I do by myself, unless it's wine. I do like wine."

"We should head to Napa when we get back and tour one of the vineyards."

Palmer smiled, but it didn't meet her eyes. Kent already knew without asking her—she didn't expect to make it back to San Francisco.

Their dinner came, and most of their conversation turned to Kent bugging Palmer to eat. She took three or four bites of her mashed potatoes, a few bites of her chicken, and then said she'd had enough and excused herself to use the restroom.

He motioned for their server. "It's my girlfriend's birthday. I want to surprise her with a piece of cake. Do you have a candle?"

The server smiled brightly and promised to return quickly. Kent watched for Palmer to return, giddy with excitement about what he'd done.

"Why do you look like you're up to something?" she asked.

He didn't have time to even shrug. The server, along with other staff members, approached the table. They started singing before Palmer's mouth dropped open wide in shock. Her eyes glistened as the server set a piece of cake in front of her with a lone candle.

"Make a wish," Kent said to her as he reached for her hand.

Palmer let her tears fall as she blew out her candle. Everyone clapped, wished her a happy birthday, and then went on their way.

"I can't believe you did this."

"Now you've had birthday cake," he said with a wink. "I know this isn't on the list and it's not either of the days, but celebrating now felt right."

"Thank you." She reached across the table and held his hand.

For every bite she took, Kent took three. She had barely eaten her dinner; there was no way he'd get her to eat cake too. He had hoped, though. As a kid, he'd much rather eat dessert than dinner.

As they walked to the car, Kent saw a bright neon sign that said **DANCING**, with a pair of boots moving back and forth. He looked down at their feet and shrugged. They didn't have boots, but they could dance. Well, he could hold on to Palmer and make sure she didn't collapse on the floor.

"Where are we going? The car is this way." She stopped them in their tracks and pointed.

"We're going over there." Kent pointed at the bar.

"We are? Why?"

"Why not? Dancing in Texas at a bar with flashing cowboy boots should be on everyone's bucket list."

Palmer hesitated for a moment. She looked from the neon sign to Kent, and then down at the ground. "I don't think we're dressed appropriately."

Kent laughed. "Only one way to find out."

He paid their cover charge at the door and escorted Palmer in. The crowd wasn't as large as Kent expected it to be, but it was still sizable. He led Palmer right to the dance floor. He didn't know a thing when it came to line dancing, but that wasn't why they were there. He wanted to dance with her. Ever since the day in the park, he'd wanted to hold her tightly and let their bodies sway to the music, and that was what he planned to do now.

"I don't think I can do this," she said. Kent watched her and not the people around them. He was head over heels in love with her and wanted to tell her. He loved seeing how something as simple as a group of people dancing captivated her interest. Line dancing was an art form, and she seemed to be in awe.

Kent leaned in. "We don't have to do what they're doing. We can just dance, or we can wait for a two-step, and I'll teach you how to do that."

He kept his head next to hers, enjoying the smell of her perfume. "You know how?" she asked. He nodded. "Teach me?"

"My pleasure."

They only had to wait for the current song to finish, and then people started to pair up. Kent placed Palmer's hands where he wanted them, and then told her to focus on his eyes and let her body feel the music. He pulled her close and gave her instructions as they moved around the floor. She stepped on his feet too many times to count, and they were definitely wearing the wrong shoes, but he wouldn't have passed this moment up for anything.

An hour later, Palmer looked into Kent's eyes and cried.

"What's wrong?" he asked.

"I'm having one of the best nights of my life," she told him.

"So, these are happy tears?" His thumb caressed her cheek and wiped her tears.

"No," she said in a broken voice. "I don't feel well."

Kent nodded and whisked her off the dance floor. He all but carried her out of the bar, and once they reached the parking lot, he picked her up. Palmer clung to him and cried into his shoulder. He had no idea what was wrong or what they were about to face. He prayed that whatever lay ahead would happen in the safety of the hotel and not in the parking lot or in the car.

Thirty-Four

Kent sped back to the hotel. He parked in the closest spot to the lobby, made sure he had the key card in his hand, shut off the car, and exited. He carried Palmer into the hotel and rushed by the desk clerk, hoping he didn't look suspicious.

As soon as he got Palmer into the room, he laid her on the bed. He had no idea what to expect. The whole "I don't feel well" could mean anything. Kent highly doubted she could feel a seizure coming, but then he hadn't been paying attention to the signs. Palmer had been moody earlier and had only changed when Kent threatened to cut their trip short. The only present sign of a potential seizure was how emotional she'd become at the bar. Initially, Kent had chalked that up to her not feeling well and them having to leave; now he was second-guessing himself.

"Here, take this." He helped Palmer sit up and then handed her the anticonvulsant medication and a bottle of water. "They should help prevent a seizure."

"Is that why I don't feel well?" Palmer handed Kent the bottle of water after she'd taken the medication. He sat on the edge of the bed and sighed.

"I don't know. There isn't anything scientific that pinpoints when a seizure will occur. I need to be better about making sure you're eating, but you do get enough sleep. You're not supposed to have alcohol, but I think it's stupid to tell you no when . . ." Kent trailed off. He ran his hands through his hair, which he desperately needed to cut. "At least you're safe here."

While Palmer got up to use the bathroom and change into some pajamas, Kent hovered. He was on edge and anxious. He couldn't get the image of her crying out of his mind or get past the thought that something was about to happen. Kent sighed when she opened the bathroom door. He led her back to the bed and helped her get under the covers.

"I'll be right back." Kent changed quickly and then crawled in bed next to her. Despite there being another bed, they both preferred to sleep next to each other. He reached for the remote, turned the TV on, and scrolled through the channels until he found a movie for them to watch.

Palmer snuggled into Kent's side, until he rolled her onto her side and spooned her. He did so because if she was going to have a seizure, she needed to be on her side. Palmer reached to turn the light off, but he told her to keep it on. "It'll help with the lights flashing from the TV."

"Oh."

The crack against his skull woke him before the shaking bed did. He groaned and then realized what was happening. Palmer's body thrashed wildly. Kent scrambled out of bed and pulled the bottom sheet down until her body was in the middle, giving her a safe space. He timed the seizure on his watch and added thirty seconds for the painful wake-up call he'd experienced. He was pretty sure Palmer had whacked him a good one with her head.

Three minutes—that was how long it took for her body to stop convulsing. He was a wreck and in tears by the time she was alert. Kent knelt at the bedside and held her hand while he sobbed. He couldn't stop them from happening, and watching her go through them ripped his heart to shreds. She stroked his hair and apologized.

"It's not your fault," he told her.

"I could've had the surgery."

"We wouldn't be here if you had," he reminded her. Kent helped Palmer sit up. He didn't bother wiping his tears as he handed her the bottle of water from earlier. "Drink this."

She did as she was told. After a couple of sips, she put the bottle down. "How long?"

"Three minutes."

"What happened to your head?"

Kent touched the bump forming on his forehead. He looked at her pointedly, and her mouth dropped open. "Oh, God, I am so sorry."

"Don't be. I'd rather it be my head than the wall or the corner of the nightstand. From now on, I'm going to put a pillow there, or you're sleeping on the other side of me." If they did that, they wouldn't be able to fall asleep in each other's arms while watching TV. "Come on, let's get you to the bathroom." Kent helped Palmer stand and then held her arm while she gingerly walked to the bathroom. He gave her privacy and went back to the bed and fixed the sheets. He was surprised she hadn't had an accident, considering the time of night.

"Kent," she called from the bathroom. He went to her and knocked on the door. "You can come in."

He found her leaning against the counter, staring into the mirror. "Are you ready to go back to bed?"

"How did I get this bump on my head?"

Kent looked at her oddly. "We conked heads when your seizure started."

She looked surprised. "Oh."

Had she forgotten, or was this a new sign that the tumor was invading more of her life? "Come on," he said as he reached for her. "The bed is made and it's late. We have a long drive ahead of us."

"Okay." Palmer went with Kent but kept her eyes on the mirror until they left the bathroom. She got into bed first and then Kent followed. He took the side nearest the bedside table, to prevent her from hitting it while she slept. She rolled onto her side to face the wall, and Kent snuggled in behind her. He wanted to hold her.

"Is this okay?" he asked her. Palmer nodded and pulled his hand under her head.

They stayed like that until the sun came up. Kent never fell asleep and wasn't sure if Palmer had either. His mind raced with what she'd said in the bathroom, questioning how she'd gotten the bump on her head and not recalling her seizure. He could easily say she was confused because of the episode, but his gut told him otherwise. Between her vision issues, the numbness in her fingers and hands, the seizures, the appetite loss, and now her forgetfulness, she was much closer to the end than he wanted her to be. Kent needed to step their trip into high gear.

After breakfast at the hotel, they were back on the road. Palmer opened the top and reclined her seat. She told Kent she was going to sunbathe. He didn't mind as long as she didn't care if he listened to sports talk radio. He turned it on and got lost in the chatter about the upcoming NFL season. Kent enjoyed all sports and never really favored one team over the other.

Halfway through the segment, Palmer sat up and rummaged through her bag for the journal she'd bought a while back. Kent wondered what she wrote about, but he hadn't wanted to invade her privacy. She slipped her glasses on and began writing.

Of all the facilities to start to lose first, he hated that it was her vision. This trip had been so important to her. She wanted to see the sights and experience the beautiful landscapes that made up the United States, and he was heartbroken that she wasn't able to see it all clearly. Yet, Palmer didn't complain. She kept on with Kent as her guide.

As they got closer to Albuquerque, Kent closed the top, much to Palmer's dismay. "With all this traffic, we don't want to inhale exhaust fumes."

"Maybe I wanted to."

Kent frowned. He hated when she talked about taking her own life, even though he understood why she did it. "Well, I don't," he fired back to match her attitude.

"You know I can get high if I want to."

Her statement caught him off guard. As far as he knew, she didn't have any substances on her or packed in her luggage that would aid her in getting high.

"Is that so?" he prodded.

"Yep. I just have to show my stupid medical card at some store, and I can do it."

Kent wanted to laugh but held back. Palmer had no idea what kind of store she even needed, but this was her way of showing him who was boss. She was right, though. Dr. Hughes had issued her a prescription for medicinal marijuana, but Palmer didn't have it. He did. She'd given it to him before they left.

"Do you want to?"

"Do I want to what?" she asked with so much sass Kent thought he was talking to a teenager.

He bit his tongue to keep from sassing her back. "Get high?"

"I don't know. You might want to make out with me."

I already do. "I might," he said, playing along.

Kent headed north out of the city, toward Raúl's. He and his family lived on the outskirts, in what Raúl's great-grandfather described as being far enough away from the big-city lights that the lightning bugs still blazed a path for followers, but close enough for everyone to visit. Kent glanced at Palmer while he waited for her response. She said nothing, making him wonder if a shift had happened. Had her mood changed again, or did she need time to think?

"Do you want to?" he asked her again. If she wanted to get high and numb the pain she was in, he was going to set things up for her, and if she didn't want to—well, that would be fine as well. She would at least know the option was there.

"Do what?"

"Get high," he said. "It can help you manage the pain. If you don't want to smoke, we can get you some edibles."

He could feel her gaze on him, and each time he took a quick peek, she still stared. "Would you think less of me?"

Kent almost ran off the road with her question. "What? Hell no. Why would you think that?"

"Because . . . well, I don't know. It's a drug and—"

Kent cut her off. "You have an octopus growing inside of your head. No, I'm not going to think less of you for finding ways to numb your pain, Palmer. Shit, I probably should've brought it up sooner, but we hadn't discussed it as part of your pain management. I'll be honest, I'd rather you get high than drunk."

"Okay."

"Okay, what? You want to get some edibles?"

"Yes," she said quietly. Kent was thankful they were almost to Raúl's because he would be able to hook them up. As soon as cannabis became legal in New Mexico, Raúl's sister had opened a dispensary.

Kent rested his hand on Palmer's leg, and she locked her fingers with his. "Thank you."

"You're welcome. I'm sorry I didn't think of it sooner. If there's something you need, I don't care what it is, just ask me. You can't say anything to shock or upset me. I'm here to take care of you, to get you what you need."

"Okay." Palmer leaned her head on Kent's shoulder. With the console in the way, he knew it wasn't the most comfortable position for her to be in, but he appreciated the gesture. He rested his cheek on top of her head and held her there while he drove the rest of the way to Raúl's.

Kent pointed to the line of people as they drove down the road. "These people are waiting for the taco stand."

"We'll never get in before they close," Palmer said as she sat up.

"Nah, we have an in, remember?" He caught her expression and saw her work through her memory bank for the answer. She nodded, but Kent was certain she had a fuzzy recollection at best.

Kent pulled into the driveway next to the taco stand and drove to the end of the dirt road. He honked the horn before parking and shutting the Jeep off. The screen door opened and slammed shut, and standing on the wide porch was one of his best friends from the army.

Raúl waited until Kent had Palmer out of the Jeep before he stepped off the porch to greet Kent in a hug. For a long minute, the men were silent as they hugged each other. "It's great to see you, man." Raúl thumped Kent's back with his fist.

"You too, brother." They parted, and Kent stepped aside to introduce Palmer. She stuck her hand out to shake Raúl's, but he went in for a hug. Kent cringed briefly, knowing Raúl's strength, but he also knew he'd never do anything to hurt Palmer.

"It's so nice to finally meet Wagner's girlfriend," Raúl said.

Palmer leaned to the side, and Kent winked. "It's nice to meet you as well," she said. "I hear your grandma has the best roadside tacos in all the land."

Raúl laughed. "That she does, but don't remind her. Her head is already big enough as is. Come on, I'll take you over."

"Before we go." Kent spoke quietly to Raúl, in case any of his nieces or nephews were eavesdropping from the bushes. Raúl nodded, told them he'd be right back, and went into the house.

"Where'd he go?"

"He had to go grab something."

Raúl was back in a flash and held his hand out to Palmer. "It's a gummy bear. Chew it like normal."

"Wait, is this . . . ?"

Both men nodded. Palmer studied it for a moment and then slowly put it in her mouth. She chewed and swallowed and then looked at the men. "Nothing's happened."

Raúl laughed and put his hands on Kent's and Palmer's backs to lead them to the taco stand. "Give it a minute to get into your system." He opened the door and hollered out for his abuelita and mom, Martina.

Two women came forward and lit up as soon as they saw Kent. They hugged and kissed him, held his face between their hands, and kissed him some more. But it was when he introduced Palmer, and Raúl's mother must have seen the love in his eyes as he spoke about her, that she welcomed the woman with open arms. All it took was one look from Kent to bring Palmer into the fold of Raúl's family.

Raúl took them around back to where five picnic tables were lined up. There were kids running around, some on a swing set, and one sitting under a tree reading a book. Kent didn't remember all their names, except for Raúl's little sister Julia, the reader. Raúl called to her. Julia sauntered forward until she spotted Kent, and then she sprinted toward him.

"Uncle Kent," she screamed as she launched herself into his arms. "When did you get here?"

"About twenty minutes ago." He set her down and introduced her to Palmer. Again, as his girlfriend. Julia peppered Kent with questions until Raúl told her to scram.

Kent helped Palmer sit down and sat next to her. He kept one hand on her until Martina came through the back door with a platter of food. "We ordered two of everything," Kent said to Palmer so only she could hear him. "This way you can try whatever you want, and if you want more, I'll get it for you."

"Why did you tell them I was your girlfriend?"

Because I wish you were. "Why not? It's better to tell them than for them to ask. They're going to see us together for a couple of days, holding hands and sleeping in the same bed. Besides, Raúl's mom senses things. So, she knows."

"Knows what?" Palmer asked.

Kent shrugged and smiled. "Things."

"I thought the gummy Raúl gave me was . . . special?"

Kent laughed. "Eat up, Palmer." He winked and bit into his own taco.

Thirty-Five

For the first time in her life, Palmer felt what it was like to belong. She and Kent, along with Raúl and his family, sat around a bonfire, despite the warm temperatures, and laughed. They enjoyed each other's company and told stories about life, love, and the art of making the best roadside taco. Raúl and Kent spoke about going through basic training together, deploying, and coming back to a country where half the people loved them, while the other half hated them because of the war. Each time one of the guys would say "Do you remember that time," everyone turned to listen. It didn't matter what the men had to say: people listened.

Everyone took turns telling a story, whether it was about their life or their day. Julia was animated when she spoke, using her hands for emphasis, and saying the hip words Kent and Palmer had laughed about earlier.

"So, like I was asked to the winter formal," Julia told her family. All the women were excited, but the men . . . not so much.

"Nah," Raúl said. "I need to meet him first."

Julia rolled her eyes; even Palmer, with her failing eyesight, could see that. Julia waved her big brother away, but Raúl wasn't having it. He went to her and pulled her into a bear hug. She screamed out and begged her brother to stop. Everyone around them laughed.

This is what it's like to have a family, Palmer thought to herself as she watched them horse around. Raúl's abuelita stood next to Palmer and put her hand on her head. She leaned into his abuelita's touch, welcoming the soft hand against her skin. His abuelita muttered something in Spanish and started rubbing an oil into Palmer's neck.

"What's this?"

"It's lavender oil. It'll keep you calm," Martina said. "You're stressed?"

Palmer nodded.

"I can tell. This will help. It's Abuelita's recipe, and she swears it's a cure-all for anything that ails you."

Kent squeezed Palmer's hand and winked. Maybe it was the gummy Raúl had given her earlier or the sheer comfort she felt around his family. Either way, she was about to open up to strangers, people who didn't feel like strangers to her at all.

"There's no cure for what I have," Palmer said to the group. She told her story to the people who'd opened their home and hearts to her. From the second she'd stepped out of the truck, she'd felt like she belonged with Raúl and his family. As she spoke, Abuelita hugged her and spoke of how God would greet her when she arrived in heaven. Raúl translated, and the once-boisterous crowd quieted and listened.

When she finished, everyone, including the people she couldn't recall names for, came to her and hugged her. Martina cried, and then cried harder when she hugged Kent. Abuelita moved her chair next to Palmer's and held her hand. This was the first time Palmer had held the hand of a grandmother. She wished she knew Spanish because she wanted to talk to the woman next to her. Palmer suspected Raúl's grandmother had a story to tell, a lifelong journey to peace, that she'd found when she'd opened the roadside stand.

As darkness grew around them, Palmer prayed for the first time in her life, with her newfound family. The thought hadn't even crossed her mind when she'd sat in the church and stared at the man on the cross. She'd been angry with him for giving her the short end of the stick when it came to life. She was a good person with shit luck, and she didn't understand why.

All night long, Kent sat on her other side, touching her in some way, being an attentive fake boyfriend. He made sure she always had water in her cup, that she wasn't going hungry, and that she was all right.

Something had shifted between them. Palmer couldn't put her finger on it, but she felt like they were more than friends. Kent wasn't pretending to be her boyfriend. He caught her staring at him and smirked a bit. It was sexy and Palmer liked it.

He leaned into her and whispered in her ear, "How are you doing?"

His cool breath along her skin made her spine shiver. Kent was everything she'd wished for years ago. He'd showed, in the time they'd been together traveling, and in one night surrounded by his friends, what life would have been like with him. If only she wasn't out of time.

"I'm . . ." She paused. What was she? Happy, yes. Sad, yes. Angry, pissed off, disgusted, all yeses. But she *was* happy because of Kent, and he needed to know that. "I'm happy because I'm with you."

Palmer was certain she heard him growl; if not, there was a coyote, or whatever type of wild dog spent time in the woods, lurking. She could feel his intense gaze on her and was thankful for the darkness.

Kent leaned in again, but this time he kissed her cheek and then near her earlobe. "There isn't any other place I'd rather be," he whispered as his hand tightened around hers.

Palmer wanted Kent, in every way imaginable, and yet she couldn't bring herself to say the words out of fear. Every day, she felt herself slipping further away, getting closer to death. Kent would be hurt. That was something he hadn't taken into consideration when he'd asked to take her on this trip. If he had, he hadn't mentioned it. Each time she brought dying up, he'd change the subject.

Kent was the reason she wrote notes in her journal. She wanted the daily reminders of where she was, why she was there, and everything Kent meant to her. He was the one aspect of her life she didn't want to forget. She didn't care about the job she'd left or the people. Palmer only cared about Kent.

Palmer looked around at everyone and saw how happy they were. The gathering was a normal night for them. They didn't need the excuse of Kent and Palmer visiting to be a family. This was all she'd ever wanted, and Kent had given it to her. She turned toward him and said, "Thank you."

"For what?" he asked in a hushed tone. Kent tilted his head and watched her. Palmer caressed his cheek, and he kissed her palm.

"For showing me what it's like to have a family. Even if it's for one night, I'll never forget this moment."

"You're welcome. I'm just sorry we didn't do this sooner."

"If we had, I wouldn't have wanted to leave, and then you wouldn't have all those magnets."

"My refrigerator thanks you," he said with a quiet laugh. "You'll tell me when you're ready for bed?"

Palmer nodded. She wanted to stay up all night but knew that would never happen. She tired easily and often, and unfortunately she'd slept through most of their driving. She wasn't a great passenger at the moment.

"So, what's next on your trip?" Raúl asked.

Kent cleared his throat and looked at Palmer. "I'm not really sure."

"Are we far from Las Vegas?"

"Seven hours," Raúl's mom yelled. Everyone went silent and looked at her. "What?" She shrugged. "I like the casinos there."

Palmer glanced at Kent expectantly. "We can definitely go, and we'll be able to knock the roller coaster off your list. The New York–New York Hotel has an arcade and coaster."

"I'd like that."

"We'll leave in the morning."

She smiled at Kent and felt a surge of love flow through them, well, at least from her to him. A man like Kent would never fall for someone like Palmer—that was what she reminded herself of each time she forgot she had an octopus sucking the life out of her. He was her friend. Best friend. Nothing more.

"Uncle Kent, have you seen your Instagram?" Julia asked as she came over with her phone. "You guys are, like, mega viral."

"There's one of those words again," Palmer chuckled.

Kent fished his phone out of his pocket, and his eyes widened. His thumb moved up the screen, and hundreds of notifications flew by. He finally cleared the screen and went to the app. "Holy shit," he said as he held the phone out for Palmer to see. "Our followers have skyrocketed."

"Uncle Kent, you have a trending hashtag."

Kent clicked on #Palmersbeforeigobucketlist and saw that there were over two hundred thousand people posting with their hashtag. He clicked on a video and turned up the volume so Palmer could hear. She covered her mouth as her coworker Shaunie started talking.

"To all you people out there following Palmer's journey, let me just tell you how selfless this woman is. Instead of breaking our hearts with her diagnosis, she told us she was moving, so naturally we gave her a going-away party. She walked out the door with her head held high and with a smile on her face, and we were happy. She didn't want to see us cry for her. Well, Palmer, if you're watching this, we love you."

"How'd they find out?" she asked as she wiped at her tears.

"I'm going to guess that Greg's video is more viral than we thought."

Kent played a few more videos for her, each one bringing more tears, and he liked and commented on a bunch of photos. He was starting to put his phone away when Palmer stopped him.

"I want to go live."

"You do?"

She looked around at everyone and nodded. "I feel like this is the right time and place."

Kent reopened the app and pressed the button to go live. Normally, they waited for a few minutes for people to join, but the room was active instantly.

"Holy crap, Uncle Kent. You guys are famous," Julia said as she waved to the camera. Kent laughed and positioned himself with Palmer in the video.

"Just Palmer and Kent here. We're currently outside—"

"Literally," Raúl interjected.

"Yes, literally." Kent laughed. "Outside of Albuquerque at the best little roadside taco stand in the world."

"That's the truth," Raúl yelled.

"Palmer and I are very humbled by all the love we're getting, and we promise to post more often. I know it's been a week or so since we did a live, but we'll be better, especially when we get to our next destination." Kent glanced at Palmer and grinned. "Is there something you want to say?"

She nodded and wrapped her arm around his and leaned into him. "It's taken me a while to adjust to this social media thing, and I know if you saw Greg's video—hi, Greg!" Palmer waved. "Then you know he told everyone about the bucket list and how I'm dying. Only a very few people in my life know the truth, with this guy right here being one of them." Palmer briefly pressed her lips to Kent's shoulder. "I'm currently at the end stages of my life with a grade-four glioblastoma. A little over two months ago the doctors gave me six months to live if I were to start treatment. I chose to live, knowing I could die at any time." Palmer swallowed hard. Next to her, Raúl's abuelita reached for Palmer's hand. "Kent, my knight in shining armor, saw the list of places I wanted to visit and devised a plan, and here we are."

"I'm very proud of you," Kent said as he kissed her forehead for all the world to see. "You're incredibly brave. Do you want to answer some of their questions?"

Palmer nodded.

"Here, we'll ask," Raúl said as he took the phone from Kent. "Julia is in your live. She'll read them to you, and I'll video."

Kent sat back with Palmer and waited for Julia to ask the questions.

"What was your favorite stop?"

"That's easy," Palmer said. "Definitely here." Everyone around them cheered.

"Why did you forgo treatment?"

"I'll answer this one," Kent said. "Palmer's reasons are hers and hers alone. We respect them."

"Wait, I thought you guys were married."

"They should be," Raúl said after Julia had read the question.

Kent and Palmer stared at each other. He was out of her league, but oh how she wished their lives were different.

Julia moved on to the next question. *"Where is your next stop?"*

"We'll let you know after we get there," Kent said, but he never took his eyes off Palmer. His intense gaze electrified her. She was almost afraid to look away but finally did so.

They answered a few more questions before signing off, and Palmer declared she was tired. Kent bid everyone a good night and walked her back to the house. Inside their bedroom for the night, she told Kent he could go back to the bonfire, that she'd be okay. She really wanted a moment—a moment where she could imagine what it would be like to be loved by him in ways he had loved another. Palmer wanted to dream about Kent—dream about him being hers and only hers. She wanted to imagine what it was like to touch him and for him to touch her. She wanted to go back to the day she'd met him and ask him to go to drinks after work, but she had not been brave then, not like tonight. Back then, she had something to lose, and now she had nothing.

Kent left the room so Palmer could change. She sat on the edge of the bed and cried into the pillow. She had wasted the only years of her life that were actually hers and not governed by a state agency. She was thirty-seven and had nothing to show for it. No husband. No children. She had accomplished nothing.

Kent returned and dropped to his knees as soon as he saw her. He held her, without saying a word, and allowed her to cry. He didn't promise her everything would be okay or ask her what was wrong. Kent soothed her and encouraged her to let it all out. She knew he understood her because she'd let him in.

When her tears dried, she pulled away out of embarrassment, but he refused to let her. "You don't need to hide from me," he reminded her. "I can't begin to fathom how difficult it was for you to tell thousands of strangers that you're dying."

"It's not that."

"What is it then?"

She glanced at him through her wet lashes. The words were on the tip of her tongue. She wanted to tell him she was in love with him, that she wanted to be with him in all the ways that counted, but she couldn't bring herself to say the words out of fear he would reject her, and rightly so.

"Tonight showed me what it was like to have a family." While she hadn't lied, she hadn't told him the truth of what bothered her.

"We can stay here," he told her. Kent didn't have to say that this could be where she closed her eyes for the last time. His face said it all.

"No, I want to keep going," she told him. "I'm not done living yet."

"Okay, we'll leave in the morning."

While Kent rolled two blankets, one for the wall and the other for the headboard, Palmer went into the bathroom. When she returned, Kent sat on the edge of the bed waiting for her. He stood and waited for her to crawl into bed. He tucked her in, giving her more blankets than he would use.

They lay on their sides, facing each other, neither of them speaking. They stared, memorizing each other as if this were their last night together.

"If you get cold, wake me, and I'll get you some more blankets." Kent pulled the comforter more toward her chin. "The air conditioner's on."

"I'll be fine as long as I can snuggle into you."

Kent smiled brightly and chuckled. "I'm always open for a good snuggle."

"I appreciate you," she told him.

Kent moved closer. "You know, you seem to forget I needed saving as well. This trip isn't about me saving you," he reminded her.

"I know, but my issues are more . . . I don't know, issues." She laughed at herself. Palmer had a hard time coming up with the right words at times, like now.

"We're in this together. We're a team."

"The perfect team."

Kent kissed her forehead. His lips lingered there for a moment before he pulled away. "Get some sleep. Tomorrow is going to be a lot."

"How so?"

"I'm afraid the flashing lights might induce a seizure."

"Oh."

"Yeah, but since none of your seizures have been bright-light-induced, we might be in the clear. It's a risk."

"I'm willing to take it," Palmer told him.

"We'll leave in the morning and be there by dinner. Now go to sleep." He kissed the tip of her nose and turned onto his back. Without any hesitation, he lifted his arm, and she moved into her favorite position, that sweet spot between the crook of his neck and his collarbone.

"Good night, Kent."

"Sweet dreams, Palmer."

Before I'm Gone

♥ Sit in the front seat of a roller coaster and feel the wind in my hair

♥ ~~Eat tacos or tortillas from a roadside stand in New Mexico~~

♥ Shop at a large farmers market

♥ Meet Lana Del Rey and see her in concert

♥ Take a picture of the most-painted shed in the US

♥ ~~Sit in the sand and watch the sunrise in Cape Cod~~

♥ ~~Take the steps to the Lincoln Memorial~~

♥ Do yoga in Sedona

♥ Tour and feed animals in a wildlife sanctuary

♥ Stand under a waterfall

♥ See Elvis on the street corner in Las Vegas

♥ Hug an elephant

♥ ~~Find my family~~

♥ Step on grapes and make wine

♥ Run through a wheat field

♥ Drive Route 66

♥ See the marquees on Broadway

♥ Ring the Liberty Bell

♥ Buy a quilt from an Amish stand

★ See the northern lights in Minnesota

★ ~~Visit Plymouth Rock~~

★ ~~Touch Babe Ruth's bat~~

★ ~~Travel the Loneliest Road~~

★ ~~Visit the Muhammad Ali Center~~

★ ~~Dance in the rain with someone I love~~

★ Take the ferry to the Statue of Liberty

★ Check out the Grand Canyon

★ Take every picture I can of Palmer ✓✓✓✓✓✓✓

★ Make Palmer smile ✓✓✓✓✓✓✓

- ~~*Eat chowdah in Boston, per Palmer*~~
- *Eat pizza in Chicago*
- *Try frozen custard in New York City*
- *Get coffee in each city* ✓✓✓✓

Thirty-Six

As odd as it sounded, Kent and Palmer were in a routine. They woke, got into their rental, and ate breakfast on the road, and while Kent drove, Palmer wrote in her journal. They were both quiet until the coffee kicked in. It was safe to say that Kent and Palmer were not morning people.

An hour after leaving Raúl's, with breakfast tacos in hand, Palmer closed her journal and opened the top to let the sunshine in. It would only be able to stay open for a couple of hours. It was already warm out, with the temperatures rising, and it would be too hot later to keep it open. Palmer reclined and closed her eyes. Kent glanced at her quickly and smiled. She lay there with the biggest smile on her face, and he couldn't help but match the gesture.

Kent reached for the bag of breakfast tacos, took one out, and worked to unwrap it while driving. He moaned as he bit in and chewed.

"Are you eating without me?" Palmer popped up and scared Kent, even though he'd heard her. He hadn't expected her to move so quickly.

"No, just testing to make sure they're not poisonous."

"Really? That's the excuse you're going with, Wagner?"

This banter from Palmer was new, and Kent liked it a lot. It might have had something to do with the gummies Raúl had given her. Kent didn't care either way. She was happy, and that in turn made him happy. "I mean . . ." He tried to shrug, but that only brought the taco closer to his mouth, and he couldn't resist eating the rest of it—including the piece of parchment paper he bit off.

"I have half a mind to throw these out." Palmer held the bag up and then started laughing.

"What's so funny? Is there something on my face?"

Palmer set the bag in her lap. "No, your face is perfect," she told him. "Your smile caught me off guard."

"What? Why?" Kent asked. He worked to keep the grin there just for her.

"I don't know, you seem different this morning. Almost like you're free of something."

Kent shrugged. "I have no idea, but if whatever it is keeps you looking at me like that, I hope it stays forever."

"Me too," she said quietly. Palmer's attention drifted toward the bag on her lap. She took out a taco, unwrapped it, and handed it to Kent, and then did the same for herself. She finished one, which was the most breakfast she'd eaten in some time. A couple of bites here and there was the most Kent could get out of her lately.

After Kent devoured the bag of tacos, he found a place for them to pull over and rest for a bit. The rest stop had a nice shady area, and he laid a blanket out on the ground, under a massive oak tree, for him and Palmer. He lay on the ground while Palmer sat up against him. Once again, she had her journal out.

"How's our list coming?" Kent asked.

Palmer looked off into the distance and absentmindedly pulled the loose-leaf sheet of paper out from the front of her journal. "I've marked off the ones we've done and added some we've mentioned in passing. It seems we have more to do, and not much time to do them in."

Kent swallowed hard and fought back the urge to cry. He cleared his throat before he even tried to speak. "What do you write about in there?" he asked and then quickly followed with "Don't answer that. I'm sorry for prying."

"You're not prying." She closed the book and set it on the blanket. "I write about the things I've seen or experienced. I write about a song we listened to or what the clouds looked like in a certain town. Sometimes I write about things I want to do and I'll never get a chance to do."

Kent rolled onto his side, and Palmer adjusted. "I told you I'd teach you how to drive."

"I don't care to learn."

"Oh. Did you write about enjoying those gummies from Raúl?" Kent teased.

"I wrote how they make me feel better and how I don't feel so much pain."

"That's good. I should've thought about them earlier."

"I appreciate them now."

He motioned toward the book. "What else do you want to share?"

She shook her head. "Nothing. It's embarrassing."

"There isn't anything you could say or put down on paper that should be embarrassing for you, especially where I'm concerned."

Palmer picked her book up and flipped through the pages. She cleared her throat and read:

We're on our way to Las Vegas, the place I once thought would be where I got married. Having no family, I figured the Little White Chapel would be a great place. Little did I know that the one relationship I had wouldn't last long enough to get to that point.

Palmer closed the book and set it aside. She pulled her knees to her chest and hugged them.

"You wanted to get married in Vegas?" Kent asked, and Palmer nodded. "So, let's do it."

Palmer's wide eyes met Kent's, and she shook her head slightly. "What? Don't be silly."

"Do I look like I'm joking?"

She didn't answer and turned away.

"Seriously, look at me." Kent waited, and when Palmer didn't budge, he adjusted, giving her no choice but to look at him. "Have I ever said something that I didn't mean?"

Palmer looked off into the distance and shook her head. "This is wholly different than agreeing to take me on a trip."

"First off, I didn't agree to do anything. I asked you, remember? And second, I'm asking you this as well." Kent got onto one knee. He may not have had a ring to give to her, but being on bended knee felt important. "I know this seems a bit unconventional, but this feels right. Palmer Sinclair, will you marry me?"

Palmer vehemently shook her head. "Sit down, you're embarrassing me." Kent reluctantly sat. Their gazes met, and Kent saw so much turmoil in Palmer's eyes that his heart broke. He caressed her cheek. "You're not in love with me, Kent. I don't want you to think you have to give me everything. I've said from day one, I didn't want any pity. I've accepted my fate, and I'm okay with it."

Kent scooted under Palmer and wrapped her legs around his waist. "I can think of a million things to say right now, but something tells me you wouldn't believe a single one of them. So, I'm going to be blunt. Palmer, I fell in love with you back in DC. I've been too afraid to tell you because I didn't want you to tell me my feelings were misguided. Every day, I've thought about kissing you to show you how much you mean to me, but I didn't know how you'd react. It's been a struggle to keep my hands to myself when you're lying next to me, when all I want to do is be with you."

Palmer's breathing hitched, and a small gasp escaped. She covered her mouth, making Kent wonder if she was at least smiling.

"So, believe me when I ask if you'll marry me, it's because I *want* to marry you. I *want* to be your person, Palmer."

Tears streamed down her cheeks. Kent wiped them away as best he could. "I'm dying."

"Don't you think I know that?" he retorted. "Every day I see a little bit of you slipping away from me, and it kills me that I can't do anything about it. Every day I see the light dim from your eyes and you fighting like hell to stay in this world. Every day, Palmer, I tell myself that today's the day—we're going to sit down and write out your requests—and I struggle with how I'm supposed to ask you—who takes care of you after you're gone?" Kent cried as he spoke. He had no idea what was supposed to happen to Palmer after she died. Was he supposed to leave her at the hospital and go home like nothing had ever happened? He never wanted to bring the subject up because it made Palmer's impending death so much more real.

"I want to be your person, Palmer," he reiterated. "I want to hold you in my arms when you take your last breath. I want to be the one who takes your body to your final resting place. I want to be your husband, and you my wife, even if it's for one day, one week, or one month, because it'll be worth it."

Palmer never took her eyes off him as he spoke, even through the copious tears. She cried hard as she nodded and mouthed, "Yes."

"Let me hear you say it. Will you marry me?" Third time's a charm.

"Yes," she said. "I'll marry you." She went to hug him, but he stopped her. "What's wrong?"

"Nothing." He looked into her eyes, wiped away her tears, and cupped her cheeks. "I love you, Palmer." With those words, he brushed his lips against hers. Softly at first until she responded in kind. Her hands gripped his wrists, as if she needed to hang on to him. She gasped and shivered when his tongue traced the outline of her lips until they parted.

Kent moved slowly, confidently. When she opened for him, his world exploded in a prism of emotion. He had never felt this way about anyone. He felt his need for her grow and his love for her deepen as she molded her mouth to his. Her fingers trailed up his arms and over his shoulders until her palms pressed against his cheeks. Kent smiled as her fingers brushed against his stubble, and he worried about giving her razor burn. He pulled away and rested his forehead against hers.

Their breathing labored, they sat there on the ground, with her on his lap, unaware of their surroundings.

"I've wanted to do that for the longest time."

"Me too."

"Ah, don't tell me that," he said jokingly. "I hate thinking we've wasted time."

"None of this time has been wasted, Kent."

He pressed his lips to hers again. As much as he wanted to make out, he wanted to get them back on the road to Las Vegas. They now had a wedding to plan. "We should get going." He tapped her hip, a signal to stand. He held her hand while she climbed off his lap and then stood. They folded the blanket together and then walked back to the car, holding hands.

"This used to be my favorite part of the day," he said as he held their linked hands up. "I have looked for every excuse possible to hold your hand. It fits perfectly in mine. Don't you think?" He turned their hands from side to side, showing her how perfect they were.

"I like it too," she said.

Kent helped her into the car, stowed the blanket, and then got behind the wheel. He handed Palmer his phone and told her what to look up. "I think we should stay at the Paris," he said as he pulled out of the parking lot. "All the hotels have wedding packages, so if they don't have a room, we'll go to another hotel."

"What do we need a package for?"

"The package is one of those all-inclusive things. They'll give us the flowers, photography, the venue, and champagne. Remember how I said the New York–New York has a roller coaster?" Palmer nodded. "Well, the Paris has the Eiffel Tower. We can get married at the top."

"And make it seem like we went to France."

"Or there are other hotels. Look around on my phone and find one you like."

"What if they're booked?"

Kent laughed. "Then Elvis it is."

Palmer put her glasses on and started scrolling. Every so often she would ask Kent a question, but he left the details up to her. His mind raced with how he was going to find her a ring and a dress. He wanted her to have and wear both. Getting married in the clothes they'd traveled in for weeks on end didn't sit well with him. They didn't need anything fancy. Call him old fashioned—he wanted a ring on Palmer's left hand, and he wanted to see her in a wedding dress.

Each time she called someone, Kent smiled. After every phone call, she'd tell him what they'd discussed and then leave a voice memo on his phone.

"The lady I spoke to says we need a marriage license from the licensing bureau before we can get married. What time will we be there?"

"Two hours, so that'll be our first stop," Kent said. He'd picked up speed after the rest stop, eager to get to Las Vegas. He wanted this. He wanted to be her husband, and the sooner they could get it done, the happier he would be.

Palmer made a couple more phone calls and then finally had a plan. She excitedly told Kent, "The only opening the Little White Chapel has is tonight at ten p.m. I booked it."

Kent fist pumped. He now had time to get the provisions he needed. "Did you find us a room?" He had heard her say a couple of times that they were coming to Vegas to get married and wondered if the person on the other end had given Palmer any special treatment or accommodations.

"Yes, at the Paris. I asked for a room with a view of the fountains. I've always wanted to see them."

"You'll have front-row viewing," he told her. "We'll go there tonight."

Palmer put the phone down and looked at Kent. He smiled and struggled to keep his eyes on the road. "Thank you."

"For what?" he asked. Kent kept his head on a swivel when all he wanted to do was stare at Palmer.

"For being this kind, generous person."

Kent took Palmer's hand and kissed it, and then kissed her ring finger. Soon enough, he'd put a ring there, giving her something to look at and remember until the end of her days. He held her hand in his lap and continued to drive.

"I forgot to tell you something."

"What's that?" he asked.

"That I love you."

Kent's smile turned into an ear-to-ear grin. As much as he wanted to pull over and kiss her, he couldn't. They had important plans, and time was of the essence. "Best damn words I've ever heard," he told her as he once again kissed her ring finger.

Before I'm Gone

♥ Sit in the front seat of a roller coaster and feel the wind in my hair

♥ ~~Eat tacos or tortillas from a roadside stand in New Mexico~~

♥ Shop at a large farmers market

♥ Meet Lana Del Rey and see her in concert

♥ Take a picture of the most-painted shed in the US

♥ ~~Sit in the sand and watch the sunrise in Cape Cod~~

♥ ~~Take the steps to the Lincoln Memorial~~

♥ Do yoga in Sedona

♥ Tour and feed animals in a wildlife sanctuary

♥ Stand under a waterfall

♥ See Elvis on the street corner in Las Vegas

♥ Hug an elephant

♥ ~~Find my family~~

♥ Step on grapes and make wine

♥ Run through a wheat field

♥ Drive Route 66

♥ See the marquees on Broadway

♥ Ring the Liberty Bell

♥ Buy a quilt from an Amish stand

★ *See the northern lights in Minnesota*

★ ~~*Visit Plymouth Rock*~~

★ ~~*Touch Babe Ruth's bat*~~

★ ~~*Travel the Loneliest Road*~~

★ ~~*Visit the Muhammad Ali Center*~~

★ ~~*Dance in the rain with someone I love*~~

★ *Take the ferry to the Statue of Liberty*

★ *Check out the Grand Canyon*

★ *Take every picture I can of Palmer* ✓✓✓✓✓✓✓

★ *Make Palmer smile* ✓✓✓✓✓✓✓

- ~~*Eat chowdah in Boston, per Palmer*~~
- *Eat pizza in Chicago*
- *Try frozen custard in New York City*
- *Get coffee in each city* ✓✓✓✓
- *Get married in Las Vegas!!!!!!!!!!!*

Thirty-Seven

As soon as they arrived in Las Vegas, they went straight to the licensing bureau. Palmer had read online that the lines could be long, depending on how many people were trying to "pull off a quickie"—the website's words, not hers.

Kent stood, while Palmer sat, in line for what felt like hours. The licensing bureau had four of their ten windows open, and each couple seemed to take their sweet time filling out their paperwork. Kent had already filled theirs out, so all they had to do was sign it in front of the clerk, show their identification, and pay the fee, and then they'd be on their way to the hotel.

Palmer sighed, and Kent tilted her chair back to plant a kiss on her lips. He kissed her every chance he got, whether it was when he parked the car or helped her into the chair. Even if he had to pause pushing her to lean down for a quick nip at her lips, Kent took every conceivable opportunity to kiss Palmer.

She giggled, like a smitten high schooler. "One of these days, you're going to tip me over," she said, even though she didn't believe he'd ever do anything like that. Honestly, she sort of liked it when he acted a bit crazy, because normally he treated her like a fragile flower. Sure, her body had weakened over time, but she still had some life left in her.

"I'd catch you." He did it again, and this time it was longer. The upside-down kiss was awkward, but she secretly loved it. If she did anything for the rest of her life, she was going to kiss him as much as he'd let her. Kent made her feel like she didn't have a care in the world, that she wasn't facing death's door.

When it was finally their turn, Kent helped her out of her chair, and they stood side by side while the clerk processed their paperwork. After all that waiting, it took them only fifteen minutes to get their license, and then they were out the door. Kent walked hurriedly through the halls to get them outside. She suspected he had something up his sleeve, but she hadn't found the nerve to ask him why he was in such a hurry. Their ceremony wasn't until later. They didn't need to rush.

"Hang on to that paper," Kent said when they got to the car. Palmer got into the passenger seat and held the envelope with their license to her chest. There wasn't anything in the world that could pry that away from her. Except for Kent.

He drove down the Las Vegas Strip, pointing out each hotel as they passed. Kent talked about having dinner in Italy later and taking a gondola ride, since they were sleeping in France. He cracked up at his jokes. Palmer liked that she could have a little bit of authenticity in Vegas. It gave their stop even more meaning.

They waited in another line after they had the Jeep valeted at the Paris Las Vegas Hotel & Casino. When Kent got to the front and gave his name, he asked, "We're getting married tonight and forgot our wedding attire back home. Is there a place where I can get a suit and my fiancée can get a dress?"

"We actually have a place right in the hotel," the clerk said as she wrote the name of the boutique down on a card. She then gave Kent and Palmer instructions on how to get to their suite.

"Wow," Palmer said when they entered the room. She got out of the chair and walked gingerly to the window. They were on the twentieth floor, and the view was absolutely stunning. "I think we should sleep with the curtains open tonight."

Kent came up behind her and moved her hair off her shoulder. He kissed the soft angle of her neck before wrapping his arms around her waist. "What an amazing view." Palmer was certain Kent hadn't even looked out the window yet. They stayed like that for a moment, until he told her they had stuff to do. Tomorrow, they could stare at the view.

Palmer walked behind the wheelchair and pushed it for a bit while Kent walked next to her. She wanted to stretch her legs, and the carpeted hallway seemed like the best place to do it. When the carpet turned to marble, she happily sat down and let Kent take over.

The hotel was abuzz with noise, lights, and cigarette smoke from the casino. All things that worried Kent. Thankfully, they headed away from where most of the people congregated. They found the boutique, went in, and were greeted by the clerk.

"Welcome, I'm Mabel. What can I do for you?"

"I'm Kent, and this is my fiancée, Palmer." He smiled lovingly at Palmer and then looked back at Mabel. "We're getting married tonight and need something to wear."

"Congratulations. If you want to head next door, Grady will help you with your suit."

Kent looked from Mabel to Palmer. She saw the hesitation on his face. She put her hand on his chest and persuaded Kent to look at her. "I feel really good right now. I'll be okay," she told him. He nodded quickly and gave her a kiss. The torment he felt by leaving her was evident on his face.

Palmer followed Mabel to a rack of dresses. Mabel guessed Palmer's size and showed her everything available. She touched each dress, rubbing her fingers over the fabric. When she lived in the home, she and the other girls would check out bridal magazines from the nearby library and dog-ear the dresses they liked. Palmer changed her mind a lot. Sometimes her favorite would be strapless or have a high neck and long train, or it would be the mermaid design and sparkles. She was never sure until now.

"I'd like to try this one on." She held out a white satin dress with a high slit. The sleeveless gown tied at the shoulders and had a white ribbon belt. Kent would love the simplicity of the dress.

Palmer followed Mabel into the dressing room and thanked her. Trying on a wedding dress felt daunting. She ran her hand over the gown and loved the way the material felt to the touch. Palmer undressed and slipped the dress over her head. Due to her weight loss, she wouldn't need to unzip her dress to get it off or on. She opened the curtain and stepped out to a waiting Mabel.

"Oh wow, you look stunning."

Palmer blushed, even though she suspected Mabel told every woman she looked stunning. It was her job to make women feel beautiful. Mabel motioned for Palmer to step up onto the pedestal and turn to face the multiple full-length mirrors. As soon as she saw herself, she gasped. The dress fit her perfectly.

"I told you, stunning." Mabel brushed her hands down the dress and tightened the belt at her waist. "Your fiancé is a very lucky man."

Palmer met Mabel's eyes in the mirror and shook her head. "I'm the lucky one. I know people say that all the time, but this time it's true. If it wasn't for Kent, I wouldn't be here right now. He's saved me more times than I can count."

"Well, you're both lucky. I'll give you a minute."

Mabel excused herself and left Palmer alone, giving her time to soak everything in. Palmer stepped off the pedestal and moved closer to the mirror. She played with her hair, pulling it up and then letting it drop and moving it to one shoulder, and then the other. She'd only imagined this day and had never thought it would come to fruition, especially in her condition. What Kent had done for her—what he was doing for her—went way above fulfilling her bucket list. Getting married was a dream she'd had as a little girl, back when she still believed in the fairy tale of life. A few aspects were missing, of course, like a dad walking her down the aisle, and a set of parents looking on proudly and with admiration, but the result would be the same. Palmer was going to get married to the man of her dreams. He wanted to be her husband, and that was more than she could've ever asked for.

Palmer sashayed from side to side and watched as her dress swished. She loved everything about her gown, but it was the way it made her feel that stood out the most to her. She finally felt beautiful. Kent had told her she was, but she hadn't seen herself until this moment.

As much as she wanted to wear her dress out of the store, she knew that was impossible. Palmer went into the dressing room to change her clothes and to rest for a minute. She wanted to keep as much strength as possible because tonight was going to be the most important and special day of her life. Once dressed, she opened the curtain and found Mabel standing there with a garment bag. She reluctantly handed Mabel the dress and followed her to the front, where Kent waited. As soon as she saw him, her entire demeanor changed. She had felt happy and reserved earlier, but now pure elation flowed through her. That man was going to be her husband. He was going to promise her tomorrow as man and wife.

"Hey." Her voice was soft and excited. She was happy to see him.

"Hey, did you find a dress?"

She nodded and bit her lower lip. "I think you'll like it."

"You could wear your blue sweatpants and I'd still want to marry you." He laughed.

"What about you, did you find a suit?"

Kent glanced at his shoulder, where his finger held a coat hanger. "I did. I think you'll like it." Palmer raised her eyebrows. Kent rolled his eyes. "I know, I know, you'd marry me if I was wearing your blue sweatpants."

Palmer laughed. She wanted to tell him she preferred the outfit he wore when he got out of the shower but couldn't bring herself to be that forward. Kent's flirting had increased greatly since he'd kissed her. Palmer wasn't there yet. She hoped to be soon, though, because there was something she wanted to ask him.

Mabel handed Palmer her dress and told her the charge had been added to their hotel bill. She wished them well as they left her store. Palmer held the garment while Kent maneuvered them through the hordes of people coming from and going to the casino, or any other part of the hotel. He directed them toward the front and turned in to a salon. Palmer looked over her shoulder and expected Kent to answer her silent question. Instead, he wheeled her up to the counter, gave the woman her name, and then looked down at her.

"Robbie is going to do your hair and makeup." Kent winked, kissed her nose, and proclaimed he'd be in the casino trying to win some money and to enjoy her pampering. Palmer's mouth dropped open, but she couldn't form a sentence. Leave it to Kent to think of everything, because she would've put on some eye shadow, curled the ends of her hair, and called it good.

Robbie washed Palmer's hair. The head massage was almost enough to put Palmer to sleep. In fact, she rejoiced when Robbie reclined her chair and told her to keep her eyes closed. While someone did Palmer's makeup, someone else did her fingers and toes. Palmer missed her weekly massages and her chiropractor. Those were the appointments she enjoyed going to.

While she lay there, she questioned her life and the choices she'd made. Would she be where she was now if she had chosen differently? Her heart said no, but her mind didn't agree. She was about to get married because she was dying, because of her bucket list. Without the tumor, there would be no Kent. Without Maeve being pregnant and married to another man, there would be no Kent. Everything Palmer had now was simply because two worlds had collided at the same time. If she had chosen the surgery or chemotherapy, she'd be in hospice right now, depending on others to take care of her. She wouldn't be in Las Vegas about to get married or have traveled parts of the country she'd only seen on television. No, Palmer had made the right choice for her—she'd chosen to live.

"Hey now, no crying on your wedding day," Robbie said softly in her ear. She dabbed at Palmer's tears and told her everything would be perfect.

Life wasn't perfect. Palmer knew this. She had lived it, and now she wanted more than anything to go back in time and put her foot forward when she'd first met Kent. He was nothing more than a client, a loan number who made his monthly payments on time. It never would've crossed her mind, all those years ago, to introduce herself socially instead of professionally. She never would've been so bold and brazen as to give him her number or ask him out for coffee. To her that would've been unprofessional, and Palmer never would've done anything to embarrass herself in such a way. Yet maybe if she had, she'd still be here, but not dying. Surely, having someone in your life, fighting for you, meant you sought help when your first headache wouldn't go away.

"Okay, let's stop for a moment," Robbie said. She sat Palmer up, and she opened her eyes. She expected to see herself in the mirror, with a red blotchy face, but someone had covered the mirror with a black drape. Someone else brought Palmer some water. She thanked them and took small sips.

"I'm sorry."

"It's okay," Robbie said. "Weddings are emotional. Hell, I started crying three days before mine and didn't stop."

"Happy tears?"

"Oh no, sweetie. I made the biggest mistake of my life. I knew it, too, but I couldn't bring myself to stop the wedding. Another mistake. But it's all good now. I'm with a great man who worships me, just like your man. He was so cute when he came in here to book your appointment."

"He was?"

Robbie nodded. "That man of yours is beaming with love for you. Said for us to make you feel as beautiful as you are. Do you want to know why that stands out over what other men will say?"

"Yeah."

"Most men say 'You look beautiful' after all the makeup is on. Your hubby-to-be wants you to feel beautiful. That's a huge difference."

"He's pretty special."

"We think you're both remarkable." Robbie met Palmer's gaze. "One of my coworkers follows you on Instagram. She showed us your page."

"Oh." Palmer's gaze fell. "So, you know?"

"I think the entire hotel knows. Word spreads pretty fast when there are celebrities around."

Palmer scoffed. "We're far from celebrities."

"That's what you think. Are we ready to try again?"

Palmer took a deep breath and nodded. "I'll try to keep my tears under lock and key."

"If you need a break, just let me know." Robbie signaled to her coworkers. She leaned Palmer back in the chair, told her to close her eyes, and went to work on her makeup.

When the team finished with Palmer, they sat her up. "Promise me you won't cry?" Robbie asked.

"I'll try," she told her.

Robbie pulled the drape and helped Palmer stand. In the mirror, staring back, was the woman Palmer had always wanted to be.

THIRTY-EIGHT

Kent's mouth dropped open when he and Palmer locked gazes. She smiled and twirled for him, even though all she'd done was her hair and makeup. She wiggled her fingers for him to see the soft-pink color she'd chosen for her nails. Robbie's words replayed in her mind, about how Kent thought Palmer was beautiful with or without any makeup, but seeing him take her all in, while still dressed in her clothes from earlier, made her feel like the most beautiful woman in the world, and not just in his eyes.

"I can't wait to see you in your dress," he told her when she came closer to him.

"Should I go put it on now?"

"No, we have a limo picking us up to take us to the chapel. We'll change there. Then I'll get to see you for the first time when you walk down the aisle."

"We do?" While she was surprised, she knew she shouldn't have been. Kent was making this a very real wedding for her. She was concerned about walking down the aisle without help. But she didn't want to say anything out of fear she would ruin the moment.

"Yeah," he said without taking his eyes off hers. "Are you tired, or do you want to go do something fun?"

"I'm up for some fun, but I need coffee." Kent nodded, and Palmer got into her chair and held on to their wedding attire. They waited in a small line for coffee, not far from the salon, and took their drinks upstairs. Palmer wanted to change out of her clothes and put something fresh on.

Palmer came out of the bathroom and walked quietly toward Kent. Dusk had settled over the desert city, and everything glowed in a plethora of neon lights. She had never seen something like this before. Kent stood there, facing the large window in their room, with his hands in his pockets. From the day he'd shown up at her apartment, with her list, he had changed her life. She would die happy and loved because of him.

"Okay, I'm ready." Palmer had put on a sleeveless sundress. Her once-pale skin had been tanned by the sun, which she was thankful for. She wouldn't be a ghost at her wedding later.

Kent took his position behind her chair and pushed her down the hall. "Did you win any money?" she asked.

"I didn't end up playing," he told her as they stepped into the elevator. "I walked around for a bit, came back to the room, took a shower, and then waited for you. How was your appointment?"

"It was very nice. Robbie was very attentive. Thank you for setting it up for me."

"Of course. Every bride needs to be pampered on her wedding day."

They exited into the casino, and Palmer instantly put her head down to avoid the lights. When they stopped walking, she looked up and saw the sign for the Eiffel Tower and looked over her shoulder. "I thought we were doing this later?"

"Slight change of plans" was all Kent said as he went through the double doors and onto the bridge that led to the Eiffel Tower. The tile walkway made for a bumpy ride, and Palmer thought about asking Kent to stop so she could walk but saw that they were almost at the end.

"Good evening," a photographer said as Kent and Palmer approached them. Kent stopped and held his hand out for Palmer to take. She did, and he led her to the side. They were only a story or two off the ground, but the view was still amazing. "If you'll turn, I'll take your photo now."

They turned, and Kent pulled Palmer into his side. They smiled for the camera. The photographer told them their photo would be ready at the stand when they came down from the viewing deck.

Palmer chose to walk and explained that the uneven pathway made her nauseous, which Kent said he understood. He apologized for not thinking ahead. They walked to the end of the walkway and waited for their elevator.

The doors opened, and they stepped in. Palmer went to the back and prepared herself for what she was about to see. Kent stood behind her, locking her in place with his arms. Palmer told herself he did this because he loved her, and for one day she was going to pretend she didn't have a tumor taking over her brain.

They stepped off when they reached the observation deck and went right to the first opening. There wasn't a crowd, which pleased both of them. The sunset cast an ominous glow over the city, and it made the surrounding mountains look like they were bathed in orange instead of brown.

"Wow," Palmer said as she sucked in a gust of wind. Kent kept his arm around her waist, and she appreciated him for that. She was also thankful for the hair spray holding her hair together because the wind was determined to ruin her hair.

"I've never seen Vegas from here before," Kent added.

Even with her vision issues, she could see the Strip and the other hotels. To one side, the fountains looked like this tiny burst of water and not the powerful jet streams they were. They laughed at their hotel being shaped like an X.

"This is what it would almost be like if we'd done the Empire State Building," Kent told her. "Only we'd be much higher, and you'd be able to see New Jersey." He turned her around, and she shivered. "We won't stay much longer." Kent dropped to his knee, much like he'd done in the park, but this time he held a black velvet box in his hand. "Palmer Sinclair, will you marry me?" He opened the box, and nestled inside was a solitaire diamond on a gold band.

Everyone around them stopped to watch, and chatter grew among them. Someone recognized them from Instagram, and the chatter turned exceedingly happy.

"What do you say?" Kent prodded.

"Of course, under one condition."

Kent took the ring and slipped it onto her finger. "What's that?"

"That we get married tonight," she said with laughter.

"You've got yourself a deal." He pulled her into his arms while everyone around them cheered. "Come on, we have a reservation." He took her hand and led her to the elevator. The people near them continued to cheer for them, and some had their phones out. Inside the elevator, he said, "Someone will post our engagement online, so we'll at least have that photo to remember today by."

Palmer nodded and rested her head on his shoulder. She held her left hand out and gazed at her ring. It was more than she ever could've wanted or expected. When Kent asked her to marry him, she figured they'd wear whatever they had on and call it good. So far, he'd given her everything he could to make her feel like today was her day.

After getting her chair, they went right to the front, where a limo waited for them. "What about our clothes?"

"Already at the chapel." He winked. She didn't know how he'd done it, and she wasn't going to question him until much later. Palmer was impressed with how organized and thoughtful Kent was and wondered if he'd forgotten anything.

He pulled his phone out and took their picture in the back of the limo and posted it immediately. The comments flooded in, from congratulations to people wondering where the wedding was. Kent went live, and Palmer waved to the camera. "We're on our way to the Little White Chapel to get married," he told the world. "This beautiful woman said she'd marry me today, and I'm not giving her a chance to change her mind." He kissed Palmer for everyone to see. "We'll update you after she's officially become my wife."

The limo pulled into the parking lot at the Little White Chapel, and the driver held the door open for Palmer and Kent. Inside, they were greeted by staff and whisked away to their own dressing rooms. Palmer's attendant helped her change into her dress and handed her a bouquet.

"This is so pretty," she said of the white and red roses.

"Your husband picked it out for you."

"He did?" She looked at the woman in shock. "Wow."

"They're ready to start." The attendant held the door open for Palmer, and she walked out. Down the hall, she could hear music, and she walked a bit faster until she rounded the corner and saw a bunch of people she didn't know, which wasn't saying much, considering she kept her circle rather small. Palmer entered the room, with her attendant right behind her, and paused. There were people there, in the small pews, standing for her.

"They're all here for you."

"But I don't know who they are." She looked around for the only face she wanted to see, and when he came into view, everyone else seemed to disappear. Kent stood next to the minister at the front of the altar, waiting for her, his bride. His hands were clasped, and he rocked on his heels.

"Are you okay?" the attendant asked, and Palmer nodded.

She put one foot forward, and then the next, until her steps became automatic. She lost count of how many steps it took her to reach Kent, but each one was worth it.

"I have never seen someone more breathtakingly exquisite than you," he said when she reached him. "I do not know how I got so damn lucky."

Palmer was speechless. The man who had changed her world, in every way possible, stood before her in a black suit, with a rose pinned to his lapel. The way he looked at her made her knees weak, and the way he made her feel kept her in a constant form of awe.

The minister spoke, and yet Palmer heard nothing until it was time for her to say her lines. She focused on Kent, memorizing every aspect of his face, his voice, and the moment unfolding between them. He would be her husband, and to her that meant something entirely different than it did to other brides. In a matter of weeks or days, no one really knew, he'd make decisions about her health. He would be the one to tell doctors she had a DNR, and what she wanted done with her body. Kent would be the one to fill out her death certificate and close out her accounts. He would be responsible for her. All of her.

She *finally* had someone.

Palmer recited her vows, promising to love and cherish every waking moment she had left with Kent. When it was time to exchange rings, she wasn't surprised when Kent put a black band in her palm to slip onto his ring finger. She held it for a moment and appreciated that it was black. Kent would mourn her when she passed.

"With this ring, I thee wed," she said as she pushed it onto his finger. He had done the same for her, completing her set.

"By the power vested in me, by the great state of Nevada, I now pronounce you husband and wife. Kent, you may kiss your bride."

Kent cupped her cheek and pressed his lips to hers. He then caught her off guard when he dipped her, much to the delight of their internet friends. Everyone cheered and had their cameras out, taking pictures and videos of them as they walked down the aisle.

Outside, they stopped in their tracks when they saw the line of people waiting for them. Everyone clapped and threw rose petals and birdseed as Palmer and Kent hustled to their limo. Tucked safely inside, Kent kissed her again and professed his love for her, which she returned wholeheartedly.

Kent opened the sunroof, and they stood as the driver drove slowly back to the Strip. Their fans lined the street for them, giving them a wedding recessional they had no idea they'd wanted until now.

They waved until the line thinned out and then sat back in the limo. "Now what?" Kent asked. As much as she wanted the night to continue, she was tired, and that likely wouldn't bode well for her later. "I need to rest," she told him, and he agreed. The driver took them back to the hotel and congratulated them.

Kent held their bag of clothes in one hand, and Palmer's hand in his other. They walked slowly to their room, stopping to accept congratulatory comments from everyone who passed by. Women gushed when they saw Palmer's dress, which caused her to blush. She would never get used to the compliments.

Kent opened their hotel room door, threw their bag of clothes in, and then scooped his bride into his arms. He carried her in and held her while she let her eyes wander around the room, soaking up every detail. Red rose petals were on the floor and the bed, and a bottle of sparkling wine chilled on the table, along with a bowl of strawberries. Hanging there, on the outside of the wardrobe, was a white silk nightgown.

"What's this?" she asked after he'd set her down.

"It's a nightgown."

It was more than an ordinary nightgown, in Palmer's opinion. It was sensual and meant to make whoever wore it feel sexy. The deep cut down the middle, the high leg slit, and the appliqué cutouts were meant to entice her husband.

Kent came up behind her and kissed her bare back. "You don't have to wear it, if you don't want to."

"I . . . uh . . . I didn't think."

He turned her around. "I want to be your husband, Palmer. In every way you want me."

Palmer thought about what putting the nightie on would mean and took it from the hanger. She went into the bathroom and closed the door behind her. Every nerve ending in her body was on fire with what waited for her in the bedroom. She wanted to be with Kent, and in a different lifetime would have been more than eager to take him up on his offer, although he wasn't exactly offering her anything, other than being her husband. It was their wedding night, and he wanted to be with her.

She slipped out of her dress and avoided looking at herself in the mirror as she stepped into the nightgown. Palmer pulled the pins holding her hair in place and ran her fingers through her curls. In her mind, she looked sexy, and that was enough encouragement to open the door.

The lights were dim, and soft music played from the speakers. Kent stood in the middle of the room, dressed in black boxers. He came toward her, and she matched his confident steps with her wavering ones.

"I'm nervous," she said as he caressed her cheek with the back of his fingers.

"I'll be gentle," he told her as he left a trail of kisses from her ear, down her neck, and over her shoulder, pulling the strap down as he went. "If you want me to stop, just say the word." His lips ghosted over her skin as his hand bunched the fabric of her nightgown into his fist.

"I'm yours." With those two little words, Kent picked his wife up and carried her to bed.

Before I'm Gone

♥ Sit in the front seat of a roller coaster and feel the wind in my hair

♥ ~~Eat tacos or tortillas from a roadside stand in New Mexico~~

♥ Shop at a large farmers market

♥ Meet Lana Del Rey and see her in concert

♥ Take a picture of the most-painted shed in the US

♥ ~~Sit in the sand and watch the sunrise in Cape Cod~~

♥ ~~Take the steps to the Lincoln Memorial~~

♥ Do yoga in Sedona

♥ Tour and feed animals in a wildlife sanctuary

♥ Stand under a waterfall

♥ See Elvis on the street corner in Las Vegas

♥ Hug an elephant

♥ ~~Find my family~~

♥ Step on grapes and make wine

♥ Run through a wheat field

♥ Drive Route 66

♥ See the marquees on Broadway

♥ Ring the Liberty Bell

♥ Buy a quilt from an Amish stand

★ See the northern lights in Minnesota

★ ~~Visit Plymouth Rock~~

★ ~~Touch Babe Ruth's bat~~

★ ~~Travel the Loneliest Road~~

★ ~~Visit the Muhammad Ali Center~~

★ ~~Dance in the rain with someone I love~~

★ Take the ferry to the Statue of Liberty

★ Check out the Grand Canyon

★ Take every picture I can of Palmer

✓✓✓✓✓✓✓✓✓✓✓✓✓✓✓✓✓ ∞

★ *Make Palmer smile* ✓✓✓✓✓✓✓✓✓✓✓✓✓✓✓✓✓∞

- ~~*Eat chowdah in Boston, per Palmer*~~
- *Eat pizza in Chicago*
- *Try frozen custard in New York City*
- *Get coffee in each city* ✓✓✓✓✓✓
- ~~*Get married in Las Vegas!!!!!*~~

Thirty-Nine

Kent trailed his fingers up and down Palmer's arm, trying to wake her. She'd surprised him by sleeping through the sunrise, which woke him the second a ray burst through between one of the other hotels. He had done as she asked and kept the curtains open while they slept. He hadn't wanted to get out of bed after making love to his wife, but he promised, and he'd be damned if he didn't follow through.

"Mrs. Wagner." He kissed her bare shoulder and she moaned. He smiled against her skin and lifted the blankets so he could move next to her. Yesterday had been a long and tiring day, and he was surprised she'd made it through the night without any issues. Kent pressed his body to hers and continued to coax her out of her deep sleep.

Palmer shifted against Kent and sighed. She put his hand on her breast, which was all the sign he needed from her. He made love to her as the sun rose higher in the sky, slowly and gently. He kept his weight off her weakening body and lavished her with every ounce of attention he could give her. Kent wanted Palmer to know how much he loved her, worshipped her, and treasured their bond. She welcomed him, loved him, and gave everything she had of herself to her husband. They were one, an inseparable pair, at least for the time being.

Basking in their afterglow, they took a bath together and soaked away the ache in her body. Kent held her against his chest and never wanted to let go. There, in their hotel room, they were in a bubble where he could pretend the real world didn't exist. In his fantasy, Palmer wasn't sick, and she was the one carrying his child. There, in the bathroom, nothing could tarnish their happiness.

They dressed and prepared for the day. They didn't have a big agenda but planned to do a couple of sightseeing activities before deciding where to go next. Palmer scrolled through Kent's phone, looking at their wedding pictures from last night. Each one brought a smile to her face, and that smile made Kent want to stay in their room all day and be newlyweds. They could order room service and feed each other. No one said they had to leave. He was about to ask her if she wanted to be naked for the rest of the day when he noticed her expression change.

"What is it?"

"Courtney emailed." Palmer handed the phone to Kent and waited while he read it.

> Dear Palmer (and Kent),
>
> I hope my email finds you well. I apologize for taking this long to respond as I've had a few things going on, but I wanted to let you know that I understand why you left, and I was heartbroken to read about your illness. Life has treated you so unfairly, I can't imagine what you're going through. As much as I wish you had told me when we met, I know why you didn't, and I respect you for that. Palmer, I am deeply sorry and wish I had the power to change things for you. Please, please know that meeting you was one of the highlights of my life, even for those few hours. I hope, in some way, I've been able to offer you the closure you need. Our mother loved you. She looked for you every day of her life, until her last. I pray, that if there's a heaven, she's waiting for you with open arms.

I have another reason for writing. Had you come to my house, I would've told you about my own health issues, one that you probably should've known about, but is really no consequence to you now. I have a rare liver disorder that may or may not be degenerative and had hoped that by finding my sister, we'd be able to test to see if you are a match for a partial donation. Even though you're out there, living your best life, would you be willing to have a biopsy done at one of the Mayo Clinics? I know it's a lot to ask, especially with everything you're going through, and I understand if you're not comfortable. I don't even know if this is possible now with what you're going through. But, if you are, please let me know and I'll set everything up.

If I don't hear from you, know this: meeting my big sister was a dream come true for me. Thank you for bringing yourself to me.

With love,
Courtney

Kent read the email and then set his phone down. Palmer wiped away the tears that had fallen. "She's sick."

"Yeah," Kent said. "What do you want to do?"

Palmer sat there and pondered, while Kent looked up the nearest Mayo Clinic on his phone. Even though he'd asked Palmer what she wanted to do, he knew where they were going. "We can be there in about five hours, depending on traffic."

"I should email her back, right?"

Kent handed Palmer his phone and went to pack their things. Palmer sent Courtney a voice memo telling her they would drive to the clinic today, if she could set up the appointment. It wasn't like time was on their side, especially if Courtney needed this from Palmer.

As they made their way to their car, Kent became irritated, which was irrational to him. It wasn't that they had plans, but he *had* plans with his wife. He felt stuck in a difficult situation. Kent would do anything to make Palmer happy, but he wanted time alone with her, and being in the car for five hours and sitting in a hospital while she got a biopsy wasn't what he had in mind. On the other end of things, Palmer's sister, the only living relative she knew, regardless of how long, needed something from her, and Kent knew how much Palmer wanted to be needed.

They drove in silence until he turned off the highway.

"Where are we going?" she asked.

"We're still on our honeymoon, and I want to show you Hoover Dam."

Palmer lit up. "That's not on the list. I'll add it." She took her journal out of her bag and jotted something down. Again, Kent found himself trying to see what she wrote, but his wife had angled herself in such a way that he couldn't see. Curiosity was about to do him in, though. He wondered if she'd written about him and their wedding night. The thought brought a smile to his face.

"Why are you smiling like that?"

"Just thinking back to last night." He winked. "I'm glad I didn't go all caveman and rip your nightgown off because I like the idea of you wearing it again tonight, and tomorrow, and the next night, and so on."

Palmer leaned her head on Kent's shoulder and closed her eyes. He kept his arm there as he navigated through town to get to the dam. He was certain she'd fallen asleep and wouldn't normally wake her, but he wanted her to experience the dam. They had come all the way to Nevada, and it was a must-visit place.

Kent pulled into the parking garage and found a spot nearest the elevator. Palmer didn't wake right away, which Kent found odd. Earlier, he'd chalked up her inability to wake up to tiredness from the previous day, but they had only been in the car for forty minutes. To him, she should've woken right up. He refused to believe she was anything but tired.

She finally opened her eyes and looked around. Kent reminded her where they were, and it took a moment for their stop to fully register with her. He helped her out of the Jeep and held her arm until she sat down in her chair.

"What do you know about the Hoover Dam?" he asked as they took the elevator down one flight. The sun blazed outside, and he kicked himself for not bringing her some water or a hat. He'd make this trip quick because he had a feeling if they went back to the car, she'd want to leave.

Palmer recited every historical fact about the dam, and even knew things he didn't. He was impressed. They started on the side that held Lake Mead back and marveled at the water. The depth of the valley, the water lines, and the rich blue-green color. Kent hopped from Nevada to Arizona multiple times, while Palmer laughed at him. On the other side, Kent encouraged Palmer to lean forward, but the wind current fought her. She gasped for air, and then did it again.

She looked at him unexpectedly and said, "We didn't go on the coaster."

He shook his head. "We can go back." He wanted to go back to Las Vegas and finish the things on their list but didn't know how to tell her without upsetting her. His only desire to go to Arizona, minus being on the Hoover Dam bridge, was to see the Grand Canyon, which Palmer hadn't put down on her list.

Palmer leaned over the side again and played with the wind. Something told Kent they wouldn't be going back to Vegas, and he had to respect her decision. This trip, regardless of him adding things to their list or not, was about her, and she wanted to help her sister.

On their way back to the car, they stopped at the gift shop. Palmer bought the baby some novelty outfits and a stuffed animal. She hadn't bought nearly the amount of stuff she'd threatened Kent with, and he was sort of sad about it. As much as he didn't have space for extra items, he wanted whatever Palmer planned to give his daughter.

Again, as soon as they were back on the road, Palmer wrote in her journal, and then reclined her seat. "Are you feeling okay?" he asked her, and she nodded.

"I'm just tired."

Kent frowned and reached for her hand. If he couldn't talk to her, he at least wanted to hold her hand while she slept. It took her a while to fall asleep, which he appreciated. She ran her fingers up and down his arm and sat up a couple of times to kiss his cheek.

"Thank you."

"For what?" he asked her.

"For changing our plans and doing so without reservation. I know it means more to me than you, to help Courtney out."

Kent kissed her hand. "I think what you're doing is admirable, but I'll be honest, I don't like the idea of you getting a biopsy. Something invasive like this. I feel it's unnecessary and a risk." He paused and shook his head. "Going to a hospital in your condition, I'm afraid they're going to fight me when it's time to leave."

"Maybe they won't ask if I have any health issues."

Kent scoffed. "Unless you lie on the intake form, you'll tell them. I'll tell them. You could code on the table, Palmer." He shook his head. The more he thought about this, the more he hated the idea. She could die in a room with complete strangers, and because of her DNR, he wouldn't be able to say goodbye to her.

"We should talk about that," she said quietly. It was the last thing he wanted to talk about, but he agreed. "In your phone, in the notes section, is the name of my lawyer. I've spoken to him on the phone and had him put you down as my beneficiary. I don't have much, just the apartment, really, and a small retirement from the bank. After . . ." She took a shuddering breath. "Call him, and he'll take care of everything. You can sell the apartment if you don't want to keep it. My payment isn't bad."

"I just want you," he said as tears escaped from his eyes. He slammed his hand against the steering wheel in frustration. Life was becoming too real, too fast.

Palmer played with the hair at the nape of his neck. "Me too," she told him. "Before it's too late, you should know, I don't have a plot or anything, and before . . . well, I thought the state would cremate me and that would be that, but I'd still like to be cremated but in my wedding dress, if you don't mind."

Kent signaled to pull over. He couldn't drive and listen to her anymore. As soon as he was safely stopped on the side of the road, he unbuckled her and pulled her into his arms. He held her while he cried into the crook of her neck and begged her not to leave him. Kent was certain the doctors in San Francisco had made a mistake and this entire time she had something curable, because no one would be so cruel as to take her away from him.

Palmer held her husband and soaked up his tears. The conversation was something she had to have with him before it was too late. He knew this but didn't want to accept the elephant in the room. Where they were headed could change everything for them. He didn't want to fight anyone on keeping her bedridden because that was something neither of them wanted. When they got to the Mayo Clinic, it would be for the biopsy and nothing else.

After a half hour of sitting on the side of the road, he finally calmed down enough to drive. He was thankful when she reclined in her seat and went to sleep because that gave him time to think about a plan of action. If her time was near, he wanted to make sure her best days were yet to come.

FORTY

While Kent loved his job as a paramedic, he hated hospitals. He loved treating people and saving lives and moving on to the next. He had never been invested in a patient before—that was until he met Palmer. She changed him. Kent couldn't pinpoint the one thing or moment when everything shifted for him—it might have been a culmination of the events surrounding Maeve, and Kent finding Palmer's list, or it could've been when she'd told him she had no one. He'd always had someone, whether it was his parents, his army unit, or the people he worked with. Kent always had someone he could call if he needed anyone. To have no one had to be the loneliest feeling in the world. Palmer had him now. He would be her champion.

They sat in a hospital room, waiting for a surgeon to come in and do the biopsy Kent didn't want Palmer to do. The stress that occupied any medical procedure wasn't good for her and could cause a seizure. She could convulse on the table, and then what? He'd be in a fight to get her out of there—against doctor's orders. He had hoped Courtney wouldn't be able to pull off a quick appointment, that the clinic would tell them to come back in a few weeks—they didn't have weeks.

Kent had never seen someone die the way Palmer was. Her tumor was killing her slowly. Bit by bit, the octopus was eating up any free space left in her brain. At times, Kent marveled at Palmer's will to live because on the outside, he could see it slowly taking her life, and she was either seemingly unaware or was fighting with what might she had left.

Palmer slept in the hospital bed while Kent sat on the window ledge, watching her. Once they'd put her in the gown for the procedure, she'd told them she was cold. At first, Kent thought it was a ploy to get some warm blankets, but then he touched her and realized she was freezing. Another sign, he told himself. They were starting to add up and not in his favor.

As he sat there, watching her sleep, he wondered if he himself had made the right decision by not encouraging her to seek treatment. If he had, they wouldn't be where they were right now. Not in Arizona, waiting for some test, and definitely not married. His entire existence these past months was a result of the one decision she'd made.

When they'd met with the staff earlier, and Palmer had given them her diagnosis, they wanted to run every test possible to see if they could help her. Palmer and Kent knew there wasn't anything anyone could do, but doctors are insistent. They think they can fix everyone, and when someone walks into your clinic, telling you they're fine with dying, there's no way you'll believe them.

That was when Kent became Palmer's champion. Her voice when the doctors wouldn't listen. They were there for the biopsy and nothing else, and once the five-minute procedure was concluded, they'd be out of there. Kent still had a tough time grasping why they were there. If she had the disease, what was she going to do, seek treatment? Tell her sister? What was the purpose?

The door opened, and a team of three walked in. Kent went to Palmer and gently woke her. It was taking longer than normal for her to wake, and that bothered Kent. He leaned next to her ear and said, "Honey, it's time to wake up." This was the first time he'd used a pet name for her, and he wasn't sure if he liked it or not, although it was entirely fitting. It took a little more coaxing from him for her to finally rouse. She looked around the room and blinked rapidly.

"We're at the clinic. Remember?" Kent recognized the panicked look on her face. "Hey, look at me." She did and smiled when he came into view. "Do you know where you are?" He hated having this conversation in front of people who didn't know her.

Palmer shook her head slowly.

"Courtney needs your help," he said, hoping she'd remember Courtney. "The doctor is going to take a sample of your liver, and then they're going to test it to see if it can help her."

"O-okay," she stammered. "Will it hurt?"

Kent shook his head. "No. Just a little pinch in your side, and then we'll be all done, and we can go to the Grand Canyon."

The Grand Canyon wasn't on her list. She had an irrational fear that she would fall over the edge if she went, but Kent assured her he'd never let that happen to her.

"Okay."

Kent motioned for the doctor to continue, and when he asked Kent to step out of the room, he refused. "I'm not leaving her."

The doctor motioned for the nurse to prep Palmer. Kent stayed by her head and talked to her through the setup and then the procedure. "Look at you, so strong and brave," he told her, even though he could barely keep it together. "I love you."

"I love you." Palmer never took her eyes off Kent, and when the procedure was over, he sighed heavily.

"We'll have the results in a few days," the doctor said as they exited the room. Once the door closed, Kent helped Palmer dress. She stood and instantly collapsed to the ground. He caught her before her head hit the floor.

"Head." Palmer could barely say the word before vomiting bile all over the floor. Kent reached for the nurses' button and pressed it. He helped Palmer onto the bed and fought the urge to cry. In a matter of hours, she had gone from doing okay to this, and he wasn't ready. She had just become his wife—they were supposed to have more time.

The nurse came in, saw the mess, and told Kent she'd send someone in to clean it up. She moved Kent out of the way and checked Palmer's vitals. Her pulse was low, and she suggested that Palmer stay in bed.

Kent said nothing until she left. He scooped his wife up and carried her out of the clinic. As far as he was concerned, she wasn't a patient.

After he'd secured her in the car, he sat outside and called Dr. Hughes and explained where they were and why, and how he thought Palmer was entering her last stage of life. When she asked what the plan was, he told her he didn't know, but he would keep her informed. Kent and Palmer hadn't talked about the period before she died, only after. He knew what she wanted to do with her body, but what about the moments beforehand?

When he got into the Jeep, he was surprised to find her staring at him. "Hey." He caressed her cheek and noticed how dry her lips were. She needed water or ginger ale. Kent reached into the back and grabbed a bottle of water. He held it while she sipped. She wasn't drinking nearly enough to maintain any sort of hydration, and it showed.

"Are you hungry?" He knew the answer before he even asked.

She shook her head.

"How about some soup?"

"Okay."

Kent searched the mapping system for a restaurant. It took him a couple of tries until he found one with chicken noodle soup. He placed a to-go order and headed there to get it. They ate in the car, mostly because Kent didn't want people staring at Palmer. She didn't look well, and she would be embarrassed.

Palmer surprised Kent by eating most of her soup and asking where they were going. Kent refused to look a gift horse in the mouth and took full advantage of the moment.

"The Grand Canyon," he told her.

"Right, I remember." She looked out the window and sighed. "Do you think I helped Courtney?"

"I hope so. We'll know soon." Kent wanted the call from the Mayo Clinic to come now, while Palmer had some lucidity left.

"That would be nice."

Kent discarded their garbage and then set their GPS to head north, back to where they'd come from. As soon as they got on the road, Palmer reclined and went to sleep. He'd expected as much and hoped the food she consumed would give her some energy. Kent turned on the playlist he'd made for Palmer and let Lana Del Rey sing to her while she slept. It was the least he could do, and honestly, over the past few weeks he had become quite fond of the singer. She delivered her lyrics with grit and passion, qualities he saw in his wife.

Halfway to their next, and what Kent suspected to be their final, destination, he heard a loud pop, swerved, and signaled to pull over. He got out of the Jeep and went around to the side to inspect the blown tire. He kicked it, muttered a long string of obscenities that he was sure would make Palmer blush, and went back to the car to search through the glove box for their rental records. He made so much noise that he expected Palmer to wake up, but she continued to sleep.

Kent didn't know whether to cry or scream at that point. This woman in the passenger seat had slowly worked her way into his heart, had become his wife, and was now dying before his eyes. Even worse, there wasn't anything he could do about it. He couldn't pump her full of IVs or perform some lifesaving surgery on the side of the road. None of his combat training would save her. Kent was going to lose her, and there wasn't anything he could do about it.

Kent chose to scream. He chose to let it all out on the side of the road, with traffic whizzing past him. He let out the deepest, most gut-pulling scream he could muster, and then he flipped the sky off. "Fuck you. Fuck you. Fuck you," he said in a low, guttural voice. Kent was angry, mostly at himself for opening his heart in a way he'd never recover from. He was in love with Palmer. He had fallen in love knowing he shouldn't, knowing her outcome. Her prognosis wasn't going to change because he loved her, and yet he'd allowed himself to feel, when he knew the damage it was going to do to him.

Kent sat against the Jersey barrier meant to keep traffic from driving down the ravine. He called for AAA to come change his tire for him.

He could do it, but he needed time alone with his thoughts, and what a better place to think than the side of a busy highway.

By the time the wrecker arrived to swap his tire, Kent had sweated through his clothes and his body was screaming in agony from sitting on the ground. He swore that businesses took full advantage of the "We'll be there within forty-five minutes" promise and showed up right on the forty-five-minute mark. God forbid they show up early.

Kent was thankful that the spare tire for the Jeep was a full-size tire. They wouldn't have to go to a tire store to wait for a new one before getting back on the road. As soon as he got into the car, he made the decision to turn around and head back toward Phoenix. The Grand Canyon would have to wait for another lifetime. It wasn't happening today, and something deep inside told him it wasn't happening tomorrow either. Not once, during the entire stop, not even when he'd fought the universe and lost, had Palmer woken up.

He found a hotel and pulled into the parking lot. Everything was automatic and played on repeat in his mind. "Hi, we don't have a reservation"—it was the same tired conversation he'd had at every stop. The clerk gave him his room keys and went through the usual spiel about breakfast, the pool, and checkout, and Kent was on his way. But this time, he drove around to the rear entrance. There wasn't a doubt in his mind they had cameras, but he hoped no one was watching when he brought his sleeping wife in through the back door.

Kent spoke to her the entire time he moved her from the front seat to her wheelchair. He asked her to please show him her pretty eyes so he could see them. He *needed* to see them one last time. Was this it for them? Was she going to die in some random hotel?

Palmer startled awake and looked around wildly as Kent pushed her down the hall. "Don't worry," he told her. "We just stopped for the night."

"Where are we?"

"Still in Phoenix."

She looked at him from over her shoulder, and he groaned. "Long story, but while you slept, we got a flat tire. I decided to turn around." He opened the hotel room door, and they went into the room.

"Oh, I'm so sorry I missed it."

He wasn't. He needed the moments alone so he could have his meltdown. Kent didn't want her to witness him going through that. He didn't want to tell her he thought her time was near. Kent wasn't ready to say goodbye, even though he could hear death knocking on the door.

The hotel had a garden tub, and Kent asked his wife if she wanted to take a bath with him. He was elated when she said yes, and he drew the water, trying not to think that this could be the last time.

Kent helped Palmer undress. He desperately wanted to kiss her, to touch her, but he held back. She tried to help him, and when she finally got his shirt off, she kissed his chest and whispered that she loved him.

They got into the tub, and Kent held her against his chest. He never wanted to let go. He brought up their wedding and how it had been the second-happiest day of his life, with meeting her being his first. She concurred and started telling him about their night together, only to stop talking. Kent sensed what would happen next. The only thing he could do was hold her head up, to keep her from drowning while her body convulsed in the water, and cry.

Forty-One

In the early hours of the morning, Kent watched Palmer as she slowly woke up. She reached for him, with tears in her eyes, and said, "I'm ready to go home."

Kent nodded and asked, "What do you want to wear?" To some, it would seem like a normal question, but to him, he'd asked his wife what she wanted to wear when she took her last breath. And while it may not have been an important question to many, it was to him.

"My gray sundress," she told him.

He helped her dress and brush her hair. She asked for a little bit of makeup, and even though they had a long drive ahead of them and it would wear off, he did as she asked. After he'd dressed, they made their way to the Jeep for one last road trip. He loaded her into the car, and then their luggage and her chair, and then climbed into the driver's seat.

"Where to, Palmer?" He choked out the words and stared out the window.

"The beach."

He nodded, scrolled through his phone for the address to Crissy Field, and plugged it into GPS. After a stop for gas and provisions to keep him alert on the long drive ahead, he set off one last time. As soon as he was on the interstate, he reached for Palmer's hand and held it. Not only did he need the comfort, but the paramedic in him needed to be able to check her pulse. As of now, it was faint, and he prayed he'd get her back to San Francisco before it was too late.

Kent drove, into the sun, through traffic, detours, delays, and into the evening. Palmer woke sporadically and would talk to him for an hour or so, and then fall back to sleep. Those rare hours were the most important to him. He recounted their trip from the moment he'd given her his pitch through them dancing in the rain. In her somewhat alert state, she'd bring up little tidbits that were meant to make him laugh, but all humor was gone. He would talk until he was sure she was asleep, and then he would go about his thoughts and how he was going to move forward with his life.

Each break, he would check her vitals. He no longer asked her if she was hungry whenever she'd grace him with opening her eyes. Kent would tell her how much he loved her and tell her to hang on because they were almost home. He sped when he could and cursed the heavy traffic of Bakersfield. He never wished more for wigwags than he did now.

When his phone rang, he answered. "We have Palmer's results earlier than expected," the doctor told Kent.

Kent looked at his wife, dying peacefully next to him. "Is Palmer's liver a candidate?"

"Yes, it's a match, and despite the tumor, Palmer could donate, since she didn't seek treatment. Her liver is healthy and a match for Courtney."

Kent nodded, even though the doctor couldn't see him. "I'll tell Palmer." He glanced at his wife. "It won't be long," he said to the doctor before he hung up. Deep down, he already knew what Palmer would say. She would want to help Courtney any way she could, and if that meant donating her liver, so be it.

When they got to Oakland, Kent called Damian.

"Wagner?"

"Are you on shift?"

"What? Not yet. What's wrong?"

"I need a favor."

"Okay. What is it?"

Kent took a deep breath. "Palmer . . . she's . . . this is it. We're heading to Crissy Field now. It's where she wants to . . ." He couldn't bring himself to say the word.

"Shit. Okay. I didn't realize you were back in town."

"We weren't until now. Listen, can you stage there? She's donating her organs."

"She should be in the hospital, Kent. You know this."

"It doesn't matter what I know, Damian. All that matters is what she wants, and this is how she wants to go. Can you stage there?"

"Let me call Greig and Matthews. I can't do it without their permission. You know this."

"Call me back." Kent hung up and looked at his wife. Her diamond ring sparkled and cast a prism of light all around her. Marrying her had been the best damn decision he had ever made, aside from taking her on their road trip.

Kent's phone rang, and Jacob Matthews's name appeared on the screen. Kent answered, and the reply from his deputy chief was gruff and groggy. Had Damian woken their boss up?

"Sorry to wake you, sir," Kent said into the speaker phone.

"You didn't, Wagner. I've been down with a cold. What can I help with?"

Kent reiterated everything he had told Damian and waited for Matthews to say something.

Matthews sighed. "This goes against my better judgment."

"I understand, sir, but I'm trying to honor her wishes. She doesn't want to die in a hospital."

The silence on the other end scared Kent. He hadn't failed on a promise yet and didn't want her last request to be waylaid by policy.

"I'll send a bus out to stage, Wagner."

"Thank you, sir."

Kent hung up and made his way through the city traffic to Crissy Field. When he pulled into the parking lot, he saw two rigs blocking the entrance path to the beach. He parked, and as much as he wanted to greet his coworkers, he had more pressing matters to take care of.

He took her chair out from the back and set it up next to the passenger side. He opened the door and gently woke her. "Hey, there's my beautiful wife," he said when she finally opened her eyes. "Look, we're home," he told her. "No more riding in the car."

Palmer smiled and tried a laugh, but it fell short.

"What do you say we go sit by the beach for a little bit?" She nodded and draped her arm around his shoulders, and he lifted her out of the car.

Kent situated Palmer in her chair and covered her with a blanket. He walked her past Damian and his new partner, and Isha and Reeva. They stood there as if they were Palmer's honor guard. When the pavement ended, Kent lifted his wife into his arms and carried her to the sand.

He didn't know how he managed to sit with her in his arms, but he did. Kent covered her with the blanket and held her.

"I've never seen the bridge look so pretty," he told her as he fought back his tears.

"You're pretty," she said quietly.

He smiled when he saw her eyes. "You're one to talk." He kissed her nose.

"Thank you."

"You saved me, don't ever forget that."

She closed her eyes and then opened them again. "I never knew what it meant to love someone until I met you. You showed me what it was like to live, and because of you, I lived my best life in a matter of days."

"Me too."

Palmer smiled and once again closed her eyes. "Promise me you're going to live for tomorrow."

"I promise, Palmer."

She gripped his arms while he held her. He told her that she was going to save her sister's life, that no one would ever forget the sacrifices she'd made for others.

"I'm sorry we didn't get to everything on your list."

"Do it with your daughter," she whispered.

"I promise you, I will."

Palmer opened her eyes again, and Kent felt this would be the last time he saw her. He met her gaze. "Before I'm gone, can I have one last kiss?"

"You can have all of them." He pressed his lips to hers, and tears streamed down his cheeks. "I want you to know that I'll love you forever, Palmer."

Kent's hold on her tightened as he rocked them back and forth. Birds chirped overhead, and he wondered if they were there to guide her. That thought soothed his soul, knowing she wouldn't be alone when she left this realm.

When he felt her heart stop, he wailed and buried his face into the crook of her neck. He wasn't ready. He would never be ready. Kent needed another five minutes, an hour, anything someone could give him so he could tell her repeatedly how much she had saved him from himself. He wanted to go back to the beginning and start over, back to when they'd first met. He would change everything to have one more day with her.

Kent peppered her face with kisses as he professed his love for her. He didn't want to let her go. He didn't want their adventure to stop. They had so much more to do. The roller coaster, the yoga in Sedona, the Liberty Bell in Philadelphia, and the roadside stands in Amish country. Right then and there, he vowed to finish their bucket list, if it was the last thing he did.

He felt the firm hand on his shoulder and nodded. Kent sat helplessly as Reeva and Isha lifted his wife from his arms and laid her on the stretcher. They took her blanket and covered her before carrying her to the ambulance.

Damian sat down beside his friend and put his arm over his shoulder. Kent cried. He hadn't just lost his best friend. He'd lost his wife. No one would ever understand the impact Palmer had on his life.

"They're getting ready to transport her. Do you want to be at the hospital when she arrives?" Kent nodded, and Damian helped him stand. He walked his partner to the back of the rig and pounded on the door before opening it. Kent climbed the step and sat down next to Isha and held his wife's hand for one last ride.

Forty-Two

Kent sat and stared at Palmer's white casket. He'd gone back and forth on what he should do. Funeral, no funeral. Casket, no casket. In the end, he decided she deserved it all. They would celebrate her life, in the best way he could. He wanted a moment alone with her, even though he had said everything he could to her before she passed.

This would be the last time he saw her, like this, with her hair and makeup done, and in her wedding dress. In a few days, he'd bring her home—back to her apartment with the view of the mountains—in a box, per her wishes.

He walked to her open casket and looked at how peaceful his wife was. Her hands rested on her stomach, with her left hand on top of her right. Before they took her away from him, he'd take her rings off and slip them into his pocket. He hadn't a clue what he'd do with them. Maybe put them back in the box and set them next to his bed, on what would be her side, or tuck them away in his drawer.

"Mr. Wagner, it's time," the funeral director said behind him.

Kent nodded and pressed a kiss to Palmer's forehead. "You have no idea how much I miss you." He knew she wasn't in there. This body of hers, the surgeons had emptied it. They took everything. He hadn't cared where her organs went, as long as her sister received Palmer's liver. That was his only stipulation. He thought about asking to see the octopus. He wanted to stab it, mangle it, and destroy it like it had done to Palmer. In the end, he changed his mind. He saw it as the giant ugly octopus that Palmer described, and that's how he wanted to remember it.

He'd called Courtney from the ambulance to let her know her sister had passed. It was the first time they'd spoken since they'd met in the restaurant. He told her to get to the hospital because they were going to call her shortly with news of a liver. Courtney had been beside herself. Her doctors had told her it would be years before she would be at the top of the list for a transplant. She thanked him and promised to call him later. She called after her surgery, but he didn't answer. He had nothing to say.

That first night without her was pure torture. He lay awake in his bed and stared at the ceiling. Each time he closed his eyes, he saw Palmer. For every happy memory he conjured up, a sad one followed. The dizziness, the memory loss, the fear and sadness in her eyes, the seizures that crippled her. Those were the times he didn't want to remember. He was so incredibly thankful the barista at RoccoBean had suggested the Instagram account because now he had something to look at every day. Sure, he had videos of her on her phone, but she rarely spoke in them. He had kept their lives in his feed, there for anyone to watch. There for him to hold on to every ounce of her he could.

The doors opened, and Kent stood next to Palmer's casket to receive people. There wouldn't be a service after the wake, or a memorial later. This was all he could muster for right now. In the coming days, he'd decide what to do with her apartment and belongings, and he'd return to the life he'd led before he responded to the 911 call that put Palmer in his path.

People flooded the funeral home. Kent shook hand after hand and accepted every condolence. When the last person he thought he'd see turned the corner, he didn't know what to think. Maeve came forward in a black dress and a protruding belly. She kissed his cheek and told him how sorry she was.

"Hi," he said as he took her in. Kent had only asked her a couple of times about her pregnancy. He had been so preoccupied with Palmer, and not wanting to believe he was going to be a dad. He looked at her growing midsection and wished Palmer could see Maeve. "I'm surprised to see you."

"I know. Maybe I shouldn't be here, but I felt like I had to come."

"I appreciate it." Kent wasn't sure he did or not, but it felt right to say. "We should probably talk."

"Later," Maeve said. "When you're settled and have had some time."

"Okay." He kissed her on her cheek and thanked her for coming. He didn't take his eyes off her until she disappeared into the crowd. Kent had been so preoccupied with making sure Palmer lived her best life with the time she had that he had pushed Maeve and the baby from his mind. He wouldn't be able to do that anymore. He didn't want to. He'd told Maeve he would be there, and he would, every step of the way, from this point on. Plus, he'd promised Palmer he would finish her list with his daughter, and he wouldn't let his wife down. Not in life or death.

Once he'd received the last person, he took his place at the podium. He looked out at the crowd. Every seat had been filled, and people stood. Palmer wouldn't believe this if he could tell her. There was a roomful of people who cared about her.

"I want to thank you all for coming. For those who don't know me, I'm Kent, Palmer's husband." A murmur rose over the crowd, and he smiled. To the side, a projection screen showed photos and videos from their trip. "Many of you knew Palmer through work. You saw the serious side of her, while I got the adventurous side. While you got years of her, I got months, and in those months, we traveled the United States on a quest—a quest for happiness, enlightenment, and answers. I believe we accomplished the goal we set out to do, and did so while falling in love. Palmer was my best friend, my partner, and most importantly, the love of my life. I thank you all for coming today. I know for some of you, her passing isn't something you expected to hear about, and she was truly sorry she couldn't tell you herself about her battle, but she'd be happy to know you're here today, to celebrate her life."

Kent walked away from the podium and sat down in the chair next to her casket. The funeral home director invited people up to speak about Palmer. One by one, her coworkers came forward and told stories about Palmer, making Kent laugh. An older woman approached Kent and asked to speak with him privately. In the hall, she introduced herself as the former director of the home where Palmer grew up and asked if he'd be okay with her speaking about Palmer.

"No, I'm not," he told her. "No one knows about her life as Faith, and she'd want to keep it that way," he explained. "Not being adopted and not knowing her family was something Palmer struggled with greatly. She would not want any of those people to know. I'm sorry." Kent was angry with this woman. Not only for showing up, but also for asking if she could speak. As far as he was concerned, she was part of the past that Palmer had longed to forget, and there was no way he would give this woman any time at his wife's expense. It was right then, he vowed to himself, he would find Sarah Cousins and get to the bottom of Palmer's kidnapping.

After they'd laughed at all the stories and shed more tears, people began to leave. Kent's parents stayed and waited for him. Tonight, he would go to Palmer's apartment and be there for the first time without her. He wasn't prepared to, but it had to be done.

The funeral director told Kent it was time. He went over to Palmer's casket and removed her engagement ring and wedding band. He slipped them into his pocket and then kissed his wife for the last time. "I love you."

Kent followed his parents out of the funeral home. The director would call him when her ashes were ready for pickup. There would be no city cremation for the woman who had stolen his heart, not that he would've allowed that to happen regardless. With or without her becoming his wife, Kent would've taken care of Palmer. He would've seen to it that she had a proper burial, or her ashes spread. As of now, he had no idea what he was going to do with her ashes, but he thought about returning to New Mexico and spreading some there or in Las Vegas next year on their anniversary.

Kent's dad drove his son to Palmer's apartment. He pulled up to the sidewalk and shut his car off. "Do you want me to come in?"

Kent shook his head. "No, I'll be okay."

"Call me when you need a ride. I'll come back to get you."

Everything in the lobby reminded him of Palmer. From the fireplace to the fake leather sofa they'd sat on as they made their plans. He took the elevator to her floor and pulled her keys out of his pocket. Somehow, in her wisdom, she'd managed to keep her stuff together for him. She'd set everything in the glove box.

Kent used her key to open her door. The moment he stepped in, he broke down. They'd been gone for over two months, and her apartment still smelled like Palmer. It felt like she was there, greeting him with open arms, welcoming him home. He set his stuff down and didn't bother to wipe away his tears; more would fall. He noticed a box on the island, addressed to him, in Palmer's handwriting. The postmark said New Mexico.

He went to her desk, grabbed her letter opener, and sliced through the tape. The flaps popped open with a woosh. Kent peeked inside and saw a red leather journal. He pulled it out, looked at the binding, and then flipped to the first page.

My dearest Kent,

If you're reading this, then that means the octopus has won. I know you're probably wondering how I've sent you this box, and no, it's not some ghostly mail delivery. Raúl was kind enough to help me out. You see, I finished this journal before we left his home, and I wanted you to have it to remember our trip. I hope you've kept the other one as well or maybe there's two. I don't really know.

In case I've forgotten to tell you along the way, thank you. I've never had a friend like you, and I know I'm going to miss you. Someday, when you're on the beach watching the sunrise, remember our trip to Chatham, and if you ever visit again, don't feed the sharks.

Please remember to live. Live for me, for your daughter, and the future family you'll have some day. Carry with you the joy you *brought to my life, in such a short amount of time, and know I was happy. You made me happy.*

You'll be a father soon, and I wish I could be there. Just know, I'll be watching over you.

In closing, if I never got the chance to tell you in person, read my words—I love you, Kent Wagner. I don't remember when I fell, but I fell hard. Thank you for catching me.

Until we meet again,
Palmer Sinclair

Kent flipped through the journal and read some of her other entries. He laughed at the doodles she'd made and looked at the souvenirs she'd added to the pages. When he came to the middle of the book, an envelope fell out. Kent set the book down and opened what he thought were her DNA results. He read the words, and then read them again. He was the beneficiary to her life insurance policy and retirement plan, as well as the co-owner of her apartment. He read the papers for a third time, making sure he hadn't missed anything. It was then that he remembered she had put her lawyer's name in his phone. Kent was supposed to call him and had forgotten.

The next letter was for *Baby Girl Wagner on her 5th birthday*. He wondered what Palmer could've possibly written to his unborn daughter, and when. He'd rarely left her side, other than to shower or get food. Kent had no idea how she had done any of this.

He stood and went into the bedroom. Her bed was made perfectly, as if she'd expected to return. Kent turned on the light in her closet and saw that it was bare. All her clothes were gone except for what he had at his apartment. He'd bring them over and hang them up where they belonged.

Kent sat on the edge of the bed and opened his phone. He went to the video of her he'd taken on the beach in Chatham. The sun glowed off her face, and he wished he could go back to that moment and tell her he was in love with her.

He paused the video on her face, and she stared back at him. "I'm so sorry," he said to her image. "I promised you tomorrow, but tomorrow never came."

Epilogue

Five years later

"Sinclair, are you ready?"

"Almost, Daddy. I can't find my bear."

Kent went into his daughter's room and stood in the doorway, watching as she frantically looked for the teddy bear he held in his hand. "This one?" He gave the bear a little shake. Her eyes widened, and she let out a screech.

"Where did you find him?"

"Right where you left him."

She put her free hand on her hip and tapped her toe. "Daddy . . ." This was her warning tone.

Kent scoffed. "He was on your suitcase. Now, are you ready?"

"Yes," she said.

"Do you have your letter?"

Sinclair thought for a moment and then nodded. "I believe it's in my bag. I'll check." She ran to the kitchen, came to a screeching halt, and dropped to her knees to go through her bag. "Yes, it's right here." She pulled out the envelope he had saved for her birthday, over five years ago.

"Okay, let's hit the road."

He loaded his arms up with their luggage while she opened the door. "Goodbye, apartment, see you on the flip side," she said as she exited.

Sinclair Wagner was a free spirit. That was the only way Kent and her mother, Maeve, could describe her. Sinclair marched to the beat of her own drum and loved everyone and everything, including but not limited to every animal on the planet. She was a devoted daughter who loved her parents and who had learned the art of pitting them against each other when she didn't get her way. Maeve and Kent had to learn a long time ago that effective communication between them was the only way they'd survive their daughter.

The day he'd met Sinclair in the hospital, he'd had no idea what to expect. Kent and Maeve were on speaking terms, but her husband was not impressed with their relationship. He wanted Kent gone as the baby's father, and he wanted to adopt the child as his own. Kent refused, and Maeve sided with Kent.

When he held his daughter for the first time, he thought his heart would explode. He had fallen in love all over again, but this was a different kind of love—a love only he and his daughter could share.

"What's her name?" Kent had asked. He'd never expected to be part of the naming process or even in the room during the birth. He wanted Maeve as comfortable as possible, and the tension was thick between Kent and Maeve's husband.

"Well, I was wondering what you thought about naming her Sinclair?"

Kent's eyes went from his daughter to Maeve. "As in Palmer's last name?"

Maeve nodded. "I like the name, and I suspect you'd like to include her in all of this somehow."

Kent said her name quietly. "Sinclair." The baby in his arms opened her eyes. "Palmer would be honored, Maeve. Thank you."

That night, he sat in their bedroom and spoke to the box of ashes as if it could understand him. He told her how beautiful his daughter was and how Maeve had surprised him with her name choice. He promised Palmer that Sinclair would always know about her, where her name came from, and how much he loved her.

To date, he had kept his promise. Sinclair knew all about her namesake, her dad's wife.

Sinclair pressed the button for the elevator and tapped her foot while they waited. "Am I getting cake?"

"Yes, there will be cake."

Suddenly, her eyes went wide. "Daddy, did you forget Palmer?"

It had been five years since his wife had passed away, and there hadn't been a day since when he'd forgotten about her. In the months they'd been together, she'd changed him for the better.

"No, I didn't forget Palmer."

"Well, where is she?"

"She's in my bag."

They got into the elevator and took it to the basement, where he kept his car parked. After piling their luggage into the trunk, he set his bag in the front seat and then checked Sinclair's straps on her car seat. They were about to embark on their first cross-country trip in honor of Sinclair's upcoming birthday, and to finish Palmer's bucket list. Maeve had agreed to let Kent take their daughter for the summer, as long as she was back in time to start kindergarten.

"Daddy, can we listen to Lana?"

"Of course we can." Kent turned on the same playlist he had made for Palmer and let Lana Del Rey's voice fill the car. Within seconds, Sinclair's legs bounced up and down and she sang along. Sinclair didn't know this yet, but they'd see her in concert before the summer was over, and Palmer would be right there with her.

"Daddy!"

"What, Sinclair?" He looked into his rearview mirror to see her.

"Did you post that we're on the trip?"

"Oh no, I forgot."

"You better pull over."

She was right. He thought about pulling over but then saw the sign for Crissy Field. He hadn't been there since Palmer had died in his arms. He turned before he could change his mind and found a place to park. Kent helped Sinclair out of her seat and held her hand while she skipped toward the beach.

Kent paused where the pavement ended, and the sand began. He could see the day crystal clear in his mind. They'd sat on the sand, with Palmer in his arms, and he held her until her heart stopped. The day was forever etched in his mind. Every day with her was.

He walked forward and stood in the spot where he'd lost his wife. He crouched down to Sinclair's level and held his phone out. Kent snapped some pictures and then went to the app and pressed the Live button.

They waited for their audience to come online . . . and then they started their journey.

Before I'm Gone

♥ Sit in the front seat of a roller coaster and feel the wind in my hair

♥ ~~Eat tacos or tortillas from a roadside stand in New Mexico~~

♥ Shop at a large farmers market

♥ Meet Lana Del Rey and see her in concert

♥ Take a picture of the most-painted shed in the US

♥ ~~Sit in the sand and watch the sunrise in Cape Cod~~

♥ ~~Take the steps to the Lincoln Memorial~~

♥ Do yoga in Sedona

♥ Tour and feed animals in a wildlife sanctuary

♥ Stand under a waterfall

♥ See Elvis on the street corner in Las Vegas

♥ Hug an elephant

♥ ~~Find my family~~

♥ Step on grapes and make wine

♥ Run through a wheat field

♥ Drive Route 66

♥ See the marquees on Broadway

♥ Ring the Liberty Bell

♥ Buy a quilt from an Amish stand

★ See the northern lights in Minnesota

★ ~~Visit Plymouth Rock~~

★ ~~Touch Babe Ruth's bat~~

★ ~~Travel the Loneliest Road~~

★ ~~Visit the Muhammad Ali Center~~

★ ~~Dance in the rain with someone I love~~

★ Take the ferry to the Statue of Liberty

★ Check out the Grand Canyon

★ Take every picture I can of Palmer

✓✓✓✓✓✓✓✓✓✓✓✓✓✓✓✓ ∞

★ *Make Palmer smile smile*

✓✓✓✓✓✓✓✓✓✓✓✓✓✓✓✓✓✓✓∞

~~Eat chowdah in Boston, per Palmer~~

Eat pizza in Chicago

Try frozen custard in New York City

Get coffee in each city ✓✓✓✓✓✓

~~Get married in Las Vegas!!!!!~~

~~Honeymoon at Hoover Dam~~

Live the way Palmer would want me to live ∞

Go to American Girl

Start kindergarten

Ask my daddy for an iPhone

See a whale or dolphin

Find a mermaid

Ride a unicorn

Palmer's Lana Del Rey Road Trip Playlist

"Beautiful People Beautiful Problems"
"Tomorrow Never Came"
"Happiness Is a Butterfly"
"Ride"
"Without You"
"Young and Beautiful"
"Thunder"
"Hope Is a Dangerous Thing for a Woman like Me to Have—but I Have It"
"Lucky Ones"
"The Greatest"
"Get Free"
"Swan Song"
"Religion"
"Love Song"
"God Knows I Tried"
"Black Beauty"

Added by Kent
"Don't Take the Girl"—Tim McGraw
"What Might Have Been"—Little Texas

Acknowledgments

Five years ago, I had this idea. There was a lot of back-and-forth with the plot, but when *that* moment finally hit, the rest fell into place. I knew going in, I'd cry. I'd choke up and have a hard time seeing the words on my screen through my tears. Needless to say, I was right. They're not tears of hard work or perseverance, but from the story of Palmer, and the life she didn't have until it was too late.

Thank you to my team at Montlake. Being a part of this family is life changing. To Lauren, working with you is a dream, and to Lindsey, your constant words (which I may have printed off) of encouragement and love for all things Palmer and Kent bring a different wave of tears each time I read them. I can never thank either of you enough.

Thank you, Kassidy. Each time I write a book, I ask you to read it. *Nope.* That was, until I told you about *Before I'm Gone*. I will always remember telling you about Palmer and the last thing she does, and how you had tears in your eyes. You said, "I'll have to read this one." But then you took your dedication one step further and had me listen to "Beautiful People Beautiful Problems" and "Tomorrow Never Came" by your queen, Lana Del Rey. Those songs, along with many others by LDR, shaped this novel, and I am forever grateful.

Thank you to Lana Del Rey. You can only put so much into a dedication, and while I suspect you'll never read this, I want to say thank you. Thank you for creating the music that you do. You're a true lyricist, an icon, and a household name. Thank you for teaching my daughter to always be true to who you are and not be someone that people want you to be.

Yvette, every word, every story—you've touched them all. I wouldn't do this without you.

Jake, thank you for the invaluable advice and guidance. Without you, this story isn't possible. I cherish our friendship.

Marisa, thank you for all your hard work.

Thank you to Erik and Madison for always being patient and understanding.

And finally, thank you to my readers. Some of you have been with me for the past ten years, and some are new. I appreciate each and every one of you and thank you for taking a chance on me with each page you turn.

Turn The Page For A Preview Of Heidi's novel *After All*

Prologue

Each morning, before the sun even rose, men and women walked the wide planks of the docks, preparing their boats for the day. The sounds of the marina echoed throughout the harbor: the scuffing of heavy boots, the whooshing of ropes coiling, the bubbling of water as the engines roared to life. They stocked their boats full of bait, loaded the ice machines to keep their catches cold, and stored groceries for those who were leaving for longer than a day. Those boats would dock days later; then the men would drop off their catches, restock their supplies, and call home to check in with their loved ones. At home, families were always on edge, watching the sky for an unexpected storm until that first call came in. They would listen to how the trip was going, happy to hear from their loved ones, but once they hung up, the worrying started again until the next call.

To some, this was their life, the way they made a living. For many, they had followed the path laid out for them by the generations before, and several worked with their families. To others, it was how they spent their summer, coming from as far north as Canada and as far south as California. Rarely would someone from the East Coast come here to earn some summer money, but it happened, and their accents made them stick out like sore thumbs in this tight-knit community.

Under the midnight-blue sky, the *Austin Woods* vessel floated through the channel and by the Driftwood Inn with its crew standing starboard, waving. They did this every time they went out, without fail, and would also do it when they returned, paying homage to their boat's namesake. No one seemed to care if anyone waved back; they knew she would be in her room that faced the water or in the inn's ballroom, alone. The way she had been for the last fifteen years.

The three-story manor looked like a mansion straight out of the *Luxury Home Magazine*, with its very own moat separating Cape Harbor from its neighboring town. The A-frame structure with its wall of windows was a sight to behold. Back in the day, the locals considered the Driftwood Inn the gateway into town—still to this day many tourists yearned to stay there just to see the purple-and-pink nightly sunsets through the massive floor-to-ceiling windows, to feel the sun's rays penetrate through the glass, and to stare at the majestic views of Mount Baker. There wasn't another hotel that could provide such a magnificent perspective. Others tried, but no one could replicate the essence of the inn, which made it utterly devastating for the community when the doors closed.

Standing in the attic window of her granddaughter's ocean-blue-and-white bedroom, Carly Woods held her mug of tea, guaranteeing that something occupied her hands when the fishing boat went by. She knew the boys meant well, but the pain she hid for most of the year crept back in. As much as it saddened her to watch, to see them wave, she never missed a morning nor evening. She always made sure she knew the schedule of the *Austin Woods* so she could keep track. Even if none of her family members were out to sea, she never gave up worrying about those who were. She glanced out to the rising sun and wondered what today would bring. They were due for a storm. The East Coast was already getting hammered, and it was only a matter of time before Mother Nature turned her attention toward the West. At this age, her heart couldn't take much more.

When the boat was out of sight, she rested her hand against the glass and dipped her head slightly. She recited the fisherman's prayer aloud, words she had learned from her grandfather and had recited when she stood with her mother in this very window when the men in her family set sail. Carly had sworn she would never marry a fisherman, and she had held fast until she had seen Skip Woods in a different light. They had grown up together, always hanging out in the same crowds.

One day, everything changed. Their friendship quickly turned into love and marriage, and with the birth of their son, they became a family.

The warm honey concoction in her mug coated her throat as she sipped. A cough tickled her throat, and she did everything she could to push it away. The last thing she wanted was to have a coughing fit that would buckle her legs out from under her. She sat on the edge of the bed, placed her hands on her knees, closed her eyes, and focused on her breathing. She had learned the technique from the doctor she saw in Seattle to calm the spasms in her chest. She didn't want her friend and housekeeper to feel the need to rush to her aid, when she knew how to control her breathing—at least not yet. The meditation wouldn't always work—it was nothing more than a temporary fix—but for the moment the urge to cough seemed to subside.

She glanced around the room and smiled. In the corner sat her granddaughter's old dollhouse, which they had converted into a bookcase one summer. They'd sat outside for days and had sanded and painted until they'd deemed it perfect. The same with her dresser. Together, they painted it a beautiful blue and added seashells for the knobs. Carly thought the beach theme was a bit odd considering where she lived, but her granddaughter wanted it, and whatever she wanted, Carly happily gave.

Her hand brushed over the mermaid quilt; the creature on it had blonde hair and a purple tail, with multiple tones of blue surrounding her. It had been a special request from her grandchild, who at the age of five had vowed she would become a mermaid and live outside her grandmother's house so they could see each other every day. That made her very happy. It would be her greatest joy to see her son's daughter every day, whether a mermaid or not.

Down the hall, she heard her best friend, caregiver, and live-in housekeeper moving in and out of the other bedrooms, humming loudly for Carly to hear. The song was unfamiliar, but she wasn't surprised that she felt calmness come over her. It was hard to put into words the kind of relationship she had with Simone. What had started out as an employee/employer arrangement had turned into a friendship. Simone had come to Carly after she had escaped an abusive relationship. Her own parents had passed at an early age, and she often thought of Simone as a sister or a daughter. At first, Simone had started as a maid before taking over the reception counter, and she had finally moved on to managing the entire inn. When Carly had closed the doors for the last time, Simone had stayed on and become everything to her. Simone was the one who'd helped her through her grieving period. And it was her friend who'd suggested the doors open again, even if it was only for the weekends.

Carly had scoffed at the idea, but Simone had refused to relent. "It would take too much to get the inn ready," Carly had said, but Simone reminded her that there was someone out there who could do the work; all she had to do was pick up the phone.

It had been years since she had opened the doors of her once-famed inn, letting strangers stay in what she considered her home, to enjoy views she loved so much, and eat the food she happily cooked for them. Losing the last piece of her life had been too much to handle. Many thought her mourning period would cease after a few months, a year tops, but when the mayor came to visit and found the door locked, even he knew Cape Harbor had changed forever. Even he couldn't change the mind of his lifelong friend.

She hated the deafening silence that her home now harbored, but the people who visited all held memories she longed to forget. For as long as she could remember, her house had been where her son's friends had stayed. Where they'd spent time together. Every day after school, the kids would bombard her kitchen, seeking fresh-baked cookies before doing their homework. She'd never minded that her home was full of children—whatever kept them safe while their parents were at work. Once they were older, they'd come after work, on the weekends, and at every holiday . . . until the day everything changed.

She stood and went back to the window. From here, she couldn't see the wharf but could hear the activity going on at the end of the channel. Despite everything, she loved knowing people were hard at work on the docks, helping the fishermen bring in their daily catch and making sure their boats were in the best shape to handle whatever nature would throw their way.

The sun rose. She felt the rays trying to burst through the window. It would be a warm day, one that would surely draw visitors out to the water. The laughter of others would carry through to her kitchen, making her smile until memories flooded her mind again.

Soon, the tourists would be here, clogging the streets and the waterway and having a good time. Still to this day, her phone rang with people asking if she was open and accepting reservations. When Simone answered, she wanted to say yes because the rooms were vacant and the inn needed life, but Carly remained steadfast. The answer was no and would always be no.

Her tea had cooled, and all the vessels were out in the ocean earning their keep. She took her leave, looking back at her granddaughter's room one last time. Years ago, it was dark green with trophies sitting on shelves and medals hanging from pegs stuck in the wall. Posters of hot rods and movies used to decorate the walls, but she and Simone had packed and stored the pictures neatly in the attic many years ago. There were days when she thought about bringing them down and poring over the memories, but she never found the courage to climb the ladder. There was so much of her life stored away in the room above her head that she often wondered what she had left.

The day was coming when she would need to clean out the attic, to finally part with the memories, but today was not that day, and tomorrow wasn't looking too promising either. Next week, she told herself. There was always next week.

Downstairs, she emptied her mug and turned on the kettle to heat more water. Her garden needed tending. Her rosebushes were struggling, as they often did with the soil on her property. Too much sand mixed with the dirt made it hard to grow anything but seagrass. She would ask Simone to go into town and buy a few bags of soil to help the roses thrive. Working on her flower bed would keep her thoughts off the inevitable.

Simone entered the kitchen, happily singing a different melody. Her blonde hair was up in a perfectly coifed bun, not a strand out of place. There used to be days when they would go to the salon together or take trips to the spa in Anacortes, but it had been years since Carly would even entertain such a thought. The idea of someone seeing her, let alone touching her, made her feel ill. Simone had done her nails, cut and dyed her hair for as long as she could remember. Usually in the summer when her granddaughter visited so they could play beauty shop.

Carly watched as she stored the cleaning supplies, washed her hands, and took a mug from the cupboard. Together, they waited for the kettle to whistle. Every so often, Simone would glance her way and smile. She refrained from asking her what she was thinking because deep down, she knew. Carly knew that Simone was right when she suggested she should reopen the inn, and at some point, she would have to consider doing that or selling—and selling the house *wasn't* an option. At least, not while Carly was alive.

The whistle blew, and Simone fixed their cups of tea. With it, she set out the pills Carly needed to take in the morning. She would also do the same at lunch- and dinnertime. Simone picked up her mug and walked to the back door. She paused and waited for Carly to follow.

They sat outside and basked in the rising sun. A few of the smaller yachts sailed by, with the people on board waving. Simone waved back, but Carly held her mug tightly in her hands. Not because she hadn't wanted to greet them, but because her hands were shaking, and she was afraid someone might notice.

"Summer will be here soon," Simone said.

She sipped her tea and closed her eyes as the tickle she had avoided earlier was back and much stronger. She coughed and felt her lungs tighten and seize, causing her to double over and gasp for air. She tried to set her mug down on the small table next to her, but it hit the edge and went tumbling down to the ground, shattering into tiny shards of ceramic as hot liquid spread across the patio.

Simone was in front of her, rubbing her back and coaxing her through the fit. Her words were soothing, but they wouldn't help the pain she felt in her chest. "It's time to make the call, Ms. Carly."

She nodded. It was all she could do, as she feared that if she opened her mouth, an anguished cry would escape. It was time for her to admit things she wasn't ready for.

Connect with Heidi Online

Website

www.heidimclaughlin.com

Newsletter

https://landing.mailerlite.com/webforms/landing/x4t5g9

Facebook

https://www.facebook.com/AuthorHeidiMcLaughlin

Twitter

https://twitter.com/heidijovt

Instagram

https://www.instagram.com/heidimclaughlinauthor/

Amazon author page

https://www.amazon.com/-/e/B00AV872O8

Bookbub

https://www.bookbub.com/profile/heidi-mclaughlin

YouTube

https://www.youtube.com/c/HeidiMcLaughlin

TikTok

https://www.tiktok.com/@heidimclaughlinauthor